THE VEILED THREAT

Book One in the Veiled Duchess Series

Sophia Menesini

CONTENTS

This book is dedicated to my husband. Bubba, you keep me
sane. And for that you will always be my forever.

*I would rather entertain and hope that people learned something
than educate people and hope they were entertained.*
—WALT DISNEY

ACKNOWLEDGMENTS

I have just a few more people to thank, but don't feel guilty about skipping ahead, the only people who read the acknowledgments are the ones who are acknowledged. So, if you even got this far, I applaud you and thank you, now go forth and adventure into *The Veiled Threat* and the wonderful world of Nereid.

Now onto thanking my incredible family, friends, and supporters: First off, I have to thank my dear best friend Lauren Young. She truly encouraged me to write this book. She gave me the strength to persevere when I wanted to give up and taught me more about the process than anyone else. So thank you my Eliza. *The Veiled Threat* really wouldn't have come this far without you.

To my editor, Kelley Frodel, for editing the re-release of The Veiled Threat. You helped my vision become a reality and brought my story to an entirely new level. I can't wait to work with you on the next books of the series.

To my oldest friend and other best friend, Julia Muth. Lady, we have been through a lot together. You pushed me to survive high school and I like to think I did the same for you. As my parents, my sister, and I have all agreed, you are not only one of my closest friends but you're also a part of this family. You're my sister and an honorary Menesini. I love you, soul sister.

My good friend Sam, you knew me as a high school artist struggling to find my limelight in the world, and honestly you kept me writing. Thank you for being a friend; you're an incredible fellow writer and eventually we have to collaborate together because I know it'd be epic.

Thank you, Lexie Moorehead, for illustrating my first novel; your map is an incredible edition and I wish you all the luck in your endeavors.

A couple of shout-outs to my extended family: Susannah, my little bookworm. I can't wait to see your own publication someday; you have the soul of a storyteller. Annabelle, you keep that big heart of yours; no one feels as much love as you do and it makes you so powerful. I know you're going to go far. Jackson, everything you need, you have. Your family will always have your back. Noah, please, please keep dancing like all the world isn't watching because you truly show everyone how to be their own rock star.

My gorgeous sister, Madelyn, I'm so glad we've come together in the past couple years and I can finally call you one of my closest friends. I believe in you, little sister, and I know the Menesini sisters have great things in store. I love you with all my heart.

Mom and Dad, I did it. I wrote a book, and I really have both of you to thank. You raised strong, stubborn, go-getter girls, and that's what I'm doing. I'm following everything you taught me. Thank you for giving me the life I have and for always being there for me even when the world felt impossible. I did it because of you both. And you're the ones who made it possible for me to show the world that I could. I love you both to infinity. Mom, you never stopped believing I could achieve something great, and for that I thank you because you taught me how to be my own support system even though I have an amazing one through you, Dad, and my family. Dad, you are the one who inspired me to be a storyteller. You've led an amazing life, and every time you told stories at Sunday family dinner of your adventures, I knew I wanted to be able to do the same and bring the same joy, sorrow, and laughter you brought me.

Nana, you have always been my loudest supporter and I couldn't be more grateful to you. I love you with all my being.

Papa, you taught me that the world is a big place and to see every inch of it, explore even the smallest corners of my backyard. You made me an adventurer and helped me create a world of my own. I love you both, forever and always.

My darling husband, I dedicated this book to you so be grateful and stop complaining about me leaving my tea bags in mugs in the sink.

And finally to all of my supporters, friends, fans, everyone who picks up a copy of this incredible story, from the bottom of my heart thank you. I love this story, I love the characters, and I hope that you love them too. So please sit back and enjoy *The Veiled Threat*, Book One of the Veiled Duchess series.

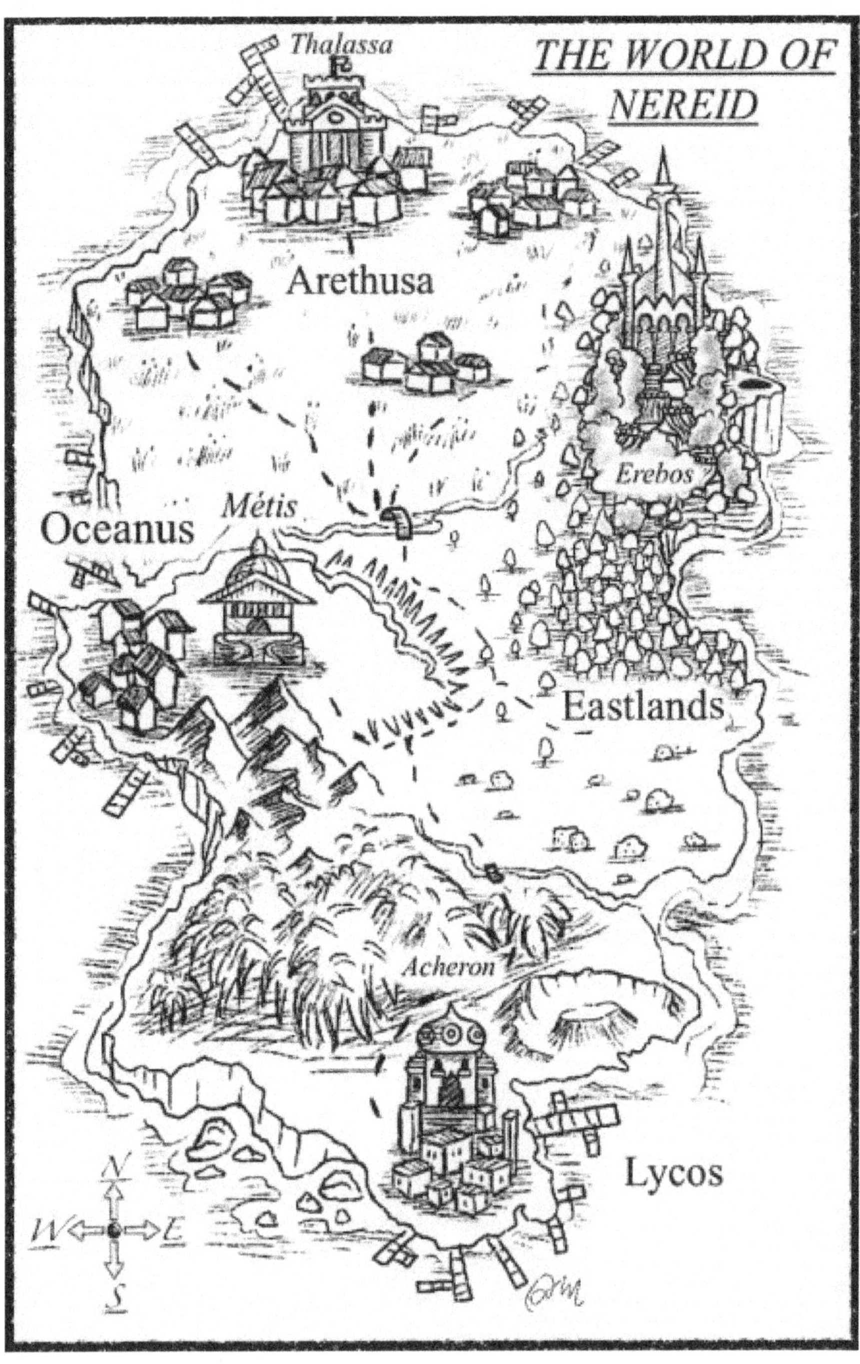
Thalassa
THE WORLD OF
NEREID
Arethusa
Erebos
Oceanus
Métis
Eastlands
Acheron
Lycos
N
W
E
S

NEREID'S SURROUNDING ISLANDS
Charis
-To the north-
Tenaro Islands
(Edge of the World)
- Far West -
Helios
-To the east-
Orena
-To the west-
Knowman's
Canyons
To the south-
Map Key
Desert
Grasslands
Tropical forest
Temperate forest
Ocean ports
Territorial barricades
Main roads
Mountain range

ENDINGS

THE EAR-PIERCING BOOM OF cannons rips through the peaceful air of the early evening and hovers above a still blue ocean.

Her ears ring from the blast as her vessel, the *Veiled Duchess*, takes another shot at the *Hydra of the Sea*, a now crippled imperial navy ship from the southern country of Lycos. Her laughter billows out from where she clings to the rope ladder on the *Duchess*'s foremast. She watches as the *Hydra* groans and shifts back from the force of fire.

Shea Lara, captain of the *Veiled Duchess*, grins down at the destruction lain at her feet. Her crew gathers below, readying to board the losing navy rig. Holding tightly to the ladder, she slides down the rope and hits the deck with a solid thud from her black boots.

"Swords at the ready, men," Shea screams. "Prepare to board!"

The crewmen launch rope claws across the water, hooking the *Duchess* to the *Hydra* steadily, in order to link the ships by plank. The *Hydra* moans in distress. The only thing keeping the hull afloat is the *Duchess*.

From her view, Shea can see the navy officers as they scramble about the *Hydra*'s deck. They scurry like rats in search of clean water, the shock of defeat coursing heavily through their veins. A proud Lycon vessel commissioned by the empress of Lycos herself to carry one of her most prized possessions, fallen.

Finally, her treasure will belong to Shea. She is handed two spare daggers from one of her crewmen and puts them both into the rear holsters of her belt. Scanning her crew, she observes her bos'n, Mister Tero, directing the men to drop the plank. The thunderous roar of the waves between the two battling hulls keeps everyone on their toes.

A bald, dark, hulking man catches Shea's attention, holding a large hammer.

"Survivors?" the giant, Caen, asks.

Shea smiles at her quartermaster and nods. Caen's her most trusted advisor and friend, ever since she wound up on the *Duchess* fifteen years ago. He's stood beside ever since.

"As long as they don't stand in my way," Shea responds, drawing her bewitched gold blade to her side.

"You've done so well and in such a short time. This is everything Paetre would have wanted. You should be proud to have finished his legacy, you bring honor to his name," Caen remarks.

There's a longing expression on his face as he mentions the former captain, Shea's mentor and surrogate father. Paetre had loved Shea enough to give her his last name, and the day he died she vowed to bring him the justice he deserved.

Caen takes a practice swing of his hammer, and it shakes Shea out of her memories.

"Don't count the coin until we have it. I've still got to get the pearl." She winks, covering the grimace threatening to overtake her features.

It's always the same when they recall Paetre, and now isn't the time to remember old wounds.

"Aye, Captain," Caen replies, shooting her a soft grin.

As soon as the wooden gangplank hits the *Hydra*'s deck, without waiting for an order, the *Duchess*'s crew barrels across to the neighboring ship. Shea commands her sixteen-year-old helmsman, James, to stay behind, as well as a few men, with Mister Tero in charge of the vessel. No use in stealing the prize if the navy somehow captures the ship.

Shea breaks into a jog, and she's seconds away from crossing the plank when a small flash of blond with what looks like a letter opener pushes past her with a war cry. She shifts gears quickly and grabs the back of the blond's shirt, effectively stopping Aster, her cabin boy, in place.

He jerks backward onto the deck, landing on his ass.

"Hey!"

"Downstairs now," Shea orders. "I don't want to see you up here again."

"But I can help!"

"I'm not arguing!" Shea searches the deck quickly for Tero. She catches sight of the old man at the forefront of the ship, berating one of the crewmen.

"Tero," Shea yells, and the sea dog turns.

"What now?" he growls.

Shea points down to the scrappy fourteen-year-old at her feet.

"You make sure he doesn't cross!"

"Aster," Tero barks, a vein popping at his temple. "Get down below before I ring your ears. I don't got time to babysit."

Tero quickly returns to checking the rigging for damage.

"I can help! You're not the only elf on this ship who can fight," Aster snaps, drawing Shea's attention back to him. He gets up, turning on his heel, and shoots her one last glare as he walks to the doors leading below deck.

Shea tucks a stray strand of vibrant red hair behind her pointed ear and laughs. "Maybe. But I'm the only one who's grown into my ears!"

Aster slams the door in response. She sighs; she'll deal with him later. Right now she's got a ship to take, and she crosses the gangplank to the *Hydra*. To her disappointment, after pausing to deal with Aster, the fight is just about over. Dead navy men lie dispersed along the upper deck. Shea spots Caen across the ship as he swings his hammer with enough force that it knocks two officers overboard.

A group of navy soldiers are huddled close together in the corner, guarded by two of her crew.

She assumes they're the surrenders. The rest still standing though, she grins, are fair game. She swings her gold sword once, showing off just a bit, when a purple plume of feathers catches the corner of her eye among the captured. It looks like the navy captain has been taken care of and now sits among the defeated.

A screaming officer breaks Shea's amusement.

He's barreling toward her and she evaluates his movements, examining his stance, his steps. His face is covered in dark red blood, and he swings his cutlass clumsily, like a novice tripping over his feet—giving Shea the opportunity she needs to run him through. He falls to his knees with an audible whimper, blood not yet gushing from the wound as her sword is keeping his essence inside his body. He coughs, gurgling, a glob of bloody spit dribbling down his lips. He can't be more than seventeen. She pulls her blade from his gut and notices the blood bloom from the injury, turning his dark red uniform black at his abdomen. She pats his shoulder, giving it a light squeeze, and steps over him as he falls, wiping her blade on his ruined jacket. At the other end of the deck, where Caen is, there is a pair of ornate doors. Unattended and waiting to be opened.

Shea surveys the last of the conflict commencing in between her and the prize. Looks like she'll just have to go through the last of the fight. The first man within the engagement storms her quick. He's got more accuracy than the first that greeted her, but Shea dodges the lunge with ease. She avoids a blow and slices her sword up his back. The soldier falls to his knees, mouth open in a silent scream, and he hits the deck writhing in pain. The next gives her more of a fight. They parry a moment and Shea chuckles, enjoying the thrill of the metal clashing as their swords meet. His foot slips in a puddle of blood, catching him off guard. She ducks under his final blow and slits his throat. The spray from the cut splashes her face—and as he falls to his knees, her clothes—before he finally manages to slap a hand over the gaping gash, attempting vainly to staunch the bleeding.

Shea gags, wiping her face with what little clean sleeve she has, and spits the man's blood onto the deck. She kicks the gurgling officer square in the chest and he falls back, dead. That's the last of the fighters, leaving only the surrendering officers alive.

Shea rolls her eyes as her enhanced senses pick up on a not-so-subtle soldier who's been hiding among the gore and is now trying to sneak up behind her. She doesn't look back at him and instead lets her eyes close. She forces her mind to go blank and reaches, pulling at that thing inside her. His steps are right behind her, but not a second passes before he starts screaming. She looks back in time to see a lasso of water wrap around his middle, and it pulls him overboard into the depths of the sea.

There's a slow clap from Caen and she meets his glaring eyes. He doesn't like when she recklessly uses her elven elemental magic, especially in front of Lycons.

"By my count, that's two more surrenders than we had last time," Shea states, batting her eyelashes with a grin.

She looks positively demonic with all the drying blood dripping down her face.

"Merciful Grace," Caen deadpans.

He throws his hammer onto his shoulder.

"I thought we agreed on no more magic around Lycons?"

"What was I supposed to do? I was defending myself."

"Right. And you don't think any of these living idiots won't tell the empress that her favorite pirate has magic? It's just one more incentive for her to catch you."

"She hasn't done it yet," Shea boasts.

"Right. So, you want me to come with you?"

He nods toward the doors. There's comfort in his golden

eyes and she's almost inclined to take him up on it. After all, this is the moment Paetre had trained her for. Everything he'd ever wanted, and her captain isn't even here to see it. Shea stares blankly at the threshold for a second and then shakes her head.

"No. This one's on me. Stay here and look after the hostages."

Caen gives her a pat on the shoulder before walking over to the group of guarded captives. She hears him giving the surrenders the riot act to empty their pockets and remove their clothes. While the clothes add to the humiliation, it's also a kindness. If, when deserted by Shea's crew, they come across a friendly vessel in their lifeboat, they won't have any colors to give away their allegiance. A rival empire, state, or queendom ship would allow the imperial officers to board.

Shea steps toward the intricately carved doors and pushes them open. Whistling, she realizes the carving is of the mythical hydra, beautifully portraying the name of the ship. She may hate the empire of Lycos but the craftsmanship of the *Hydra* is a marvel and a pity to sink to the bottom of the sea.

Down the stairs, she finds herself at a crossroads, and not wanting to take too much time, she automatically takes a left just as she does on her ship to go to her own cabin. With luck, she comes across a door entitled "Captain's Quarters" farther down the maze of halls.

She notices the blood on her blade has dripped to the floor like breadcrumbs from where it's holstered at her side. It makes her chuckle. Her sword is a pure, solid gold blade crafted in the independent state of Oceanus by an elven blacksmith. It had cost a pretty favor, but it was completely worth it and enchanted to be lightweight and durable.

She stops, stalling, but then brushes her nerves away. She pushes the door open and enters the quarters. It's disappointing to say the least. Considering how magnificent the ship is, she figured it'd be a lavish suite. But the cabin is quite bare and dull. Though her eyebrows do quirk at the wall of mirrors in the back of the room.

A small cot lay off to the side and a desk takes up most of the cabin. Maps are strewn across the table, and heavy books fill most of the chairs. Shea's prize, a magnificent chest, sits directly in the center of the desk among the maps and captain's log. It's the most beautiful thing in the cabin, made of shards of black onyx and obsidian, just like the high towers of Lycos.

Shea catches her eyes in the back mirrors, and for a moment, she imagines Paetre in the image. She smiles, remembering the details of his worn face. The triumph is bittersweet, but she doesn't let that bother her, at least not now.

She draws her sword and breaks the lock on the box with the hilt of her blade, then tosses the broken iron aside onto the floor. Such a pretty box with such an unimpressive lock. The empress must have thought no one could get past the ship.

Shea sheaths her sword and opens the chest. The pearl inside is the size of a young child's fist, lain atop purple velvet lining. Gold and silver octopus tentacles encircle the circumference of the sphere. Its black pearlescent sheen shines in what little light filters into the plain-mirrored cabin. She examines the pearl closer, and spots inside the tentacles small emeralds and other precious gems resting within the suckers.

The Pearl of Lycos, the country's most sacred treasure passed down from ruler to ruler. And Captain Shea Lara, an enemy of the empire and of the empress herself, is stealing it.

The ship groans, catching Shea off guard, and she feels the boards under her feet falter. The *Hydra* is running out of time.

Shea takes one last look around the unimpressive cabin. She contemplates taking the onyx chest but ultimately decides against it. She has what she needs and makes her way back up to the top deck, whistling a merry sea tune along the way.

She strolls across the deck and takes in the Lycon soldiers sitting in the ship's pinnace—the large lifeboat hangs over the water, and two of her crewmen stand at either side ready to cut it loose.

Shea winks exaggeratedly, mocking their current situation.

The navy men and their pompous captain clad in only their undergarments. She resists the urge to laugh as she sees Caen has generously allowed the captain to keep his ridiculous ceremonial feather-plumed hat. The other captain glares daggers at Shea as she stops at the *Hydra*'s rail.

"Empress Ceto will have your head for this," he growls.

Shea quirks a brow, trying to imagine Ceto's face when the imperial bitch realizes just who has stolen her pearl. A ghostly pain blooms in her chest; her hand absently rubs the spot above her heart, tainted by her first meeting with the evil empress.

"I'm sure she would," Shea sighs, "but seeing as it hasn't happened yet well…By the way! Love the undergarments, the lace suits you."

She blows them all a teasing kiss and gives the signal for her men to cut the rope. The Lycon captain's hat stays in the air a fraction of a second longer than the pinnace as the lifeboat free-falls to the ocean's surface, and she can't hold back her chuckle at the Lycons' high-pitched screams.

"Gentlemen"—Shea smiles, taking the pearl out of her pocket for them to see—"I think our work here is done!"

The crew cheers upon seeing the pearl and they all follow her back over to the *Duchess*. Once they are all safely on board, Tero orders the deck crew to cut the claws stringing the *Hydra* and *Duchess* together.

Lastly, Shea orders a round of cannon fire to sink the enemy ship. The *Duchess* pulls away as the blasts brutally rip through the *Hydra* one last time. The beastly hull creaks and moans as it begins its slow descent to the depths.

Shea can hear shouting from the navy men below on the water. They watch their precious vessel begin to slip down into the dark fathoms of the sea where only the gods can see. She closes her eyes, feeling the sun on her face, and the pull of the sinking ship, her magic dancing along the wreck as it's pulled down and out of sight.

Caen shouts to James to sail away toward Arethusa, the

northern queendom on the other side of Nereid from Lycos.

Shea crosses to the handrail, watching the last tip of the *Hydra* sink below, and laughs softly at the men scrambling around the pinnace to row away faster so they're not pulled below with the once glorious ship.

Just like that she finishes what her mentor had started. It's been two years since Shea came into her inheritance of the most successful pirate ship in all of Nereid. She absently wonders if Paetre would be proud of her as she takes the pearl out of her pocket to examine it. She scans the pearl, pushing herself to feel the accomplishment, but all she's left with is the bitter memory of the man she'd considered a father.

Shea pushes the grief to the back of her mind—this is the moment the crew has been waiting for—and hardens her resolve. Turning around, she finds herself face-to-face with the said crew.

They've gathered around her, eager to see what they've waited desperately for: the prize of a lifetime. She summons a genuine smile from just the thought of her sworn enemy. Imagining Empress Ceto's face at the discovery, that once again, she's been swindled by the woodland elf of the sea. She adjusts her grip on the pearl and holds it to the sky.

The men cheer, clapping each other on the back for a victory well earned and the thought of the price the pearl will catch on the black market.

"Enough to retire," Tero shouts.

Shea laughs along with the other men. But a selfish little voice whispers from the back of her mind: she's only just become captain. She's not ready to retire. She suppresses the voice to the depths along with the *Hydra*.

"Alright," Shea orders lightly, "enough lagging, there's still a ship to be run. Mister Caen?"

"Yes, Captain?"

"Get these men back to their posts."

"Aye, Captain." Caen bellows orders to get back to work.

As the men break apart and scatter to wherever they're

needed, Shea notices Aster across the deck.

He's leaning against the double doors that lead down below. There's an annoyed look on his face that only a teenager can pull off. His gaze must finally find her, because he straightens abruptly.

She stops and watches as he makes his way to the staircase leading up to the steering deck. Probably to complain to James about how awful she is. Shea sighs. Guess that means he's still mad at her.

Caen claps her on the back, and the man's strength nearly knocks her off her feet. But being the graceful elf she is, she steadies herself, giving him a wry look.

"Kids. He'll get over it. I seem to remember a young lady giving her captain just as much grief for being benched during battle." Caen winks.

Obviously he had noticed the silent exchange between her and Aster.

"That was different, Paetre was more like a father to me," Shea exhales.

"Motherhood is hard."

He's mocking her and Shea smacks him hard on the shoulder for it.

"He's fourteen, I'm twenty-three. We're only nine, ten years apart," Shea objects.

Caen holds his hands up in surrender. "Whatever you say."

"Ugh, I'll be up in the nest, let me know if I'm needed," Shea replies, trying to end this conversation.

"You don't want to go talk to him?"

She can't resist. She pulls at that energy once more inside of her. Caen squawks as a whip of water comes over the ship's edge and smacks him on the back of his head.

"Oi! Alright! Alright! I'll let you know."

Caen takes off to his own post, rubbing the back of his head, and it's enough to bring a smile back to Shea's face.

She makes it the rest of the way to the rope ladder at the foremast, slipping the pearl into her long green coat, and begins to climb while surveying the *Duchess*'s massive breadth. She stops about halfway, spotting James standing proudly at the helm, and notices his admirer creeping at the bottom of the steps.

"James," Shea calls down, catching the young man's attention.

Aster also turns at the sound of her voice, where he's perched on the stairs, and scurries off before she can note his presence.

"Yes, Captain?" James shouts back.

He's grown so much in the last five years since he joined the crew, Shea thinks, taking in his maturing jaw, the sharper edges to his face.

James took over as Paetre's cabin boy for her after Shea was promoted to first mate at eighteen. He served Paetre until the captain's death two years ago. After Paetre died, it had not only been hard on Shea but James as well, who had grown close to the man the three years he'd been in service to him. He may not have been like a son to Paetre the way Shea was a daughter, but Paetre had cared for him. Not long after Shea's inheritance of the *Duchess*, James had come to her frightened, worried that he was to be thrown overboard since he no longer served a purpose. In that moment Shea had seen a scared fourteen-year-old boy with nowhere to go, so she'd assigned him to old Mister Brandon, their previous helmsman who had retired about a year back now.

James had taken up the mantle swimmingly and now works with Caen, getting to know the mapping and duties of a quartermaster.

Shea reckons he'll make a fine quartermaster to any captain someday.

So naturally when Aster joined the crew, Shea had pointed him in James's direction, so he could learn the ropes on how to be a cabin boy and get to know the dynamics of the ship. Not surprisingly, from that first moment Aster was smitten.

He spends most of his off time up on the poop deck talking

at James who, thank Poseidon, takes it all in stride. At sixteen, he's two years older, while Aster is fourteen, and Shea laughs every time she sees her boy trying his best to get James to notice him.

"Mister Caen has some business to attend to below, think you can manage the deck for him while he's gone?"

Caen, who had actually been at the bow, looks upward at Shea questioningly and she nods as best she can.

Caen smiles knowingly. He'll get to use Shea's teaching moment as his naptime, and so he starts walking toward the double doors.

James glances down nervously at Caen, who waves back to him in approval. By this time next year—though Shea would hate to see him go—if James truly wished it, she'd find him a quartermaster position on an allying ship. Aster would be devastated, but James deserved the advancement if he wished it.

After Caen's approval, James shouts back to Shea, "Aye, Captain! I can manage the deck."

"Good. Mister Tero?"

Mister Tero, who had also been at the bow, looking over the edge at the damage taken from the *Hydra*, looks up at Shea on the rope ladder.

"Aye?"

"You'll take your orders from Mister James until Mister Caen returns."

Tero scoffs as he glances over to the teen at the helm.

He sighs in agreement. "Aye."

He'll take James's directions seriously but everyone knows that it's really Tero who leads the deck; the captain and quartermaster simply supervise.

Once that's decided, Shea continues up the ladder. The figurehead never fails to impress, and Shea smiles at the dark wooden lady carved magnificently into the bow of the vessel. Her face is shielded by the wooden veil, but her eyes are cast out at the darkening sea.

Shea quickly climbs the rest of the way up to the crow's nest, noting the beauty of the horizon. The wind picks up speed and the ship picks up knots. The dark cherry wood, almost black, casts a harrowing aura around the *Duchess*. Her burgundy sails are red with what fools and rumors call the blood of her enemies.

Finally, Shea heaves herself up into the nest and slides her back to the walls of the lookout, feet pointed toward the hole.

A screech echoes across the water as she pulls the pearl out of her pocket and begins rolling it along the inside of her palm, the precious gems and metal scraping along her calloused hand. She looks up in time to see a blue blur of sapphire circling above.

Caeruleus, an Azulean Lionbird who had once belonged to Paetre. But after his death, he'd continued to stick around and became Shea's familiar. His kind is almost extinct. They were popular pets for royals decades back, creatures with the body of a cat but wings of a large owl and green feather's that mix with blue fur. His facial features are that of a regular house cat, with silver-blue eyes and gorgeous markings, except like an owl he can turn his head all the way back. His reflexes are quick and each paw has five-inch talons that extend out, sharp enough to disembowel his enemies. Caeruleus revolves overhead, keeping watch on the crew below while Shea is preoccupied.

She can always count on Caeruleus to keep things in check while she keeps to herself, to be her second pair of eyes. He'd done the same for Paetre and would remain loyal to Shea until her death or his own. The Lionbird swoops down briefly and drops a cold piece of parchment out of his mouth and onto Shea's lap. His reason for his absence during the battle.

She smiles, closing her eyes for a second so she can smell the lavender off the parchment before opening the letter.

Placing the pearl back into her pocket, she breaks open the wax sealing the parchment together, then skims the contents. V will be expecting her; she smiles and hands the letter back to Caeruleus, who takes it easily into his large paw.

He takes off from her side to sail down below, and she chuckles, noticing a couple feather's missing from his tail. Lionbird feathers fetch a nice price on the black market; he must have had a rough journey back to the ship.

Shea removes her hat, placing it on her lap, and slowly weaves and unweaves her bright curly red hair into small braids, staring off into the darkening sky.

Caeruleus knows to drop the letter on her desk, and soon enough he yowls, alerting her that he's once again above, but only for a second. He swoops down below faster than any normal bird, so that even a trained eye would have trouble knowing he hadn't disappeared into thin air.

Shea hears an indignant yelp from one of the crew members, which she quickly places as Aster, and purses her lips to hold back a snicker. The boy should know better than to waste time with Caeruleus in charge.

A sharp gust of wind rises behind her as he returns to his flight position above the *Duchess*. Even with the setting sun, she can feel the golden rays tanning her skin, giving her already golden complexion a kind of glow, highlighting her sage-green eyes.

And while thoughts of Paetre are easily suppressed, the questions of whether her captaincy is at an end plagues her waking mind. She knows that if she wishes to sail, she only needs to tell the crew and ask. But what about the men who decide the pearl is enough; can she do without Tero? Without Caen? Does she even want to?

But even as she contemplates it, it's all she knows. She's not ready to retire. The pearl had been Paetre's dream; Shea needs to find her own score. Taking the pearl back out, she already has an inkling of what her final score might be.

As a child, slavers in the Eastlands of Nereid had taken her from her childhood home of Erebos, the elven capital. She'd been sold to Captain Paetre Lara in the southern slave markets of Lycos, and while she considers the crew her people, her elven race is dying.

More and more elves are enslaved every day. Even in Arethusa, where slavery is outlawed, the elven people starve if they do not serve. She'd always hoped that one day she could be a part of the disbanding of the markets, the freeing of the elves. But even now she can hear Paetre's voice echoing with finality: *We do not interfere with the land folk's quarrels.* He could never understand her desire to get involved.

But Ceto, the empress of Lycos, had made it personal the day she'd carved her name and her country's sigil into Shea's chest at the ripe age of sixteen. A phantom pain shoots through Shea's shoulder at the memory, and her hand rubs the brand cut by a glowing enchanted knife. Can Shea really just retire and ignore her call for vengeance?

Paetre gave her the tools to fight; wouldn't going quietly into the night dishonor his memory? These questions continue to haunt her mind hours later when someone finally disturbs her solitude.

The sound of feet climbing the rope ladder tells her he's nearing her destination. Caen's ebony bald head pokes through the hole in the floor of the crow's nest.

She can feel his piercing gold gaze narrowing into the side of her face, examining every twitch. There's a permanent worry line etched into his forehead all because of her. Even when she was only a cabin girl, years ago on this ship, he'd taken her under his wing. He'd taught her most of what she knows, except for the parts Paetre had instilled. For the hulking man that he is, taller than any other on the ship at a staggering height of eight feet, he was mother as much as Paetre had been father to her, comfort and care. He was and always will be a part of what makes this ship her safe harbor. There had been no other choice when it came to a quartermaster.

Their words crash together.

"Are we there yet?" Shea asks.

"Are you alright?" Caen inquires.

She smiles, leveling her eyes with his, keeping her breath

steady.

"I'm happy. We have the Pearl of Lycos; we're rich."

Caen rolls his eyes. Caeruleus lands on the edge of the crow's nest and they exchange glances, the Lionbird's ears flattening against his head.

Shea merely keeps a soft smile on her face, hiding the turmoil behind that easy facade, and snatches her hat off her lap. She places the cap on her head and stands, stretching her back, looking out over the horizon.

The wind has warmed, and there's a smell in the air like burnt rain. Shea can feel the friction dancing along her sun-kissed skin as she leans against the railing of the nest.

"It's going to storm."

"Aye," Caen agrees, leaning his arm briefly on the wooden floor of the nest.

"I've set the orders to port, I believe we should stay on the *Duchess* tonight," Caen tells her before beginning his descent to the deck.

Shea leans her head over the hole. "I'll be going ashore, and I'll be keeping the pearl with me."

Caen stops. He looks back up, glowering. "Captain, I think —"

"Caen, I believe I've made my orders clear," Shea responds, and though he grumbles, he doesn't argue.

Shea turns to climb down herself, but her gaze settles on Caeruleus, who is sitting on the edge of the lookout. She can feel the judgment.

"Oh hush," she tells him, and he meows at her, ruffling his feathers. "I'm fine. Besides, V is expecting me."

Caeruleus hisses and she figures it's probably an insult as she descends down the rope ladder after Caen.

THE SLIPPERY SERPENT

Shea

THEY MAKE IT INTO port quietly in the capital of Arethusa, the city of Thalassa. The port master knows better than to ask questions, and with their standard payment, they supply the necessary papers to keep the Arethusian guards off Shea's back.

Caen handles the paperwork, and the men continue with their ship work as it begins to lightly rain.

Shea runs below deck to grab her coin pouch off her desk and decides on a change of clothes, as she doesn't want to scare the locals with her bloody appearance. Shrugging her jacket back on, she climbs the stairs, examining her blade for a moment before slipping it back into the side holster. She makes it through the doors onto the quarterdeck when she hears someone shout her name.

"Captain!" Shea turns, stopping as she sees Aster running over himself to catch up to her.

She smirks. "You need something?"

Aster purses his lips and drones, "I know that I put you in a hard position and that"—he sighs—"that I still have a lot to learn. And…I'm sorry for my actions."

Shea gives him a grin. "Okay."

Aster huffs. "I really am sorry."

"I know."

There's a pregnant pause, and she reaches out and pats him lightly on the shoulder.

"How about training with me tomorrow? I should be back early," Shea informs him.

She turns to leave and finds the blur of blond in front of her again. "That'd be great, but, Cap?"

"Yes, Aster?" Aster straightens his posture, standing a little taller.

He clenches his jaw, but it does nothing to harden his pretty features; the tips of his ears peek through his curly, strawberry-blond hair.

"I think I should accompany you tonight to mistress's tavern. It's storming, and it'd be good to have a second pair of eyes. I've been practicing. I'm much better with a sword! Plus, Caen told me he'd teach me how to use the trident. I'm better than most the guys on the ship, in fact, I mean, I could have handled the siege just fine honestly..."

Aster continuously rambles.

She groans and places a hand over Aster's mouth to stop the jabbering, a fond smile gracing her features. The pointed tips of his ears tinge pink. He removes her hand from his mouth.

"I can help."

Shea laughs in exasperation and ruffles his blond curls. "Aster..."

She thinks, his wide eyes pleading for something to do. She looks up, her eyes catching the brim of her hat, and she can remember a conversation much like this one long ago between a young elf and her captain. She takes her hat off her head and hands it to Aster.

"Here, I'm going for a drink, and it's nowhere you should be. So you can stay here and guard my hat."

"What," Aster yelps, looking down at the old captain's hat.

"Be careful, it's priceless," she teases.

Aster starts to argue, but Shea cuts him off, "Captain's orders."

Aster's mouth snaps shut.

He groans, "I never get to do anything."

"Well you could go scrub dishes in the kitchen with Strom. I'm sure he's got lots of stuff for you to do." Shea grins and points back to the double doors leading to the deck below.

Aster's eyes widen and he offers her a sheepish smile. Muttering a never mind, he quickly heads for the door with Shea's hat in hand before she makes it an order for him help the cook. She stares after him and shakes her head.

He's been on this ship nearly as long as Shea has been captain. It had been two months into her voyage as leader after Paetre's death when she found him. They'd been scavenging a small slave-trade island off the coast of Nereid called Helios. As much as she would've liked to have blown the entire slave trade off the face of the island, they had reliable contacts for both masters and slaves all over the system. A new investor Paetre had acquired while he was alive had invited Shea to his home, to see if she was as good as her predecessor. Especially considering her "disability" as he called it. Her being elven.

His plantation had rested on the far side of the island. After playing the market earlier in the day, she figured she'd conclude the evening with dinner at his place with Caen and James. Shea knew she needed to show him that his investment in her ship was still good, so she'd sucked up her pride and turned on her charm.

Upon arriving, she'd met Aster, only twelve at the time. An elven boy from Erebos just like her, sold into slavery. But unlike Shea, who'd been purchased by a man who considered her a daughter and returned her freedom, Aster had been acquired as a pleasure slave for the fat smuggler she was trying to impress. She'd met with Aster's owner, discussed business, and had been so close to leaving without a word against his slave use. But as the night progressed, she hated him more and more. The final straw finally came when Shea had gone to her chambers provided by the master on his insistence. It'd been too late to head back to the ship, and Aster had been sent to Shea's room to pleasure her. Her pleasure was quickly found in beheading Aster's owner and setting all of his slaves free.

Shea gave Aster the choice of passage to the mainland or a position on her ship—a free position, and she'd teach him everything she knew.

She sometimes wishes she had taken him back to Erebos, given him a shot at a normal life. But there was something in her that couldn't let him go. Now he's one of her most loyal crew. She feels like his older sister and, even though they're only nine years apart, at times even his mother.

All this reminiscing only brings more grief, but Shea continues to bury it deep within and instead strolls toward the gangplank connected to the dock.

Nearby Tero orders a few of the deck crew to double check the tender and rigging before retiring for the evening.

"Mister Tero," Shea shouts and Tero, like the old pirate he is, stands at attention.

She withholds a chuckle; honestly, the man is so previously navy.

"I'd like you to take a look at the rigging on the foremast, something in my gut tells me it needs some care."

The bos'n looks to the mast and makes an audible note. He begins to head off, but Shea stops him once more. "One other thing, please make a note of anyone who requests leave off the ship. They're fine to go, but I'd be curious to know who does. I'll be back before the morn."

"I don't think any of the men will be leaving tonight. We're in for an Underdeep of a storm, Captain," the old sea dog calls after her.

She walks down the plank and onto the dock while he heads to the rail at the ship's edge, peering down at her.

Stopping a moment, she looks up at the billowing clouds. He may be right.

"Thank you, Mister Tero, but I'll be fine. I..." Shea responds but trails off just as she sees Caen striding toward her down the plank, dressed in town clothes and with a purse of his own at his belt.

"Where do you think you're going?" Shea demands as Caeruleus lands on Caen's shoulder.

"I'm going for a drink," Caen replies, walking past her.

She looks up at Tero, who is watching, amused, before he catches sight of Shea's glare and pushes himself away from the rail to return to the foremast.

"Shouldn't you stay with the ship," Shea urges.

Caen simply looks over his shoulder. "No."

She thinks about stomping her foot and telling him she doesn't need a babysitter but instead leaves him be, grumbling quietly to herself.

"Fine," she groans.

She pushes past Caen at a brisk pace, forcing herself to look straight ahead. The port is like a ghost town; anyone with any sense is already inside for the night and out of the rain.

The stone houses dance in the torchlight, lit at all the street corners and outside some of the establishments.

"So what's got you all in a rise?" Caen asks, jogging lightly to catch up.

"Nothing."

"Right."

"Really!"

"I hear you."

She stops, turns, and glares him down, but Caen only smiles at her softly. The rain's coming down harder, and her clothes stick to every inch of her muscled frame. Her hair looks crimson in the dark, like she's bleeding from a head wound.

Caen is drenched as well, and Caeruleus ruffles his feathers, trying in vain to stay dry. If she doesn't get the creature inside soon, he might bite the tips of her ears off. She huffs in defeat.

"Why can't you let me wallow?"

"Because you're my kid." Caen smiles.

There's silence. With a sigh, Shea reaches her hand out for

his arm and hooks it through. He's still smiling at her so she leans her head against his giant bicep. Caeruleus purrs from where he's at on Caen's other shoulder, and using his nails, much to Caen's displeasure, steps around the giant's head so he's sitting on the shoulder she's leaning on. Once there, he leans down, pushing and rubbing his head against hers.

They walk the rest of the way together to V's establishment through the winding streets of Thalassa. The roofs jutting off the wooden and stone homes do nothing to keep the rain from soaking them to the bone. The small alleys open up into a huge courtyard with a signpost in the center and a lantern on top. The flame is flickering from inside the glass until a final wind snuffs it out, plunging the courtyard into semidarkness. Past the signpost, on the other side of the courtyard, is the Slippery Serpent, the only pub Shea frequents this side of Nereid.

Good mead, great company, and the owner is just who Shea's looking for. Thunder quakes overhead as they make it through the threshold of the tavern. Shea smells lightning strikes in the distance.

Rain drips from their clothes onto the floor, and the bartender, a strapping young lad Shea hasn't seen before, whistles to the whores, who are already walking toward them with some towels.

Caeruleus meows in relief, shaking off the water onto Caen and Shea. He briefly nuzzles the inside of one of his wings before flying off into the rafters where a small bed awaits him.

Shea knows she won't see him for the rest of the night.

There's a few patrons scattered around the relatively large pub, but no one dares lift their heads or meet her gaze. Shea whispers a few pleasantries to the ladies toweling her off before she catches sight of a blond-haired beauty she's spent more than one night with in the quiet evening and the dying candlelight.

The blonde shoos the other ladies away and wraps a towel around Shea, pulling her in close with a wink.

"Venus," Shea acknowledges.

Venus holds her hand out, and Shea kisses the back.

"Got your message, you're right on time," V remarks teasingly.

Her low-cut seafoam dress highlights her skin, and in the firelight, she looks damn near pearlescent. Shea appraises Venus with a flirtatious smile, then frowns when Caen clears his throat, breaking up their interaction.

"V, lovely as ever," Caen says, grabbing V's hand from Shea and kissing it as well.

They share pleasantries while Shea finishes drying off and hands her towel to a raven-haired girl who she notices is staring at her hair. Her long curls are practically standing on top of her head in a frizzy state.

"Caen, you're as charming as ever," V giggles. "Why don't you let my ladies take care of you tonight. I have a feeling your captain and I have business to attend to."

"You're too kind," Caen rumbles as the group of ladies who greeted them begin pushing and prodding Caen toward the stairs near the back that lead up to the bedrooms. Shea rolls her eyes.

Caen gives her a short wave on his way up the stairs.

V steps toward Shea, and Shea offers her arm as they make their way to the bar. She pays the brave, prying eyes around her no mind. They know who Shea is and if they want to stay alive, they'll stay away. They reach the bar swiftly. Shea pulls out a barstool for V and one for herself, but the lady of the Slippery Serpent doesn't take it, so Shea sits down without her.

The captain's eyes wander to the gorgeous blond Adonis working behind the counter, passing out beer and liquor to the various ghosts at the bar. She glances over at V and laughs at the amused expression on her face as she'd been watching Shea admire the young man.

"New hire?" Shea smirks.

"You like?"

"I do."

"Perhaps he might join us upstairs sometime," V purrs, and

the sound of her voice sends shivers up Shea's spine.

Gods that voice is like magic, Shea reflects.

"Any prior engagements this evening?"

"I'm always free for my favorite customer," V whispers, her long golden hair falling like a river down her back and to her waist.

V's enchanting eyes catch Shea's, and she notices once more that they always seem to swirl with what looks like the lightest shade of purple.

V reaches out, softly playing with Shea's hair, and leans down close to Shea's lips. She places her hand on Shea's, ready to take her upstairs. And while Shea is more than willing, there's still a small part of her that needs a minute to herself and she turns her head away so V kisses her on the cheek instead of her lips.

"Not yet," Shea tells her.

"You always were surprisingly resistant to my charms," V remarks. Stepping back, she gestures for the barkeep to come closer.

Shea shoots her a gloating smile and turns her body to face V's, leaning against the counter. She pushes a blond streak of hair over the mistress's shoulder, exposing her ear.

Sitting straight, Shea whispers into the sensitive flesh, "I have something that might interest you."

V steps closer, and Shea's grin widens as she hears V's breathing shallow.

She continues, "But first I need a drink. So I'm going to order myself a pint of ale and then I'll meet you upstairs"—Shea kisses the skin right behind the blonde's ear—"to conduct our business."

Her breath catches. And with that Shea pulls back, leaving a flushed V scowling. She revels in the triumph, chuckling to herself.

In retaliation, V grabs Shea's chin tightly, causing her to gasp. Her hand flies to the handle of her blade on instinct.

"You best hurry that pint," V hisses, holding Shea's head so their eyes are level.

The redhead's jaw tightens, but she nods as best as she can. V releases her and Shea resists the urge to adjust her jaw. V signals the bartender for a pint of ale.

"On the house," she tells both Shea and the Adonis.

He nods. With V's offer fresh in her mind, Shea can't help but groan at the image in her head of Adonis and V, all three of them in bed together. Well, some other time. Shea swings her legs back toward the bar and leaves V off to her side. But V, never to be outdone, slips behind Shea and runs her hands over her back in a massaging gesture. She squeezes Shea's shoulders gently and leans her mouth close to her ear.

"Don't keep me waiting."

"Yes, mistress," Shea quips.

"Good girl," V whispers.

Shea scoffs as she feels Venus's wandering hand heading deliberately toward her pocket with the pearl.

She catches V's hand gracefully, like a dance.

"You best be naked when I get up there," Shea growls, releasing V, who pulls her hands back in a surrendering gesture.

"If that's how you want to play it," V mutters with a wink, "Captain."

And with that, the mistress of the Slippery Serpent ascends the stairs, leaving the elf alone with her drink.

A PROPER EXCHANGE

Shea

WITH VENUS GONE, the warmth from their exchange fades away. The candles on the bar do nothing to lift the chill in the room.

Shea drinks from the wooden tankard, staring unseeingly into the flickering light. Questions come flooding back now that's she left alone with her thoughts.

The memories of Paetre bleeding out on the deck of the *Duchess* blends into the melted candle wax she picks on the bar table. His face is as clear as the day it happened. She knows it's only so vivid because of the pearl. She doesn't even realize her hands are shaking until she hears the mug softly clattering against the wooden counter. Letting go of the cup, she huffs.

What's dead is dead, she thinks. Shea pushes away from the counter to head upstairs to V, abandoning her drink, when a hooded figure stops her.

He settles onto the barstool that she'd pulled out for the blond mistress. Shea subtly scoots back toward the bar, as she's unsure of the mysterious fellow beside her. Her hand comes to rest on the hilt of her concealed blade.

"A beautiful woman," the hood speaks.

It's definitely male, but there's a lilt to his voice that sounds feminine and refined. He gestures a gloved hand up the stairs and Shea realizes he means Venus.

"Aye, though if you're looking for an appointment with the lady, I would go now. She'll be preoccupied for the rest of the evening." Shea smirks, nonchalant, but she finishes the rest of her drink quickly.

She's not in the mood to start a scene.

"A fine woman," he agrees, "but not the one I seek."

He flags down the attractive barkeep, gesturing to Shea's pint, and the boy brings a round of ale filled to the brim.

"Then I wish you luck," Shea murmurs.

She goes to stand, pushing the barstool back again, but the man puts his hand on top of her left.

"As luck would have it, it's you I'm looking for."

Shea tightens her grip on her sword and lifts her eyes, meeting only the side of the man's brown leather hood.

Caeruleus growls a warning from above that the stranger pays no mind.

"I suggest moving that hand if you plan on keeping it."

He lets go immediately and sets his palms flat on the table as a peace offering.

Shea relaxes but only just, sitting back down in her seat lightly. She keeps a steady grip on the gold longsword.

"My apologies for startling you," he soothes.

Shea laughs darkly and his shoulders tense.

"Look, I'm not for sale the same way the other ladies are. Not all elves serve," Shea mutters, "so if you'll excuse me..."

"No," he says quickly.

He lifts his palms off the bar but instead stops, flexing his fingers then relaxing them flat back onto the counter.

"Please. I mean to hire you for another reason."

Shea stays where she is. She doesn't know why but the man piques her interest as she observes his submissive position. She stands, turns, and leans her back against the bar. She notes how the hood averts his gaze away from her so his face is still obscured.

"I'm not sure you know who I am," Shea chuckles, raising a

brow.

"I know who you are," he states.

"Then what could you possibly need me for?" Shea asks, genuinely curious.

Surprisingly, it's not often that dark strangers find her in the night to propose business propositions.

"I need you to steal something. From what I know, that's kind of what you do."

"Depends on the something."

"Something of great value," he explains.

"Right," Shea deadpans.

"A princess."

"Of course."

"This is serious."

"I bet." Shea grins, because come on. "Which princess?"

"The crown princess of Arethusa," he whispers.

"Careful, mate." Shea's eyes narrow, glancing around casually. "Around here that's treason."

"Among me and my fellows, we're calling it a political coup."

"Don't they all."

Shea turns back to face the bar, letting her hips lean against the edge, and downs the new tankard.

"And what do I get out of this arrangement?" Shea inquires, wiping her mouth with the back of her hand.

"The thing you desire most."

"And what's that?"

"Money," he says.

Though the answer sounds more like a question.

Shea snorts. "For a princess? It'd have to be a lot of money. Even so, if you know anything about me, I don't carry live cargo, mate. You picked up the wrong pirate."

Shea takes a step away from the bar and he tenses, but she doesn't walk away. She stays close and that seems to calm him.

"Then what you need most," he tells her.

And she doesn't have to see his face to hear the pleased

smile in his voice. He knows she's interested.

"I'm aware that you have an ongoing…" he continues, but it seems as if he struggles to find the right word, "…relationship, with the empress of Lycos?"

Shea nearly laughs. Yes, that's one way to put it. Her hand settles over her heart, rubbing the area slightly.

"Would you help me if I told you I have the map and entrance key to her private vault? Where she holds her most damning evidence on the major elites of Lycos and Arethusa?"

The information doesn't quite process. Shea looks at him, really looks at him. His clothes, his boots, the not very well concealed dagger at his side. Whoever this is, he's powerful. And that means he's dangerous. She takes a seat on the other side of him, her hands folding onto the counter.

"Now how the Underdeep did you get that?" Shea asks.

The Lycon Vault: the largest archive in existence filled with blackmail, threats, and the secrets of every powerful person out there that Ceto has acquired over the years. Every nation in Nereid wants that vault.

And not all are completely sure it exists.

With it, someone could control Ceto herself. It could bring down the elven slave trade, that nasty little voice in Shea's head whispers. It's impossible to get into though. She's looked into it more than a few times. The only reason she knows it's not a myth is because she tortured it out of some Lycon spy that had tried and failed to sneak aboard her ship. It could bring the whole nation down overnight.

"I have my resources," the hood explains.

To hold that power, Shea could bring the whole elven slave industry down to its knees and slit them at the core. She keeps her face neutral. This isn't like taking down a navy ship. This is a mainland job and that means this could go very wrong.

"Now while that is an extremely generous offer, I hate to mention stealing a person, a crown princess in fact, is a larger operation than stealing a crown jewel."

"You don't think you can do it?"

Concern filters through his voice. Shea rolls her eyes. He's an amateur. In this one moment he's let her know that he needs her as much as she needs him. But it also means he's never done this before and it makes him a liability. But for the vault? She has to risk it.

"I didn't say that," Shea responds.

"Then what are you saying?"

"It's a great score, but I can't just pull this off tomorrow."

"I need this done tomorrow."

Shea huffs, "Won't work. To break into the castle and steal the princess it'd take me months of scouting and trials of breaking in."

"And if you had a way in?"

"A way in and a prize? You really want this girl gone," Shea mutters. This time he turns toward her but only slightly.

She catches sight of a short beard before he corrects himself, keeping his features hidden. "But you'd do it?"

"Maybe," Shea remarks, pretending to examine her nails.

She can tell she's starting to get under his skin and that's exactly where she wants to be. She has no plans of being surprised upon taking this venture. And even if she wanted to take it, when Paetre had been alive he'd had a thing about working for other people. *We upset the status quo*, he'd say, *we don't get involved.* The crew might not like this business deal.

"This is more than just a kidnapping. You'd be helping Arethusa." His hands move from the table, but she's not entirely worried.

She watches his movements, intently searching for any kind of identifying marker.

"You could almost consider it a courtesy to the country. A contribution to the liberation of old tradition. A revolution!"

There's a pause and he draws back into himself as if he's forgotten where he is. He adjusts his posture and places his hands back on the table, awaiting Shea's answer to his great cause.

"A revolution?" Shea reaches over the hood, which makes him recoil in order to hide his face, and clasps his untouched pint, bringing it to sit in front of her.

"A moment ago you called this a political coup, now it's a revolution? Make up your mind, are you a grand hero or a usurper to the crown?"

"Can't it be both?" he inquires.

"Only to the winners."

There's another pause. Shea considers her options; she subtly slips her hand into the pocket with the pearl. She wasn't ready to give up this life, not yet, even for the prize of the pearl. This wasn't her final score; the pearl would always be Paetre's, but the vault, the vault could be hers.

"I'm not saying I'll do it." The figure's shoulders crumple but Shea continues, "But I'm not saying that I won't either. First things first, I take the girl. Then what? You want her dead?"

"No need," he replies. "Just out of the way. Do you know the Tenaro Islands?"

"Of course," Shea acknowledges. There's another pause and she realizes he's actually waiting for her to explain. She groans. "The Tenaro Islands. The westernmost islands hundreds of miles off the coast of Nereid. Many are uncharted and some believe it to be the edge of the world."

Shea has to admit that's one way to get rid of someone. "So you do want us to kill her," Shea questions; it'd be a lot simpler to just cut her throat instead of sailing all the way to the world's end.

"No," he sighs as if he's dealing with a small child. "Just maroon her on one of the islands. You could even give her some supplies."

Shea ignores his tone and returns the condescending attitude in full. "With all due respect, she's a princess. Even with a box of supplies she won't make it through a night. Even an experienced survivalist...the rumors about those islands, not even the heroes of old would have stood a chance."

"There's always a chance," he whispers.

Shea nods absently. It's horseshit, but if it eases both their souls, she'll take it.

"Aye," Shea voices her agreement but it's hollow. "So...last question: What's the way into the castle?"

The man reaches into his dark coat, pulling a card from a pocket. He places it on the bar in front of Shea. "An invitation to the traditional pre-coronation ball tomorrow night."

"The pre-coronation ball? The biggest event, besides the coronation itself, of the season? Not to mention the most guarded."

"Not good enough?" he asks.

She doesn't need to see his face to hear the loud amusement in his voice. "Look, mate, the invitation gets what? Maybe four of us in? But people are going to notice if I've got the unconscious future queen heaped over my shoulder."

He laughs.

She finishes off his ale with a soft shake of her head. She should have known this was too good to be true. She'll just have to live without the Lycos Vault. Maybe retirement won't be so bad. Though now that she has confirmation the vault exists, she might just have to look into it again.

But then he speaks, "Let's just say that tomorrow night around the south-facing wall of the castle, where the royal gardens are, the guards will be particularly lax. In fact, you may just be able to walk out the servants' quarters."

And she's back to considering this insane idea. There's something off about this guy, but the vault clouds any fault she might find.

"And how long would this window last?" Shea inquires.

"Around midnight, at the guard change, to about two in the morn."

Shea's had smaller windows. She keeps her face guarded with the same nonchalant smirk. "Interesting."

"Curious as to why?" he asks.

Shea merely shrugs. "Not really," she lies. "Though I'm guessing you're not a servant? Perhaps a lord?"

"Forgive me if I don't tell you."

And there are those manners again.

She shakes her head, clapping him on the back; he flinches. And that's when she notices, in the corner of her eye, two men at a far back table stand quickly. They're watching her hand but are careful not to draw her attention.

"Secrecy is my business, mate. I don't need to know shit about you as long as you can pay."

He laughs, she grins, and the men at the far table sit back down. He pushes the stool back to stand, and she grabs the invitation off the bar, slipping it into her inner chest pocket before he can take it back. He plops some coin on the counter, enough to pay for both the drinks, though Shea doesn't correct him that hers are free.

He's about to step away when she asks, "How'd you find me anyway?"

He stops, and she gets a chance to examine the way he stands, how tall he is, his posture, filing the information away for later. Definitely a lord if his posture has anything to say about it.

"Asked around," he chuckles, and then lifts his hand to shake his finger at her teasingly. "You're quite popular, you know? It was rumored that you frequented this tavern from time to time when you entered the queendom."

Shea takes note of that as well. As much as she enjoys V, it's dangerous for a pirate to become predictable. That's how you get caught, or killed.

"So...what?" She continues, "You came in every night just hoping I'd be here?"

She's joking of course, but he answers quite seriously, "Something like that."

Shea laughs at him; everything about him has been ridiculous. "So if I agree to your deal, how exactly will I get paid? If I take who you're asking, I have no plans of sticking around."

He walks closer to her, looking around the tavern as if expecting a loyalist to shout traitor. But no one in here cares, that's why they're in a place like this.

"Keep a man here or perhaps a woman." He points up toward

the ceiling and she gets his drift. Venus. He'll give the payment to V and Shea knows she'll get what she wants.

"Aye, I get your meaning. When and where could payment be expected?"

"Neutral meeting ground." He gestures with his hands. "Perhaps the white cliffs, easily accessed by horse or carriage and private enough to get away clean."

Shea nods. It's the perfect setup, it would just be convincing V.

"And should you ever need Arethusian assistance, you can rest assured a pardon will await you here. You have my word. Should you, I don't know, do pirates retire?"

"If they're lucky enough," Shea laughs.

He gives her a moment to take everything in.

"Do we have an accord, Captain?" he whispers, leaning forward.

"Perhaps," Shea murmurs back. "You'll have to wait and see."

She can feel his eyes raking over her body and it's eerie since she can't see his obscured face. She breaks the trance by stepping around him and toward the stairs leading to the upper level of the tavern.

"You seem to have thought of everything," Shea remarks, turning back to the hood one last time. "You're definitely committed, I'll give you that. Though really, I'm not that good."

He nods his head, one hand flat on his abdomen, and bows.

"From what I've heard? You are. Have a pleasant..." Once more he pauses, looking for the right word, and even if she can't see the smile, she knows it's there. "...evening, Captain."

She returns a sort of mock bow and he turns his back to her first. He walks through the doors and Caeruleus growls again. The men at the back table step out behind him, no longer concerned about being seen.

Shea watches the door for another moment, and the tension from the encounter seems to drain from her body, leaving her light-headed. She leans against the banister, but not enough for any of the sea dogs in the room to notice, and heads up the steps to her awaiting lady.

JUST REWARD

Shea

S HEA MAKES HER WAY up the rest of the steps until she sees the large ornate door at the end of the hall. It's the largest room in the house of ill repute and on the front of the door is a painted oyster shell with a swirling pearl inside. This, of course, is Venus's room. Where only the most esteemed guests visit.

Shea slinks down the long hallway, stopping when she hears Caen's mighty laugh roaring from one of the closer rooms to the steps.

It's like hearing a parent have sex. Shea gags.

She quickly steps away, not wanting to hear any more. With a final deep breath, she puts on her sexiest smirk and steps through the door.

The fireplace lays off to the left and a roaring flame lights the room in a soft glow. The walls are covered in scenes of myth, love stories mostly, from the gods of old as V has pointed out to Shea in the past. White and red roses litter the room, some in vases and others only petals on the floor. Furs scatter the floors as well, keeping the chill out of the wood and away from bare feet. There's a lounge chair and large armchair over by the fireplace with a short table in between. A bottle of rare red wine and a bottle of amber liquor are placed neatly with four crystal glasses.

But the crowning jewel of the room is V herself, lying naked in the center of the massive bed. Blankets of silk and fur surround her.

She watches intently as Shea enters the room, her flowing blond hair barely covering her breasts.

Shea carefully masks her lust, keeping her features neutral.

V sensually sits up in bed, her blond curls beautifully messy.

Shea spares her a small glance as she strides across the room to the table with the wine. She methodically shrugs off her large overcoat, folding it over the back of the armchair. Her purple dress shirt is still slightly damp and the puffed sleeves stick to her tan arms. She opens her belt, sliding the sword and leather strap off her waist, then leans the blade up against the chair, draping the belt over the back, and kicks off her boots. Shea uncorks the bottle of wine on the table, ignoring the blond vixen writhing on the bed, trying vainly to get her attention. Instead she pours the bloodred liquid into one of the crystal glasses and sits down in the armchair, studying the crackling logs crumbling under the burning fire, and waits.

Soft moans and rustling blankets can be heard from the bed, but Shea merely sips her wine and gazes deeply into the blaze. She doesn't wait long, as she hears the blonde give a deep, suffering sigh and the bed creaks as V makes her way to the redhead.

Her long red hair is almost dry and flows loose past her shoulders, stopping about mid-back.

V slides her hand along the back of the chair, brushing the material of the coat, and then down the side to the chair's arms. V's hands fall to her side gently until she's facing Shea, breasts at eye level. Shea admires them with a soft expression but doesn't meet V's gaze. Sensually she kneels down in front of the elf, laying her arms on Shea's knees, using them as a headrest.

They're face-to-face.

Shea is completely clothed, V completely naked, but under

those violet prying eyes it is Shea who feels the most vulnerable.

"What took you so long?" V inquires with no real interest.

"I had things on my mind."

"A woman?"

Shea laughs at her. She finds the idea of her jealousy more than a little amusing.

"Perhaps." She grins.

V frowns, focusing on the strings coming apart in a hole in Shea's pants.

"You should mend these," she comments, ignoring Shea's answer.

"Aye," Shea responds, sipping the red wine.

She's never really cared for the stuff but it's expensive and it's there. They fall into silence, Shea's eyes slipping back toward the flames and V's hands dancing along her lap.

"What is it?" V asks.

Shea takes a moment to consider the cost of telling the truth and then proceeds, "It's been two years since the mutiny." Shea doesn't have to see V's face to know she suddenly remembers. The dancing hands come to a halt. "It's been two years since Paetre died. Two years since I became captain of the *Veiled Duchess* and I still can't get him out of my head," Shea continues, taking another sip of wine.

The flames are hypnotizing and she has the urge to touch the fire.

"It couldn't have been avoided," V tells her, and it's exactly what she said two years ago when Shea came to her bloody and stricken with grief.

She'd taken Shea to the tub in the far right corner of this very room and had washed her body until she was clean.

"A year ago I would have disagreed. But now I know. It's not that," Shea whispers, breaking her gaze from the fire and instead concentrating on the liquid in the glass.

Anything to keep from looking into the mistress's calculating stare.

"What then?"

"Paetre Lara was my mentor, my father in many ways. I continued his legacy as captain, but I fear that while worrying about his legacy and name, I've forgotten mine." Shea stands, dislodging V from where she sits.

V, ever the feline, gracefully moves to the lounge chair and watches as Shea begins to pace with the crystal glass still in her hand.

"You have done well for the *Duchess*. You have made a name for yourself, as an elf and as a woman. A difficult task in our world, and the reputation and legacy of the ship lives on. You've even settled his final score. The *Hydra* was everything he wanted."

Shea grunts. She's not surprised V already knows about the *Hydra*. Caen has loose lips when he's drunk and no doubt one of the whores was instructed to keep tabs. Shea places the glass on top of the fireplace and grips the edge, leaning over the flames. The heat warms her skin and she closes her eyes against the intensity.

"And now am I expected to retire? What do you do when you've caught the final score so early in your career? Is it right by your crew to keep going when you are the one unsatisfied?"

"You're captain."

"So what?"

"Don't stop. Not if you're not ready," V states.

"But is that fair? To the crew?"

There's a silence and Shea glances over to V, who's staring at her with an amused raised brow.

"You don't think they'll follow you?"

"Should they?"

"Shea," V laughs, "you're amazing. You picked up where Paetre left off and you've kept the *Duchess* together. You've even finished his legacy! They'd follow you anywhere because they'd be crazy not to."

Shea turns her head to gaze at V and smiles sheepishly.

"Look," V continues, "you don't want to stop sailing, fine.

Don't. If you care for fair, when you give the crew their wages, give them a choice. They can take their earnings and retire or continue to sail with the finest siege of the sea that Nereid has ever seen. But trust me, it's no hard choice. They'll sail for you."

"You sure know how to make someone feel good," Shea chuckles at her own double entendre.

"It's my job," V purrs.

Shea smiles, leaving the glass on top of the fireplace, and sits back in the armchair. Once comfortable, she reaches for the pearl in her jacket pocket. Producing the treasure for V, she holds out her hand, closed around the pearl. V stares at the outstretched palm, confusion evident on her features, until understanding seems to dawn on her.

She smiles, edging off the chaise lounge and crawling until she's kneeling right in front of Shea and the closed hand.

Shea gasps softly, entranced by V's seductive form erotically stopped between her legs. V kisses Shea's fingers surrounding the pearl, a silent request for her to reveal what's inside. Shea's eyes are hooded with desire; she exposes Ceto's pearl to the firelight.

V grins at the sight of the Lycon treasure. "The Pearl of Lycos..."

She peers up at Shea through her long eyelashes. "Why you little thief," she teases. "It's more beautiful than I could have imagined."

V reaches out to touch the pearl and Shea lets it fall into her hands.

"So, think you can snatch a high price on the Arethusian black market?"

V raises a brow. This thing will sell for millions of gold.

"I can expect my normal percentage?" V inquires.

"Fourteen percent and not a diamond more," Shea orders.

V grumbles slightly but accepts the price.

"Well, my dear." V stands, taking the pearl with her.

The cup Shea left on the fireplace sits near a wooden box

on the center of the mantel. She opens it, revealing a red velvet casing inside, and places the pearl in the safe, then mutters softly under her breath in a language Shea is familiar with. There's an audible click of a lock that can be heard from where the captain sits.

"I think you've earned your keep quite nicely," V murmurs and turns back to Shea.

She's still completely naked, with only her hair hiding her soft round breasts.

"Is that so?" Shea drawls breathlessly, her legs spreading.

V nods and returns to her position in between Shea's knees. But before kneeling all the way down, V holds herself up using the arms of the chair and leans forward until she's inches from Shea's full red lips.

"You asked me to be naked, Captain, I'm naked." V hovers close, almost touching.

"Yes…" Shea reaches her hand out, brushing V's blond curls away from her face before gripping a tight handful.

It draws a gasp from Venus.

"I did."

Shea pulls V close and kisses her harshly as she fights for dominance.

V wins the battle, sucking Shea's bottom lip into her mouth. She controls Shea's every move, whether the elf knows it or not. Their lips move together languidly.

Shea releases V's hair and trails her hand down her shoulder, farther, until her hand lies on V's breast. She grips the supple flesh, squeezing with just the right amount of pressure. She flicks her thumb over a nipple, eliciting another bite on her lower lip from V.

Shea chuckles into the kiss and responds with a pinch that will have consequences later.

V's soft, nimble hands casually but firmly make their way to Shea's fastening on her pants, unlacing them quickly. She arches her back, but the blonde uses a solid grip to keep her in place, then slides the too big pants down Shea's sun-kissed thighs.

Once the pants are pooled on the ground, V breaks the kiss. The blonde falls completely to her knees to tenderly peck the inside of the captain's legs.

Shea releases V's breast and lets her hands fall to her mistress's head as V dips her face nearer to Shea's womanhood. Her legs fall farther apart in anticipation. Their eyes catch for just a second, bright green melting into the shining lavender, before V's mouth is upon her.

Shea's hands tighten, a soft moan escaping her lush lips. Clenching the blond curls, Shea arches further, pressing herself against V's sweet mouth, who moans in encouragement.

The redhead's hips jerk involuntarily and the suction from V's plump lips leaves the elf on edge.

Then the panic comes like always: the feeling of not being in control.

Shea begins to struggle slightly, her hands tightening around the strands of hair in her grip. With as much mind as she has left, she removes her hands from V's curls and clutches the arms of the chair desperately. She's in and out of consciousness, then suddenly the pleasure is gone, and her face is being gripped between two soft hands.

Green eyes find the light purple, focusing in on the strange specks of gold floating within those enchanting orbs. Once more their foreheads come to rest together, breathing as one. Shea comes back to herself and pulls away slightly.

Her eyes scan over V's delicate form, watching how the light dances off her skin and how her lips glisten. She reaches out with her own lips to taste. The captain helps V onto her lap as they hold each other close. V pulls away from Shea, reaching for the hem of Shea's dark peasant shirt, then pulls it up over her head before allowing it drop on the ground. The bandages hiding the brand on Shea's chest and binding her breasts will be much harder to take off, so they leave it for now.

Their mouths crash together, struggling once again for dominance. V wins again. She always wins and encourages

Shea to squeeze the ample flesh of her ass, pushing their groins closer together. V positions her hips just so, sensually controlling their every move.

Finally Shea's grip tightens on the blonde's thighs and she uses her strength to stand up with V's legs wrapped around her waist. Their tongues dance together in a deep kiss and Shea groans as V squeezes her right breast through her bandages.

Carefully she walks unseeing to the bed in the center of the room and lowers Venus to the mattress in one suave move. Lying together, she lets her hand wander down and grins at V's hitched gasp as she her fingers find their way inside.

V's head hits the mattress and her hands claw at the silk sheets. Sweat mingles between their joining bodies.

The candlesticks drip onto the short table by the fire, and the night fades into heated bliss.

(DON'T) THINK THINGS THROUGH

Shea

"**Y**OU IDIOT!"

Shea opens her mouth to respond to V's insult but instead ducks for cover behind the chaise lounge as another solid object—a candlestick—comes flying for her head, slamming into the wall behind her.

V's hair is a sexy mess down her shoulders and her hastily thrown-on silk robe just barely conceals her heaving chest. The rage in her eyes almost keeps Shea locked in place as another candlestick from the side table comes flying her way.

Her own red hair falls in a tumbled mess, even curlier than V's, and her peasant blouse stops about mid-thigh, providing her with at least some modesty through this attack. Her chest bandages lay forgotten near the top of the bed where they'd used them as handcuffs during sex.

"Are you insane?" V growls.

"That's been up for debate," Shea jokes, straightening and placing her hands on her hips. "But this time I think this plan is quite sound."

"Stealing the crown princess of Arethusa is sound?" V screeches.

This time V goes for the bottle of wine that's still filled. She pelts it at Shea, who luckily dodges it, ducking behind the chaise, and it explodes against the far wall. The wine splashes the surface and the bottle shatters with a loud crash into a million tiny pieces.

Honestly Shea had thought the conversation was going to go a lot better. They'd just had amazing sex. And coming off that delicious high, she'd figured it'd be the perfect time to relay the job opportunity she'd decided to accept from the hood.

Obviously V hadn't seen it the same way.

"Frankly I thought you were going to react differently," Shea mutters, scanning the side table for more objects.

The door to the bedroom slams open, making both women jump as Caen, barefoot and clad only in his trousers, comes stomping in. "What the bloody Underdeep is going on in here? It sounds like a storm caged between the walls."

"Caen! Maybe you can talk some sense into your delirious captain. Otherwise I'd very seriously start thinking about mutiny," V snaps, crossing her arms over her chest.

"What happened to 'Shea, you're the best captain ever,'" Shea misquotes V's speech from earlier, making the blonde roll her eyes.

"That was before I knew you'd lost your bloody mind."

Caen steps farther into the room, narrowly avoiding the glass shards on the floor with his bare feet. He decides to close the door behind him as he notices other guests of the establishment are peeking their heads out from their rooms trying to discover what is going on in the mistress's chambers. Caen sighs, envying their ignorance, but returns his attention to the plot unfolding.

"He wants you to kidnap the crown princess of Arethusa and you entertained the idea. I think that calls for mental evaluation!"

V growls, picking up the final candlestick off the table, and takes off in a run toward Shea with the intention of smacking her over the head.

Shea holds her ground, quite through with V's tantrum, chin up in defiance.

But Caen steps in between them. He grasps V's wrist tightly, stopping her in place.

"Hold your roll, sweetheart."

V drops the candlestick and in return Caen drops V's hand. She shrugs him off with a surrendering gesture but keeps a cold glare in Shea's direction.

"Since when did you grow such a moral code? It's a kidnapping. I've done a lot worse, and with your help," Shea argues, matching her steely gaze.

"You can't tell me you agree with this." V turns on Caen, who looks at her with wide eyes. "As quartermaster, you must think of the crew."

Caen steps away from the mistress, keeping his body tense in case she decides to throw more things. "I don't know what you're talking about! Now somebody wanna explain this or do we all have to keep listening to you fools jabber all night."

"We were offered a job," Shea answers, keeping her features cool.

"You were charged with a suicide mission," V snarls, adjusting her robe, tying the strings around her waist tighter. "Shea has been hired to steal the next queen of Arethusa."

"Stealing what?" Caen asks, turning a sharp gaze to his young captain. "You want to kidnap the Arethusian heir?"

"Personally? No. But the man we'd work for does and, Caen, the score is good! Retirement good," Shea reasons with a huge grin.

Caen turns his back completely on Venus to face Shea. He ignores her state of undress with a grimace. "We have our retirement, the pearl."

"But that's not my legacy," Shea tells him earnestly, trying to get him to understand.

He stares at her with confusion deeply etched into his brow before his eyes widen. "You don't want to retire the *Duchess*,"

Caen states, understanding replacing the bewilderment on his features.

"You have to hear what he's offering—"

"It doesn't matter," V interrupts.

"Shea, you know I'd follow you anywhere," Caen says, and the elf's pleading expression turns into a beaming smile. "But I don't know about this. Even before your captaincy. Paetre knew better than to involve himself in the affairs of the land folk. There are too many things that can go wrong. We disrupt order—"

"We don't change it. I know, I remember," Shea finishes. "But I have a good feeling about this."

She stops talking to allow Caen a moment to process as he mutely thinks it over.

"This is a whole other level," V insists. "This is dangerous; this man could turn around and put your head on the line for this 'revolution' just to come out on top."

V crosses to the armchair and sits heavily in it. She leans forward, her forehead coming to rest in her palm.

"Do we know who the man is?" Caen asks.

"No," Shea reveals honestly.

Caen nods, his own hands going to his hips. "What's the offer?"

"You can't seriously be considering this?" V whispers, straightening up.

She reaches for the remaining bottle, the amber liquor on the tray, and pours herself a heavy drink in one of the crystal glasses. She takes a sip and then pours two more glasses, extending one out to Caen, who takes it and gulps a drink.

"I'd follow her anywhere," he repeats with a glance toward Shea, and the captain offers a small smile. "But," he continues, "I do have to consider the crew, so I have to know…what's the offer?"

"The entrance key and map to Ceto's private Vault of Secrets," Shea states. "Every piece of blackmail, every dark history of the reigning families of Lycos and Arethusa, and who knows what else. Along with sanctuary in Arethusa after we get the vault. All for the taking."

Her claim is met with silence as both V and Caen try to process the reward.

"This is my legacy, V," Shea whispers. "It's my…our"—she gestures to Caen—"chance to go down in history. I could take down Ceto."

Shea shoves her shirt aside, away from her chest, showing them the carved brand above her heart: Ceto's initial surrounding the dark seal of Lycos. A half circle representing the first letter of the empress's name surrounds a perfect sketch of Scylla, the monstrous she-beast of the sea and the patron goddess of Lycos. Sea serpents ascend from Scylla's head along with tentacles like that of a giant squid. They curl along with Scylla's hair around the tearful woman's face within the crescent, a repugnant sight. Her monstrous face is correctly detailed because of the magic blade used by the royal slave carver, who helped Ceto cut the brand into her chest under his supervision. This brand is, and was, a message that someday Shea would belong to Ceto as nothing more than property.

Caen has to look away, the memory of that day still vivid in his mind. V refuses to even glance in her direction at the disgusting mark. Shea waits and finally V looks at her. Really looks at her. From the brand to the solemn, decided look on the captain's face, and there seems to be a battle warring behind those translucent lavender eyes. Shea releases her shirt, letting it settle back over the brand, and readjusts it so it falls back down to mid-thigh.

"No one other than the ruling family has ever sat on the Arethusian throne," V begins. "It's impossible. And besides, you sashay out of town and I'm left to collect? That puts a lot of pressure on me."

"You're right, which is why, if you wish, I'll find someone else to take the payment, and meet them in Lycos."

Caen starts to object, but V beats him to it.

"Who?" she growls. "Who are you going to get? Are you

going to leave Caen? Not bloody likely."

Shea chuckles and V gives her an aggravated glare. "Look, you're my fence," Shea tells her, then leers. "And occasionally a great piece of ass."

Shea laughs at her own tease while V rolls her eyes in response.

"But other than that," she continues, "my business doesn't concern you. For what it's worth, I'll calculate a risk factor into your earnings. Say, twenty percent of the pearl?"

Again the blonde's mouth opens to object but then shuts unexpectedly. There's a look of defeat etched into the subtle lines on her face. It's as if she's aged a millennium in the last ten minutes of talking. She gives a small nod to Caen, who shrugs in silent agreement.

Shea smiles widely.

The decision settles in continued silence. Caen breaks it first.

"Okay," he mutters. "So how do we plan on getting in? A mere chance of the changing of the guards?"

"An invitation," Shea answers.

She walks toward V and rummages through her jacket hanging on the chair, then produces the invitation from the inner pocket to the pre-coronation ball, handing it to Caen, who quickly examines it and hands it to V.

"And the way out?" Caen asks.

"Servants' entrance. We have to lead her out to the gardens and take the south exit, a path has been cleared."

"That's not going to be the hard part," V states, examining the invite.

"Then what is?"

"Getting in."

"But we have an invitation?"

"Yes, and if you had bothered to read it, you're playing a part," V drawls, handing the parchment to Shea, who takes it to read.

V continues, "Lady Anavella of Lycos. You have to convince

them you're a refined lady, and not only them, but Princess Joana herself."

"Shit."

V hums, then smiles sinisterly. "Do you know why they hold the pre-coronation ball?"

Shea looks up from the invite and sends a glance to Caen, who shrugs. "To celebrate the impending coronation?"

"It's a mating dance," V clarifies. "It's where the sovereign chooses her future consort."

"You're kidding," Shea deadpans.

"We're screwed," Caen mutters and Shea shoots him a sharp glance.

"Actually, most Arethusian royalty lean toward the fairer and more delicate sex," Venus states.

"So?"

Caen laughs. "Shea wouldn't know delicate if it ran up and smacked her over the head."

"Do you mind." Shea glares. "Besides it doesn't have to be me that seduces her."

"They just need to look the part."

V gets up, crossing the floor to the other side of the room where a giant chest resides. She opens the chest and out floods materials of silk, tulle, and taffeta. Then she rummages through the unexpectedly deep chest and pulls out a beautiful ball gown. The top of the bodice is deep black velvet, with twin off-the-shoulder straps. Shea pushes off the wall she's leaning against and strolls closer to V and the gown. The firelight glints off the dress, exposing subtle beading on the bodice of dark leaves spiraling up to the neckline. From the corset bottom, deep forest-green material with a shimmery surface flows into a train on the floor. V shakes the dress and as the bottom material moves, it sparkles like moving water.

"Perfect," Shea whispers. "So we dress you up. I go as one of your handmaidens and we help you lure the princess to the gardens. This may just work."

"I've already met the princess," V says, shaking her head. "So no. We're going to dress you up."

"What?"

"We just need to make you look the part. As long as you don't say too much, no one will notice."

"No, you heard Caen. I don't do delicate."

"Oh I don't know, darling, you can be quite delicate under my touch," V teases.

Shea turns a bright shade of red and glares.

"Actually, that could work," Caen replies.

He sets his glass down and starts walking toward the door like all of this is set and final.

"No, it can't, guys, are we forgetting something?"

Caen stops and V looks at Shea, confused. Shea huffs and points to her ears.

"How do we explain this? No way the princess will give us the time of day."

"Shea. Arethusa is not like Lycos. Elves are actually widely accepted and in some provinces coveted. There are many ladies in the Arethusian court who are elven. And you'll be seen as even more rare to be of such high status from Lycos. I'm telling you, this will work. Besides, you like a challenge, wouldn't you like to have the gloating rights of seducing a crown princess?"

Appealing to Shea's pride, that's low even for V.

Shea notices Caen's shaking shoulders as he keeps from laughing out loud. But V is right. It could work.

"Alright. You've got a day to make me look like a lady. Caen"—Shea turns to her quartermaster, who salutes, to which Shea rolls her eyes—"get back to the men, tell them the plan. I can have three for the party inside the castle, so take Aster and one other, you'll be coming with me."

Caen nods. "We'll need a carriage for tonight."

"Find one, pay someone if you have to. We don't want to make too much noise by stealing. Send a group out to canvass the south wall and find our exit. Once we do this, we'll have two hours to get her to the garden, knock her out, escape, and get back to the ship."

"That's not a lot of time," Caen remarks.

"And you've got a day to figure it out."

Caen leaves quickly after that and V calls for two of her girls. One to clean up the mess of glass in the corner from all the thrown objects and the other to help her with Shea. V holds the dress up in front of the captain to see if the color matches her skin. A black-haired prostitute, who Shea's been with before, holds her hair up in a mock updo to get an idea.

"You've got a day," Shea repeats, frowning at her reflection.

V smiles slyly and kisses Shea on the cheek. Lavender meets green. "That's more than enough time."

MASQUERADE

Shea

EVENING ARRIVES QUICKLY AND Shea's head is filled to the brim with etiquette lessons and manners. She takes another gander at the mirror, making sure there isn't a single hair out of place.

She smooths her hands down the green dress that sticks to her curves, leaving nothing to the imagination. The bodice gives her a small, desirable waist, though she thinks it might have broken two of her ribs in the process of tying it. And the corset forces her boobs to stick out like a sore thumb. The neckline of the gown exposes her upper chest much to her distaste, and so she's had to cover Ceto's brand with a small concealment charm she'd picked up years ago.

Some days she wishes she could use the charm all the time to cover the brand, but the magic takes concentration, and Shea would still know it's there even if she couldn't see it. Hopefully it holds through the night.

The dress falls in waves, and she thanks Poseidon that it's long enough to cover her boots twice fold. Discarded heels lay on the floor in a disheveled heap, and she hopes V won't argue.

Her ears are uncovered by her hair and it makes her want to cover up and hide. The black straps fall off the shoulder, and V has accompanied the outfit with black pearl earrings along with a single pearl necklace on a petite gold chain. The necklace falls perfectly within the hollow of her collarbone and she reaches up and touches the pearl, smiling at the irony and glancing to the box over the fireplace that holds the Pearl of Lycos.

Her red hair is beautifully intertwined in a waterfall-braided updo and small ringlets cascade around her face. On the right side is a golden hairpiece that looks like ivy wrapped around a rose and is tucked between the curls.

She doesn't recognize the creature staring back at her; it's otherworldly with all that makeup. Shea can't say she hates it, but that's perhaps what disturbs her the most.

"Shea? The carriage is ready. Caen, Aster, and Mister Sanders are downstairs. I set them up with the extra suits I acquired."

V walks in after a quick knock but doesn't wait for a reply. She stops in her tracks as she sees the captain. Shea turns to look at her and immediately notices her staring; the tips of Shea's ears tinge pink.

"Great! I'm ready," Shea tells her.

She breaks her gaze with a cough and grabs black gloves off the bed. She manages to slip the first on but has trouble with the second.

"Here let me," V murmurs, her temporary trance over. The mistress walks over and takes the remaining glove gently from Shea. She holds out her bare hand and watches as V swiftly works the long glove up her arm.

V straightens the material on both of Shea's forearms. "There. A perfect fit."

Shea nods but keeps her gaze on the floor, afraid she'll see V staring again.

"You look beautiful," V tells her.

"I look like a snob."

V laughs but her face turns somber, almost wistful, like she can see something Shea doesn't.

"I wish you didn't have to go tonight," V states, fixing the tulle at the bottom of the dress.

"Not this again."

"No, I'm not fighting you. I fear I must let you go now," V hurriedly explains.

You never had me, she wants to respond, *no one ever will.*

But instead she says, "You could never lose me."

"The Fates are cruel women. They've set you on your path," V mutters, stepping away.

She wraps her arms around herself as if suddenly cold. She looks at Shea like they'll never be the same again.

"We're not controlled by fate, Venus. There's no such thing as gods or weavers controlling the future."

A pained smile graces V's features. "But there are monsters just like in the myths of old. You've seen them, you've fought them. So doesn't that mean the gods who created them could be real too?"

Shea shakes her head no. Because if there were such things, she would never leave the comfort of this room again; the world is full of dark and formidable monsters. Every voyage brings them closer to an unimaginable end. If there really were immortal creatures out there, there'd be no point in trying because how do you best a god?

Shea steps closer and kisses V deeply, cutting off this line of thinking. It feels like a goodbye, but Shea doesn't voice the concern. She keeps V close and rests their foreheads together.

"It'll take just under two weeks to get to Tenaro. And don't forget, the *Duchess* is just about the fastest ship on the sea," Shea reassures her, looking V in the eye. "And then about a nine-day journey to Lycos where we'll meet at the capital."

"I'm still not sure if Acheron is the right place, the capital of Lycos is too dangerous for you to dock. Especially after stealing the pearl." V worries her bottom lip between her teeth. "Perhaps farther up the coast in Oceanus at their capital of Metis?"

"No," Shea orders, "it has to be Acheron. Once we take the princess, every country in Nereid, including Erebos in the Eastlands, and Oceanus, are going to tighten their borders.

Once we have the map we'll need to make quick work of stealing from the vault."

"Are we going or not? What in Hades is taking so long?"

Caen barges into the room, causing V to step out of Shea's arms before she really notices.

"Triton," Caen breathes, giving Shea a once-over. "You look great." Shea winks, lifting up the skirt and showing him the long dagger holster connected to her thigh.

"Perfect." He grins. "Caeruleus is at the south side entrance. Once he sees us, he'll notify the crew to get the ship ready. We'll be coming in fast. Mister Sanders will drive the carriage around the back and then stake out the garden exit. Aster and I will stay by your side until you manage to snag the princess. Shall we?"

Caen holds out his arm for Shea to take.

Shea nods and takes one last look at V before mockingly curtsying to make her laugh.

"It would be an honor, sir," Shea drawls in an exaggerated falsetto.

The Arethusian palace towers at the top of the inner walled city. Mister Sanders drives from the Slippery Serpent up to the royal city entrance casually enough not to raise suspicion.

Once through they follow a line of extravagant carriages up the narrow cobblestoned roads to the castle, passing homes of the lords and ladies of the Arethusian court.

Upon arrival at the front of the palace, hundreds of carriages fill the giant courtyard. Men and women in stunning clothing span the magnificent marble staircase that leads up to the golden doors of the Arethusian castle. Guards stand at every step to either side of the stairs and there's even more at the entrance behind the squires announcing each royal's arrival.

Shea watches from the window of the carriage as it slowly comes to a stop in front of the intimidating staircase covered by a long ocean-blue carpet.

Aster rides on the back of the carriage in pale green squire clothing, while Caen dons a traditional Arethusian blue suit. Dark blue pants and a dark blue jacket with gold buttons down the front. The seafoam sash around his waist is tied with the correct fisherman's bend knot. He sits across from Shea checking the parameters before knocking on the roof of the carriage to signal Aster to let them out.

"We could still ride away," Caen tells her, staring Shea down, searching for any kind of doubt. He won't find any.

Shea's made up her mind. "This is it, Caen. Once we have the map and key to the vault, Ceto loses everything."

It's that simple. Shea met Ceto when she was fourteen; it was on the empress's royal voyage vessel. Paetre had stormed it in an attempt to steal the pearl, but unfortunately it hadn't been there. Shea and two other crewmen were supposed to find the empress in her personal cabin, take care of the guards, and keep her there until the captain could arrive. It had been her first real mission during a siege and it had gone easily enough.

They'd dispatched the guards and even found Ceto. They waited for Paetre in the empress's cabin while Ceto tried to make a deal with Shea to betray her captain. The offers had been good and Shea was so young that in that second the empress's promises caused seeds of doubt.

It had almost worked until she had said, "Think of how well off you'd be compared to your subhuman brethren. You'd almost be human. Free like me. Not a slave like the rest of your kind."

Shea had outright refused after that. Another hour and Paetre finally arrived, but by then Shea had forced Ceto to remove her garments and wait naked on her knees for the captain. She had humiliated the empress and it felt like justice. Paetre made his remarks, as did the rest of the male crew in the room, and then Shea had left her tied and bound for her guards to find her.

Sometimes Shea wonders, if she'd just kept her cool, if things could have turned out differently—because Ceto got her revenge when Shea was captured on a mission a couple years later. Ceto ordered her bound to a table, naked from the waist up, and had carved the seal into Shea's chest herself, above her heart so she would always remember that she belongs to Ceto. Even with a concealment charm, it would still always be there hiding behind the magic.

It was quite a scene when Paetre and Caen found her. From that point on, Shea has made it her personal mission to be a delectable thorn in Ceto's side. Her bounty in Lycos is so high, she's considered number one on the most wanted list. This vault will be Shea's legacy. And if she can bring Ceto down a peg while stopping or hindering the slave trade, then it'll all be worth it.

Even if it means this young woman's life, because after all, the princess is only human.

"Let's go," Shea orders.

Aster opens the carriage doors and pulls out the steps. Caen gets out first, taking a look around before stepping aside and holding out his hand, along with Aster, to help Shea out of the carriage.

Once she's out, she tries not to let the atmosphere overwhelm her—the lights of the palace and the beauty of the scenery feels breathtaking.

Caen whispers to Mister Sanders to take off after Aster puts the steps back and closes the door. The carriage drives away as does any thought of retreat. Aster and Caen wait behind Shea for her to make the first move.

She looks up the steps to the open doors, watching the shadows dance along the high vaulted stone ceilings of the inner hall, and then takes a deep breath. She walks up the steps with Aster to her left and Caen to her right. She realizes she almost forgot to tell Aster how handsome he looks and she whispers it off to the side. His ears blush, much like hers did before, back at V's.

They make it to the top of the steps and the captain glances back to look out at the view from the palace entrance. The vast ocean can be seen from where she stands and the moonlight dances off the waves, calling for her to return. She turns her back on it and instead focuses on the squire ahead accepting the invitations.

"Caen," Shea murmurs, nodding her head toward the squire, and he easily produces the invite as the line moves forward and it becomes their turn.

"Lady Anavella." The squire smiles, bowing deeply as Shea returns a small curtsy. "An honor, my lady. Boy." He thrusts the letter toward Aster, who takes it clumsily.

Shea pretends to ignore the situation and instead makes an air of taking in the castle, which isn't hard to do.

"You will give this to the squire at the balcony over the ballroom to announce your lady's arrival, understood?"

"Understood," Aster mutters, averting his gaze. Shea notices how the squire leers slightly at Aster and pointedly glares at Caen to do something.

Caen coughs and closes in on the squire, towering over him. The obnoxious servant squeals and hides slightly behind the list in his hand.

"Are we free to go?" Caen rumbles.

"Yes, of course, sir, please go in." The squire trembles.

Shea curtsies once more and walks away without a word. Aster and Caen follow quickly behind.

Once they're out of sight and away from the squire, Shea lets her left hand fall to her side. She reaches back subtly, her hand almost lost in the green tulle of her skirt, but Aster puts his hand in hers and she gives it a quick squeeze.

He squeezes back with a thank you.

They step away from each other after.

Finally the moment arrives and they're at the top balcony over the ballroom. The announcer is to Shea's left just ahead, and the first couple goes in.

"Lord Kelpren and Lady Algaea of the Rivren province, Arethusa," the announcer bellows.

The ballroom is magnificent. Water cascades over the windows like curtains and in the center of the room is a fountain carved of Queen Amphitrite, the patron goddess of Arethusa and the wife of Poseidon. Fabrics of varying shades of blue are woven around the white marble columns and the material drapes along the ceiling. At the far end of the room from Shea are the thrones. The larger chair for the queen is empty, and an older man who looks to be in his fifties, Prince Mariner if Shea remembers correctly from V's studies, sits in the small consort throne.

Standing at the edge of the steps leading up to the thrones are three women. The one in the center is wearing a stunning white-and-gold gown; her skin shimmers as if it's been painted by glitter and her long blond hair flows down her back with white seashells intertwined in the curls. On top of her head is a tiara made completely of gold with chips of diamonds and seashells on the ragged points. It looks beautiful and expensive. Her bodice of gold reminds Shea of armor. It's formidable and makes the woman appear strong while the white tulle flowing gracefully to the floor accentuates her figure nicely. At the lady's sides are two older women in blue dresses: one in a light seafoam and the other in a night sky that without the candlelight would look black.

"I think I see her," Shea murmurs.

Caen subtly looks down to where Shea is staring.

"Yes," he whispers. "That's Princess Joana in the center."

"Next," the announcer commands, and they step up to the entry. The squire smiles warmly and Shea realizes he's elven.

"Now after I announce your name," he explains, "you'll follow the blue carpet down the steps and to the princess, where you will introduce yourself. You will do so quickly and then join the rest of the ball. Be careful not to waste Her Highness's time."

Shea glances back at Caen, who shrugs.

"Very well," Shea tells the announcer, who bows to her, taking the invite from Aster.

"Please." He gestures for her to stand at the front of the balcony.

She steps forward and Caen holds Aster back as he tries to follow. This presentation is everything and she has to do it alone.

"Lady Anavella of Cocytus, the elven province, Lycos."

She curtsies low, with a pointer finger eloquently placed at her chin as V taught her to do in this moment. It feels like forever but then she's straightening once again. Just in time for her eyes to meet with Princess Joana herself. It's only for a second and even though it's far, Shea feels as if she could give extreme detail to every intricate feature of the princess's face.

Shea is the one to break the gaze, but it's like she can still feel those vibrant eyes watching her as she makes her way down the carpeted steps to the grand ball.

Caen and Aster follow behind, making a subtle effort to keep up with their captain.

ISN'T SHE LOVELY

Joana

CROWN PRINCESS JOANA OF ARETHUSA stands at attention, playing the part of royalty to perfection, and wishing she could be anywhere else.

The pre-coronation ball is a sham. Her grandmother, the late Queen Doris of Arethusa, already laid down in her will who she wants Joana to marry if she doesn't find someone at the ball. And so far it seems highly unlikely that some magical true love will appear. Everyone is the same, all in their varying blue gowns, their sugary smiles, and their constant blather.

She glances back subtly to her distant father sitting behind her in the consort throne.

He catches her expression and tries to give her a comforting smile, though it looks like no more than a vain attempt.

She tries to smile back but her eyes catch on her mother's empty throne—how she wishes she were here. Just one of the many wishes Jo has had in her life. In this moment she wishes that her older sister hadn't died at birth with the royal surrogate due to some foreign complication. She wishes that her mother hadn't been forced to then carry Joana for an heir. That her mother hadn't suffered from the effects of childbirth, dying when Jo was eleven. She even wishes her mother could be here just for the day to celebrate her most recent birthday of twenty-five. And that she would tell Jo what to do now, whom to choose, and who would make her happy.

Another brunette in a sparkling dress makes her appearance, bowing shortly to the court and offering some sweet nonsense about how beautiful Joana looks tonight.

"Lord Kelpren and Lady Algaea of the Rivren province, Arethusa," the announcer bellows, and another young gentleman shuffles down the aisle, looking dejected to the entire world.

Men are always less eager to meet her, since even if they married her, their position would be consort and not king. In Arethusa, it's normal to grow up appreciating both sexes since it's often common to marry either, like her great-grandmother who had married a Lycon woman. And the Lycon woman had then carried their heir, Jo's grandmother Doris.

Queen Doris and Jo's mother, Queen Triteia, had both married men though. Sometimes Jo wishes she could find someone like her father, who had married her mother because he loved her with all his being. He's never been the same since she died, though he's always been a quiet man. He didn't care that he wouldn't have the power, all he wanted was to see Triteia and the queendom succeed.

But Jo prefers women anyway and finds them to be more interesting partners than men. So she ignores the preening male standing before her as he rambles through his forced manners. Jo curtsies to him politely and casually looks up to see the next announcement.

"Lady Anavella of Cocytus, elven province, Lycos." Jo's eyes widen as she takes in the gorgeous sight of Lady Anavella. Her red hair is pulled up in a braided updo with small tendrils escaping and a beautiful golden comb embedded in the vibrant curls. Her green dress complements her sun-kissed skin and it's a refreshing change from the rest of the blue attire throughout the ballroom.

Then Anavella looks up and the world stops as Jo loses her breath. She is absolutely the most stunning creature Jo has ever seen. Her ears at the tips are pink and Jo tries to stay still instead of attempting to draw the lady's attention back to herself again. The redhead sneaks one more peek at the bottom of the steps and quickly looks away when she sees Jo is still watching her. Jo smirks.

"Rhea?"

The old albino woman in the dark navy velvet dress turns to her, stepping closer to the princess.

"The woman coming down the stairs? Who is she?" Jo asks.

"She's an elf," Rhea remarks, looking at the redhead with veiled disgust.

Jo frowns but lets the comment go, if only to get a straight answer from her chaperone.

"She's beautiful. What do you know about her?"

"I've heard rumors of an Anavella, but I didn't realize she was so young."

It's Gaea who speaks instead, Jo's other chaperone and Rhea's wife, in the light blue dress. They've been Joana's handlers ever since her mother died, hired under her grandmother, who thought it prudent for Jo to see what a strong marriage can do.

"There's not many elven courtiers in Lycos; she must be married to someone powerful," Rhea responds, stepping away from Jo as Lady Anavella makes her way down the aisle.

"Or the daughter of one," she whispers hopefully.

Finally the lady stands before her, and up close the gown is even more beautiful. The green is almost black on the corset and her hair is a vibrant red. Her eyes take Jo's breath away. Viridian with specks of silver, they almost glow in the firelight. She curtsies low in the same old style she did at the balcony, just like Jo's mother used to do. It makes her smile. The boy and large man behind Anavella bow deeply as well. Jo curtsies back.

"Your Highness, thank you for the invitation to this evening, the ballroom looks exquisite tonight." Anavella smiles, her voice perfectly level. Her eyes dart around the room as if careful to meet Jo's gaze.

"The pleasure is ours," she returns, purring.

There's an awkward moment of silence as Jo waits for her to continue, but it's not until her escort coughs subtly that Anavella resumes her spiel, as if she'd forgotten about the whole performance of the courtiers.

"Congratulations on your coronation. This must be an incredible time, have you thought about what your first act as queen might be?"

Rhea huffs loudly and the question brings a rather large smile to Jo's face.

"Young lady, even if Her Highness did, she has no reason to discuss it with you or during such an event as this."

"What act did you have in mind, my lady?" Jo asks, completely ignoring Rhea's outburst.

Anavella, frozen by Rhea's reprimand, slowly grins at Jo's approval though she almost looks surprised. She intrigues Jo even more.

"Perhaps dock regulations, Your Highness? Arethusian trade is a powerful emissary among the entirety of Nereid. Perhaps allowing regulations to bring in more smaller independents to create outlander trade." Anavella almost seems likely to keep talking, obsessively interested by the subject, but her escort coughs again and she stops smoothly.

But her ears give her away with a pink tinge at the points.

"To be honest, that is not an avenue I've explored," Jo admits, and while the smile on Anavella's face doesn't deflate, the sparkle to her eyes slightly fades and she feels closed off again.

Jo quickly tries to save the moment. "But after your comments, I will definitely be exploring the law there, a most excellent suggestion."

And there's that gorgeous smile again. Jo just might melt. She decides right then and there that this is a girl she's got to get to know.

She steps closer into Anavella's personal space and extends

her hand out in an open gesture. "Do you dance, my lady?"

There's a pause, and the lady chuckles. "You could say that, yes," she responds with a coy smile.

"Well then, may I have the honor of your company?"

"Your Highness," Gaea interrupts, "perhaps later in the evening after you've seen to more prospective guests."

Rhea shares a look of displeasure with Gaea, and Jo finds it all the more reason to dance with this beautiful elf. Jo smiles sweetly, the intent made clear that she doesn't care about their disapproval and they nod, bowing. She can't help the small glance back at her father, who is leaning forward as if trying to get a better look at Anavella. Jo shoots him a questioning look, raising a brow. He takes another second to evaluate Anavella before expressing a gentle smile and a nod. That's enough for Jo.

"My lady?" Jo prompts again.

Anavella hesitantly takes Jo's hand, and when they touch, a spark shivers down the royal's spine. She notices Anavella shivers as well. The lady is staring at their touch with an odd expression, but at Jo's prompting, she follows the princess to the dance floor.

The crowd parts for the future queen and they stop at the center of the ballroom, as is custom. Jo takes first position, waiting for Anavella to take the second dominant position. When she pauses, Jo looks into her eyes and sees fear, almost like doubt. A small thrill of pleasure runs through Jo, who decides to take control and instead dance the dominant position in a dashing rescue to the lady's aid. Jo already likes how this is turning out.

She puts her arm around her waist, pulling her close, which causes Anavella to place her hand on Jo's shoulder. She then offer's her left hand and the lady places her palm on top. The crowd gasps at the breach of protocol. Jo grins at the break in tradition, delighted to be offending the court's delicate sensibilities, as they obviously know that isn't how the royal Arethusian waltz works.

Screw custom, Jo thinks as she holds this beautiful redhead in her arms. They fit perfectly together and the music starts slowly. Whispers have already erupted for the change in dance position, and it feels like an enhancement of the music to her ears. Anavella's short for an elf, which Jo takes small pleasure in as it leaves her more than a few inches shorter than her six feet. They begin to sway, turning around the dance floor as they begin the traditional Arethusian waltz. She's clumsy for a lady, but it makes Jo smile, and before long, every missing step or bump becomes a giggle between the two and there's a genuine light coming from Anavella's eyes.

"You are very beautiful, my lady," she tells her as they turn around the floor softly.

She guides her on almost every move as if the lady has never danced a day in her life.

"Thank you, Your Highness, but please, call me Ana. You look really great tonight too, or lovely, as it were," she corrects herself and it almost seems as if she might curse, which Jo would have loved to see, but Ana holds her tongue.

Jo wets her lower lip, and she notices Ana's gaze on her mouth as she follows the movement.

"You're definitely not from around here," she jokes, and it catches Ana's attention.

She looks up with a coy smile.

"And why is that?"

"Well for starters, no Arethusian wet nurse would have let you attend a ball with these dancing skills."

It catches the lady off guard and because of that, she throws her head back with a boisterous laugh. The princess grins at the beautiful curves of Ana's sun-kissed neck.

"You know, for a princess your manners need work," she teases back, and suddenly her movements are becoming more natural.

"I think that's the best compliment I've received all evening." Jo smirks. "Hold on."

Ana gives her a questioning look when Jo tightens her hand

at her waist and spins her out, leading her across the floor. The music becomes more intense, the violins growing harsher yet slower, until it leads to the semifinal dip.

There's a slight panicked expression on Ana's face and Jo wants to wipe it clean off.

"I've got you," she whispers, and it seems that Ana trusts her hold as she lets herself fall back slowly in a perfect Arethusian dip.

The princess's hand is placed lightly upon Ana's chest. In this one moment, she feels as if she experiences a forever within the held note, holding this gorgeous woman perfectly in her arms. Together they move as one.

Jo wants to talk to her and hear more of how she knows about trading policy but she stays reserved. There will be time for that. She brings Ana back up as the music returns to normal and the dance continues.

"You're an incredible dancer, Your Highness," Ana murmurs as they're pressed close together, almost forehead to forehead.

Jo can't quite believe her luck. She came to this ball knowing that the person she would be forced to spend forever with may be good for the queendom but not for her. Doesn't romance begin with attraction? Maybe this could be more. She has pushed away any dream of falling in love the normal way because to be a queen means sacrifice. But now, staring at Ana, she realizes that maybe it can be both. She lets the idea of love at first sight sink in, she allows all the fairy tales her mother ever told her to be true. That this could be the start of her story as Queen Joana of Arethusa.

Because all Jo wants is to press a kiss on those beautiful lips but instead she pulls back and smiles broadly.

"Thank goodness too, or we'd both be tripping over ourselves." And there goes that laugh again and, oh yes, there is no way she's letting this girl get away. Because now Jo has hope. In time she can even see herself marrying this wonderful girl, and with any luck, they'll fall in love later.

THE NOT SO GREAT ESCAPE

Shea

So PERHAPS SHEA SHOULD have paid attention to all those dance lessons V tried to instill over the years. But hey, somehow her dancing actually seems to be working.

The princess took control much to Shea's relief, and she felt herself being guided gracefully across the dance floor without much effort. The music has steadied after the grand dip, and slowly courtiers file out onto the dance floor, each of them trying to create a distraction so that the crown princess might notice them.

But so far Joana's eyes seem to only be for Shea, much to the captain's embarrassed discomfort. Shea keeps up the pretenses of the charmed lady from far away, completely entranced with the princess. But the more time spent with this royal, the more the pretenses are becoming real. Her Royal Highness is actually quite funny. So Shea makes the decision to stop laughing at the young woman's jokes.

Focus, her mind screams.

"So you're from Lycos?"

The question stumbles out of nowhere and it catches Shea

off guard, making her trip slightly. Shea withholds the groan but it makes Joana chuckle anyway.

"Yes," Shea responds with a polite smile.

"Do you like it there?" Joana continues, "I've only had the pleasure of meeting Empress Ceto once when I was younger, but I remember her being very beautiful."

Shea suppresses the eye roll and instead nods graciously.

"It's nice. The country itself is beautiful. Though there are things that make it hard for me to see it all. Empress Ceto has a...prominent presence," Shea falters, spinning her story quickly.

Joana must read in between the lines of her guarded statement because she brings her closer and their faces are now inches apart.

"That was insensitive of me. I'm aware that Lycos has a more closeted outlook on elven culture."

Right, there's that, Shea thinks. The comment itself catches Shea off guard though, and she finds herself absently staring at this intriguing royal. She's played many courtiers before, taking them for all they're worth, and yet Shea feels like a con artist on her first job trying not to be caught by this very impressive woman.

"What? Is there something on my face?" Joana jokes and Shea forces herself out of her reverie.

"No, it's just not often you hear someone of the court"—Shea gestures around—"with much sympathy to the elves."

Shea kind of resents the pity that appears in Joana's eyes, but it doesn't make the respect she feels for her comment fade.

"You would find more acceptance in Arethusa. Is there a reason you do not leave, a parent or spouse perhaps?"

A smile draws across Shea's face, and if she weren't trying to kidnap this princess she'd almost be impressed. Sneaky girl, Shea reflects to herself, and the princess ducks her head, obviously caught off guard by her own bluntness though she recovers quickly.

"A father. I'm not married yet." Shea smiles, batting her eyelashes.

But instead of causing Joana to blush, like she had intended, the gesture merely makes the princess chuckle. The song draws to an end and Shea removes herself gently from Joana's arms as they clap for the orchestra.

Shea takes her chance to glance at the massive sundial in the room that hangs above the thrones. It's midnight, which means they have their two hours. Her eyes drop down to the man sitting in the throne below the dial, and she's surprised when their eyes meet. She can't say if he was watching her, but he turns his gaze away to another part of the ball.

The princess thanks a couple that walks past, complimenting them on her dance, and Shea takes a moment to catch Aster's and Caen's eyes from the crowd and signals for them to head to the garden. They begin to slip away.

"My lady?" Joana calls and Shea turns back to her.

"It's a beautiful night, Your Highness. I thought I might take some air in the garden," Shea says.

She hopes the princess will take the subtle offer and she begins to turn away when Joana grabs her hand, stopping her. Shea smirks, but when she turns back to Joana, her features are the picture of innocence.

The blonde smiles. "Would you be willing to take a turn around the gardens with me? It's my favorite part of the castle. And they've been lit for the ball tonight."

"Without escort, Your Highness?" Shea gasps with wide eyes.

Joana glances back at the two older ladies glaring at the captain and nods defiantly.

"Just the two of us," Joana replies.

It'll be your ruin, Shea muses, taking Joana's offered arm as they walk toward the gardens.

Caen and Aster are already outside; all Shea has to do is get Joana alone and wait. They pass through the large pillars that lead out into the royal gardens.

Shea has to admit it is beautiful. They seem to be the only

ones out, everyone still in the ballroom. The trees glow as if they've been lit up from the inside. It's obviously elemental magic, but she's never seen it used so casually by courtiers before. Most disdain it, considering usually only those of pure elven blood can perform it. Shea can remember, before she was taken as a child, the few elves with the special gift given to them from the Underdeep, the kingdom of Poseidon. The elder elves taught those of Erebos that all magic is sacred. She wonders now what her people would think of the display. Would they think it beautiful or blasphemous?

The paths are made with crushed seashells that have been smoothed down to the point where they wouldn't cut your feet if you walked on them barefoot. The plants are foreign and strange, as if they're walking on the ocean floor. Marble statues that look like coral span the grounds. It's incredible. Shea could spend days just living in these gardens.

"Do you like it?" Joana asks.

Shea almost forgot she was here.

"Yes," Shea answers honestly. "It's the most beautiful thing I've ever seen."

There's no need to lie. Her answer seems to make Joana extremely happy because she takes them out farther into the gardens, toward the south wall and away from the ballroom. Shea is almost skeptical of her luck. After walking for a few minutes, they make it through the other side of a labyrinth and arrive at a magnificent fountain surrounded by a glistening saltwater pool.

The fountain's center statue is of Amphitrite and Poseidon. Poseidon holds Amphitrite close, their chests touching. She's wrapped her arms around him, and as they walk to the other side of the pool, Shea sees from a new angle that Poseidon and Amphitrite are in fighting stances. Poseidon has his trident across Amphitrite's back, pointed out, and Amphitrite has a staff protecting Poseidon pointed toward invisible enemies as well. It's incredibly carved.

"This was my mother's favorite spot," the princess breaks

the silence. She releases her hand from Shea's hold and steps closer to it.

"It's called the Lover's Fountain. King Poseidon and Queen Amphitrite hold each other so close that nothing comes between them. But as their backs are open to the world, the other protects them with everything they have. They will always have each other no matter what. Just like my parents did. I always wanted a love like theirs. This place, after she died, quickly became my favorite," Joana explains. "I spend much of my time here, reading and sparring."

She looks back and takes Shea's hand, pulling her toward the fountain. They sit on the edge of the pool listening to the trickling water.

"It's amazing, Your Highness, thank you for showing it to me," Shea whispers, letting Joana keep her hand in hers. "So, Anavella, tell me more about you. Why are you here?"

Shea chuckles but begins to weave her tale, waiting for the ambush.

"There's not much to tell really, and I suppose I'm here for the same reason as everyone else."

This seems to disappoint Joana, who then asks, "And what's that?"

Shea begins to continue the con but finds that the truth might enthrall even more. "I'm here to get what I've always wanted: change."

The answer seems to jolt Joana out of her disappointment. "I think that's a very different response. Most would have said power. And have you found what you're looking for?" Joana whispers.

Joana reaches out with her free hand and pushes a stray strand of hair away from Shea's face. She lets the hand fall to Shea's shoulder, and she squeezes gently. Shea involuntarily scoots closer. She almost laughs, finding it weird to be on the other side of a seduction. Joana's hand sensually moves up Shea's neck until her jaw rests in the palm of her hand. She allows the princess's thumb to swipe over her bottom lip. Shea's eyes flutter closed—and she really shouldn't be doing this, but as Venus said, she's never kissed a princess before.

Their lips touch and it's like everything in this world has been leading up to this moment. It's soft, gentle. And Shea feels a hum fall over her fingertips.

She opens her eyes, noting that Joana's are still closed, and starts when she sees the water from the fountain is hovering at least three feet off the marble. Shea gasps involuntarily, breaking the kiss, and the water splashes back into the fountain. The water lightly splashes the two of them.

"What the—"

Shea's eyes widen in panic; her magic has never acted on its own before. But luckily Joana starts to laugh and Shea's body relaxes at the sound. The princess wipes the light water droplets from Shea's cheek.

"Strong wind," she chuckles, and Shea laughs nervously with her.

Joana is just about to say something else when the bushes off to their left start to shake. The sound of branches breaking cause both of them to stand on guard, forgetting the strange water incident from moments ago until Shea remembers exactly who she is and what she's doing here.

The princess extends her arm out in front of Shea, pushing her back behind a protective stance. Shea smirks, shaking off the nerves from her almost blown cover; if only the princess knew, she wouldn't have Shea protecting her back.

"Who's there? Show yourself! And you will not be hurt," Joana commands.

Shea subtly moves, trying not to draw any attention, and reaches down, bunching the tulle of her dress into one hand while grasping for the dagger pinned to her undergarment.

"I thank ye, princess! But I'm afraid I can't guarantee your safety the same," a voice sneers from the shadows, which Shea quickly places as belonging to Mister Sanders.

He steps out of the bushes, followed by Caen, who has ditched the suit for his vest, pants, and black leather boots.

And Aster, who is back in his old clothes as well. Swords hang at Sanders's and Aster's sides while Caen carries his hammer.

"Now, Sanders, there's no need to get violent," Caen murmurs.

"You have no right to be here. I demand that you leave at once, or I will have no choice but to call the guard," Joana threatens. "It'll be okay, Ana, I promise."

Shea nimbly grasps the dagger and lets her dress fall back without notice. She keeps the blade hidden, mockingly playing the part. "Joana, I'm scared."

The use of her given name seems to be a great touch as Joana stiffens, standing even taller she keeps her gaze ahead, focusing on the intruders, and protecting Shea from them.

"I've got you, Ana," Joana states.

Shea raises the hilt of the blade and slams the butt of it directly into Joana's head. The princess crumples to the floor silently, her tiara hitting the ground with a clang.

"Nice!" Aster yells and both older men shush him, Sanders even hitting him upside the head. "Ow, sorry."

Shea sighs, burying the nonsense guilt tugging in the back of her mind until it dissipates. "Guess I'm not the one who should be watching your back," Shea whispers down to Joana.

"Great work, Captain. Though you wanna explain the water show back there?" Caen acknowledges, glaring at her for her unexpected use of magic.

He clips the hammer to his back on its leather strap.

"Don't worry about it, we need to get her out of here," Shea orders, ignoring the weird hitch and thanking the gods it didn't cost her the con.

Sanders jogs over to the entrance of the courtyard from where Shea and Joana had come in and stays on guard, watching for anyone else from behind surrounding trees.

"Thanks. Aster, you alright?" Shea questions, scanning him over for injuries.

Caen reaches down and places Joana in his arms. He quickly checks her head for bleeding but doesn't see any and lets her head drop back over his forearm.

"I'm fine," Aster complains, waving Shea off and picking up the tiara. He holds it up to Shea, and she nods, allowing him to put it in his bag over his shoulder.

"Captain," Sanders alerts her, and she turns to him. "We need to go."

"Thank you, Mister Sanders, lead the way."

Sanders nods and gestures for them to follow him out the far exit, past the Lover's Fountain in the south wall. They move carefully through the shrubbery until they reach a wooden door with heavy beams carved as the frame, and with ease and no key at all, Sanders opens the door.

"I'm not going to lie, Captain. This is where it gets weird," Sanders admits, holding the door open for them.

She gestures for Caen to go first with Joana, then Aster, then Sanders, and she follows behind, closing the door. The room inside is surprisingly bright, lit by torches along the walls. They find themselves in some sort of barracks with multiple bunk beds against the walls.

Sanders goes ahead as he knows the path, and they exit the room quickly, going down hallway after hallway. They walk carefully behind him at first, noting the odd ease in his strides, but as each hall is found empty again and again, they begin to move more quickly.

"Sanders, what in Hades is this?"

There's not a single person down here. It's almost as if this whole exit was cleared just for this escape. As if Shea and her men had done it herself, and she begins to wonder, not for the first time, just who the Underdeep she's working for.

"It was like this when I came through," Sanders claims. "Didn't run into anyone, and didn't have to kill no one either; it's as if we're being let go."

"Even before the clock started?" Shea murmurs, checking open doors off the halls with her dagger in hand, but there's no one there.

"Yes. Same as when I came in."

"Courtesy of our employer?" Caen inquires.

Shea frowns, not entirely sure how to answer.

"Let's just get to the ship. Now," she commands.

Once they're out the final door, a yowl echoes across the sky and Shea sees Caeruleus flying off in the direction of the port to alert the crew.

Sanders leads them to the carriage, where he's already disconnected the four horses to make the journey faster.

"Caen, I'll take her," Shea says, hopping onto the black horse.

"You sure?"

Shea nods and he helps Joana onto the horse in front of the captain, who wraps her arms around the princess to keep her in place. The blonde's head rolls back onto Shea's shoulder, and the other three hop onto their horses. Shea doesn't wait, she spurs the horse on and takes off with her men following into the night toward the port. To the *Veiled Duchess* to set sail for Joana's fate at the Tenaro Islands. And if Shea holds her a little closer than needed, the elf pretends not to notice.

DEATH'S MISTRESS

Joana

THE POUNDING IN JOANA'S head as she comes to almost knocks her out again as the pain ripples through her body. Her stomach lurches as the room rocks, and she suspects that it's not her concussion. The black recedes and her eyes finally focus on the room around her.

She's lying on a bed and it's definitely not her own. A table sits in the center of the chamber and it's filled with papers and maps. Clothes are strewn across the floor and a hammock is hanging in the corner. Fabric and gold trinkets are wrapped around a standing mirror, obscuring the reflection. Two closed doors can be found on opposite sides of the room. Light streams in through the wide windows behind the bed; the glass is colored and it casts beautiful shadows through the area.

Slowly Jo sits up and endeavors not to spew her stomach contents on the floor. She's still dressed in her gold-and-white ball gown, and upon reaching up to feel the bump on the back of her head, she notices the seashells and tiara have been removed from her disheveled blond hair.

She crawls to the back of the bed. Squinting her eyes against the light, she peers out the stained-glass windows. She nearly chokes on the air because all she can see is water for miles and miles out. She's on a ship.

Jo tries not to panic, she's never really been fond of sea travel, not since the summer her family had agreed to sail to Lycos for the season. To say it hadn't agreed with her was an understatement. Again she pushes away the nausea. It's just mind over matter, she thinks, or at least hopes as she pulls herself to the edge of the bed.

It's only a matter of time before someone comes in, and she doesn't want to be unprepared when they do. Jo stands, swaying slightly, but as she tries to collect her bearings, an unsuspecting memory crashes into her, nearly knocking her back onto the bed. Anavella.

Her kidnappers could have her as well; the elf was with Jo in the gardens. And if they don't have her, they could have killed her. Jo slams the thought away. No.

The vertigo ends and she begins searching the room for anything that can give her an advantage. She finds clothes and a ribbon and makes quick use of them. She changes into the pants. They're loose, but she takes what is probably a stolen scarf anyway from one of the piles of treasure. She hooks it through the loops, tying it off to one side of her hip. She leaves the corset from the dress on and shrugs a teal peasant top over the stiff material. Finally, with the red ribbon, she ties her hair back in a simple ponytail. It's enough that at least she won't be clambering along the deck in heels and a petticoat.

She loses the shoes, opting to go barefoot; she won't need them anyway unless she can't find a better weapon than her heels. She's the daughter of a queen; they're stupid if they think she's never prepared for this possibility. The problem is if they're intelligent enough, they will have removed all of the weapons from the room, and after a quick scan, she realizes that's true.

So there are two options: the right or left door.

And she prays to Amphitrite one of them is open and unguarded. Jo takes a quick look at the giant mirror again, before shrugging it off—she doesn't want to slice her palms open if she can't find something to hold the glass, just one more dis-advantage. Her eyes shoot back and forth to each side of the room. She chooses the left. Carefully, she creeps toward the door. One of the planks squeals as she comes close enough to touch the nob and she thinks she can hear rustling from the other side of the door. She puts her guard up and looks back at the heels discarded on the ground. Making a split decision, she goes back and grabs one before walking back to the door with the shoe raised up over her head. She's ready to strike.

Slowly, Jo pushes the door open, and as she looks inside she stops herself from hurling a battle cry. In the far corner of the closet-spaced room is a bed with a little blond boy curled up inside. There's a tiny desk where bandages and books are scattered, and leaned up against the table leg—Joana almost squeals in delight—is a sharp-looking cutlass.

She eyes the cabin boy, the term coming to her from her tutoring sessions with Rhea and Gaea, and carefully reaches for the sword. He shuffles lightly in his sleep, but she grasps the sword before he can wake. She recognizes his sleeping face, though she can't place from where. Taking in the room and his clothes, she realizes he looks well kept. His clothes are clean and he looks fed. He's valuable, perhaps, and valuable is some-thing she can trade. She squares her feet and places the sword at his throat. The moment he awakens, she pushes her sword closer to his fragile skin.

Every inch of his body stiffens. His eyes open to reveal a beautiful light green that looks so pale she thinks he might be blind. But then his eyes narrow and focus on her face. He goes to say something, but she presses down once more with a warning, making him arch his back so he doesn't get cut.

"Not a word," Jo growls.

Her hand wraps around his upper arm as she helps him out of bed, keeping his back pressed close against her front. Her grip is iron tight and she brings the sword to rest at his throat. He struggles briefly but curses when he realizes he's stuck.

"Where am I?" Jo murmurs into the boy's pointed ear; his

beautiful features begin to make more sense.

He's elven. He stays silent, and she can see the muscle of his jaw clench under his baby fat. She swiftly flicks the blade, making a superficial cut along his cheekbone.

He hisses from the pain.

She pushes down the wave of guilt, not enjoying the violence, but for now it's necessary.

"Answer," Jo threatens.

"The *Veiled Duchess*."

"The pirate ship?"

"Yes. Captain will want to know that you're awake."

"Will he?" Jo snarls, rolling her eyes.

"She will," the boy growls, and Jo can feel his frustration radiating off his stiff form.

"Well then, let's not disappoint her. Lead me to the deck," Jo commands, and she pushes the boy through the door to the other side of the captain's quarters, staying on top of him, chest to his back.

He groans but doesn't object, leading her on. They run into a couple of the crew on their way and each freezes when Jo threatens to slit the boy's throat. Instead of stopping her though, they follow the two of them up the remaining steps and to the doors that lead to the quarterdeck. There must be three or four pirates behind her, so Jo keeps her grip steady. The doors open and the sun hits her face. It's warm and calming, and she takes in a deep breath of sea air, enjoying the heat on her skin. The ship is huge.

The deck spans far in either direction, and the burgundy sails nearly take her breath away—the rumors do them justice. They really look stained with blood.

More pirates acknowledge their presence as they begin to circle around the two of them. There's a large hole in the deck with a square grate off to the side, which she realizes is a large scuttle, used to hold supplies, but Jo drags her attention back to the pirates.

Once she is closer to the center of the ship, the boy cries out,

"Captain!"

She presses the blade to his neck, cutting him off, and his body goes rigid.

"I see you have my cabin boy!"

A familiar voice yells and Jo startles, looking up to the afterdeck where the beautiful Anavella resides with an enormous Azulean Lionbird perched on the rail beside her.

The elven woman leans against the railing, lazily looking out over the deck in dark brown pants, a purple peasant blouse, and a long black jacket with tan leather boots. Her hat rests over her braided red hair with a large blue feather plume on top of the deep velvet material.

Beautiful, passes through Jo's mind until the realization seeps in and all that beauty is replaced with a black ugly pile of betrayal and anger.

"You," Jo seethes.

She almost slits the boy's throat right there as Anavella or whoever she is takes off her hat with a mocking bow. She remembers now the large man behind the redheaded elf, his arms crossed over his chest as he observes the scene. He was her escort, and she remembers how she knows the boy. He was her squire. The Azulean growls, and it echoes across the sea.

"Hello, Your Highness, wake up on the wrong side of the bed, did we?"

There's a shit-eating grin on fake Ana's face, and to Jo, it's difficult to equate the cocky pirate to the sweet lady at the ball. A pirate from behind Jo tries to grab her arm, but she dances out of reach.

"Touch me again and I'll kill him," Jo snarls.

"Hold," Ana orders, and the pirates step back, giving Jo more space.

Anavella straightens up from the railing, the Azulean hissing at the princess before taking off into the sky. She pushes back the fear as she notices him circling above her. Ana walks around to the steps that lead down the afterdeck. She's quick yet graceful as she descends, with the giant man from the ball following behind her.

The circle of pirates opens, allowing Anavella and her escort entry before closing the circle again. The giant stays back with the rest of them, but Anavella continues until she's mere feet from the boy and Jo. She begins to orbit around them like the Lionbird above but more slowly. Jo turns as well, not wanting to allow her back open to the pirate…again.

"Where are we?" Jo snarls, keeping her gaze steady on the redhead.

"About forty miles off the coast of Arethusa, far out of reach from any of your countrymen. Why don't you let the boy go? I'll tell you what you'd like to know," Anavella suggests.

The way she moves reminds Jo of a cat waiting to pounce. There's a sort of calculation fluttering behind those bright eyes and Jo shakes her head.

"No, I think I'll keep my leverage," Jo spits. "I see no other woman on the vessel, and according to the boy the captain is a she. So, I address you. I command you to take me back."

Anavella chuckles wickedly and it painfully reminds Jo of her laugh from the ball.

"I am the captain." She nods and curtsies just like she did when they first met.

The crew laughs around them.

"Captain Shea Lara of the *Veiled Duchess*, and I'd really like my cabin boy back."

"Not until you take me home," Jo snaps, tightening her grip.

And while there's a wide smile on Anavella's—no, Shea's face, Jo can see the way her eyes narrow when the boy cries out from the pressure.

"No can do, princess, we're on a tight schedule so as to get you to your destination."

"And where might that be?"

"On an island at world's end. Tenaro."

And suddenly the vertigo is back.

The edge of the world.

Jo wants to wipe that smug look off the pirate's face, but she holds back, looking up at the sky for a brief moment to clear her thoughts before returning her gaze to Shea.

"Why are you doing this?" Jo pleads. Her voice is strained and she can feel her eyes glossing over, but she refuses to cry.

"Because someone paid me to," Shea answers honestly. "Now, one last time, I've been very accommodating answering all your questions. Release Aster or I'm going to have to make you, and you don't want that."

It's the condescension in Shea's voice that breaks Jo. She screams and throws the boy aside, thrusting her sword toward Shea's chest, ready to kill her. Shea's hands move faster, and she catches the blade between her palms. There's silence and Jo can't help but gawk as Shea holds the blade of the cutlass. She's staring down at it but slowly brings her gaze up to Jo's with a wicked smirk. Jo tries to push the blade forward, but Shea is stronger and she keeps the blade where it is, inches from piercing her chest. Quicker than Jo can follow, Shea suddenly turns the blade, stepping to the side and in, pushing the cutlass aside and nailing Jo in the jaw with her elbow. Jo hits the ground, her back slamming onto the deck, and the cutlass clatters to the side. She stares at it briefly and then notices Shea standing in front of her, hands on her hips like she's dealing with a small child.

"You feel better?" Shea asks, and Jo's vision goes red.

She pushes herself off the wood and tackles Shea to the ground, who uses her legs to flip Jo over her head. Shea lands straddling her, pinning her arms to the wood, their faces close together.

Jo struggles and Shea sighs. "Are you almost done, Highness?"

Jo glares and Shea chuckles. Shea pulls them both off the ground, her hands closed on both forearms tightly as she drags her toward the other end of the ship. The crew follows closely behind, cheering and hollering.

Jo can see the boy, Aster, who she used to make her way up. He's still sitting on the ground where she threw him, watching, while the giant comforts him. They stop suddenly and it's only now that she can feel the blood dripping from the open cuts on Shea's hands from the cutlass. It's a small victory that makes Jo smile, but it's short-lived.

Shea pushes her backward, and then Jo is falling. It's a decent drop and when her back hits the straw floor, she can barely catch her breath. Jo's vision grays from the force but soon clears. She realizes she's in the scuttle as a group of men place the iron grate over the top of her new prison. Shea stands, hovering overhead, looking through the metal bars down at her. Off to Jo's right, there's a wall of bars with a door that looks into a larger room filled with smaller cells. She's in the brig. Jo looks back up, watching as someone hands Shea a piece of cloth, and the pirate begins wrapping it around the cuts on her hands. The princess sits up gingerly.

"I think you'll find us most forgiving hosts, princess," Shea yells, keeping her attention on Jo.

The crew laughs and Shea barks a couple orders for them to get back to work. Soon all she can see is Shea's face and everything about it feels like a betrayal.

"My people will come for me," Jo shouts, pushing herself up. She's standing as tall as her hurt body will allow, glaring up at the pirate. "My father will save me, and when he does, you will die."

Shea smiles darkly. It gives Jo chills, and she knows she's not dealing with the woman from the ball.

"It was your own people who hired me. You must not be as valuable as you think."

Jo scoffs, about ready to argue, but Shea cuts her off, continuing, "They hold no love for you, princess. It's not I who will die somewhere alone and forgotten. Let your father come. It will make no difference."

Shea doesn't remove her gaze and Jo attempts to stay strong, but the more she looks into the captain's eyes the more she begins to believe she's telling the truth. She can't stop the emotions from flashing across her face. Hope slowly withers and Jo collapses to her knees on the straw, letting her tears fall softly without sobs.

"The other night…I trusted you," Jo growls.

"I wasn't your love, princess," Shea states, and Jo glares up at her angrily. "I'm the villain in your story."

Shea steps back and away from the top of the brig, allowing Jo to stew in her hatred.

FREEDOM

Shea

Days pass since the deck incident, and Shea keeps herself busy and away from the brig.

Aster is in charge of bringing Joana her food and Caen visits from time to time to check on the state of the prisoner. Other than that, she tries not to think about the woman sitting in her brig. They're hundreds of miles off the coast of Arethusa. There's no way the Arethusian navy can catch up to them.

Shea keeps her focus on the map in front of her as she stews alone in her chambers. The path to Tenaro is filled with dark creatures and rough seas. Some believe it to be the work of Poseidon himself creating a barrier between Nereid and the edge of the world. That is if they believe in the old religion, but the monsters are real enough. Which is why she's here chartering the safest course and coincidentally it also keeps her far away from the princess.

And if the course she plots is a slightly longer journey than it should be, she knows it's concern for the safety of her crew and not lingering thoughts of a magical kiss shared in some faraway castle gardens that makes her choice.

Shea leans over the table, glancing at the compass for the fourth time today as she traces the path over the charts. She thinks about lighting a candle as the sunlight wanes through the windows. Caeruleus is sprawled out across the desk, asleep on his wings and snoring away; occasionally a paw takes a swing at the air, but as long as he's not blocking any of the maps, she lets him be.

She's got enough scars from startling the damn Lionbird. A knock echoes from the door and Caeruleus wakes, turning his head to see the intruder.

"Enter."

Caen walks in, shutting the door behind him. He comes to stand in front of the table and waits until Shea is done marking the map.

She tries to hold out, making unnecessary dashes, but he's patient, which makes him unavoidable. So she sighs, putting the quill down, and sits back in the desk chair to stare up at Caen expectantly.

Caeruleus purrs, wriggling on his back to get Caen's attention, and Caen reaches out and scratches the Lionbird's belly.

Shea waits for whatever Caen has to say, but he continues to pet her familiar.

"Yes, Mister Caen?"

"The boys are just wondering about the arrival. I figured I'd update them with some news," Caen replies, picking up Caeruleus, who meows until he readjusts so he can sit on Caen's shoulder.

The animal wraps his feathered tail around Caen's neck possessively. Shea returns the smile.

"We're four days off from Orena and then another seven days from the Tenaro Islands. Perhaps a little less if the wind stays good. I figure we should resupply at the final outpost on Orena."

Shea stands and points to the places on the charts so that Caen has a good visual. He nods in agreement.

"And then we'll hook around Tenaro toward Lycos. We can be there with good winds in nine days. We meet up with V, get the goods, and plan our final score."

"Very well. We're close," Caen acknowledges.

Shea nods, stepping away from the map table toward a side desk where a goblet of rum and the bottle sit. She grasps the goblet and all seems well until Caen speaks again, "And far away from Arethusa. Far, far away…Very far. It's amazing we've come so far in the last few days. Miles out really."

Shea sighs, putting the goblet down and shaking her head.

"You've been talking to her, haven't you?"

Caen ignores the question and continues, "And really there's no way for her to change the course, she's trapped. You win."

"Caen."

"She's very persuasive."

Shea rolls her eyes, sitting back heavily in the chair. Caeruleus trills and takes flight out the back toward the open port window. Shea looks after him wistfully, wishing she could escape the same way.

"We don't carry live cargo. Your rule. And the men have become accustomed to it. We've stuck to your law and I believe we're the better for it. Better pirates. We kill when we have to, we don't take these jobs."

She growls, "Blast it, Caen. I know."

"Do you? I know we can't turn back, it's too late now. I know that and I'm not suggesting it. But maybe we can give her a peaceful last few days or leave her on Orena with—"

Shea snaps her head around, glaring, daring him to continue that line of thought.

Caen sighs. "Where does she have to go? She's going to her death whether she stays on board or jumps over. You and I both know this is it. As you said, we're less than a week to the last supply before the Tenaro Islands and then she's history."

Caen places his hands on the table and leans over the charter, staring fixedly at Shea.

"She's cargo," the captain argues, ignoring his gaze.

"You know better than anyone that's not true," Caen refutes. "She may be a means to an end, but come on. If this were anyone else, you'd have let them wander."

"If this were anyone else, we wouldn't be having this conversation," she snarls and Caen acquiesces, gesturing a surrender.

"She could have killed Aster."

Caen chuckles. "Please. Never would have happened. Unless…"

Shea eyes him. "Unless what?"

"She did manage to stand up to you." He gestures toward her hands. "Which must have been pretty surprising. I don't remember the last time that happened in any fight."

She glances down at the bandages surrounding her palms.

"It's not about me." Shea frowns.

"Then let her out. Give her last rights; we're pirates, sure, but it doesn't mean we can't give mercy. We don't even know if the kid deserves this. I hate to say it, but this is why we don't take political jobs."

"Since when did your moral compass get tightened so straight?" Shea bites.

Caen merely shrugs in response.

"I don't have time to babysit some princess."

"I know," Caen replies.

"Neither do you."

"I'm aware."

There's a small pause of silence.

Shea sighs again. "So?"

"Mm?"

"Who will you get?"

"Oh you know. Someone who'd like his honor back."

"No," Shea chuckles, shaking her head. "No way."

She gave Aster the job last time and that brilliantly blew up in her face.

"He's not ready."

"I'll get James to help him out. Come on, Captain."

Shea knows this will end badly, she can feel it in her bones. She closes her eyes, but what in Hades does she have to lose? Opening her eyes, she solemnly agrees, "Fine. Is there anything else?"

Caen gives her a look like he's thinking of leaving it there, but she gestures for him to get on with it.

"I've seen you watching her. When you're up on deck. I see you stand near the brig and listen to her talking to Aster," Caen says, and this is so not what Shea wants to hear.

She gets up, walking away from the table and stepping past him to march out the door.

He quickly dodges her and blocks her exit.

"Now wait, hey, I'm not saying you're having second thoughts, but you can't tell me you don't feel funny doing this."

"Was there something you wanted to ask me, Mister Caen?"

Shea can feel her cold mask slip into place, but Caen merely laughs, keeping his warm grin on his smug face.

"Well, it's just a thought."

And then she gets it. And no, no way is she going anywhere near that woman, not even to offer her a small amount of freedom.

"No."

Shea pushes past him. He valiantly tries to stop her, but she jabs him in the side, throwing open the door, and takes a step out.

But Caen bounces back and manages to grab her arm. "Look, it seemed like you two had some kind of connection at the ball," Caen wheezes, bent over at the waist from the jab.

"Oh yes, I'm sure that's still simmering, what with the kidnapping and the bringing her to her death."

"Right," Caen breathes, removing his hand from her arm and choosing to lean against the door frame instead. "So I'm thinking you should be the one to tell her."

"No."

"Shea."

"We could always keep her in the brig," Shea threatens, but it's no use, Caen's made up his mind.

"Shea," he repeats.

There's no way she can be around this woman, let alone help her.

"She's dead anyway, what's the harm?" he asks.

Shea chuckles darkly and wipes a hand across her forehead. Her eyebrows furrow as she looks Caen in the eye.

"She doesn't wanna see me."

Caen shrugs. "It's not her decision."

Shea stalks toward the brig with Aster following close behind. She twirls the iron key around the metal ring, nervously fidgeting with her hands. She hasn't spoken to Joana since she left her in the brig days ago. Shea doesn't plan on the conversation being pleasant.

"How is she?"

"Cranky, usually, but I don't blame her," Aster responds, catching up to Shea and walking alongside her.

"Even for marring your pretty face," Shea teases, glancing at the cut healing well on his upper cheek.

"Actually I thanked her for that one." Aster grins, showing off his wound.

Shea decides not to tell him it's too light to scar. Finally they round the corner in the dying afternoon light as it filters into the relatively dark brig. On the far side of the room she can see the huge cell Joana is currently being housed in. Normally it's used for cargo such as fabrics and other expensive wares. But this voyage they'd left it empty so that they could acquire some new items on Orena. There's bedding on the floor, Shea notices, as she gets closer. She supposes it's courtesy of Caen, the only one ballsy enough to do it without Shea's permission. Near the cage door is a tray full of half-eaten food.

Shea makes her way until she stands in front of the cell, her hands dancing on the hilt of her sword, and Joana sits leaning against the wood at the back, staring up at the sky. Shea looks up out of curiosity and is surprised to see Caeruleus circling above.

"Captain, what a surprise." Joana's voice nearly makes Shea jump, but she resists the urge and her gaze lands on the princess, who is watching her with obvious hatred.

"I honestly didn't expect to see you back here."

"My lady," Shea responds, tipping her captain's hat.

Joana just about comes unglued; she stands from where she was and storms over to the bars, stopping in front of Shea, grasping the iron.

"Don't call me that!"

"As you wish. Do you prefer Your Highness, Your Majesty, Enthralling Mistress?"

Shea laughs softly at her own joke.

Aster groans, his head falling into his palm as the unanswered question hangs in the air. Joana cuts through the humor with a hardened glance.

"Joana," she responds.

Shea grimaces. She doesn't want to say Joana's name aloud. She hasn't said it since she was Ana, but she discards the thought and pushes on.

"Joana," Shea repeats.

The silence stretches once more, setting the captain's teeth on edge.

"Are you comfortable?" she asks and keeps her face neutral at the look Joana gives her.

"What do you want?"

"It's been discussed that, perhaps under the circumstances, you would like a little more access to the ship. With Aster to assist you, we were wondering if you would like—"

Joana scoffs and pushes away from the bars. She turns her back to Shea and states, "No."

Effectively cutting off the rest of Shea's speech.

"No?"

"No," Joana replies.

She turns around and leans against the far wall where she was sitting earlier.

"Well. It seems you've made up your mind so…" Shea smiles and turns to leave, quite content with this turn of events, when Aster steps in front of her.

After watching the whole thing with silent judgment, there's a look in his eyes that says Shea's not walking out of here. She groans. Okay, let's try this again.

"You'd rather rot in here?"

"As opposed to a wooden box? Oh wait."

"I'm just trying to make this better for you," Shea snaps.

She takes off her hat, running a hand through her hair. Joana pushes off the wall and takes a step forward. She's still in the clothes she stole from Shea's room the first day, though her hair is not braided, instead it's in a ponytail.

Joana snarls, "For who? You or me?"

I don't know, Shea wants to shout back, but she keeps quiet, silently scowling at the top of her shoe, avoiding Joana's and Aster's scrutiny.

"It's too late to play the hero, Captain." The princess mocks, keeping her stance solid and firm. "You've already said yourself, you're the villain of this story."

At that, Shea's gaze snaps to her, and Aster shifts uncomfortably. It feels as if the room has dropped several degrees below freezing.

"Was that how you saw me before, a hero?" Shea asks, stepping toward the cell and running her finger down one of the bars.

Joana rolls her eyes, one eyebrow arching as she crosses her arms. "Not exactly."

"Really? Perhaps the sweet love interest? Maybe now I can play the redeemable villain?"

Shea boasts with great sarcasm.

"Better yet: the heartless monster who gets slain in the end," Joana coldly responds, shooting daggers in Shea's direction.

Shea turns her face away from that one, holding back the wince. Who cares what she thinks. Shea shouldn't. It's not like they know each other that well. But Shea's been watching. Caen wasn't wrong. And the more she's watched her the more she feels like Lady Anavella at the ball, and she can't be that.

She's not the love interest; this isn't a story. This is a job. She runs her hand along the bars and turns back to Aster, who looks as if he'd like to melt into the wooden boxes he's leaning against.

"I guess that makes you the damsel in distress," Shea mutters.

"Is that how you see me?" Joana coos tauntingly with a smug expression.

Shea snorts and smiles sweetly in return. "I would have said a profit, but a damsel is fine too."

"You disgust me," Joana barks, her hands flying to her hips. Shea takes in the view, studying the anger in those blue eyes, a little vein visible just above her brow, a snarl upon her lips.

Shea studies it and accepts it. "Is that so, Jo." Shea lets her face rest on the horizontal bars. "That didn't seem to be the case that night."

Joana storms toward her until their faces are inches from each other, her hands grasping the bars. Both women's bodies are now inches from the barrier between them.

"That night wasn't real, and don't call me that," Joana growls. They peer into each other's eyes, searching for any kind of reprieve from the exhaustion of hating each other.

"You think you can come down here, with a false olive branch, and that'd make you feel better. Rationalize what you've done to me. No. In order to do that, you'd need a concept of right and wrong. The woman I met that night, she was kind, thoughtful of people who'd been slapped in irons and stolen away."

"Hades," Shea says, pulling back slightly from the bars.

There's a pause and Shea's hand comes to rest on her chest; she looks up at Joana with wide eyes.

"You're right," Shea breathes.

Joana's own eyes widen, a ghost of a smile resting on her

lips.

"I can see it now." Shea nods and then cruelly laughs. "I do feel better. Because I'm doing what's right for me. Thank you, princess, for helping me understand so fully. I think I'll keep calling you Jo, it's a cute nickname, don't ya think?"

Joana recoils and nearly trips over her feet as she stumbles back like Shea has slapped her.

"Get out!" Jo snarls.

Shea hollowly chuckles. "Darling, I'm the captain, I'll go when I want—"

A loud shout from a crew member can be heard overhead.

More voices join the panicking man's yells and suddenly the sound of boots pounding against the deck echoes across the brig.

"Somebody get the captain!"

Shea looks through the bars toward the grate above Jo's cell. She can see the clouds quickly billowing, turning dark and black. Jo yelps, and Shea glances back to her. She wipes her hand against her forehead before reaching out both her palms up to the sky.

"Great," Jo growls, "it's raining."

Shea turns quickly to Aster, handing him the key. "Stay here and keep watch. I'm needed on the quarterdeck."

"But, Cap," he attempts to argue.

"Stay."

And without looking back, she takes off in a run out of the brig. She passes crew in the hall who let her pass on her way up to the helm.

Finally, she breaks through the doors and is almost blasted back by the sheer force of the wind; she's caught by James and her hat goes flying down the hall.

"Ah bloody Underdeep," she snarls dejectedly, looking after her flying hat.

"Captain, you alright?" James yells, trying to get his voice to carry over the sound of the wind howling.

"Aye. Talk to Mister Tero before getting to the helm, I'll help

Caen man the wheel. I have a feeling this storm isn't natural and Tero's going to need all the help he can get," she screams back and forces her way onto the deck.

The waves crash against the ship, electricity sizzling through the dark clouds, and rain falls like frozen knives, slicing against the skin. She shouts commands to Mister Tero, who is ordering the men to batten down the hatches and prepare for the oncoming storm. He sends James off to tie down the cannons.

"Mister Tero!"

"I've got it, Captain! Best get up to Mister Caen," the old boatswain hollers back. "Get up there, men, we don't need a fallen mast."

Shea takes off for the steps, her whole body slamming into the rail with a shout. She wraps her arm around her middle and continues on up. She finds Caen without his usual vest, straining against the wheel as he attempts to hold the ship steady on her course. The wheel groans against the force, and the veins in Caen's neck look as if they'll explode at any given time.

"Captain," Caen groans, gesturing her over with his head.

"What happened?" Shea cries, grabbing onto one side of the wheel and pulling with all her strength to relieve some of the pressure on Caen.

The sky thunders above and it seems as if miniature hurricanes have sprouted along the deck, knocking crew off their feet, attempting to drag some of them over the ship's edge. "It came out of nowhere! Mister Sanders was up in the crow's nest, he spotted a gathering storm, a black barrier as if there were waves in the sky barreling toward us!"

"Where is Mister Sanders now?" Shea bellows, squinting past the sharp pricks of rain barraging her face.

Caen nods toward the front of the ship. "He was knocked from his post."

Shea looks out past the dark termagant waters and sends a silent prayer up to Poseidon. This would be a great day to finally answer her prayers. Her ears twitch as she hears a wailing shriek carrying along the wind and a light goes off in her brain.

"Caen," she shouts, "it's started."

"What?" he hollers back. She lets go of the wheel and Caen grunts as he takes the full force of the ship again.

"James! Come help Caen!"

Shea bellows down to the young man. He finishes his knot on the cannon and runs full force for the steps, sidestepping the small gusts of wind attacking the deck. His foot is only caught once, but as he hits the deck he rolls as another shriek echoes through the air. He takes the steps two at a time until he's finally at the wheel.

"I've got it," James says, grasping the side Shea was on.

Caen blows out a breath of relief, his muscles stretched.

"What is it?" Caen asks once more.

"Aurai," Shea responds, as she unsheathes her gold sword. The rain falling from the sky simmers upon touching the blade and she holds it up, adjusting into a fighting stance.

"Aurai!" she screams, and as her voice hits the deck, the wind spirits appear in their ghostly forms, screeching and crying, trying to pull the men overboard.

Their bodies twist and mold into the rain and wind, scratching at the crew. One of the spirits catches sight of Shea's sword and comes flying toward her with a high-pitched scream.

Shea slices through her body, the Aurai's form disintegrating and sizzling as the gold pierces her invisible flesh. The crew cheers for the minor victory before going back to their own battles. The good thing about Aurai, purity is their weakness and that's just what Shea's sword is made of, pure gold gifted to her by an elven blacksmith in the state of Oceanus.

She scans the horizon, watching for the eye of the storm, and her gaze catches on the edge of the Aurai's hold. The problem with the seas at the end of the world—they're filled with monsters.

"There!" Shea screams, pointing ahead.

"I see it," Caen yells back.

"I'll keep them off the helm!" Shea responds, guarding the steering. If they can get out of the storm, they can make it.

"That'd be most appreciated!"

A couple more Aurai come flying toward her. She dodges the first, thrusting her body to the left, and it flies past her with no control. The second hurtles at her more directly. It blasts her with wind and she blocks it the best she can with her blade. It pushes her back a few inches just by the sheer force, but as the creature gets closer, she ducks under the pressure and turns, slashing through the beast's middle. She pulls the water to her aid, sending tentacles of pure saltwater toward the Aurai on the lower deck. The water slashes through each ghostly frame, giving each of her men a reprieve before dropping back to the ocean.

She cheers, slightly out of breath, turning to look toward Caen and James with a gloating smile.

Caen rolls his eyes, yelling for her to get back to work.

Shea laughs, readying herself, and notices too late the first Aurai from before is coming from the back of the ship straight for her. She turns at the last minute and is lifted into the air with a shout, hoisted above the crew and flung backward. Caen sees her and screams, almost losing the wheel, but he holds his place at James's insistence. Shea hits the mainmast beam and cries out in pain. The spirit makes a high-pitched chattering noise like laughter. It flings her to the side and she falls stomach first onto the horizontal beam. It knocks the wind out of her and her ribs scream from the earlier abuse on the rail.

She feels her body slipping and scrambles to hold on, scratching at the wood until she finds a solid grip and pushes herself up. There's barely a moment of reprieve, but she manages to see they've hoisted the foremast sails and it's carrying them as best it can to clear waters. Once they're at the edge, she can cast the barrier charm, once the Aurai's hold isn't as strong, but not before.

Shouts echo from below and she hears something burst out of place; the ship rocks and groans, and she knows if they don't get out from under these Aurai soon they're going to bring down the ship. She's managed to keep hold of her sword and sheathes it, looking up above her at the crow's nest. She hears the damned thing screech and knows it's coming back.

So she does what any person would do—she jumps. Shea clasps the rope hanging from the crow's nest that's meant to secure the person in case of rough weather. Though it seems it didn't favor Mister Sanders. Her ears pick up on the approaching screeches and she knows there isn't much time.

She climbs.

DISTRESSED DAMSEL

Joana

THE RAIN IS COMING DOWN HARD. Joana stares through the grate as strange movements in a visible wind carries men across the deck.

"Aster, what the Underdeep is going on up there?"

He isn't listening though.

She watches as he paces back and forth in front of the cell.

"Aster!"

He looks up just as a harrowing screech echoes overhead.

"Aurai," he mutters, walking up to the bars and pressing his face against them. He tries to get a better look at the world overhead.

"What in Hades are Aurai?"

"Wind spirits. Guardians of the Aiolos reef. Their existence is to make sure no one makes it past the reef and into the waters of the world's end. Some say Poseidon placed them here himself in the beginning. And now only skilled sailors know how to get past them. We should have been a few days off. Shea must have thought so too. We're close to Tenaro."

Jo ignores the bit about being close to the island she is supposed to be marooned upon forever and instead focuses on the insane explanation for what's going on above.

"Aster, there's no such thing."

"Don't you believe in the gods?"

"Of course."

The response is automatic, practiced from hours in the temples as a young child.

"Then why wouldn't the monsters be real as well?"

Aster makes a fair point, she thinks, but her answer is stolen from her lips when a loud female scream echoes from overhead.

"Shea!" Aster shouts and pushes off the bars, making for the door to exit the brig.

"Wait!" Jo shrieks.

Aster stops, almost losing his balance, and turns back to Jo with an annoyed expression. "What?"

"Take me with you. I can help," Jo pleads while reaching her hand out through the bars.

Her hair is sticking to one side of her face from the rain. She's soaked and the water keeps coming down anyway.

"No," Aster scoffs and moves to take a step away, but Jo yells at him again.

"There's nowhere for me to go! I don't—I don't want to die. So if helping you all will give me a few more days, then I will," Jo confesses.

The elfling looks down, contemplating whether releasing Jo will land himself in the brig if Shea finds out.

"Please," Jo begs, "I haven't lost hope just yet."

Aster groans. He looks up at the ceiling and then lets out a long-suffering sigh. "Trench of Poseidon!"

He runs back over to the cell and uses the key given to him by the captain to release Jo. The door swings open, but Aster stops her from coming through.

"I swear to the gods though, if you try to hurt anyone, you try to betray me, I will throw you overboard myself, got it?"

And she can tell he's serious. Jo nods her understanding and he nods back in agreement, stepping aside to let her through.

"Lead the way," she teases in reference to her words from the other day.

He gives her a half smile and takes off toward the quarterdeck. They run through the hallway, not stopping by the weapons bay. The quarterdeck is visible through the broken double doors at the top of the stairs. They run through it, taking in the situation. The men are holding off the Aurai as the Aurai scream from the crew's pure iron swords. Wind tunnels spiral across the deck, attempting to drag men overboard.

An older gentleman who looks too old to still be a pirate is running toward the foresail with two other men behind him. A crack sounds from above and Jo watches as two of the wind spirits pull on the rigging, trying to bring down the foremast. "Let's go help Mister Tero. They bring down that mast and we're finished," Aster yells over the whistling winds, and Jo nods, following him as they try to avoid the Aurai dancing along the quarterdeck.

Jo looks back to the afterdeck wondering (definitely not hoping) to see Shea there, but all she sees is Caen and another boy holding the helm steady.

A female shout draws their attention, and Aster and Jo both look up to find Shea in the crow's nest fighting against a particularly nasty wind spirit. Her gold sword glitters in the rain and her red hair is drenched, flowing like blood down her back. She slashes at the creature, causing it to scream out in agony.

Jo is so busy watching Shea that she forgets to look where she's going and is knocked off her feet. She screams as she bounces off a wind cycle and nearly goes overboard. Half her body is hanging over the gunwale of the ship as the waves gnash and claw their way along the bow.

"I got you," Aster screams, his arms wrapped around her waist.

He watched her hit the cycle and ran after her, jumping to catch her body before it went over. He hauls her back onto the deck and they both gasp for air.

"Thank you," she breathes, wiping the rain from her eyes.

His strawberry-blond hair lies dark on his head and he simply says, "Tero."

They run and finally make their way to the foresail. Tero stands on the ground as the two men ascend the rope ladders to the beam, hoping to reconnect the rigging at the top of the foremast.

"Mister Tero! Anything we can do to help?" Aster shouts.

"The boys need some cover while they reattach the rigging, and with my back, I can't get up there; think you can give them a hand?" Tero hollers back and extends two cutlasses that must belong to the two men above. Tero is hesitant to give it to Jo, so he looks to Aster.

"It's alright. We can do it! Right, Jo?"

"Right," Jo bellows and takes the sword. She watches the wavering rope ladder as it snaps in the wind and turns to Aster.

"After you." She smiles.

He laughs and starts to climb while she follows quickly behind.

"Mister Tero!" a voice screams and Jo recognizes it as Shea's. Jo looks up quickly to see Shea slice through the apparition and then follows her as she leans over the edge of the crow's nest surveying the damage below.

Shea shouts, "We're close to the edge of their domain. Have they reattached the rigging yet?"

"Working on it, Captain!"

Shea looks as if she's about to answer when she's thrown back. She hits the side of the crow's nest, the Aurai putting more force into her attacks.

Shea manages to choke out, "Hurry!"

Jo pushes herself to climb faster, though not because of Shea. They make it about halfway to the men and the two guys are weaving the rigging tighter through the wooden pin, holding on for their lives. Aurai are coming in hot, and they manage a perfect shot at one of the men, who loses his grip. He falls to the deck screaming. The other crewman can barely look up; he knows he has to get this rigging tied off.

Aster makes it up first; the Aurai comes at him and he slices it with the cutlass. The spirit doesn't sizzle on contact like they do with Shea's sword, but they do disappear and that's enough. Jo gets to the top of the rope; Aster keeps one arm around the beam to the foremast and Jo does the same.

The remaining crewman is just about done when an Aurai comes screaming down the middle of the ship.

Aster thrusts the blade out, but the Aurai dodges and hits the kid off the side. He loses his grip on the beam and starts to fall. Jo makes the choice and drops her cutlass, jumping onto the ladder and catching the rope with one hand and Aster's arm with the other. She cries out as his weight wrenches her arm almost out of the socket, but she swings him toward the rope, and he grabs onto the ladder.

"You okay?" she yells.

Aster nods, his teeth chattering as he clenches the rope tightly.

"Got it!" the crewman yells down and Tero cheers.

"Captain! Ready!"

Jo looks up to see Shea roar and carve her sword through the Aurai once more.

As it disintegrates, she thrusts her gold sword up in the air and shouts, "Akousé me! Kairós gia Peiraiá kai Kidemónes tou Poseidóna, den tha perásete pléon to monopáti mou! Sas dia-tázo!"

Lightning strikes the sword but she doesn't waver. The rain falls harder and the wind blows so fiercely it feels as if the pressure alone will split Joana in half.

Shea brings the sword down hard, stabbing it into the floor of the crow's nest, commanding, "Méso tou, entolí. Iremía."

Light blasts from the crow's nest and a force more powerful than the Aurai sweeps over the ship, forcing them back and away from the vessel.

They shriek and cry in agony and anger. Jo closes her eyes and waits. Seconds go by, and she realizes the rain has stopped. When she opens her eyes, she sees the clouds have receded to the distance, bright stars burn overhead, and the light from the early evening moon shines from above, masking the ship in bright white light. The waves roll calmly and the air is silent, there's barely a breeze to be felt. Jo looks up, and she can just barely see the top of Shea's head as she kneels over her impaled sword in the crow's nest floor.

The crew yells and cheers for the victory, but Shea doesn't move. Jo looks away and instead smiles at the men below laughing and pushing each other around.

Caen is sitting on the afterdeck looking up at the sky, shaking his fists at the heavens; Aster must see it too because he points and starts laughing.

The crewman who fixed the rigging is swinging down quickly to the deck, and when he lands, he runs over to where Tero and someone who she assumes is the ship's doctor checks over his fallen friend. Their heads are bowed and she can hear the softest of cries. She looks away and down to Aster, who looks back at her with a sad expression.

He shrugs but she understands. In this life not everyone makes it. They climb down the ladder, and once their feet hit the quarterdeck, she sees a few of the crew have gathered around her. She expects a fight and looks up to the crow's nest to see Shea descending.

Caen shouts to Shae, and she looks over to see him pointing in Jo's direction.

Shea meets Jo's gaze and she turns back to Caen with a nod and continues her descent from the nest.

Caen barrels his way toward Jo and Aster, and Jo waits for the inevitable explosion but is surprised when Caen says, "It's fine, guys, she's alright. We should start getting the evening routine started; someone let Mister Strom know he can start supper. Aster go help him."

They all grumble and walk away without another glance at Jo. Aster gives her a smile and a "Thanks for saving me."

He takes off toward the broken doors leading down to the galley.

"You did good, kid," Caen smiles. "You okay?"

Pain ripples through her arm from where she caught Aster and she rubs it absently.

"Your arm?" he asks and Jo nods.

"When I caught Aster, I felt like I pulled it out or something."

Caen whistles sharply to the group of men surrounding their fallen friend. "Dr. Nol?"

A man with specs and a green velvet vest turns at the sound of his name and once he spots Caen, he walks quickly in their direction, giving Jo a thorough once-over.

"Think you could check out Miss Joana's arm?"

Nol is already on it, poking and prodding her shoulder.

She cries out softly at a particularly hard poke and his face turns red as he stutters out an apology.

The doctor smiles reassuringly to Jo before speaking to Caen, "Yes, definitely, although if you could convince the captain to come see me. She dodged me a moment ago, and I believe she'll be needing my attention."

Jo can't help it; she smiles a little at that, and Caen salutes the doctor. "I'll take care of it. And Nol will take care of you, Joana. We'll see you both at supper."

He takes off, presumably after Shea.

"Miss Joana? Shall we?"

Nol holds his arm out like a gentleman. She takes in his specs and semi-suit and suspects he's not like the rest of these pirates on this galleon.

Nol guides her down to his own little quarters, filled with physician's equipment and books. Tons of volumes fill the floor, the walls, and even parts of the bed. Though it seems as if most of them were knocked down in the Aurai attack, as he sits her down on the table, she realizes it might just normally be this messy.

At first she stays silent, not really sure of what to say, and she lets him take off her blouse to get a better look at her shoulder. Her corset is loose, as she's been taking it off at night to sleep and it's much harder to put back on without her lady's maids. Still he doesn't look and focuses on weaving the bandage.

Finally she asks him what such a refined doctor is doing on a pirate ship.

"I don't look like a pirate?" he asks, laughing.

"No," she answers honestly.

"Well if you must know, I was once an honorable doctor of society serving Empress Ceto in Lycos. But I—I had the unfortunate circumstance of falling in love with an elven man, a slave who worked in the palace. We tried to suppress the attraction, but we couldn't. So we made plans to run away together to Oceanus and become a part of the freefolk."

"I could never understand Ceto's hatred for elven kind," Jo murmurs, thanking him as he helps her put her blouse back on.

"It runs deeper than you know. We were found out, of course, and Maren was killed for trying to escape his service."

Jo can't believe how calm he is as he talks about his former lover.

"I'm so sorry."

"It happened a long time ago. I was sold into service for my own crime to a plantation on Helios that Shea liberated. She gave me a choice of freedom or a post on her ship. I chose the ship."

"Over your freedom? I mean, aren't you just trading one master for another?"

Jo grunts as he tightens a fashioned sling out of a belt over the blouse.

Nol adjusts his specs and for a second she's embarrassed for all her questions. "I'm sorry, I didn't mean to pry. You don't have to answer."

Nol shakes his head, smiling gently. "I know what you must think of her. After what she's done to you. But she has her reasons, as horrible as that may sound. She's not evil, though she may pretend to be. She's a pirate, and yet, she's a good woman. And as hard as this is for you, I know it's just as hard for her as well."

"She won't die from this," Jo snaps bitterly, "I will."

"She may not lose her life for what she's doing to you," Nol responds, "but condemning you may kill her all the same. And I'd hate for that to happen. Because the part of her that sees you is what made her see me too. And save me."

Nol walks away and places the extra bandages in the cabinet from where he got the belt.

Jo's thoughts wander back to Shea fighting the Aurai and the strange conversation with her in the brig. Regardless of what Shea's reasons are, is it really fair for her to ruin someone else's life for the sake of her wants?

"Well I seem to have worked up quite an appetite, care for dinner?"

He helps her jump down off the table and Jo chases her thoughts away.

"Sounds good."

The dining quarters are hopping as Jo and Nol arrive downstairs.

She notices familiar faces, some she's seen walking around from below and others most recently in the fight.

Tero and the crewman who saved the foresail are sitting sullenly in the back corner alone with two bowls and a jug of what's probably alcohol.

Nol jogs down the steps with ease, striding toward the line at the end of the room where a huge man with white hair and white eyes is serving up something from a large pot.

Aster is beside him, occasionally adjusting the older man's hands so the stew pours into the bowl and not onto the floor or a poor crew member. Aster glances up and catches sight of Jo. He waves at her with a big grin and she can't help but wave back at his cuteness. He points over to one of the neighboring tables and she sees Caen with a couple of men.

Nol is already halfway through the line, so Jo follows suit.

She waits and when she gets to the front, she's greeted once again by Aster.

"Joana, welcome to the galley. Okay, I hope," Aster says, examining Jo's sling.

Jo shrugs, which makes her wince, but other than that: "I'm okay, thank you, Aster."

"This is Strom, by the way, he's the cook," Aster explains, grabbing a bowl from behind and holding it out to Jo, who takes it graciously.

"The same one who's been making your dinner these last couple days, decent I hope." Strom grins and Jo can't help but shake her head in amusement at there being another nice pirate.

"It's been very good actually, thank you," Jo responds, happy to know her royal manners are still intact.

And truthfully the food has been good. Even living in a coastal nation she'd never had as much seafood as she's had in the last couple of days.

"He's blind," Aster tells her in case she hadn't noticed, and Strom turns his head in the boy's general direction.

"What, I am? You're kidding? Well nobody thought to tell me! Why the bloody Underdeep am I cooking then?" Strom jokingly yells and Aster turns about ten shades of red while the room erupts in laughter.

Strom hands Jo a piece of bread on her stew with a wink, and even though he can't see it, she sends him back a huge grin.

Aster then asks if he can go sit down and eat, which Strom answers with a smack upside the head and a "Not until we serve our final crew member," whoever that is.

Jo sits down next to Nol at the table with Caen, who sits on the other side, eating.

He gives her a salute with his spoon.

"Looking good, princess." Caen smiles before directing his next comment to Nol, "Sprain?"

"Bruised really." Nol laughs and Jo smacks him lightly on

the shoulder. *Thanks.*

Caen laughs along. "So what'd you think of your first monster attack?"

"I had no idea they existed. I mean, I believe in the gods of old, but to think that the creatures from the stories could be true is...intriguing."

"Mine was a sea serpent, just about pissed myself," Nol chuckles and Jo feels proud of herself for getting in on the fight then.

"You saved Ollie up there; he won't thank you now with his brother in that position, but I know if things were different, he'd be here telling you thanks," Caen explains with a head nod to the back table where Tero and Ollie are sitting.

"It was the right thing to do," Jo murmurs.

Caen shrugs. "Maybe, but you didn't have to." And at that, Jo takes the compliment and leaves it there.

"So what was that? With Shea, I mean?" Jo asks.

Caen coughs, choking slightly, and Nol leans over, patting him on the back. He looks at her with wide eyes and a gasp before grumbling to himself. As he opens his mouth to reply, Aster sits down between Nol and Jo, making the doctor scoot over with an eye roll, and beats Caen to the explanation.

"Magic."

Jo stares at Aster, who begins digging into his bowl next to her, before asking, "Magic?"

"Yeah, you know elven wards? Haven't you ever heard about the elves? You had elven magic at the ball," Aster says around a huge bite of bread in his mouth.

Caen leans over the table and smacks him on the head with a spoon, which makes Aster yelp.

"You, shush." Caen points at Aster, who rubs his head, and then points his spoon at Jo. "And you, you wanna know? You gotta ask her yourself."

And right at that moment it seems that opportunity comes knocking because down the stairs comes none other than Captain Shea herself.

Her head is bandaged and her hair is braided into a high pony, which shows off her pointed ears. She's holding one arm around her middle; her clothes look fresh, new dark green pants, her boots the same tan, and a scarlet-red blouse that highlights her skin in the firelight. It almost looks as if she sparkles. As she enters the room, she scans it almost like it's her custom, before her eyes land on Jo. Shea stares for barely a moment and then her eyes flutter to the ground, and she acts as if she didn't see her. She strides into the room and greets Strom, who only has big smiles for her.

He asks if she's okay and she answers she's fine.

Jo watches her every move, and soon Caen and Aster notice Shea's arrival as well.

"Captain, over here!" Caen gripes, settling back down into his seat.

"Shea, you were amazing out there!" Aster hoots, and the rest of the crew cheers, saluting the captain with mugs and cups of rum.

Shea smiles and grabs her bowl from Strom. At first it seems as if she might take a step toward their table, but then she turns away and starts to walk back to the stairs.

"Is there a problem, Captain? Please, join us," Jo dares, keeping her eyes on the elf.

The redhead pauses, still facing the stairs, but responds, "I think not, but thank you for the invitation."

"Scared to look at your mistakes?" Jo snaps, and she sees the remaining energy drain from Shea's form and suddenly even she feels exhausted from all the bickering and pain.

Aster is staring at his food along with Nol, while Caen is glaring at Jo as if he could stare a hole right through her head.

"My apologies, princess, but perhaps another night." And with that Shea exits the galley without another word.

Jo sits there trying to keep that smug feeling, but it withers at the crew's silence and is replaced with exhaustion and disappointment.

She looks up at Caen, who is still glaring at her, and sighs,

"Excuse me."

She gets up. She's not exactly sure what she'll do when she finds her, but she goes after Shea.

YOU'VE GOT STARS
IN YOUR EYES

Shea

SHEA SETS THE FINISHED BOWL of gruel down beside her makeshift seat on the bow, staring off at the horizon. She pulled some boxes that needed to go below and put them together to create a lounge chair. It works for the most part as she leans against the back crate and lets her feet rest on the rail. Something whooshes past her head and she tenses before Caeruleus meows, landing on the box above and letting his tail fall over and smack her in the face.

"Where in Hades have you been?" Shea accuses, pushing his tail away.

She reaches up and pulls him onto her lap. Caeruleus protests and presses his front paws against her chest, looking into her eyes. She pets his head gently, making him purr.

"Too busy for an Aurai raid?"

Caeruleus trills and Shea rolls her eyes.

"I could have used you, you know? Silly bird," she mutters and he nips at her fingers.

She hisses, shaking her hand out, and holds up a surrendering gesture. "Alright, sorry."

He chirps a truce, pushes off of Shea's chest, and walks down to her feet before plopping over and promptly going to sleep. There's footsteps coming up from behind the crate chair, but Shea doesn't bother looking back. She knows its Caen coming to check on her. That man doesn't know how to leave well enough alone.

Caeruleus meows loudly at Caen but remains where he is lying at Shea's feet. The captain keeps her gaze out on the dark horizon. Candles burn in the lanterns along various points of the ship but it's no warm comfort. Shea's always preferred starlight to fire, perhaps because it gives off a familiar glow, beautiful rather than the harsh orange of fire. They wait in silence, either Caen working up what to say or waiting for Shea to start. And after a moment she does.

"You were right," Shea confesses, grateful for his silence. "Everything you saw, everything you said, and I can't do a damn thing about it."

Shea shakes her head and suppresses the rush of emotion that almost keeps her from speaking again. "She hates me, and it's okay really, because I can be that for her, I can do that. But this was just supposed to be a job. Get in, kidnap the girl, get the key, and drop the problem off where it would never be heard from again."

Shea's laugh is quick, and sharp like ice, and she thinks Caen is about to speak but she cuts him off, "She's real now, and she's so difficult to explain. She saved Aster today. Even though her own life is on the line and I don't think she thought about it. I came in knowing what I was doing and now…How can something be right and hurt so damn much? Because I wonder. I wonder, if she'd been someone different or if I had? I wonder now. I didn't used to."

Shea sniffs, running a hand over her face with a cough. "Ugh. I'm being stupid."

"Not unusual," Jo responds as she steps up beside Shea, and Shea just about has a heart attack with a particular urge to jump from her own ship right about now.

"Where in Hades did you come from?"

"You're not going to believe this, but I actually felt bad for snapping at you."

Shea blinks. "Okay."

Jo laughs for real and the captain nearly faints.

"I didn't know it was you," Shea tries to explain herself.

"I figured."

Shea can't figure out how to respond so instead they stare out at the water together. She searches for something to say but everything's blank. Because what do you say to the woman you're starting to crush on and plan to leave on an island to die?

"You were amazing today," Jo tells her, and Shea can feel the tips of her ears blushing.

"It's my job."

"You're good at it."

And the blush intensifies; Shea tries to suppress it and rolls her eyes at the smug grin Jo shoots her way.

"So you can do magic?"

"What gave it away?" Shea jokes, her head coming up until bright green meets silver blue.

"The spell you did with the sword? What did the words mean? I've never seen anything like it. Have you always known how to do that?"

"It's a small charm really. A command spell. Simple. When I was younger, I learned it from my—" Shea bites her tongue because, no, they're not having this conversation about Shea's childhood. "I learned it a long time ago."

"Aster said it was elvish."

"Well Aster is correct," Shea sighs.

She clambers out of her makeshift chair and goes to the rail, bringing her elbow up to sit on the wood and letting her head rest in her palm. "You two seem to be getting along."

"Yes," Jo laughs, thinking about the teen. "He's a good kid. Eager."

"Oh you noticed that too?" Shea teases.

"Of course," Jo chuckles, sobering, as if she's just remembered where she is, but there's a soft smile still lingering on her lips and it feels good to see it. "You guys have a lot in common."

Shea points to her ears and Jo rolls her eyes, amending the statement, "Besides the elven thing."

Shea grins.

"It seems like you guys have a common experience, it's made you kindred to one another. He really cares about you."

Shea nods. There's nothing she wouldn't do for that kid.

"You weren't so bad today yourself." Shea nods, changing the subject, to which Jo thankfully doesn't object, but she does take notice. "Where'd you learn how to fight?"

Jo snorts. "Why? Because I'm just a pretty princess who lives in a shiny castle and knows nothing of the world?"

"I mean, you said it." Shea chuckles, and Jo takes her good hand and pushes Shea over with enough force that she stumbles.

"My mother's captain of the guard. He was like an uncle to me. Before she died, she asked if he would train me a little, just the basics in case anything ever happened. I guess it came in handy." Jo wryly gestures to the ship.

"I guess it did," Shea repeats, her face returning to neutral.

And there it is. The reminder that they're not a princess and an admirer alone together at some ball but a captor and captive stuck together at sea. Shea turns her head in her palm so she can watch the princess looking out at the stars—she enjoys the way Jo's face lights up as she spots each one.

"They're incredibly clear out here," Jo gasps. "In the city they're beautiful, but it's as if they don't shine as bright. Like they were made for the open world. Free." And at that last comment, Jo catches Shea's gaze and really looks at her.

It feels as if Jo is examining pieces of Shea's own soul and Shea wants to look away, but she can't; she feels completely entranced.

"You were very beautiful that night," Shea says, and Jo breaks the gaze. Shea closes her eyes in pain, in regret; it feels as if the world has gone away and Shea ruined it.

"It's getting late, I should get to bed." Jo steps away before asking jokingly, "So should I go back to my cell or...?"

"Jo, wait—I mean, Joana," Shea says, reaching out for her, but Jo dances out of reach, holding her injured arm closer to herself.

"Jo's fine. I prefer it anyway. Now where am I sleeping?"

"Fine, Jo. I know it doesn't make this any better, but there are reasons for this, why I'm doing it—"

Jo holds up her good hand. "Please, stop. I'll just ask Caen—"

"If there was another way," Shea stresses, "I would do that for you. I think you're an amazing person, but I can't give this up."

"You can!" Jo snaps, tears are now in her eyes and Shea groans.

"Just let me go, you can release me. And I'll make sure no one comes after you."

"You don't understand what's at stake!" Shea objects, slamming her fist into the wooden railing. "If I could let you go, I would, but I have to do this. And my feelings on the matter cannot come between this job, not even for you."

They stand there frozen, glaring at one another, neither willing to stand down.

"Feelings?" Jo scoffs.

Shea nods tightly.

"Oh, Shea. You don't have feelings," Jo states coldly. "Because if you cared for me at all? You'd take me home. Because nothing would be worth my life. If you do this? You don't get to be the redeemable villain or the sweet love interest from before."

"Jo..." Shea's eyes glaze over with unshed tears, but she doesn't let them fall, just allows the grimace to settle over her features.

"What exactly is my life worth?" Jo rages into the night.

"My people."

"What?" Jo whispers, tears openly falling now.

"If I take you away and make sure you never return, a man will give me the key that will end the elven slave trade. And that's why I can't take you back. That's why I can't save you and it kills me that I can't."

The tears still don't come; they remain unshed and Shea offers a broken smile.

Jo shakes her head. "Damn it..."

She whispers it over and over again, like a prayer, wiping a hand down her face.

"You were supposed to be a monster," Jo accuses, her voice cracking. "You said you were the villain."

Shea offers a watery smile. "I still am, Your Highness."

But Jo shakes her head, biting her bottom lip with enough force that it splits.

"No," she growls softly, "but I wish you still were one."

Then she turns and starts to walk away.

"Jo!" Shea calls after her.

Jo stops, turning at the urgency in Shea's voice.

"Just...Talk to Caen. Tell him...I've given you his quarters and in the meantime, tell him to come see me. I'll assign him new sleeping arrangements."

Jo nods and again turns away from Shea, but she calls out once more, stopping the princess in her tracks.

"And if you like, we tend to get a lot of injuries on board," Shea continues; she takes a step toward Jo and Jo takes a step back. "Surprisingly a lot."

Shea laughs nervously and forces herself to stay still. "Nol has been begging me for an assistant; perhaps while you're here you'd like to help him out? It's a place for you for now."

And Shea doesn't know what she expects—a fit, snarls at the idea of working during what may be her last days, more tears over Shea not changing her mind—but instead she gets a small broken smile and there's a twinkle in Jo's gaze.

"I'd love to."

Jo's blue eyes almost glow in the darkness, and Shea finally realizes why they're so hypnotizing. They burn just like starlight.

SOMETHING 'BOUT YOU

Shea

ORENA'S OUTLINE FINALLY appears on the horizon. It's a small island but a major trading outpost if you can get to it, and luckily they had. Regardless of the incredible bounty Orena was said to hold, most didn't travel near it—considering the monsters that surrounded these waters in between Nereid and the small isle. And even if you got through, there was never a guarantee that the cargo or ship would make it back alive to be sold.

Shea stands on the afterdeck watching Orena grow larger on the horizon and it makes her wonder. Since the strange conversation the other night, Jo had joined Nol in the medical bay.

Shea can't help smiling, thinking about Jo's way with the crew, and she can't help the pleasure it gives her to see the princess becoming part of the ship. It takes everything in her not to give in to the request of those dazzling blue eyes and return her to Arethusa, but Shea can't. Not now, not with the reward so close. Her smile edges away and she loses sight of the horizon up ahead, getting lost in her thoughts. Shea's evaluated the job. The hooded man had simply asked that Jo disappear so that she couldn't return to Arethusa and reclaim the throne. Sure, he had mentioned the Tenaro Islands, but it had been more of suggestion than a real part of the deal. Jo couldn't return to Arethusa. Not without destroying this chance. So with that in mind, Shea had taken on a small mission of her own to make Jo as comfortable as possible on the *Veiled Duchess.*

Shea went so far as to turn a small old storage room on the galleon into a new cabin room just for Jo. The island's shape becomes clearer by the second and another thought whispers easily from the back of Shea's mind. Perhaps if she showed Jo around Orena? Maybe give her an idea of a life to be offered here on the island? It would be difficult to visit often, but Jo would be alive, and safe. And perhaps after it all goes down eventually in Lycos—the key, the blackmail, and the end of the slave trade? Maybe if Shea manages to stay alive? Maybe a retirement on Orena could be possible with a charming princess at Shea's side.

The captain snickers, shaking her head out of the fantasy. It's a nice wish. Aster shouts from the quarterdeck, drawing the redhead's attention back over the rail to her crew working along the deck.

"Captain! We're nearing Orena, Caen would like to know the list for the landing party!"

"Tell Caen it matters not, but Jo and I will be accompanying him to port," Shea responds.

Aster gives a stiff nod, taking off back to the bow where Caen is. Shea catches sight of Jo and Nol as they stroll out from under her.

"We are?" Jo asks, picking up the end of Shea and Aster's conversation.

Jo cranes her head around the balcony edge to look up at Shea. The captain admires Jo's powder-blue blouse, and the dark black pants tied at the waist with a white satin scarf, the blouse tucked in. She's barefoot, which lifts the edge of Shea's mouth slightly, and tanning from the amount of sun. Her blond curls are lightly tied behind her back. Shea almost falls over from the brightness of the smile she receives from the princess.

"Might I come as well, Captain? I have some herbs I'd like to pick up from the apothecary," Nol explains, using his hand to block the sun from his face.

Shea cuts her attention away from Jo, who is smiling at her almost knowingly, and focuses in on the graying doctor. "Very well, Nol," Shea agrees.

She takes out her spyglass from her jacket pocket and peers through, surveying the Orenien dock. Shea murmurs to James at the helm, telling him to dock in lot seven.

He acknowledges her without a word and adjusts his position accordingly. Shea announces the ship leave across the deck as she slips the spyglass back into her pocket. Nol and Jo haven't gone far and so Shea waves their attention down once more, interrupting their discussion. "We can meet up at the Fire Daisy's Tavern an hour after we dock, Caen and I have a meeting with a supplier. I sent Caeruleus ahead with the message."

"Can't I go with you?" Jo interrupts. "While I'd love to go with Nol"—the blonde turns slightly to the doctor to appease him—"I wouldn't mind meeting one of your suppliers."

"Maybe next time," Shea states, dipping her hat in apology. "I need to meet with this client alone."

Nol nods, and Jo seems as if she might object when Nol cuts her off, "I remember you saying you took horticulture with a tutor back in your palace days."

Jo nods reluctantly, and Nol continues, "I'd appreciate a second eye then, mine aren't what they used to be."

Jo glances up at Shea again, who shrugs, and finally Jo agrees.

"Good, let's say about noon," Shea remarks.

Looking at the shadows on the deck, she'd say it's still about midmorning.

"Take us in, Mister James."

"Aye, Captain." Shea knocks the railing twice with her fist and heads down the steps, passing Jo with a small wink on her way to the door.

Jo smirks and Shea carries that with her as she goes to get ready for the day ahead. The ship docks with ease.

MEET THE TRADERS

TERO TAKES CARE OF THE DOCK MASTER, under the table of course, but considering the territory isn't under Lycon or Arethusian rule, Orena just might be the one place the *Duchess* is not considered a criminal vessel and instead just a normal trading ship.

Shea reaches for her purple velvet hat that she'd luckily found in the anchor room after the Aurai attack; to say she'd been ecstatic was an understatement, considering it had been Paetre's before hers.

Shea pockets a coin purse filled with Orenien currency and shrugs on her dark brown overcoat. She clips the leather belt with her sword holster into place and checks herself out in the mirror. Her hair falls down her shoulders and back in sea salt curls from the ocean air. Her face is a mess of freckles and tan from the hours and days spent working in the sun. A thought crosses her mind and she glances back toward the door to her cabin, biting her lip. She thinks about locking it but shrugs it off. If anyone comes in here, she'll just threaten him or her under pain of death not to say a word.

Shea walks toward her desk and opens up the quill box, pulling out a piece of charcoal. Walking back to the mirror, she tries to relax and remember how Venus had used it when she was helping Shea get ready for the ball. Carefully and steadily, Shea draws one line across her eyelid and then on the other. She curses slightly when it smears, but with a little saliva, it's a quick fix. Her eyes intensify with the black liner. They look brighter, and slightly bigger. A cough startles her from behind and she turns back to find Caen leaning in the doorway with a smirk.

"You ready?" He grins.

And of course it's the one man who will ignore all of her threats.

"Not a word."

"I wasn't going to say it."

Shea slams the charcoal on the desk, not bothering with putting it away, and pushes past Caen. They meet on the quarterdeck: Caen, Shea, Aster, Nol, and Jo, all of them dressed and ready for port. Mister Tero greets them at the gangplank, giving Shea the rundown on what they can carry on the ship for the return journey and the supplies they need replenished.

"Thank you, Mister Tero," Shea acknowledges, folding the list and placing it in the breast pocket of her coat.

Tero nods and goes back to barking orders at the various deck crew checking out Joana. They head down the gangplank and Shea can't help but laugh at the awed expression glued to Jo's face as she looks over the Orenien port. Ornate and magnificent colors span over the tops of trading booths and storefronts.

Orena is known for their silk. The extravagant designs on each tapestry are enough to entrance anyone. The water is bluer closer to shore, and it's so clear you can see all the wildlife swimming beneath as they descend down the plank. Merchants and people of all design wear tunics and robes of varying wealth and color. Buildings made of sandstone, specially crafted on the island with precious gems uncaringly mixed within, span as far back as the eye can see, a sparkling tawny sea of various heights. Orena is the hidden jewel of the west and as the last member of their meager party steps onto the port, Shea begins the separation.

"Nol, you know where the tavern is." Nol nods and Shea continues, "Good, we'll meet there in about an hour or so."

"Great, let's go," Jo says excitedly, gesturing for Nol to take the lead to the apothecary.

Shea laughs, stopping them. "Aster will be accompanying you."

Jo and Aster object at the same time. "But, Captain, you promised I could be there for the negotiation—"

"Shea, is that really necessary—"

"Aster will be accompanying you. Are we clear?" Shea commands, leveling her gaze on both of them with a raised eyebrow.

Aster grumbles a "yes, ma'am" and Jo rolls her eyes.

"Worried I might run?"

Jo's eyes narrow as she waits for Shea's answer.

"Yes." Shea smirks. "One hour. Caen, let's go."

Caen grunts and the two of them start off toward the meeting point with the traders. By chance, Shea sneaks a look back at the other three before stopping in her tracks as she can see all of them still standing there arguing with each other.

"Oi!" Shea shouts, catching their attention. "I suggest you take off, times a-wasting. And you wouldn't want to be late."

Aster's and Nol's faces lose all color while Jo shoots her a confused expression. Next thing Jo knows, Aster and Nol are ushering her off to the apothecary. Shea laughs and turns back to Caen, who asks about the amount of cargo Tero had mentioned. They navigate through the winding streets of Orena; rich silks of blue and gold hang from building to building over the alleys and streets. As they venture deeper into the exotic city, the plant life begins to take over more and more.

Vines creep up the tawny sandstone, and twist against the marvelous gems peeking through the rock. Palms can be found at almost any corner. And it's a relief when they finally arrive at their destination. There's blue ivy crawling along the massive face of the home in front of them. A beautiful fountain stands on the cobbled stone and sits between Caen, Shea, and the front door.

The fountain's carved stone depicts the scene of Poseidon slaying the last kraken, its giant tentacles crawling menacingly toward the statue of Poseidon as he stabs the terrible creature right to its core. The water spews out of the kraken like blood. It's visceral and for some reason it always causes a shiver to run down Shea's spine. Not the violence but the face of Poseidon—it creates a feeling of familiarity before Shea is shaken out of the trance.

Caen knocks on the large, dark wooden doors, each knock louder than the next. It doesn't take long before a man who barely comes to Shea's waist steps out. Behind the small man stands a silver-haired elven woman who is missing one of her arms.

"Caen, Shea," the man bellows, his arms stretched out, and Shea sidesteps around Caen, kneeling down to embrace Phoebus. Shea meets eyes with Phoebus's wife, Dari, and shoots her an affectionate smile.

"We got your message! Welcome back, my dear," Phoebus continues.

Dari presses past Phoebus and Shea to give Caen a one-armed hug.

"You're looking well," Dari murmurs to Caen, who returns the sentiment.

"Is Caeruleus here?" Shea asks, standing and giving Dari a hug as well.

Caen picks Phoebus up in a bear hug, causing both men to start laughing hysterically. Dari and Shea share an exasperated look as Caen puts Phoebus back down, and Phoebus turns to answer.

"Oh yes, he's bothering the other cats, getting a thrill of them hissing." Phoebus chuckles.

Shea glances into the large home, catching sight of Caeruleus sitting on a perch in the front room that also serves as a shop. There's a door at the back that leads to the rest of the house. Shea points her index and middle fingers at her eyes and then points them back at Caeruleus, who yowls belligerently before merely going back to ruffling his feathers with his muzzle, unbothered.

"Come in, come in please, you've come at a good time." Dari grins, beckoning them inside.

The front store of the house is a large room, with shelves on every wall, and a marble table used for transactions. The couple leads Shea and Caen past the store into a huge ceilingless dome. The architecture is like nothing Shea has ever seen anywhere else—in the center of the dome is an incredible oak tree that spans up to the top of the room and then stretches out with its branches creating a ceiling of leaves.

Magic guards the home with multiple glamours. If anyone saw the house from the front, they'd never know what hidden treasures lie within.

Sun streams through the branched ceiling and there are rooms connecting off the main living space leading to the kitchens, bedrooms, and baths. This was Shea's favorite place to visit as a child.

When Paetre couldn't handle her or needed to put Shea somewhere for safety, when she was too young to attend a mission, he would take her here to live briefly with his old friend and former captain, Phoebus, and his wife, Dari. Somehow this small island in a sea of monsters was where Shea felt most at home besides the ship.

Dari exits the room briefly before coming back, carrying in her one hand a tray of tea and cookies, while Phoebus leads Caen and Shea to the sitting area. The furniture is made of wicker, and branches form the couch and sitting chairs with a small table in between. Oak leaves obscure the floor entirely, and with the help of Dari's nymph magic, the leaves feel as soft as petals.

When Shea was younger, Dari—being the only elf she really knew—helped Shea through her awakening, when she presented with magic. As a specific god had never claimed her,

Dari had tried to offer her guidance in Taurus magic, a common gift of the elves and one that solidifies a bond with the earth. But Shea had always felt more in tune with the sea.

Instead Shea practiced charms and other small pieces of the god's magic, using small glamours and communication charms and building her water magic skills on her own. All elves are born with magic, and while some are never able to access it, for others it springs forth like a fountain.

Shea for the most part suppresses her gifts except in hours of need, but most elves in the old lands practice from a young age, coming into their abilities before being claimed by one of the old gods.

Often they choose an elemental specialty, like Dari. From what she knows, there are four elemental specialties: Tauri are earth elementals and Libras are air, but the names for fire and water escape Shea's memory. After coming into their specialty, elves can become tree nymphs, protectors, river folk, and even wind sprites, depending on their claiming.

Caen and Shea take a seat on the wicker couch and Phoebus sits across in an armchair as Dari moves closer, carrying the heavy tray with a pot of tea and four cups. Caen goes to stand and help, but as always Shea remains seated—she's been at the end of Dari's speeches for trying to help.

"I've got it." Dari glares, practically forcing Caen back onto the couch with a single look. Phoebus chuckles and Dari sets the tray down, swiftly pouring the rose petal tea into four cups. She takes a seat as well and sits down in the wicker chair next to Phoebus.

"Well, let's get work out of the way. I've got some big shipments of textiles, silks, and a crate of sandstone that has to get to the freefolk in Oceanus," Phoebus says, taking a delicate sip of the tea from the small china. Shea takes a sip as well and holds back a snort at Caen staring down at the tiny cup of tea almost engulfed by his large hand.

"We came with an empty scuttle, so we'll take as much as you'd like and smuggle it through," Shea responds, and

Phoebus grins, smacking his hand on his knee.

"Excellent, then I'll also send over this elkhorn coral that was shipped over here from the reefs of Tenaro; it'll fetch a pretty price in Arethusa. I reckon you know how their gardens are."

Shea nods, recalling the night not too long ago and how beautiful the water gleamed in the Lover's Fountain, much different than the fountain out front here. Her silence comes off as awkward and Phoebus and Dari exchange glances before they turn their eyes toward Caen, who stiffens at the acknowledgment.

"Why are you here so early? We're not complaining, we love having you here as well as the business, but you're two months early. What brings you out this way? You both know how dangerous it is to deviate from the schedule," Dari states, staring Caen down until he seems to be shrinking in his seat.

The *Duchess*'s encounter with the wind spirits was just one example of what deviating from the schedule can do, as many of the creatures on the outskirts swim farther down the Aiolos reef. The mistake in timing can be deadly.

Caen opens and closes his mouth, not really sure where to begin, and the inquisitive glares on Dari's and Phoebus's faces do nothing to reassure him. He shoots Shea a sharp glance, hoping it'll get her to talk instead. Shea, who has been at the end of those stares more than a few times, specifically when she's in trouble, stays silent and avoids Caen's eyes as she pretends to focus on Caeruleus chasing the cats around the hall.

"Yes well," Caen begins, clearing his throat. "We have something on board that is time sensitive. We were charged with bringing it to the Tenaro Islands."

No one speaks and Shea can feel the twin glares switch over to her. She looks up with an innocent expression.

"The Tenaro Islands? What the bloody Underdeep could you be bringing there?" Phoebus barks, setting his tea down firmly.

"Shea, you promised that if you ever needed anything from

there, you'd let us hire someone who knows the islands. Someone who could be in and out. Those waters are dangerous. Even a skilled sailor such as yourself would need years and years of mapping just to take a small trip to the outskirts," Dari calmly asserts, trying to keep Phoebus's temper from flaring.

The captain sighs and then speaks, "I was charged with kidnapping the crown princess of Arethusa." She rushes the statement, partially hoping the two elders won't actually comprehend what she said. "The Tenaro Islands were simply a suggestion of where to drop her off."

The tension in the air solidifies until Shea could run her sword through it. By the time she looks up, Phoebus's face has slowly turned from tan to bright red. He jumps from his seat, his graying beard looking positively stormy among his angry features. "Are you insane? I knew women shouldn't be allowed to sail, I told you all she should stay here on the island with us," Phoebus bellows as he storms over to Caen, who is looking down at the small teacup in his hands.

"You told us you'd keep her safe, that you'd keep her well informed! Rule number one, we don't get involved with the plots of the land folk, we take from the mainlanders, we trick the mainlanders, and we sell to the mainlanders! But we don't work for them!"

Shea resists the urge to flinch as he keeps shouting—she's no longer a child in his household—and she lifts her gaze to his face.

"It was my decision."

"Yes, I can see that," Phoebus snarls, walking over to a double-shelved glass cart stored against the wall near the entry to the kitchen.

He grabs a bottle on the lower shelf, popping the cork off with his teeth, spitting it out, and pouring himself a glass.

"Might I get one as—" Caen starts, but Phoebus slams the bottle down, effectively silencing him. "Never mind."

"Phoebus, please," Dari asks, but he ignores her.

"I don't understand after everything you went through as a child—how you fell into Paetre's and our custody—you said you would never trade life. What was the price?"

Shea starts to answer but Phoebus cuts her off. He stalks toward her, pinning her with a disappointed expression, and his glass falls to his side in his other hand.

"Paetre would never have done this."

The blatant comment is well placed and Shea can't help the way her stomach turns inside her. He's right, but it doesn't calm the storm that brews within her.

Shea stands, and she can barely hear Caen whispering to her, "Shea, don't."

Even Dari is shaking her head, her one hand gripping her forehead in exasperation.

"You're right," Shea says, her voice deadly calm, clear and sharp. "He wouldn't have taken the job."

"You bet your ass," Phoebus growls.

"But Paetre is dead," Shea responds.

Phoebus objects vehemently, "Watch your tongue, young lady, you have some respect."

"I am not a child anymore. I am the captain of the *Veiled Duchess*, not some little girl, and yes if I knew then what I know now, maybe I wouldn't have taken the job. But you have no say over what I do. You will show me respect."

Phoebus opens his mouth to cut Shea off, but she leans over him, staring him in the eye.

"I know Paetre was your friend. Hades, he was my guardian, but he wasn't perfect. I'm not him. And I don't want to be him. So you can decide whether you would like to do business with me," Shea snarls, her heartbeat thumping loudly in her ears. She can barely hear her own voice.

The red drains from Phoebus's face and he looks solemn; he opens his mouth to speak but Shea shakes her head. She can't do this right now.

"Save it." Shea turns and walks toward the entry on the back wall, toward her old bedroom.

Caen and Phoebus flinch as the door down the hall slams closed, but Dari looks back, pensive. Phoebus groans, sitting down heavily in his seat. Caen on the other hand gets up and shuffles over to the glass-shelved cart, taking the rum off the top level and pouring himself a glass as well.

"She's different," Dari acknowledges, and Caen chuckles before drinking a big gulp.

"Aye, she is."

"I just don't understand why she took the job. Paetre taught her better, we taught her better," Phoebus exclaims, reaching out his left hand for Dari's right, who takes it with ease.

"We don't have to understand," Caen states, turning back toward the two of them. "She's the captain of the *Duchess* now. She's right. She's not a child. She saw an opportunity that lay in her best interest and she took it. As much as she hates to admit it, she's a lot like Paetre."

They all nod in agreement.

"She likes her," Dari assumes, and Caen laughs. Dari has always been so damn perceptive.

"Likes who?" Phoebus asks, but they ignore him.

"Bring her here, all of them. I'll make dinner," Dari states, smoothing out her dress.

"Dari, I don't think Shea would like that," Caen murmurs, setting his glass back on the shelf.

"She doesn't have to, my daughter needs me," Dari replies simply. "Bring me the girl."

Caen still seems reluctant, and finally Phoebus catches up.

"The princess?" Phoebus exclaims.

"Caen," Dari repeats. "You know where they'll be, she'll be safe here. It's now or this deal could change who Shea really is."

Caen agrees and so he nods.

"Will somebody please explain what is happening?" Phoebus yells.

But instead Caen whistles and Caeruleus flocks to his shoulder. He bows to Dari with respect, and she giggles before he walks out the door in search of a princess.

LOVE'S FOOL

Shea

SHEA SITS ON HER OLD BED in what became her childhood bedroom. The dark blue blankets are stitched with silver dots that appear to the world like the material has been woven with pieces of the night sky.

The room is just as she left it; the back wall is nonexistent as it opens up onto a large balcony that looks over the inner gardens of the house. Two pink trees encompass either side of the balcony and the whole room's floor is covered in the tree's soft light pink petals, magic sustaining them from dying. The walls are covered with mosaics that depict scenes from the bottom of the ocean: some of the scenes are dark while others are light and beautiful.

Sunlight streams in from the day, and Shea knows that she can't sit in here forever staring out at the beautiful gardens she'd grown up playing in.

The twinkling center pools in the courtyard glitter under the sun, and screeching monkeys yell at poor Lena the elephant bathing in the pool.

Lena had been a gift from Phoebus when Shea turned sixteen, a gift that was given with the intention of her staying with them forever. She wasn't their child though—she used to say that in her mind over and over, but the more Paetre left her on Orena the harder it became to believe. They may not have been her blood parents, but they were hers all the same.

Shea jolts from where she's leaning against the mosaic wall on her bed when a knock sounds at the door. She's sure it's Caen coming to remind her that they're supposed to meet Jo, Aster, and Nol at the tavern and nearly curses. Here she is having a tantrum like the stubborn child she was denying to be and her crew is out there waiting for her. She doesn't like tardiness.

Shea jumps up from the bed, grabbing her belt and hat off the vanity chair, where she had laid them down briefly.

"I didn't forget, let's go," Shea calls as she opens the door but finds Dari standing there instead.

Her long white hair is tied off at her waist in a loose braid, her blue eyes sparkling like the pools in the garden, and they complement her black skin. She's waiting on the other side with a bag of something in her hand.

"Can I come in?" Dari smiles.

Shea leans against the door frame with a sigh.

"Actually Caen and I are expected somewhere," Shea responds, focusing her eyes on her boots.

"He's already gone," Dari states.

Shea's eyes jump to Dari's, and there's a twinkling, knowing look in them.

Shea groans.

"Dari, no."

"It's been done, she's coming."

Shea groans again.

"Oh hush," Dari admonishes.

She shoos Shea back into the room. The redhead shuffles in, dropping her captain's hat on the floor, and sits heavily on her bed with her belt and sword in hand.

"I didn't really get to mention it over tea, but I'm happy to see you," Dari notes.

Her bony, thin frame is draped in a blush-pink wrap tunic and she walks gracefully over to the balcony. She sets down a bag Shea hadn't realized she'd been carrying, and from the bag the older elf pulls out a bit of fruit. Sliced pear, from what Shea can see.

Dari steps closer to the edge of the balcony, her braided white hair falling over her shoulder, and she beckons for Lena to come closer. Lena, as big as she is, walks over slowly and Dari kneels down at the edge of the balcony. Once Lena is below her, she passes the fruit to the elephant easily as the ledge is low enough for Lena to reach up. Dari stays there like that; her dark complexion glowing in the sunlight, and Shea huffs, knowing that she's expected to go over there.

She goes and kneels down next to Dari. Lena smells her and gets excited, running her trunk all over Shea, poking her and causing her to laugh.

"So what's her name?" Dari finally asks when Lena relents and Shea has a moment to breathe.

The captain rolls her eyes, grabbing a piece of pear from the bag and giving it to Lena.

"I'm not doing this."

"Okay, what's the cargo's name?"

Shea grimaces, hating the way the question simply runs off Dari's tongue. Shea may have been kidnapped from her home and sold as a slave, but Paetre had purchased her—she never really was a slave. But Dari was. Her mistress, the queen of Arethusa at the time, Queen Doris, caught Dari stealing food for the younger slaves when she was fourteen and ordered her men to cut off her arm. According to Phoebus, she didn't even scream.

Back when Phoebus was captain and Paetre merely his quartermaster, they saved Dari from the Arethusian slavery. It wasn't long after Queen Triteia came into power and outlawed slavery from the queendom. It was a tale that wasn't often told, the story of how Dari and Phoebus had fallen in love. Later, after an adventure or two, Phoebus and Dari retired here on Orena together to live out the rest of their days, and Phoebus passed the ship on to Paetre.

Because of Dari's cruel mistress she wasn't able to have kids, but Phoebus never minded; he had never seen himself as the father type anyway. Then several years later, Paetre shows up on their doorstep with a seven-year-old girl trailing behind him, with a request that they take her in for a little while. Dari likes to say it was her little miracle day and that she treasured every time Paetre brought Shea to them.

"Her name is Joana," Shea finally tells her after all the memories subside, and Dari smiles.

"Joana, what a beautiful name."

They sit there in silence and Shea holds her emotions at bay, but her voice comes out hollow and cracked, "I don't know what to do."

Dari turns Shea toward her until they're both facing each other, still kneeling. She places her hand on Shea's face; a single tear falls but Dari swipes it away with the pad of her thumb.

"You don't know what to do?" Dari repeats.

"I like her," Shea scoffs, shaking her head.

"That's good," Dari coos, brushing a stray strand of hair behind Shea's pointed ear.

"If I save her, I risk so much more."

"What do you mean?"

"The payment is the vault," Shea explains. "Ceto's vault. I could take down the slave trade, I could take down Lycos. But if I let her go? All of this would have been for nothing."

Dari snorts, and it startles Shea.

"My darling, you're already losing something far more important." Dari points her finger straight at Shea's heart. "You want to end the slave trade by taking someone else's freedom? That's not the right way. And who says she'd go back anyway."

"Of course she would."

"She's met you. And if you like her half as much as I know she can't help but love you, then she'll stay. Screw the deal. You're a pirate. We don't play fair, we get what we want, and sometimes we don't give what we promised."

"You're asking me to take this on faith," Shea murmurs, rubbing a hand over her face.

"You've been paid, I assume. The moment you took her?"

"Supposedly," Shea answers, thinking of V.

"So you have the vault."

"Maybe, but it'll mean nothing if the man I'm working for alerts Ceto. Or if Jo tells her herself by escaping and going home. I'll lose everything."

"That's a risk you need to take. You need to know if she could give up her home for you."

"She's loyal in nature, she wouldn't—"

"As was I, before I ran away with Phoebus, and as was Phoebus when he left the crew for me."

"What would we do? Keep her on the ship?"

"Or another place," Dari suggests and glances around the room with a smirk.

Shea looks around. "Really? You'd let her stay?"

"I may not be a mother to you, but you will always be a daughter to me."

Shea smiles sadly at the comment. "If people found out about her, you could be killed."

"We can handle ourselves. Remember who you learned it from."

Shea is trying to find the right words to communicate how she feels but instead she reaches forward and hugs Dari tightly, who laughs in response.

"Thank you," Shea tells her.

"I would do anything for you," Dari replies.

They relax comfortably and Shea reaches down to Lena, who is nosing along the edge looking for the bag of sliced pears.

"So tonight, you'll have to convince her to stay," Dari remarks.

"Yes."

Shea gives Lena another slice. Lena takes it and begins to walk back to the pool.

"Are you planning on wearing that?" Dari questions as she looks down at Shea's ratty pants and loose peasant blouse.

"Well yeah," Shea responds, surveying her own clothes. "What's wrong with the way I look?"

"Nothing, but perhaps something that will surprise her?"

Shea rolls her eyes.

"What did you have in mind?" Shea grumbles and Dari's eyes light up at the prospect of dressing the redhead up.

"Well, now that you mention it, I do have this old dress of yours that I just so happened to have spruced up a bit."

Dari stands as quickly as she can and bounds over to the tall dresser in the corner of the room, just before the balcony, and opens it. She pulls out a lavender dress, simple, with off-the-shoulder sleeves and a slight thigh slit. The tropical fabric looks almost sheer and there's a silk base underneath it. It's not too long; in fact, it looks as if it'll stop just above Shea's ankles.

"Dari, I'm not wearing that," Shea says, looking at the slip like it's poison.

"Why not?" Dari inquires and Shea almost regrets her position as she can see the hurt in Dari's eyes.

Shea looks over the dress.

"It just looks very...elven."

Dari stares at her and then laughs. "My darling, you are elven."

Shea wants to object but she can see the eagerness in Dari's features, and she can't bring herself to disappoint.

"Fine. Hades, it's tonight or bust, do what you want," Shea chuckles.

Dari squeals in excitement. She demands for Shea to take off her clothes and try on the dress. As Shea starts undressing, Dari stares at the redhead's hair, telling Shea she'll fix that too. And as Shea relaxes into her pseudo-mother's touch, she allows herself a small amount of hope for tonight, and draws on a little faith.

I'D LIKE TO HATE YOU

Joana

THE APOTHECARY IS LESS THAN extraordinary but the city of Orena itself is magnificent. Jo finds herself falling in love with the scenery at every turn of the street. All of the people are so different—their clothes have so many colors, some she's never seen before—that it makes her feel as if she sticks out like a sore thumb.

Nol gives her a few notes on the local herbs and things that have even been shipped from Tenaro that are incredibly rare and useful. Aster makes the trip entertaining as he continuously touches everything in the apothecary, getting yelled at by Nol and eventually kicked out by the owner.

Once Nol acquires everything on the list, Aster calls into the store, careful not to step inside as the owner glowers at him. He alerts the two of them they should all be heading toward the tavern. Every inch of the streets are filled with carts and people, and while everything is beautiful, Jo can't help but feel homesick for Arethusa. Many of the silks she recognizes as pieces she's seen in the palace, and she's amazed that she never knew the trinkets of her culture come from Orena.

Jo misses her father and even Gaea and Rhea, the meddling witches they are; Karnon, her captain of the guard; and even a few of her friends from court. And these growing feelings for

Shea only confuse Jo more—there's so much that she should hate Shea for, but there are even smaller voices inside that whisper to Jo that she could forget it all, her father, her ladies, her country, and just be with the redheaded captain.

The three make it to the tavern on time and without delay. They get a table in the back near the door and Aster goes to the bar to grab them drinks, coming back with three jugs of ale.

Jo stares down at the mug wistfully and thinks about how much she misses wine. They wait, knowing they're there a bit early. But as time passes, worry starts to set in. Aster ventures outside to see if he can spot them.

"They've probably just lost track of time, they'll be here," Nol explains, looking through the herbs he bought at the apothecary.

"And here I thought Shea had a thing about being on time, she can't even keep to her own rules," Joana jokes, but Nol looks up with a somber expression.

"She worries. She likes us to be on time because anything can happen; she's always looking out for the crew. In her line of work, if someone's late it usually means they're in trouble."

Jo's eyes widen and Nol shrugs in response. "One of the last times we were at some port, it was another outlying island similar to Orena. Aster had been given his first solo mission, accompanying me to a rare bookstore for information on something we'd been looking for. We ran into a bit of trouble on our way out."

Jo listens curiously to the tale and nods for Nol to continue. "Aster recognized a sailor as we walked out of the shop, a man who'd known his master from his old life. He wanted to arrest Aster for escaping slavery and force him back into service. I was merely a lucky catch to go along with the boy. Somehow Shea found us and saved our asses. We do well to listen to her."

"Someone was just going to take you? I'm sure others would have objected!"

Nol smirks wryly. "The world is a much darker place than you know, Your Majesty."

Jo says quietly, "So then, does this mean Shea's in trouble?"

Jo glances back at the tavern door once more and begins to worry her bottom lip between her teeth.

"I don't know," Nol mutters, nursing his drink. "But if she is, there's not much we'll be able to do."

Time passes slowly and it feels like an eternity before Jo stands, her body shaking from reluctant nerves. "Something's wrong, we should get back to the—"

Aster comes running through the door and Caen swaggers in behind him with Caeruleus perched on his shoulder.

Jo waits another moment, but Shea doesn't appear behind them. Her emotions get the best of her and she strolls up to Caen purposefully, glaring him down. He looks at her with a raised eyebrow but doesn't say anything.

"Where is she?" Jo barks, looking Caen over for any injuries.

"She's fine," Caen counters, waving his hands in a placating gesture. "You worried?"

He smirks and Jo turns red from the implication and takes a step back with her hands on her hips. "No. She's late."

Aster laughs and Caen rolls his eyes with a huff.

"Where is our lovely captain?" Nol echoes Jo's previous question with softer intensity.

"She's still with the traders, we've been invited back to their home for a meal," Caen confirms, and much to Jo's surprise Aster hollers with excitement.

"Yes! I hope Dari makes my favorite." Aster smiles and even Nol is grinning at the mention of these traders.

"Shall we?" Caen asks, and Jo nods—it's not like she has a choice—and follows Caen and Aster out the door with Nol behind her.

Caeruleus flies ahead of the crowd as Caen takes them deeper into the city. It seems as if the farther into the city they get, the more the alleys curve and cross like a winding labyrinth.

Jo marvels at the greenery and asks Nol about the excess of plant life climbing the inner city walls and buildings. "Orena used to be an elven city, before the traders made it across the sea. Some of the older folk have tried to preserve the olden kingdom. The elves were the ones who taught the people of Orena to make sandstone, but they believed that true shelter came from life itself."

"The plants?" Jo asks, staring at the palms on the corners holding up structures and the vines almost overtaking some of the buildings with vibrant flowers Jo has never seen until today.

"Yes, Maren taught me that. We had planned to live out our days here after we made it to Oceanus before he died," Nol confides wistfully.

Jo grants him a somber smile, thinking about her own precarious position. Finally they make their way to a courtyard where a massive fountain stands tall; the architecture is similar to that of the Lover's Fountain back home, the same lines, though a much cruder scene.

She's caught staring at Poseidon's face; something about it is almost familiar and yet she can't place where. She's so busy studying the fountain that she never hears the giant door open.

"Do you like it?" Jo jumps a good foot in the air, turning to look at whomever spoke but finds no one.

"The fountain I mean."

The voice comes from below, and Jo looks down to find a very short graying man with a peppered beard and dark brown eyes. Jo can't help but stare before finally gathering her wits.

Blinking, she says, "Yes, thank you, there's one back home that reminds me of it. The styles are similar, the way the Poseidon is crafted."

The man nods. "The Lover's Fountain in Arethusa?"

"Yes," Jo confirms, smiling in return. "You know it?"

"Quite well," he continues. "I knew the man who carved it."

"Really?" Jo exclaims.

"Is that surprising?"

"No," Jo startles; she does find it a bit hard to believe, but here another fountain exists and she can't deny the similarities.

"Is this done by the same man?"

"Oh yes, my father made quite the collection. There are many scattered around the queendom and empire."

"Your father?"

"Mm, he was commissioned by your grandmother when she was a young queen to build it. And I'll let you in on a little secret." He gestures for Jo to lean down.

Jo looks around, slightly awkward, as she notices that Aster and Nol are already inside. Caen is the only one still left with them in the courtyard and he watches amused. She leans down.

"He was a pirate."

The confession takes a second to register and then Jo laughs because of course he was. The small man is grinning and he holds out his hand for Jo to take.

"I'm Phoebus, a trader." Phoebus takes Jo's hand in his and kisses the back, making Jo giggle.

"Joana, crown princess…or was," she murmurs.

"Life makes you many things, a father, mother, a wife, you learn to take titles with a grain of salt," Phoebus advises and gestures for her to follow him through the massive front doors.

"You two seem to be getting along," Caen observes, and Jo nicks him with her shoulder as she walks past and enters the home.

Inside the doors there's a little shop, but they don't stop there; instead they head past the trading post and through the door at the back. As Jo steps inside the dome, everything stops, the massive oak tree in the center takes her breath away and the floor is so soft she can't really believe she's walking on leaves. There's a sitting area of wicker furniture and to the left of that a long table with different size chairs down the sides and at the heads. The light through the branches is fading and floating balls of light, not fire, twirl slowly and softly around the dome, illuminating the room.

Aster is nowhere to be found, but Nol is talking with a one-armed elven woman carrying a tray of food toward the long table.

"Dari, come and meet Joana. Shea's ward," Phoebus calls, and Jo tries to object to the wording but the older woman captivates her.

She can't help but eye the scar on her left shoulder where an arm should be, but it doesn't deter her beauty, and the way she holds herself. She's gorgeous, with long white hair that falls in ringlets connected by a ribbon at her waist. She wears a tawny sheer silk dress, much like the color of the sandstone that complements her black skin, and Jo has to stop examining the woman as she is suddenly engulfed by her with a one-armed hug.

"It's so wonderful to meet you!" Dari exclaims, pulling back to get a better look at Jo. "Even more beautiful than I imagined."

There's a knowing twinkle in her eye and it sets Jo on edge. She looks around for her annoying elven captain, but still Shea is nowhere in sight.

"Shea is here?" Jo asks before she can stop herself.

"She'll be out soon, just freshening up," Dari explains before gliding out of the room into what Jo assumes is the kitchen.

"Please come sit," Phoebus announces, pointing to the wicker chair that looks out over the room; he sits on the other armchair.

Nol follows Dari into the kitchen and Caen sits on the couch. There's a loud yowl from above, and Jo looks up to watch Caeruleus land in the branches of the massive oak tree, chasing what she can't believe are small spider monkeys. She's only ever seen drawings in her castle books.

"I'm sorry but how do you know the *Duchess* crew?" Jo asks, more than a little confused.

"I was a part of it. The first captain of the *Veiled Duchess*," Phoebus explains, "and a friend of the former captain. Dari and I used to sometimes care for Shea for him, when she was young."

The whole situation feels utterly bizarre, the idea of Shea having a semblance of a family and the way the redhead turned out makes Jo's head ache. But looking around at the laughter coming from the elven woman and Nol bringing out another plate of food, the way Caen speaks with Phoebus with such ease and the way Aster gushes over Shea as she walks out from one of the back entryways in a lavender dress—Jo's attention stops there and her head snaps back as she watches Shea enter the dome wearing nothing but the thin lavender dress stopping just above her ankles.

The captain's barefoot and the dress has two slits, one on either side of her strong muscled legs. Her hair falls loosely down her back with pink petals woven within the curly strands. There's a shine to her cheekbones that reflects off the floating balls of light in the room as the dying sun of early evening filters through the open dome. Her green eyes are so bright, and when they catch Jo's, the air leaves her lungs. Aster bounces around Shea like a squirrel chattering in excitement, gushing and teasing her about how beautiful she looks.

Caen looks back briefly and smiles, returning to his conversation with Phoebus, who ignores Shea entirely as she ventures closer. Her eyes hold steady under Jo's gaze, which stays frozen on her tan, muscled form.

Dari moves gracefully to the captain and embraces her lightly. Nol remains at the table and Dari gestures for Aster to join him, and he eagerly bounds toward the food. Dari rests her hand on Shea's naked shoulder, and Jo suppresses a growl that surprisingly rises sharply in her throat. The older elf lets go and they seem to have a silent conversation between them before Dari walks away toward Caen and Phoebus, then shoos them to their seats at the table.

Shea looks so small in the dress, and it makes Jo feel strange inside. The elf steps toward her and Jo stands abruptly from her armchair, like she would do if approached by a lady of the court. Shea either doesn't know the protocol or pretends not to notice as she walks a few steps closer before she's in front of Jo.

"My lady," Shea whispers, granting a small curtsy, and it reminds Jo of before.

"Hi," Jo responds, searching Shea's eyes for answers, but she finds none.

"I wanted to ask," Shea murmurs stopping briefly to clear her throat before continuing, "that is, I hoped…you might like to join me for dinner?"

Jo stares, bewildered. All of this just to sit at the table with a bunch of strangers. Jo shrugs and offers her hand for Shea to take. Shea does, smiling softly, and Jo begins to escort her to the long dining table when Shea stops her.

"No," Shea objects.

Jo stares at her confused, and she tries to concentrate on what Shea wants, but she's having a hard time as she feels how their hands are intertwined, noticing how perfectly they fit together, and committing the feeling to memory.

"I was hoping you might have dinner with just me," Shea explains and she pulls on Jo's hand in the opposite direction.

Jo's brows furrow and she gives one glance back to the table, where Phoebus and Caen are high-fiving and Dari is yelling at them both to be quiet, but nods in acceptance and follows Shea away from everyone else.

YOU'VE CARVED
YOUR WAY INSIDE

Joana

SHEA LEADS JO BACK through from where she had come, down a white hall that looks to be made of dry white clay. The hall is narrow and they make their way down two turns of corridors before arriving at a blue oval door, a similar color to the Azulean vine that wraps around the front of the home. Shea stops them and turns to Jo.

"I don't know why I'm so nervous."

"I don't know either," Jo teases, and it seems to make Shea relax.

They both realize that they haven't let go of each other's hand and Jo gives Shea's palm a quick squeeze just because she can before letting go.

"You look very beautiful," Jo tells her.

Shea steps in between Jo and the blue door with a challenging grin.

"Close your eyes," Shea demands.

"Excuse me?"

"You heard me, close 'em. And no peeking!"

Jo gives her one last questioning look but closes her eyes.

"Don't look."

"I won't."

"Promise?" Shea asks and there's this beautiful hopeful lilt to her voice that makes Jo melt.

"Promise," Jo whispers.

She hears the door creak open and Shea steps in first, guiding her through the entryway. Shea leads her to a certain spot and then stops, letting go of Jo's hand.

"Almost, stay still for one second." Jo waits and listens as she hears the door close behind her.

She's a woman of her word so she doesn't look, but she reaches out with her senses. There's a smell of sweet blossoms cascading through the air, invading her nose, and she can hear the soft trickling of water and the wind navigating through branches. She can feel the warm breeze on her skin, and the sound that surprises her the most is something like a trumpet mixed with something guttural. She's never heard it before in her life and it almost makes her open her eyes as she stumbles back, scared.

"No, it's okay," Shea says, coming up behind Jo, placing her hands gently on her shoulders to steady her. "It's okay. Are you ready to look?"

Jo doesn't trust herself to speak so she nods.

"Open."

She opens her eyes and looks around in awe. She's standing in a bedroom, she realizes as she notices the dark blue bed in the corner, but what takes her breath away is the balcony that looks out over a fantastic garden. Trees with pink leaves sway in the evening wind and candles lay all over the room in lanterns. There are pink petals covering the floor from the trees near the balcony. Various silks have been laid out and there are small platters of food among the pillows. Jo looks up at the ceiling and walls and notices enchanting mosaics of mythological battle scenes and love stories scattered around. The artistry is amazing.

Shea steps around her and hugs her arms to her chest. "So what do you think?"

"What is this place?" Jo breathes, stepping toward Shea and the balcony.

She looks over the edge, down into the magical garden. Pools of water reflect the evening sky, the setting sun shimmering in the small pool below. Various animals scatter around the grass, creatures Jo has never seen before. Her eyes land on a huge gray…thing of sorts. It's massive, with huge ears and a long snout that hangs down with protruding talons or horns growing from the side of its mouth.

"What is that thing?" Jo asks, careful not to get too close to the edge, as the balcony has no railing. She stares at the creature curiously.

"Phoebus called her an ellie-phant, she comes from islands up north past Nereid. Dangerous waters, but he used to have traders that would venture that far. She was a gift," Shea explains, walking to the edge and kneeling down.

She whistles and the sound is so sweet it reminds Jo of a bird. The elephant turns at the sound and comes closer to Shea, its long nose feeling along her hand. Shea turns and looks over her shoulder to Jo.

"This is Lena. She's very friendly."

Jo hesitantly moves closer, walking around the picnic to kneel down next to Shea. She keeps her hands in her lap, watching as Lena nuzzles Shea's hand.

"Here," Shea says, grasping Jo's hand before the princess can do anything about it, and thrusts it down to where Lena can reach. Jo squeaks and glares at Shea when she laughs at her. Lena noses along her hand and Jo smiles at the way it tickles. She laughs nervously when Lena wraps her nose around Jo's wrist, pulling on her, but with ease Shea gets the animal to let go and they stand together, looking out over the garden.

"I don't get it," Jo states, walking back until she's standing on the silks looking around at the platters of food, stuck in utter amazement.

"Don't get what?" Shea asks, grabbing a piece of fruit off one of the platters and popping it in her mouth.

She sits on one of the pillows, adjusting it so that she can lean back against it with ease. Jo sits as well.

"Where you come from? How you became you? How this place is a part of you?" Jo rambles, spouting all these questions and waving her hands.

Shea nods, her lips quirking in one of her frustrating smiles, and Jo almost wants to reach over and smack her over the head.

"Alright."

"What?" Jo asks, an eyebrow rising.

"I'll give you three questions."

"What?" Jo stutters again.

"I'll give you three questions, that I have to answer truthfully—"

"Ten," Jo counters, jumping at the chance to figure out just who Shea is.

Shea laughs, shaking her head. "Five. I'll give you five questions and I'll answer truthfully, but only five."

"Five questions?" Jo confirms.

"Five questions," Shea answers and places another piece of fruit seductively into her mouth.

"Are these truthful answers going to be one worded? Or will I actually get an answer?"

Shea rolls her eyes at Jo's skepticism. "If you want me to, I'll explain to a point. But I reserve the right to stop where I want."

Sounds fair enough. Jo sighs and mentally weighs her options.

"Okay. Well then, I'll do the same," Jo returns, which surprises Shea but she doesn't object.

Jo is never one to back down from a challenge.

"You first," Shea hums.

Jo's curiosity gets the best of her and she asks, "Where are you from?"

"Erebos in the Eastlands of Nereid," Shea responds easily with a smile.

"Okay, but how did you get here, why are you a pirate?"

"Technically that would be your second and third question. You asked a first question, and now it's my turn."

Jo gives her a look.

Shea sighs theatrically. "Fine, cheater. I was taken by slavers when I was seven and sold at the slave market in Lycos to Captain Paetre of the *Veiled Duchess*," Shea begins, and a wistful look spreads over her features.

Jo's surprise must show quite easily because Shea laughs at her wide-eyed expression.

"That's it really," Shea chuckles. "I was sold by slavers and purchased by a pirate and became his cabin girl. I asked him once when I was older why he did it, why not one of the boys, but he would simply say he saw something in me. He raised me the best an old sea dog could; Dari and Phoebus helped and so did Caen. And I worked my way up to his first mate. He made me captain when he died and the rest is history."

"But why—"

"Nope. I answered, more than I even had to! So, my turn," Shea interrupts, effectively cutting her off, and Jo's mouth closes into a pout.

"Fine, what is your question?" Jo grabs a grape off the tray and pops it into her mouth.

"Have you always been into women?" Jo coughs, relieved that she'd swallowed the grape, and blinks; she hadn't been expecting that.

The wind continues to blow warm, and Jo wishes she could take off the corset she'd put on over her peasant blouse. She does reach for her boots and pulls them off her feet, throwing them behind her deep into the room, trying to avoid the question. Shea smiles, watching as Jo fidgets with the pillows and makes herself comfortable against the fading light. Pink blossoms fall from the tree overhead.

"Are you avoiding my question?" Shea teases and Jo rolls her eyes.

"No," Jo answers, "I'm just thinking how to answer this politely.”

“It’s a yes or no question.”

“Perhaps, but nobles have something called tact.”

“Yeah, well pirates call that bullshit.”

The response catches Jo off guard and it causes her to laugh.

“Right. Well to answer your question,” Jo begins, grinning, “yes, I’ve always preferred women over men.”

“Scandalous, redheads in particular by any chance?” Shea smirks and Jo throws a grape at her.

“My turn?” Shea nods and leans over. She grabs a silver pitcher next to the blankets filled with an amber liquid and pours it into two cups. Shea holds one out to Jo, who sniffs it, and her heart nearly bursts when she recognizes the scent. White wine. She takes a sip and revels in the taste. Shea tips her glass in a gesture for Jo to go ahead.

“Why didn’t you run?”

“What do you mean?” Shea asks.

“When you got older, why didn’t you leave the ship? Didn’t you want to go home?” Jo clarifies.

“It is my home, the *Duchess*, I mean. I was seven when I was taken, and there was no way Paetre could have taken me back. Outsiders can’t cross the borders without permission. That’s why the elves rarely leave, and the ones who are taken by slavers are those lost in the woods or exiled or young enough to wander off. If he’d taken me back, I would have been picked up again. Paetre gave me two outs, though, later on. One when I was sixteen and one when I was eighteen. I just knew where I wanted to be.”

“What did he do?” Jo asks and Shea laughs at her again.

“You’re not very good at this, you know? One question per turn.”

“Hey, you said you’d explain if I asked,” Jo demands, reminding Shea of what she’d said earlier. Shea takes a sip of the wine and looks down into the gardens, watching Lena spray the chattering monkeys with water from the large pool.

“When I was sixteen, Paetre dropped me off here on Orena.

There was a job, a big one, and I was begging him to take me with him; instead he took me here. He told me if, when he got back, I told him I wanted to go back to the ship, he'd take me on his next job. If I didn't, I was free to stay on Orena with Dari and Phoebus."

"But you didn't?"

"No. They wanted me to stay, and I think Paetre did too. He didn't know if I was right for this life, but I'd seen too much out there. I knew what I was. That I was elven, and to grow up on a ship of men who treat you no different than they are? Well, it's hard to go from that to planting and growing magical trees for the rest of your life. Phoebus even bought me Lena as incentive to stay, but come the next fortnight, I was sailing the open seas once again."

The lanterns grow brighter as the sky turns darker, turquoise, pink, and purple melting into night, and the lanterns shine brightly through the room and onto the balcony, basking both women in soft orange light. Laughter from the other dinner party can be heard in the distance, but Jo keeps all of her attention on Shea.

"And when you were eighteen?"

"He sent me a woman," Shea tells her matter-of-factly, and Jo blanches, making Shea laugh.

"A woman?"

"An elf, a prostitute. I was sitting on the ship's deck after dark, looking up at the stars; it was a favorite of mine to do," Shea explains, glancing up at the sky above, loosely pointing at the awakening stars, lazily tracing out constellations with her finger.

Jo looks up as well, but she doesn't see the trace.

"The woman comes stumbling out of the doors onto the quarterdeck, she's looking around, and I watch her for a few seconds more, recognizing her as the woman Paetre had taken down below a couple hours before. She sees me, starts walking toward me, and says let's go."

"She wanted you to leave?"

"I was confused," Shea remembers with an amused expression. "I told her thanks but I didn't want any company for the night. Then she told me that she'd drugged Paetre."

The turn is startling, and Jo can't imagine how she would have reacted in that situation.

"I was instantly on guard. I asked her who she was and she told me she'd seen me in the brothel with him and she thought I was his slave. She told me she could help me escape, break the chain. Hades, she'd even connect me with a merchant who could take me back to Erebos after all these years." Shea chuckles, and it makes Jo smile. "All I had to do was take her hand."

Shea reaches her hand out as if she is going to take that imaginary offering, but she hesitates and her hand drops back down to her lap.

"I gave her a gold piece for her trouble and headed down to the room off the captain's quarters where Aster sleeps; it was my old room. Paetre was waiting for me. He told me he was glad I didn't take the offer."

"It was a trick?" Jo exclaims, scooting closer, and she ignores the eyebrow raise Shea shoots her way as their legs touch.

"A test. He handed me a dagger I still have to this day and asked me to be his first mate. And then he gave me his name. From that day on I was Shea Lara. He trained me to eventually become captain."

Jo lets the entirety of the information settle in, committing each detail to memory.

"He must have loved you," Jo whispers softly.

"Yes," Shea breathes with a light smile, "I suppose he did."

Jo catches sight of the moon now shining brightly in the small pool where the fading sun used to be. She gives Shea a moment to recover. The whole place feels magical.

"Did you always want to be a princess?"

Jo turns back to Shea, meeting her green eyes, her red curls having fallen forward over her right eye, and Jo reaches forward, tenderly taking the curl and tucking it behind Shea's ear.

"Yes."

"You never had any doubt?" Shea inquires with a laugh. "Singer, tavern owner, farmer?"

Jo shakes her head, grinning, trying desperately to remember something else she wanted to do but there was nothing. "No. I knew who I was, who I am," she amends. "I loved my people and my country. Sometimes the rules were a bit strict, but it's who I am."

The simplicity catches both of them off guard, leaving them in brief silence.

"I see," Shea acknowledges.

Jo tries to ignore the ache in her chest; she pushes it far away and instead hides it with a big smile. "Where did you learn magic?"

Shea snickers. "I knew you were going to ask that."

"Well then, you should have an answer prepared," Jo teases.

"We're born with it. Every elf has it inside of them, some can access it and some can't. Some are young when the awakening happens, while others can be about Aster's age, but not many after that. Elvish can invoke it, if a person's connection to the energy is strong enough, even some humans, but it's rare. I spoke elvish as a child, pieces anyway. It's not as common as you might think. Many elves in Erebos adapted to the common tongue for trade. Only the priests really spoke it. Dari taught me most of what I know."

"You never wanted to learn more?" Jo asks.

"Again with the secondary questions," Shea lectures, and Jo ignores her, waiting for her answer.

They have a small stare off as Shea refuses to explain further, but Jo doesn't relent until Shea gives a loud sigh. "It reminded me too much of where I came from."

Jo stares at this new version of the mysterious, cocky sea captain who had taken her captive; it's a vulnerability Jo tries not to extort.

"I'm sorry. For what happened to you," Jo tells her sincerely.

"It was a long time ago."

They leave it at that.

"First crush?"

"A man," Jo tells her, and Shea pretends to sit back with fake shock, her hands covering her mouth.

"No!"

Jo rolls her eyes. "Karnon, my mother's captain of the guard and now mine. He's quite handsome."

"And old," Shea comments and gets another piece of fruit thrown at her. "Hey don't play with your food. The manners on you."

"Do you remember your parents?"

Shea nearly does a double take. She picks up her glass from where she set it and downs it before pouring another glass as Jo laughs. "You don't pull your punches do you?"

"You don't have to tell me," Jo relents.

But Shea does.

"I remember my mother, some. Not really my father. I can't picture them anymore. I can remember her hair like mine and his eyes, a flash of green." Shea shrugs.

And Jo tries to stay silent, biting her lip.

Shea watches her a moment before throwing her hands in the air. "Oh alright, spit it out."

"Do you wish you would have gone back, to find them? I mean have you? Gone back?"

There's a beat. "No."

"No you haven't gone back or no you didn't want to?"

"Both?" Shea answers with a question of her own. "That life is gone. By the time I could go back I was so different. I'd rather just be gone to them than come back and be a ghost of someone they once knew. I mean, I don't think seeing me now, seeing what I've become, would reassure them," Shea jokes, saluting her cup before taking a sip.

"A strong beautiful woman, what's not to like?" Jo replies and grins as the blush reappears at the tips of Shea's adorable ears.

"What about you? Who raised you?" Shea inquires, picking off the other platters that lay around.

"Well," Jo starts, but first adjusts the pillows she's lying on.

She pushes them back so she can lay her head down and stare up at the stars. Shea sees what she's doing and quickly moves the remaining trays off the silk blankets, carefully placing them behind. Shea pushes her own pillows back until the two of them are lying next to each other staring up at the incredible night sky before them. Jo has never seen anything like it; stars fill the entire black cosmos and there are splashes of purples, reds, and pinks as if they were both floating together in the middle of the universe.

"My mother," Jo starts, "was Queen Triteia, she died when I was eleven. She ascended the throne when she married my father, Prince Mariner. Her mother Queen Doris had to step down because of her health. When my mother died, Grandmother had to step in again and became queen ruler once more instead of queen mother."

"There's one thing I never understood: Why didn't your father rule?" Shea asks, honestly interested about how the only rulers of Arethusa are women.

"Well, he's a man, only a woman can rule Arethusa. Grandmother didn't have any other children besides my mother, so she was to take over until I came of age. Unfortunately she died last year, so my court council—with the advisement of my father—have been ruling until my coronation."

Jo freezes, but now there wasn't going to be a coronation. Who would rule?

"That's a lot of politics." Shea grimaces, oblivious to Jo's inner plight.

Jo chuckles in response. "Yes."

"So who raised you?"

"What do you mean?"

"I mean, I get that after your mother passed away, your grandmother became queen, but who was with you through it all? You know the scraped knees, the chills, and the studies, the playing? Your father?" Shea inquires, and she rests her elbow on the silk pillow, placing her head in her hand as she looks down at Jo, who catches her gaze.

"My father is a distant man, it became worse after my mother died. He has trouble expressing himself. My grandmother wasn't particularly warm either, even before. Plus Gran was constantly in meetings and overseas. But I had Rhea and Gaea, they were the ladies who stood with me when we met."

"The two crones from the ball?" Shea deadpans, remembering each of their wrinkly faces with a frown.

Jo smiles. "That's them. They've been preparing me to ascend the throne. Ascension usually takes place at the heir's twenty-fifth birthday."

"How old are you now?"

"I turned twenty-five last month, hence the coronation."

"Right. Sorry, I guess I'm having a hard time seeing the crones as the…motherly type."

"They were kind. In their own way, they cared." Jo shrugs.

Shea laughs, nodding. "I guess that's all we can really hope for."

"Last question," Jo reminds her, and Shea grins, letting out a huge sigh.

"Best make it good," Shea teases.

Jo closes her eyes, searching for a question she hopes will give her more than one answer.

"How did Paetre die?"

The smile fades from Shea's face and she looks away. Jo almost wants to take it back, but a part of her really needs to know.

"It was boring really. I don't want you to waste your last question, I'll let you pick something else," Shea excuses with a fake grin, but she still won't look Jo in the eye.

"How did he die?" Jo asks again.

Shea sits up from where she's lying, bringing one of her knees up and resting her arm on it, staring out into the garden.

Jo sits up on her forearms and waits.

"It was two years ago," Shea mutters. "When—when Paetre bought me from the slave market in Lycos, there were two human boys he bought as well. One was small, Basil was his name, he worked with Strom, and the other was Orin, mentored by our former gunner. Basil was a sweet kid, me and Orin used to push him around a little, but we were kids together. The whole crew is like a family. When we were all about thirteen, Basil was killed in an Arethusian navy raid."

Jo sits up at the mention of the Arethusian navy, and she feels a pit form in the center of her stomach. Her eyes close. Under her grandmother's reign there was a strict no-tolerance piracy law, any person found on a pirate vessel unless wearing Arethusian military colors was to be killed. Jo has always been ashamed of that, and especially now.

"I'm sorry," Jo murmurs, but Shea shrugs.

"You didn't kill him. It was a long time ago. After that, the former gunner I mentioned, his name was Mani. He felt that Paetre had lost his touch allowing the ship to get raided like that. Strom lost his sight and his boy; he was never really the same. Paetre dealt with Mani's complaints but mostly just shuffled it under the rug. After that, the crew seemed to split, some siding with Mani while most sided with Paetre."

Shea swallows loudly and reaches for her glass, as if her mouth has run dry.

"Orin stopped talking to me shortly after that; we grew distant. Time passed and for the most part the crew operated under Paetre until about two years ago. We were closer than ever to Paetre's final score, the *Hydra of the Sea*. He'd been chasing the Pearl of Lycos for a few years then. The job went a little south, lost a few good men but gained a charter with the dates of when and where the ship would be. It was Mani's last straw."

"We can stop if you need to," Jo tells her, but Shea shakes her head.

"No, I want to tell you about it. I was asleep downstairs when the mutiny started. I heard yelling overhead, grabbed my things, my sword, and headed upstairs." Shea closes her eyes and drags her hand over her face, remembering the night like it was yesterday.

"When I got up top"—Shea focuses on the flickering lights in one of the lanterns, watching the flame dance behind the glass —"there were torches everywhere. Paetre and Mani stood inside a circle of the crew, Orin behind Mani, and Caen behind Paetre. I watched quietly, listening the best I could. I didn't want anyone to notice me just yet. Mani was yelling about how it was time for a new captain and that Paetre was no longer fit, having an elven girl for a successor, having Caen as a quartermaster, for chasing after the *Hydra*...just a bunch of crap. He challenged Paetre to a duel; the one alive at the end would be captain.

"Paetre agreed, of course, he was never one to stand down from a challenge. They drew their swords and I could feel my heart burst when the iron connected with a solid clap. I slipped in behind Caen, watching the fight. Mani was strong, but Paetre's footwork—he'd trained in sword combat for years. Mani didn't stand a chance; it didn't drag on long, as Mani's thrusts became more and more violent and often. Paetre waited for the right time and sidestepped Mani coming up behind him, slitting his throat."

"He won?" Jo stutters.

"Aye, he did. Mani fell to the floor, blood flowing from the wound, his hands wildly flying to his throat, trying to staunch the bleeding. He kept wriggling almost like a dying fish as he choked on his own blood."

Jo flinches at the graphic description; but upon looking at Shea's expression, she realizes she's not really here, but back two years ago on the night this all happened.

Shea continues, fixated on the flickering flame. "Anyway everyone thought it was over, Paetre had won, that was that. I even turned away. I didn't see him."

"See who?" Jo asks.

Suddenly Shea looks up and meets Jo's eyes, and the guilt

and despair swirling in the bright green irises steals Jo's breath away.

"Orin," Shea answers. "Mani was my enemy, but to Orin he was like Paetre. He watched the man who raised him die and all he saw in Paetre was the murderer who'd done it. Paetre wasn't watching, none of us really were, when Orin quickly picked up Mani's sword and swung at Paetre. Paetre blocked it, but he was caught off guard; Orin came down hard and fast and Paetre was just shell shocked—he wasn't really thinking. He blocked and parried as much as he could, but Orin was young and he just kept coming at him hard. Finally, Orin stepped past Paetre's block and carved the blade straight through him."

Shea's eyes never leave Jo's, and Jo watches as fleeting emotions flicker endlessly across Shea's face: grief, anger, frustration, and shock.

"He pulls the blade from Paetre and Paetre falls to his knees, holding his side, and Orin lifts the blade to bring it down. And he's going to kill him, he has killed him, and I don't even remember moving. Caen tried to grab me, but I've pulled my sword and I swing it around"—Shea gestures her hands, holding the imaginary sword—"and I slash my sword down his back. He turns, ready to fight and he sees me." Shea pauses. "He remembers me. And he freezes."

Jo listens as Shea's voice chokes, and Shea closes her eyes.

Tears fall down her cheek as she opens them and continues, "And I kill him. I run my sword through his chest. I look into his eyes and I turn my blade, watching as I massacre his heart beyond repair."

She's shaking. Jo wants to reach out and hold her, but at the same time she's afraid to touch her.

"He falls. I go to Paetre; I kneel down to hold him. No one picks up another blade; I don't think anyone had really understood what happened yet. You see, last one standing doesn't have to be the two original duelers; anyone can pick up the sword. It's the last one standing after it all, when no more contenders are left. By killing Orin, I was captain. Fair. I held

Paetre in my arms, and he told me, 'You did good, kid, you did well.' He asked that I would fulfill his final request to steal the Pearl of Lycos and then he told me, 'Retire, kid. Get out while you can still live.' He died. Obviously." Shea sniffs, wiping her nose with the back of her hand, shooting a watery smirk toward Jo, who scoffs, wiping her own tears away. "Why I'm telling this story of course."

Jo can't take it anymore. She moves closer and wraps her arms around Shea, pulling her in for a tight hug. She feels Shea let her head rest upon her shoulder, but it's brief and then she's pulling away and they're staring into each other's eyes as the night sky twinkles above.

They're inches from each other, their lips close enough to touch, just barely.

"Thank you for trusting me with that," Jo whispers.

"Anytime."

"You have one last question," Jo reminds her.

Shea chuckles and pushes herself even closer until her body is up against Jo's, and Jo's hand comes to rest lightly on the thin material above Shea's hips.

"What'd you think of the kiss?"

"The ki—"

Shea cuts her off. She presses her soft lips to Jo's, and Jo melts into the touch. Her mouth falls open and it's all Shea needs as she pushes her tongue in. They reposition, pulling each other as close as possible, both of them on their knees. Shea's hands wrap around Jo's shoulders as Jo pulls Shea in by her waist, gripping her hips tightly, moaning softly at the feel of their chests pressed together. Jo gasps as Shea tugs on her bottom lip, worrying it between her teeth.

Finally they break apart with slow breaths, the electricity still running between them. Their foreheads lean in together. Jo notes every detail, every beautiful piece of the way Shea looks. Shea's eyes glance around them and she laughs to herself.

"What," Jo breathes.

"Nothing's floating," Shea chuckles, and Jo quirks a brow.

"So, what'd you think?" Shea questions with a wry smile.

"It'll do," Jo teases.

Shea grins. She grasps Jo's face between her palms, looking into her bright blue eyes. "Then stay."

"What?" Jo murmurs.

"Stay. With me on the ship or here on the island. I can't take you to Tenaro, but we can stay and we can make a life here. We can be together. Tell me you feel what I feel, I know it's not Arethusa, but we'd have each other. I would be there for you, always."

It's hard to breathe. Jo tries to concentrate on those beautiful emerald eyes sparkling with encouragement.

"Stay with me," Shea repeats.

Jo wants to say yes. She wants so many things that seem so far beyond her reach. She wants to take Shea to the bed in the corner and show her how to be loved. She wants to stay with Shea on the *Duchess* forever, sailing away to many more adventures. She wants to hold Shea in her arms every night just like this and care for her when her demons come howling. She'll push everything away, and forget about the world of politics and palace intrigue.

She wants to stay.

Of course she should stay.

Jo looks up, tucking that stubborn stray curl back behind Shea's ear, and kisses her softly on the mouth once more.

"I can't."

SO MAYBE I'M NOT OKAY

Shea

"WHAT?" SHEA CHUCKLES, not quite understanding, but when she pulls away from Jo, she can see the regret clearly written across her face.

"I can't," Jo repeats. "I can't abandon my people, my queendom."

Jo tries to explain, reaching out, but Shea pulls away. Her heartbeat is heavy in her ears. After everything tonight, Shea had thought Jo understood. She thought she could be enough. Apparently she was wrong.

"Jo, I don't think you understand, I can't take you back. I can leave you here on Orena, if you don't want to be with me…"

"I do want to be with you," Jo exclaims, reaching again for Shea's hand.

Shea laughs hollowly. "Then stay with me."

"I can't. I want to, but my people need me, and if you leave me here I will return to Arethusa because I have to."

"You know I can't let that happen," Shea barks, starting to get frustrated.

She runs a hand through her hair and ignores the pink petals falling to the ground.

"I know."

Shea looks at her shrewdly. She stands, moving away from the silk blankets, and begins to pace.

"This isn't a game, Jo! You're leaving me no other choice." Shea can feel the volume of her voice rising.

Her hands are clenched at her sides and she moves farther into the room, as if trying to get as far away from the balcony as possible. She looks back at Jo, who's still kneeling on the blankets.

"If you don't stay, then I have to do my job." Shea stares Jo down. "If you go back, I lose everything—you, the key. I can't let that happen, there's too many other lives at stake. This is how I save you! We can be together!"

Jo's head drops slightly and Shea can see her body shaking, but she pushes herself up gracefully, standing among the silks.

"I know. You are much more than I thought and I care for you, I do. But I told you once my people are a part of who I am. I can't just give that up for my own selfish feelings."

"Do you think this was easy for me? Letting myself feel for someone like you?"

"This isn't simple for me either."

"Right. It seems extremely difficult for you," Shea snarks, pulling the decorative petals out of her hair.

She wants to rip this ridiculous dress off her body but instead settles for knocking over the vanity. She turns away from Jo, covering her mouth with her hand to withhold her scream. Shea can hear Jo's steps behind her and quickly turns, finding the princess close. Their shadows flicker on the walls from the lanterns, and it casts dark shapes, obscuring parts of their faces. The mosaics on the walls have taken a menacing turn from the harsh light, the once magical setting now filled with darkness. The laughter from down below is silent; the only sound is the howling wind through the trees and the chattering monkeys running along the ground.

"Do you want to die?"

Jo sighs. "Of course not."

"Then why?" Shea yells.

She's hoping Jo will relent, but Jo keeps her stance strong and her gaze firm.

"I can't sacrifice my people. I was supposed to be a queen; I can't afford to be with you. And if you can't take me back, then you will have to leave me on Tenaro, because if you leave me here, I will stop at nothing to get back to my queendom. You leave me on your ship, and the first port I see, I'll make a break for it."

Everything drains from Shea's body, her shoulders droop, and her face pulls into a grimace.

"Then it seems you've made your decision."

"I have," Jo states. "But maybe you could change your mind."

Shea laughs coldly. "But of course, because what could be more important than a whole country?"

"You can't blame me for wondering. Maybe I could help you as queen. What are you getting in exchange for me?" Jo snaps.

"You're out of questions, Your Majesty."

"No. I don't accept that. You said this deal is worth a lot of lives and that it could help end the slave trade. If you tell me, I can help you. What is worth the price of my life?" Jo seethes.

Shea wants to yell at her, her hands curl into fists, everything feels tense, but instead she lets go. "The map and key to Empress Ceto's vault and a full pardon with sanctuary in the Arethusian queendom."

There's a pause.

"Come on. Seriously?"

Shea shrugs. There's a short burst of laughter from Jo, but it quickly subsides.

She studies Shea with a harsh glance. "Secrets? My throne, my reign being taken from me, is all for a neighboring empire's secrets? Why?"

"It doesn't matter," Shea snarls, but Jo walks closer until they're a mock of the image they were before.

Shea looks up into Joana's now cold eyes.

"It matters to me."

Shea's guard is wavering, she can feel it. So she uses her patented smirk to mask any trace of her true feelings. Before Jo can notice.

"I have a personal history with the empress," Shea states.

She pushes aside the neckline on the left side of her dress and shows Jo the symbol of Lycos that was carved into her flesh. It looks like a *C* with the emblem of Lycos situated within, the ghastly face of Scylla, the monstrous patron goddess of the southern empire.

"When I was fourteen, I ran into her on a job. Paetre was after the pearl. Our men captured her, she tried to turn me against Paetre but I humiliated her instead. A couple years later, she carved her initials into my chest. Elves are no more than property, she said."

She lets the fabric fall back into place. Shea scoffs at Jo's softening expression.

"Don't pity me. With Ceto's vault, I could control Lycos. Gods, I could control her, and make a better life for people like me. So don't worry, your life is worth a lot more than you realize," Shea spits.

Jo's expression turns thunderous.

"It's not enough," Jo growls.

It's stupid, but Shea can't help herself; she pushes Jo back. Jo stumbles but catches herself before she can fall.

"Neither am I, apparently. Right? I'm not enough," Shea snarls and turns to head for the door, but Jo is quick.

She moves and grabs Shea's arm roughly, turning her around until they're face-to-face. Jo grips both of Shea's forearms, holding on tightly, almost to the brink of pain as Shea struggles to step away.

"You're worth everything to me," Jo grinds out.

Shea brings her arms up with enough force to break the hold. "Then the choice should have been easy."

They've stepped so far back into the room that the door to the bedroom is close behind Shea. She just wants to get out.

They're both standing there, just breathing at each other. If Shea can turn fast enough, she can make it out the door and away from Jo, but it's too late.

"You're asking me to give up everything!" Jo screams and charges toward Shea.

Shea doesn't have time to move as she's slammed up against the door, the back of her head hitting the blue wood. She struggles against Jo's hold, but her adrenaline has made the princess incredibly strong, and she can't push her off. She doesn't want to hurt her.

"You get what you want," Jo shouts. "Your ship, your lifestyle, me. The vault! But then you're asking me to sacrifice my life and what matters to me!"

Shea lets her head fall back against the wood. "I'm offering mine in exchange," Shea begs, forcing back the tears.

She hasn't been this close to tears since Paetre.

"You don't understand the cost," Jo reiterates, moving her hands from Shea's shoulders up to her face, cupping her cheeks in her palms, bringing their foreheads to rest against each other.

"I can't abandon my people."

Shea again tries to pull away, but Jo keeps her where she is.

"A relationship is built on give and take, and if we do this? Ours would be built upon you taking me and me giving up everything, giving up who I am. I can't do that," Jo says.

She pulls back and she's staring at Shea in a way that makes the captain feel like she's naked. Jo swipes the pad of her thumbs across Shea's face. The captain can't quite understand what she's doing or why Jo looks so blurry until Shea realizes she's crying, and the tears are dripping down her face.

"And I cannot believe you want that either."

Jo drops her palms down to Shea's shoulders.

Shea reaches up and rubs her hand down her face, wiping away as many tears as possible. She looks at Jo, really looks at her, and suddenly she feels broken and tired.

"I guess we'll never know," Shea murmurs.

The wind howls, washing over her and leaving a cold chill in her bones. She shivers.

"I care for you," Shea tries one last time, pleading. "Deeply."

Jo tightens her grip on Shea's shoulders for a small moment and then steps away. She puts some space in between them. "I wish it was enough."

Shea nods. Her head falls back once more and then she lets her body roll off the door.

"I'm sorry," Jo tells her.

Shea turns her back on Jo, reaching for the handle. "Me too."

Once she steps though, she casts one last glance back, her eyes roaming over Jo's strong form before meeting tearful blue eyes. "We sail for Tenaro tomorrow."

With that, Shea shuts the door firmly. She can't bring herself to let go of the handle, and she just stares at the chipping blue paint on the wood, her eyes blurring. She lets go of the knob and presses her pointed ear against the door, listening. Sobs. Shea listens as Jo cries softly through the door and her own breaths come shorter. She leans her head against the cool wood and feels her body weakening, slumping against the door. She presses her palm against the hard surface. She should have kissed her goodbye.

"Oh, my love."

Shea startles sharply, looking down the hall. Dari is standing there with tears in her own eyes. Shea shuts hers, clenching them tightly. She shakes her head and then stands from her kneeling position by the door.

"Are you okay?" Dari asks even though she knows the answer.

Shea turns her back on Dari as well and whispers over her shoulder, "No. I'm not."

She leaves her in the hall, going nowhere in particular, just away from it all.

THIS LOVE DOESN'T BREAK

Shea

THE MORNING COMES TOO quickly in Shea's opinion. Her head aches from the bottle of rum she'd borrowed off of Phoebus's liquor cart. She wakes in a guest room and groans—the shades have been pulled back from the windows. Trying not to move too quickly, she pushes away the feelings of nausea and pain. She can hear a strange humming noise coming from across the room, and it takes a moment for her eyes to adjust.

Finally her vision clears and she sees Dari placing her clean pirate clothes over a chair and her boots on the floor. Shea looks down and smooths the material of the lavender dress. She slept in it.

"Morning," Dari comments softly, not bothering to look up from her task.

Shea grunts in acknowledgment, worrying her lip in between her teeth. She doesn't want to talk about last night, and if that's why Dari is here, she can leave as quickly as she appeared.

"I brought you your clothes. I know you have plans to leave early today. Caen is waiting for you, and Aster and Dr. Nol have escorted the young lady to the ship already."

Shea breathes a sigh of relief; at least she won't have to deal with the princess this morning. She attempts to stand from the bed, her arms swinging out as she tries to balance while her head swims.

"She asked for you."

Shea ignores her and walks gingerly over to the chair with her clothes, pulling them off the back, then returning to the bed.

"I just. I want you to be sure," Dari continues, and Shea scoffs, glaring at her harshly.

"I am sure, she made her choice. And you were right before, you're not my mother. You're just some childless woman Paetre dropped me off with when he didn't feel like dealing with me. So good for you! Do you think you're a good person for babying the elven orphan nobody wanted?"

Dari stares, shocked at Shea, as if the redhead had actually struck her physically, but Shea doesn't stop there. Instead she ignores the look of devastation on Dari's face.

"Good news though, I'm all grown up so you can stop pretending, stop mothering. Because I don't need you anymore!"

Phoebus, who must have been walking by, storms into the room, taking in the last of the conversation. "Shea, that's enough!"

He comes to Dari's side, as she tries to recover from Shea's words. She mutters to Phoebus that she's fine.

"How dare you speak to her like that," Phoebus fumes, and Shea rolls her eyes, grimacing from the headache throbbing in her temples.

"Shea, please," Dari attempts, but Shea stands, still seething.

"Just forget it, I need to get out of here. I'll change on the ship."

Shea stomps out of the room with her clothes in hand. She can hear Dari calling after, but she keeps going. She's almost to the door that leads out to the shop, at the edge of the dome. With every step she takes, her own words echo throughout her mind, everything she just said to the woman who practically raised her. Caen enters through the same door into the dome with her belt and sword in hand. She's almost to him, but Dari uses her nymph abilities and creates a thin wall of leaves between them, stopping the captain in her tracks.

"I know you didn't mean it," Dari says. Her breathing is heavy from running after her, but she walks closer until she's right behind Shea.

She doesn't want to turn around, but at Dari's pushing, she does and she sees Phoebus standing beside her.

"You're my daughter, and I know you're hurt. And you are enough for me," Dari tells her and then holds out her one arm.

Shea gasps, her chest tightening, and her eyes start to glisten. She's so afraid she might fall as she drops her clothes to the floor and stumbles into Dari's arm, hugging her like she's the only thing keeping Shea from floating away.

She doesn't cry, she did too much of it last night, but she just holds Dari and it's enough. The leaves rustle as the wall between them and Caen collapses. Shea pulls back just enough for Dari to kiss her forehead, making Shea chuckle. She picks her clothes up off the ground, along with her boots. Then she reluctantly looks down at Phoebus and is relieved to find him smiling at her widely, his wrinkled cheeks pink.

"See you around, Pops," Shea jokes, and Phoebus reaches up, grasping one of Shea's hands and kissing the back of it.

"You're ours, kid," he tells her.

Shea nods and gives Dari one last smile before turning away. Shea keeps going this time and she doesn't look back or say goodbye. She walks out the door.

Caen doesn't say a word, and they walk in silence all the way back to the ship. Her hair is loose, and she's still wearing that ridiculous lavender dress with her clothes bunched up in her arms, barefoot. They make it to the ship and everyone stares, not used to seeing the captain in such a state.

Jo is nowhere to be seen, and Shea breathes another sigh of relief. She takes her belt and sword from Caen as they make their way to her quarters; still he doesn't say a word. He hands her the pieces and then walks out the door, closing it behind him gently. She stands in the middle of her room, staring out the back windows dumbly; she's not really sure where to start. So she strips the dress. Part of her wants to burn it and the other part of her wants to keep it forever. So for now she throws it in her closet and doesn't look back.

She grabs a black peasant top and a rolled-up bandage, and then she takes a black ribbon and ties her hair back and out of her face. She walks over to the mirror and begins to bind her breasts against her chest, careful not to look at the brand. Once that's done, she pulls on the pants and shrugs on the shirt. The whole ordeal wears her out, but she keeps her head high. She slips into her boot—they fit like a glove—and breathes. All that's left is the hat. Resting on the bedpost is a plain black captain's hat, this one without the blue feather.

She reaches over, turning it in her hands and remembers the way it had looked on Paetre. She places it on top of her head. She's done playing the love-struck elf, now it's time to be the *Duchess*'s captain once again. There's work to be done and she can't avoid it any longer.

IT'S A MATTER OF HEART

Shea

O N   D E C K ,   T H E   C R E W   P R E P A R E S   F O R   D E P A R T-U R E .

Mister Tero is barking orders, and Shea sees Aster among the men getting the *Duchess* ready to sail.

She looks around further for Caen and instead hears a loud meow from above. She looks up in time to see Caeruleus swooping down and then back up to the foremast to rest. Shea ventures to the afterdeck and finds Caen and James looking over the maps on the table next to the bittacle, periodically looking up at the compass and then tracing their fingers along the maps. Shea casually makes her way to them.

"Caen, Mister James, are we ready to set sail?"

Caen looks up but, instead of answering, steps away from the table and walks back toward the helm.

James shoots Caen a sidelong glance but doesn't acknowledge the snub. He nods, giving Shea a small smile.

"We are, ma'am, we should get to the Tenaro Islands in good time. Mister Tero and I went and talked with a few experienced sailors, they told us the best course with the least amount of obstacles for this time of year. It'll still be tricky, but hopefully we can make our way through."

"Very good, James," Shea responds with a smile.

She takes a step toward the helm to find out what's gotten into Caen but decides she really doesn't have the energy to care. So instead she walks over to the railing and faces out over the quarterdeck, overseeing the rest of the crew.

"Mister Tero," Shea shouts.

Tero turns from his position by the foremast and looks up at her. "Ready, Captain!"

"Very well. Mister James, take us out."

There's grumbling from behind, but she doesn't bother to look as James replaces Caen at the helm. Caen crosses the afterdeck, and journeys down the stairs onto the quarterdeck.

"Weigh anchor!" Caen hollers and Tero repeats, other members shouting down to the below crew to raise the anchor in final preparation.

The chains begin their slow ascent, the anchor rising from the water. Shea enjoys the view and then all at once her heart stops beating.

Jo arrives on the quarterdeck dressed in fresh clothes, a powder-blue peasant top, green work pants, and black boots.

Aster follows closely on Jo's tail as she steps out onto the forecastle watching the horizon as the ship heads out from port. The wind is strong and the sails greedily fill, pushing the *Duchess* forward until Orena is a mere speck in the distance.

Caen finally trudges back up the stairs and Shea makes a point of ignoring him, giving him a taste of his own medicine. Not liking being ignored, he strides over and takes his place at her side.

"Talk to her," he says.

"There's nothing to say," Shea responds.

He shoots her a look.

"It's decided. Nothing to be done."

"We have seven days before we arrive at the Tenaro Islands. Four. I've never known you to give up so easily."

"You heard everything at dinner last night, don't try to

deny it. Those walls are paper thin."

He doesn't.

Shea tries to ignore the way her hands tighten on the railing, watching Jo laugh as Aster prances around her like a stumbling fawn. Caen looks almost embarrassed but he pushes forward.

"Try again."

Shea sighs. "There's nothing I can say to change her mind."

"Then maybe you should change yours."

"Don't be ridiculous."

"There are other scores," Caen chides and walks away to speak with Mister James before Shea can argue.

Shea growls to herself, doesn't he know she's already tried to change her mind? To try and get past the vault, and let it all go? She watches Jo and Aster smiling like fools, and then for a moment, Jo looks up to the afterdeck and their eyes almost meet. There's a wistful smile playing upon the princess's lips and then her gaze is gone and she's talking to Aster again.

"Pointless," Shea mutters.

She eyes the stairs, and before she knows it, she's walking toward them. Just as she hits about halfway down, she looks up past the right side of the *Duchess*. Out in the water, Shea sees another ship in the distance. It stops her for some reason. To be able to see such a ship from this distance it must be a big one. She studies it, trying to make out the details. But it's moving fast. It's far but it's coming in closer, approaching quickly.

Instead of striding to Jo, she stalks to the gunwale and stops in front of the banister, pulling her small spyglass from her jacket pocket. She adjusts the position and looks through, and at first she doesn't really understand what she sees, and then she does.

"Arethusian navy vessel off starboard!" Shea bellows.

The whole ship goes silent, and then running footsteps break out everywhere.

Shea shoots a quick glance up at Caen, who takes his own spyglass and looks through. She watches him curse and she knows she's right. He shouts at James to bring the ship around. The crew runs, gunners man their stations, and the deckhands start pulling their energy to turn the ship to face the navy.

"Get her down below!" Shea snarls at Aster, who loses Jo as she runs toward the gunwale, looking out upon the horizon.

A smile spreads across her face, but as she looks back at Shea, the smile fades and instead a look of horror overtakes her features.

Shea turns away; she's got too much to do if they're going to come out of this with their hides intact. How the Underdeep did they get out here so fast? And how in Hades did they know where to look? There's no way they could have made it here —even with the stop, they were too many days ahead. It's not possible.

She turns away, heading to Mister Tero. There's only one way they could have beaten them here and that's if they'd been waiting here all along.

Shea curses. She could rip her hair out at this double cross —but she's jerked back and thrown around until she's face-to-face with Jo, who now has her arm in a tight hold. Shea harshly shakes her off.

"Aster!"

"Shea," Jo pleads, "let me talk to them, this doesn't have to end badly for you."

"They're not here to talk."

"They're here for me," Jo exclaims.

Shea laughs because she's not so sure.

"Maybe, but there's no way they could have gotten here so fast. Even with the stop," Shea adds before Jo can interrupt.

Jo's mouth closes as she processes the new information; crewmen push past them and the ship jolts as they correct course.

"Man the cannons," Shea commands, pushing past Jo, but she's grabbed again and turned around.

"You mean they might have been out here all along?"

"Good, you're caught up," Shea sarcastically praises, getting a narrow-eyed glare for her trouble. "Yes, so either the hood isn't as clever as he thought he was—"

"Or this was his plan all along."

"Everyone hates loose ends. Now if you'll excuse me, I've got a navy vessel to take down. Aster!"

"Sorry, Captain." Aster suddenly appears at their side, looking deeply out of breath.

"Escort the princess down below," Shea orders and turns her back on the both of them, running to catch up with Caen to tell him what she suspects.

Jo objects as she's dragged down below by Aster, who gets an elbow to the face for all his effort. The navy ship is quickly approaching.

Caen runs a hand over his face as he hears Shea's speculation when she catches up with him.

"Damn it," Caen growls, slamming his fist onto the table with the maps.

"We've got minutes. We find out the truth," Shea tells him.

Caen grits his teeth. "We're going to come out bruised, but we can take it; the *Hydra* was by far worse."

"We were prepared for that one," Shea huffs, and Caen groans, yelling the orders down to Tero.

The men arm themselves, Shea draws her sword, and Aster comes running up the stairs trembling with Caen's hammer. Once Caen has his hammer, Aster draws his own sword and descends to the quarterdeck where the men have readied themselves.

The ship approaches and Shea can see every detail. Queen Amphitrite is carved onto the bow. The Arethusian colors wave in the wind, flashes of midnight blue and gold, around the insignia on the flag: Amphitrite's face with a dolphin in the shape of a half-moon around her head. They have many cannons.

But nowhere near the amount the *Duchess* has.

Shea hollers down to the crew below to unleash the second row. An underlying stretch of planks unfolds down the side of the ship, releasing a second row of cannons. The port of the navy ship is almost off the starboard, and Shea waits a second longer; she won't hesitate to waste a couple cannonballs as long as she's the first one to shoot. She yells down to Tero to only fire the second-row cannons, and as soon as she can hear the naval captain yell *ready*, she yells *fire*. The second row fires, splitting apart the bottom ship planks on the Arethusian vessel. The massive navy ship groans and it catches the soldiers off guard.

The Arethusian captain roars for the men to fire, and as they do, Tero releases the top row of cannons. The Arethusian cannonballs rip into the side of the ship, but Shea's crew has already loaded the second set, and as Shea's top row rips apart the navy quarterdeck, Shea's hidden under cannons rip the bottom apart even more.

She orders the men to shoot the hooks, and eight of the crewmen use crossbows to connect the ships together. Aster along with Tero and a few other men push the gangplank over, building a bridge across the sea.

"I want whoever's in charge and their second-in-command, they'll come to no harm," Shea dictates. "The rest do as you wish."

The pirates begin to board.

Just as Shea is about to step over the gangplank herself, she can already hear the screams from the naval men. Some are begging and some are already confused by the outcome; they came unprepared.

Surprisingly enough, Jo bursts out from the underdeck.

"Jo," Shea fumes.

She glares over at Aster, who looks about ready to keel over at the sight of Jo.

"I locked her in your cabin," he shouts and then runs over the plank to the navy vessel before she can stop him.

Shea groans, storming over to Jo, who has an iron sword in her hand. "Where in Hades did you get that?"

"The armory," Jo responds plainly, stepping past Shea toward the gangplank.

Shea grabs her arm. "You're not going anywhere!"

"I'm here to help."

"Who?" Shea snaps.

"You."

And Shea stops. The sincerity in Jo's eyes confuses the Underdeep out of Shea.

"Are you crazy?"

"I want to help. I need to know how they got here!"

Shea stares at her for just a moment longer. She looks back at the navy vessel as the fight marches on without them and shakes her head, weighing the options.

"Damn it! Alright, fine, but you stay close to me, you hear?" Jo nods and Shea just hopes either side doesn't accidentally kill her.

They make their way steadily along the gangplank. Shea eyes the churning water below, daring it to try to rise up and take Jo. The quarterdeck of the navy ship is in chaos. There's fire burning along the edges of the deck, and blood flows in rivers along the creases of the wood floor. Shea keeps Jo in front of her, watching the fight whirling around them.

They're winning and Shea pushes back the guilt of Jo having to watch her people die. They brought this on themselves. A young navy man shouts a battle cry near them, charging forward with his blade raised.

"Stop, please," Jo screams. "You don't have to do this! I'm alive."

He's coming straight at Jo, and Shea can already see the bloodlust tunneling his vision. He can't hear her; he can't hear anything besides the erratic beat of his own heart. Shea sidesteps in front of Jo so she doesn't have to do what needs to be done and quickly buries her blade through the young man's stomach, slicing through the organs and muscles.

He gasps and falls to his knees as Shea rescinds her blade.

Jo gags. She takes a step in the fallen man's direction, but there's nothing to be done. Shea stops Jo with a firm arm around her waist and pushes her forward.

"Keep moving," Shea whispers.

Caen is up ahead, thankfully with Aster at his side. Shea releases the breath she'd been holding, hating how much she cares for that kid and the stress he causes. Caen and Aster are advancing through the doors to the lower deck with three men behind them, and there's a hostage at Caen's side that he's subdued. The captain must be below. But instead of fighting with his men on deck, he's hidden away like a coward. The Arethusian men and women are dwindling; Shea shouts orders to start preserving the officers for questioning. The rest are easy to subdue.

Shea guides Jo toward the afterdeck up the stairs, and she sits her down in the chair attached to their navigational table. Shea returns to the quarterdeck knowing Jo will wait. Her crew ushers the remaining soldiers to the side of their own gunwale. They push them onto their knees and order their hands on their heads.

"Any of them moves, kill the person next to them," Shea orders.

She keeps her focus on her own men, who nod in understanding, and tries to ignore the burning gaze on her neck that she realizes is coming from her princess. Shea gives the orders to loot the ship and sends a handful of men back to their own to alert Mister Tero that the battle is over.

Finally Caen emerges from the lower deck with Aster following closely behind him. Aster now has the first hostage Shea saw from before, and he pushes him toward the remaining officers who are kneeling on the deck.

Caen has two new prisoners and he marches the men to Shea. He pushes them down at her feet. She examines them both and it's simple to discern who the captain is. His clothes are too fine for a working officer and his hat rivals that of the captain from the Lycon *Hydra*, with a huge gold plume sticking out of it. The other she assumes is his quartermaster; he dresses more plainly, though his coat does hold badges of honor down the sides of his arms.

"Take them both to the afterdeck, we'll question them there."

Caen pulls them up by the backs of their collars, the Arethusian captain objecting the whole way.

"This is an outrage! Do you have any idea who I am? You dirty little elf, you'll pay for this!"

He continues to seethe, but Shea ignores him. Instead she favors the quiet man beside him who she's come to realize is also studying her. Shea follows them up the steps to the afterdeck, and as she reaches the top, she chances a glance in the direction of the hostage crew. She frowns—some are murmuring to each other, others have their mouths dropped open, and they've all suddenly become quite restless.

Shea bites back a groan, hoping Caen hasn't killed the captain in annoyance to cause such a stir, but instead she finds Jo standing at the rail of the afterdeck. She has her feet planted and her right hand over her heart with her left hand saluting the navy officers below. Shea walks over and pats her on the shoulder.

"Enough," Shea mutters.

Jo relents reluctantly and Shea keeps moving. Caen's got the captain and the quartermaster on their knees. The captain is still threatening everyone in sight. Aster stands by Jo's side, making sure she's okay while Caen looks like he's about to slit the captain's throat. But it's the quartermaster who captivates Shea's attention as he stares solemnly at Jo, never breaking his gaze. Shea stands in front of the two men.

"How long have you been here?" Shea questions, but she doesn't point the request toward the captain.

She stares down the quartermaster until he finally acknowledges her. The solemn man remains quiet, but Shea keeps her gaze on him.

The Arethusian captain, of course, speaks. "I don't know what you're talking about. No one can outrun the Arethusian navy," the captain sneers. "You have murdered our princess and future queen, you will die for your treason."

Shea turns to him slowly, a cold smile breaking out across her face at the sniveling man. "As you can see, your princess is alive and well. I have not committed the crime you accuse me of."

The captain rolls his eyes. "Please."

He gives Jo a once-over, feigning ignorance, but Shea sees the recognition in his eyes. "An imposter, clearly. The princess is gone. The country must move forward and it begins with your death."

Jo steps toward him, staring the officer down. "Captain, I am Princess Joana. I am alive. What has been the indication of my death?"

"Imposter! We will not hear your lies. Lieutenant Soren, avert your gaze," the captain snaps at the lieutenant, and after some reluctance Soren looks away.

Shea watches as the lieutenant's hands fidget, and even though his head is pointed at the ground, she can see through his hair that his eyes are straining to see Jo.

"Why did you believe her to be dead?" Shea questions Soren.

Soren looks up; he bites his lip as if trying to stop himself from answering.

"Remember your duty, Soren! You cannot threaten us, you murderess sea witch."

"Oh shut him up," Shea mumbles.

Caen grins—"With pleasure"—and takes the blunt end of his hammer, knocking the captain to the ground with a hard hit to the head.

He's knocked out cold.

Soren doesn't flinch. Instead he keeps his gaze entirely on Jo.

"Soren," Shea demands softly, and he turns to her. "How did you get here?"

He grimaces, his teeth grazing his bottom lip.

"Please, Lieutenant," Jo requests.

That seems to do the trick because he speaks.

"We were sent here to capture the *Duchess*. There was a tip our intelligence had acquired that you would be sailing this way toward Tenaro. So we set out. But the captain attacked too soon. Our orders were to kill you and destroy your ship only when you were sailing back from Tenaro. We were to follow your ship at a distance from Orena. According to the orders, it was important that whatever you were taking to Tenaro made it there."

"That doesn't make any sense," Aster grumbles.

Shea agrees. For the navy to receive a tip like this and follow it without question, the hood was higher up the political food chain than Shea could have imagined.

"The captain was eager to return to Arethusa. He believed we'd find you off guard after the port and so he attacked early."

"When did you receive this tip?" Caen asks.

"Four weeks ago. We sailed out three weeks ago."

"That's almost a fortnight before we kidnapped Jo," Aster realizes.

Shea's blood is starting to boil; the hood set her up.

"You said Joana was dead. How did you know she was even missing?"

"A messenger bird arrived a week into the mission saying that Princess Joana had been kidnapped and slain by the captain of the *Duchess*. It gave the crew encouragement to see you dead"—he gestures to Shea—"apparently a body dressed in the same gown as the princess the night of the coronation ball was sent to the council, headless."

Joana gasps, a hand flying up to cover her mouth. Aster puts his hand on her shoulder to comfort her.

"With the corpse came a letter from you, claiming you would only send back the head with a settlement of the Arethusian coronation crown. A crown for a crown, it said."

"Oh god," Jo mumbles; she looks faint and Shea gestures for Aster to help her back into the chair.

"Who gave the tip?" Shea questions.

"I don't know," Soren shrugs.

"This doesn't make any sense," Caen growls, pacing behind the lieutenant.

"Who gave the orders to sail?" Shea demands, folding her arms over her chest.

"I can't say."

"Who gave the orders to sail?" Shea snarls, grabbing the lapels of Soren's shirt and yanking him up to his feet.

The surprise on his face would almost be comical if Shea wasn't so gods damned pissed at this backstab. He struggles briefly but finally relents at the elf's strength, staring down at her. Caen steps up behind Soren, looming over him. The lieutenant's body shrinks against the massive form, his brown wig shaking along with his pale body.

"Lord Tyber," he finally relents.

"Lord Tyber?" Jo's head shoots up at the name.

"You know him?" Aster clarifies.

"Yes, he's a member of the Council of Nobles, the council that's been ruling until I'm crowned. He's always been a friend of my father's. A bit of a radical though. Did he say why?"

Jo is up out of the chair before Aster can stop her and moves quickly until she's standing by Shea's side examining Soren.

"I wouldn't know," Soren mutters.

Shea doesn't believe him.

"Answer her."

Soren scowls. "Look, I read the letter from the admiral that came to the captain through the messenger." He nods to the man unconscious on the floor. "Captain Finse had me read the message out loud to him in his quarters. We were given news about the princess and that once the pirate captain of the *Duchess* was dead, Prince Mariner would be taking the throne. The matriarchy would finally fall, and from its ashes the patriarchy would rise."

"Mariner?" Shea murmurs, turning her head back to look at Jo. "Your father?"

Shouting erupts from below and Aster goes to the rail to see what the commotion is about. "It's fine," he assures, "the men need help loading the food rations from the storeroom onto our ship."

Shea nods and tells him to go.

Caen gives Shea a look, asking if he should leave too, but she shakes her head; he's needed here.

"That doesn't make sense," Jo falters.

"His coronation is in days. Captain Finse sent back a letter promising the *Duchess*'s demise. Lord Tyber convinced the council to crown Mariner as king upon your death. Once Captain Shea is dead, we return home with proof and Mariner becomes king."

"My father would never agree to this. He believes in the matriarch monarchy," Jo snarls; she grabs one side of Soren's lapel, and Shea releases her hold, allowing Jo to deal with him. She keeps her hand on the hilt of her sword, but after nearly falling, Soren stays his balance and keeps still at Jo's command.

"Only a man would think it's a good idea for men to rule the world, a bunch of penises running around measuring and blowing countries up. Sounds like paradise," Shea mocks.

Caen chuckles in response.

"He doesn't have a choice, it's all been set in motion," Soren explains to Jo, ignoring Shea's quip. "He's been in mourning since the news. Barely anyone has seen him."

Shea watches as Jo's face crumples and it makes Shea grimace.

"Shea," Jo murmurs and she releases Soren. Caen stays close behind him, but Soren makes no move to run.

Jo clears her throat, and then turns to face Shea. "Captain. I need your help."

"Jo."

"Please. They will tear everything my ancestors have built apart."

Shea shakes her head. She got involved with the hood and look where that led her. She can't make another deal. Jo growls in frustration and reaches forward, grabbing Shea by the arm. She pulls her close.

Caen takes a step forward, eyeing the iron blade still resting in Jo's hand. There's an audience below—the crew can see what's happening on the afterdeck—and Shea sees her men from the corner of her eye go for their swords. She tells Caen to stand down. He motions for the crew to keep moving and suddenly the audience is gone.

"The night Paetre died," Jo says, and Shea's eyes snap to hers, narrowing in warning, "you sacrificed everything to keep this ship going. To keep Paetre's legacy from ending. I'm asking you to help me do the same."

"There's no stopping it," Soren warns. "I believe you are the princess, and just you being alive means that all of this has been orchestrated from within. At this point what if it's Tyber? There's no stopping whatever he has planned. He's too powerful."

"It's not my fight," Shea states.

Tears gloss over Jo's eyes. Shea stays very still, ignoring the desire to comfort her. She can't do this again to her crew. This whole mess started because she got involved with the land folks' problems.

"I'm asking you to make it your fight," Jo pleads, and before Shea knows it, Jo moves in too quickly for Shea to react, hugging her tightly.

"If you care for me at all, I need you."

Shea is frozen in the embrace, and all the emotions from last night come flooding in. She manages to break free from Jo, stumbling slightly so that she has to grip the railing.

Caen grabs Soren's arms, holding him in place in case he tries to pull a fast one. The captain is still unconscious on the floor. Shea forces herself to look out at the never-ending sea and her gaze settles over her crew. Even considering this choice changes everything. Shea was fooled and set up by the same faction that Jo now wants to fight. This isn't her legacy. Her mind wanders to the hood and his power. He planned everything down to the last detail, and it probably would have worked if the captain hadn't been so eager, which makes him dangerous. For all those pretty words that stroked her ego, Shea should have known. But he should have realized who he was dealing with. He underestimated Shea.

"Alright," Shea agrees.

"Alright?" Caen repeats surprised.

"We give them what they want."

"Excuse me?" Caen exclaims. "And what's that, to kill you? 'Cause I'll tell you right now, that's not happening!"

"You're going to help us?" Jo breathes excitedly.

Shea ignores them both for the sake of working out the plan. "We're going to send the newly appointed Captain Soren here back to Arethusa. He'll tell the court of my 'death.'" Shea looks Soren dead in the eye. "You'll tell them that Joana's head went down with my ship and you'll bring proof of my demise. Then we"—Shea gestures to Caen and Jo—"are going to go for reinforcements and catch the Arethusian traitors off guard by storming the castle and foiling the coup."

"You want to head straight into the lion's den that set us up in the first place?" Caen glowers.

"Yes. I don't take threats to my life kindly. They've just committed an act of war on the captain of the *Veiled Duchess*."

"Thank you." Jo smiles and Shea grunts, brushing off her gratitude.

"Don't thank me. For now, your needs align with ours, saving your queendom is just a side effect."

Jo smirks, spotting the bullshit easily, but Shea keeps up the facade. She's not ready to play nice just yet. She'll deal with Jo's gloating later, or better yet, never.

"Captain, with me a second."

Caen demands and he leaves Soren to step to the helm.

Shea bumps past Soren but on second thought stops. She uses an old trick she learned from Paetre and puts a hand on the lieutenant's shoulder. She squeezes the point precisely until his knees hit the deck and he yelps.

Jo attempts to object, but Shea shoots her a look that silences her on the spot.

Soren glares up at Shea, wounded.

"Stay," she whispers.

Finally she comes face-to-face with Caen.

"I thought we would have learned by now not to mess with the land folks' problems. We've defeated the navy ship sent to kill us, now, we disappear. And we can send Jo back with them," Caen harshly whispers, casting a scowl in Jo's direction.

"I can't leave her, Caen, not yet. If she goes back by herself, they'll kill her. And as much as it pains me, I can't let that happen."

Caen sighs. "This isn't the crew's business."

"She's earned her place, please. Go with me for a little while longer on this."

Caen groans. "Gods this is going to be the death of us."

His shoulders drop. "Fine, I'm with you, but I doubt the crew is going to storm any castle to help reinstate royalty."

"No, they won't. And I wouldn't expect them to. Which is why she's going to need help," Shea admits.

She already knows where this is headed and so she's not surprised when Caen raises a brow, confused. Shea leaves Caen at the helm, stepping around Soren with a condescending pat on the head and a *good boy*. She makes her way back to Jo.

"So how in Hades are we going to storm a castle?" Caen inquires after her and Shea's smile is hollow.

"I have an idea."

"I doubt the queendom is going to take kindly to a bunch of pirates invading the castle," Soren throws his two cents in.

Shea laughs. "No, but they wouldn't help anyway. Not on this."

"Then who?" Jo asks.

Shea bites back her groan and instead grins widely. "What are neighboring empires for if not to start invasions?"

Caen starts laughing hysterically, and even Soren chuckles.

Jo's expression is not as encouraging, "You want to get help from Lycos?"

"This is great," Caen growls. "Forget Arethusa, we'll never

make it through Lycos."

"Good news, Captain Soren," Shea exclaims.

She pulls him back up onto his feet with a big fake grin. "You're going home and you're going to tell the court I'm dead. And that you all destroyed my ship at the cost of many men."

"And you think they'll believe me? If I were found out, Tyber would have me killed. No way," Soren objects. "You might as well kill me here."

"If you like, we got plenty of other people below willing to play captain." Shea winks, pulling out her sword, but Jo stops her with a hand on her hilt.

"Why are you here, Soren? Why did you join the navy?" Jo questions, taking a step toward the man who is now looking down at his feet.

"To serve and protect my country, ma'am."

Shea watches the exchange, hoping something will come out of it.

"Enemies of the state are attempting to overthrow the monarchy and take my throne." Jo pauses, and before continuing, she grabs Soren's chin in her hand to turn his face upward, so he can look her in the eye.

"Are you loyal to your queen?" Jo demands.

Shea holds her breath, keeping her hand on her hilt, but it's as if Soren finds what he was looking for when he examined Jo at the beginning of all this.

He kneels on the deck in front of her.

"Yes, I am."

"Then your queen needs you to fight for her. I promise to set things right. But I need your help to do it."

"I apologize for my cowardice, Your Highness. I will help in any way I can." Soren stands but not before adding a quick bow, and Jo nods regally like the queen she should become.

"Do you have any men you think are still loyal?" Shea interrupts.

"I can think of a good few," Soren answers.

"Then you may take them with you."

"And the rest?" Soren asks, gesturing to the former captain still on the ground.

"You'll leave them to me," Shea responds, this time drawing her sword. "Will that be a problem?"

Captain Soren pauses, staring at the man who'd been his superior, but he stands straight and assumes a strong position with a salute. "No. I understand."

"Then let's begin. We've got a country to take back."

IS IT TOO LATE TO TURN BACK?

S HEA ORDERS CAEN TO INFORM their crew of their new course, while Jo goes with Captain Soren to deal with the rest of the Arethusian crew. Shea is quick with the execution, and when she's done, she throws the former captain overboard.

There's no time to waste.

But as Shea looks past the quarterdeck and out to the horizon, she can't help but feel haunted by the decision she's just made. Going to Lycos was more than a risk and docking in the capital city Acheron, there's no way Ceto won't find her. This could be the end for Shea Lara.

But as she watches Jo with her subjects and the way not one of the remaining naval officers rejects her, she knows this is what she has to do. They salute Jo proudly.

Shea can finally feel herself changing; two weeks ago she would have run just like Caen suggested. But now she's throwing herself headfirst into danger just because of a girl. Paetre would be smacking her upside the head right now, telling her she's thinking with her balls and it'll get her killed. Pirates don't do the right thing; they do whatever is in their best interest. Then why the Underdeep is she doing this? Maybe because Jo is her best interest.

And on that note, Shea readies her crew, crossing back over to the *Duchess* to grab the proof needed to fake her death from her cabin. The naval ship is in rough repair, but they'll at least make it to Orena where they can take a smaller ship the rest of the way to Arethusa. It'll take them a couple of days, but they'll be there just before Shea, Jo, and the crew make it to Lycos. As a consolation prize for her crew, she allows them to keep the supplies stolen from the Arethusians, much to Jo's displeasure, but Shea frankly doesn't care.

The naval crew won't be needing it all anyway, and Shea considers it compensation for these idiots trying to blow up her ship.

The rest of the crew, including Jo, withdraws from the navy vessel, leaving Shea the last on board. She shakes hands with Captain Soren, who surprisingly gives her a nod of respect.

"Protect her," Soren tells her.

"For some reason, I always will."

Soren smiles. "Good, and the proof? That you're dead?"

"Yes," Shea mutters and pulls out the two severed elf ears from her pocket. Soren's eyes widen dramatically as she hands him the preserved ears, and he stutters trying to ask.

Shea waves him off. "Don't. The removal of an elf's ears is a great insult to my people. I bought those at a flea market in Lycos. They come in handy for faking your own death. The council will know they were only taken after you killed me."

"Understood." He closes his fist around them, looking a little green. "Good luck."

"You too," Shea murmurs and steadily crosses the gangplank back to her own ship.

They cut the ropes connecting the two vessels together. Shea makes her way to the steering deck, where Mister James is already at the helm, and Caen is barking orders below.

Caeruleus trills overhead and she finds Aster in the crow's nest, batting his hands at the annoying blue Lionbird, trying to get creature to stop pawing at him. Jo stands alone at the map table in front of the helm. Shea leans against the rail, her hands clasped behind her back, and she calls over her shoulder to Mister James, "Take us out."

"Aye, Captain!" James shouts down to the crew to release the sails and Tero orders the deck crew to work.

The ship lurches forward as it catches the wind, and Jo stumbles slightly, almost falling over. Shea sees Jo in the corner of her eye and catches her arm just in time.

They come together, with Shea's arms around Jo's waist and Jo's hands on Shea's shoulders. Their eyes meet and before they know it, they hear James's throat clear. Jo quickly steps away, embarrassed, while Shea shoots James a glare.

Shea follows Jo back to the map table and the blonde points out the charted course.

"We should make it to Lycos in about four days," Jo tells her.

"Good, that's good," Shea acknowledges, studying the maps.

"Are we really going to Lycos?"

Shea chuckles. "Yes."

"We're really going to save my queendom?"

"Yes."

"Are you okay?"

Shea shakes her head and looks up at Jo. "I'm not sure."

Jo bites her lip and then forces herself to ask her next question, "Do you think Ceto will kill you?"

"I don't know," Shea answers honestly.

It'd be a surprise if she didn't.

"I'm scared." Jo laughs nervously.

And Shea smiles at that. "It'll be okay."

Shea tries not to jump when Jo places her hand over hers on the table. Instead of saying anything, they just look out at the horizon. There's change in the air. And after all, where does this leave them?

Shea tries not to focus on them right now; instead she has to plan and figure out exactly how she's going to get Jo to Empress Ceto.

THE ENEMY OF
MY ENEMY

Shea

THE DAYS PASS BY QUICKLY, but the unease of the crew remains in the air. After stealing the Pearl of Lycos and kidnapping the heir to the Arethusian throne, most are restless to return back to the mainland so soon.

Shea attempts to appeal to them, calling a meeting in the galley.

Caen of course is her biggest supporter, but even Mister Tero feels uneasy of meddling in the land folks' affairs again. After a vote, she luckily convinces them to follow her lead. No one wants a mutiny, but they do have concerns about this new plan. They like Jo, which helps, and they're loyal to Shea. But she's starting to wonder if it's fair, asking them to risk their necks for something they don't believe in.

Caen and Shea stay up almost every night until the wee hours of the morning thinking up ways to get into the palace.

They send word to Venus through Caeruleus, hoping she's alive. After all, she was supposed to meet the hood to collect the reward. The message tells V everything that's happened and they patiently wait for her response.

During the first day after the navy altercation, Jo asks Shea to work with her and teach her the basics of sword fighting. They only have four days, but Shea gives it her best shot. Every time they meet they practice a new technique, and Shea finds something new she loves about Jo. The last day they're supposed to meet, Shea can't bring herself to go and so she sends Aster in her place, avoiding Jo for the rest of the day.

It's late, they only have about six hours until they arrive in Lycos, and Shea requests her dinner in her quarters; they have a plan and now it's just perfecting it. It's the witching hour and the desk candle has been replaced twice. Every moment feels like a minute closer to her execution. Shea leans back in her desk chair, taking in a sharp breath before she reignites the incense she'd lit to calm herself. She startles at the sudden knock at the door.

"I'm fine, Caen, go to bed," Shea calls out.

She slumps farther back into her chair, her head leaning against the wood.

The knock sounds again.

"Aster?" Shea questions.

But Aster responds from his room off of her quarters. "Yes?"

"Nothing. Never mind," she soothes.

He doesn't answer again, so she figures he's gone back to sleep.

There's a third knock, so this time she gets up and goes to the door. Before opening it, she adjusts her braid until it falls down her back, wispy tendrils curling around her face. The top of her blouse is untied and anyone can clearly see the bandages of her bindings through the thin ivory material. She thinks about lacing it up, but if it's just a crewmate, she doesn't want to go through the trouble.

"Just a second."

Her pants are rolled up comfortably below her knees, and her sword and belt along with her shoes are back by her desk.

Finally, she opens the door, taking cover behind the heavy wood, and much to her unwanted surprise, she finds Jo leaning against the door frame. The blonde's hair falls loosely over her shoulders and she's wearing a long blue nightdress that ties at the top. She's got two wooden mugs and a bottle of what Shea recognizes as rum tucked under her arm.

"You should be in bed," Shea says softly, careful not to let her eyes wander.

Jo raises a brow. "You're probably right, but I figured I'd keep you company since you've been avoiding me all day."

"I haven't been avoiding you," Shea responds, moving around the door and crossing her arms over her chest.

Jo begins to argue but a gasp cuts her off as she notices Shea's chest.

"Are you okay? What happened?"

Shea's eyes widen and she looks down, her eyebrows furrowing at whatever Jo is looking at, when she realizes Jo can see her bandages under the blouse.

Shea quickly pulls her shirt closed, her ears reddening.

"I'm fine," Shea stutters.

Jo looks ready to object but then notices the tinge of red on Shea's ears, so she doesn't press. Instead she gestures down to the rum under her arm and forces a smile.

"Come on. Are you really going to let a fine bottle go to waste?"

Shea snorts. "If you found that bottle in the kitchen, I think I'll survive."

Shea examines the stubborn features on the princess's face and sighs. She's not going to leave, and so Shea steps aside, allowing Jo access to her quarters.

Jo smiles in approval. The princess strolls inside and sets the cups down on the desk where Shea had been working. She tries to open the bottle of rum but can't quite pull the cork out. Shea chuckles at her and extends her hand in an offer to help, and to her surprise, Jo hands her the bottle graciously. Shea pops the cork with ease.

"Nice," Shea teases after smelling the rum.

She hands it back to Jo, who rolls her eyes and pours the

liquor into the two mugs. She hands Shea the first one and Shea takes it with a thank you, sitting back down in the desk chair.

Jo briefly examines the desk, her mug in one hand, and Shea is about to offer her the chair in the corner when Jo pushes some of the papers aside and hops up on the desk.

She sits on the table, her feet just touching the floor, facing Shea with an adorable smile. Then they just sit together for a few moments, taking sips of the rum and enjoying the taste.

"It's weird being in here," Jo says, breaking the silence.

The princess looks around the room as if seeing it for the first time. Shea hums in acknowledgment, her eyes following Jo's movements.

Jo slips gracefully off the desk, looking around at the stacks of jewels, gold, and other various trinkets haphazardly placed around the room as if they'd unwittingly stacked up over the years. There are subtle differences since the morning Jo awoke on the *Duchess*. Fewer clothes scatter the floor. The hammock is in the corner, now resting with assorted books lying on it. The standing mirror is still wrapped with precious gem necklaces and gold string, along with a copious amount of fine scarves and wraps.

And for the first time, Jo really notices how many mirrors there are in the cabin. Intricate and plain mirrors cover the walls of the room, making the chamber appear larger. Shea observes Jo examining all the mirrors resting on the walls. The blonde even walks closer to a couple of them, going so far as to brush her fingertips over one of the surfaces.

"I found that one in Knowman's Canyon, in a small trading post on the Pieria Islands just south of Lycos," Shea recounts, remembering that particular job with edging fondness.

It was one of Paetre's last missions.

"They're beautiful," Jo murmurs. "All of them. But—"

"But why all the mirrors?" Shea voices the unasked question with a smirk.

Jo returns the smile and nods. "I picked up this trick from another elven pirate who had brief passage on this ship," Shea explains. "I was young. And I was starting to forget my life before the *Duchess*."

Jo steps away from the wall and settles back to her spot on the desk, giving all of her attention to Shea's story.

"It's funny, I can't even remember the man's name, but he found me one night on deck sitting behind a water barrel. I was crying, I think, and he talked with me for a while about elves, and about the world. He told me that even though he was no longer a part of Erebos, he still missed them. The wood paths and the vines. The way the light filters through the trees," Shea recalls wistfully.

"He asked me to hold out my hand, which he took, and then he closed his eyes. And when he opened them, his eyes were the most magnificent shade of gold. He told me to stand up and he popped the top off the water barrel."

"Why?"

"I didn't understand either. Then he drew a symbol in the water over and over again with his finger. Back and forth almost like a rainbow. He concentrated on the water. Then suddenly, there was an image. In the water there were trees and sun," Shea remembers.

Shea's fingers twitch, wanting to draw the symbol with her own hands.

"I still don't understand."

"Magic, Jo." Shea smiles. "He gifted me with my first spell."

Shea stands, leaving her mug on the desk.

Jo stays where she is but turns her head so her eyes can follow the captain as the elf steps toward the mirror she was just examining.

Shea places her fingers on the reflective surface and begins drawing the symbol back and forth until she feels the energy rush through her hands. Electricity prickles across the pads of her fingers and a strange fuzzy feeling starts at the base of her neck.

She remembers the night, not so long ago, and the way the water had sparkled and the lines curved and carved in the stone. It doesn't take much before she hears Jo gasp behind her, and soon the warmth of the princess's body is at her back.

Jo's breath tickles Shea's ear as she gazes into the mirror and sees the Lover's Fountain at the castle of Arethusa.

"Is this real?" Jo chokes, her emotions warring and partially stealing her voice.

"Yes," Shea replies but then retracts, "and no. It's not an image of what's happening or something that will happen. It's a memory, my memory. Of the fountain that I've placed into the mirror to hold the image."

"I like this spell," Jo laughs in wonderment and the sound goes straight through Shea, so that her concentration falters.

The image fades.

"Sorry," Shea mutters and goes back to her chair. Jo stays, staring at the mirror as if hoping the image will reappear.

Her shoulders sag slightly when it doesn't, but when she turns around, her face still has a soft smile spreading across her features.

"Any more tricks I should be aware of?"

"I'm no use to you if I give you all my secrets," Shea jokes into her glass.

Jo grins but relents. She wanders around the room, stopping at a pile of treasure back near Aster's door, but as Jo gets closer she notices that not all of the things in the piles are as valuable as gold. Some are wooden trinkets and others are pieces of cloth. Jo turns back to Shea, and the captain startles when she feels the heat of the princess's gaze. Her pointed ears tinge pink and she has to look away, staring instead at the contents of her cup. Jo returns to the desk once more.

"So how's the plan coming along?" Jo starts and Shea finishes as the same time with, "Do you feel more confident with a sword?"

They laugh, recalling their talk under the stars and how each had been so awkward that their sentences had constantly crashed together like waves on a rock.

Shea apologizes softly and then clears her throat. "It's coming together well, the plan, I mean. I know a guy. A guard by the southern gate who should be able to get us in. Caeruleus brought him our message and he confirmed. He's optimistic. From there, an elven slave the guard works with will take us to Ceto's quarters. We'll only be able to take a small party, but the smaller the party the easier it will be to slip back out."

"Amazing," Jo praises "You put all of this together in such a short time."

"It's what I do," Shea brags teasingly.

Jo nods and answers Shea's initial question. "I feel much more prepared, thank you," Jo admits. "Although I missed my teacher today. Aster was not nearly as…well equipped."

"I'm sure he was fine. Trained him myself, so trust me, I know what I'm talking about," Shea laughs.

"I do," Jo responds. "Trust you, I mean."

"Jo."

"You can't fool me. You're doing this for me, I know it. It's not some revenge mission because some guy led you on. You care about me; you've found this excuse, but I know you're doing this for me."

"What if I am? Where are you going with this?"

"Thank you," Jo states with great sincerity.

"Jo. Nothing has changed. I'm still the same person."

"No."

"Yes. I'm still the one who kidnapped you," Shea states, "the one who lied, who even after it all was going to take you to Tenaro. My interests changed, not me. I'm still the same person."

"I don't believe that," Jo argues, setting her cup down on the desk.

"I don't care if you do,'" Shea remarks coldly. "So what? Now you want me? Because I'm giving you what you want?"

Shea pushes her seat back abruptly and stands, causing Jo to have to look up at her. "You had reasons for not being with me. You couldn't sacrifice your people. Now, you're going back. You're going to be queen. Where do I fit in to that future?"

Shea walks away toward the bed, leaning against one of the tall bedposts, her back facing Jo.

"We'll make it work," Jo declares, hopping off the desk.

She comes up behind Shea and reaches for her hand. Shea turns so they're face-to-face and looks her dead in the eye.

"I'm a wanted criminal. I stand against everything you stand for. I don't belong to any country. Princesses and pirates don't belong together."

"You're more than a pirate," Jo snaps, "just as I know now that I'm more than a princess. I care for you Shea; I've just learned that a faction within my people wants me dead. Tomorrow, you, the crew, maybe even me, could all die. For all we know Ceto could stand with them. I'm tired of putting the rest of the world ahead of me. I'm trying. And I won't stop trying to save and take back my throne, but I'm done taking one or the other."

She pulls Shea against her body till their faces are inches apart.

"We're fighting for what we want," Jo purrs, and Shea is mesmerized by the cold fire behind those cobalt eyes. "I want you. And I'm going to get what I want."

"Jo—"

Jo moves forward. She presses her lips to Shea's in a passionate kiss. Shea stands shocked, unable to move, but the intensity makes her feel as if she might faint. Jo's hands wrap around her waist and she's pulled even closer, until they feel like one. Shea's hands come to rest on Jo's chest. Her eyes flutter shut and before she knows it, she's kissing back. The captain moans as her mouth grants entrance to Jo's unrelenting tongue and gasps when the princess's teeth drag across her bottom lip.

Shea chases Jo's mouth as she pulls away slightly, her knees bending, and suddenly the elf can feel Jo's hands venture farther down until they're on the back of Shea's thighs. Later she'll deny the squeak that escapes her mouth in surprise as Jo hoists Shea into the air, the captain's legs quickly wrapping around Jo's waist. She revels in the strength displayed by the blonde and holds on tightly as Jo carries her the rest of the short distance to the bed, laying Shea gently down.

Jo crawls on top of her, adjusting the redhead's back until her head rests on the pillows. The captain moans at what feels like currents of electricity humming along her body, raising soft hairs all over. Their mouths move together, creating the most delicious friction. While Shea isn't paying attention, Jo's hand sneaks up under Shea's untucked blouse. Shea yelps into the kiss as Jo expertly finds her nipple beneath the bandages restricting her breasts and pinches.

She gasps, Shea's right hand clenching the top blanket on her bed, and she can feel Jo pull away slightly.

"Huh," Jo breathes, looking up.

Shea has to open her eyes to find out why Jo has stopped when she sees the rum that was in their mugs and the bottle swirling above them in delicate patterns. Shea's mind goes blank and the rum plummets toward them.

She raises her hands with a gasp, catching the liquor with her magic before they find themselves soaked with rum and the mood ruined. She concentrates and flings it out the open window at the back of the cabin.

Jo laughs a fully belly roar at this most recent development, and Shea can feel her ears burning.

She expects Jo to clamber off of her, but instead she leans down and kisses Shea even deeper than before.

"Hades, you're amazing," Jo whispers in between the many kisses.

Her fingers find Shea's nipple again and the captain is back in the throes of the mind-numbing pleasure. The pain from the pinches melts into pleasure and Shea wants to stay here forever, but after the magic use, a small voice in the back of her mind whispers for her to stop. *You're out of control.* This is the second time she's used magic around Jo without realizing it.

She needs to stop.

"Jo," Shea gasps.

She tries to push the nagging voice away, but it keeps coming back louder.

Stop.

Stop.

Stop.

"Jo, please, wait," Shea tries again, this time her voice sounding panicked.

Jo stops, holding herself up over Shea, and she watches the captain's green eyes fluttering as the redhead tries to catch her breath.

"If we do this," Shea whispers, "there's no going back."

Jo smiles, a flash of relief flickering across her features. She takes a strand of Shea's hair and pushes it away from her face.

"I don't want to go back. You're mine, Shea," Jo states as if it's that plain and simple.

"Jo—"

"Shhh..." Jo comforts and leans her forehead against the elf's.

"I'm just going to hold you, okay? Is that alright?"

"All night?" Shea asks.

"All night. For as long as you'll let me," Jo answers, and she falls beside Shea, pulling her close.

Jo leans her face in, lazily kissing Shea. They kiss until the candle burns outs and then they sleep happily entwined within each other's arms.

FEEL MY WRATH AND EXTREME SELF-DOUBT

Joana

JO WAKES UP ALONE with a blanket laid over her body. The top of the bed is wrinkled from where they slept all night, but that's all that remains from their night together.

Jo scans the room but finds no trace of Shea anywhere. The maps from last night that were on the desk are now gone. It's quiet, and Jo notices that at the end of the bed, pants and a new peasant blouse have been laid out for her.

"Aster?" Jo calls out, but there's no reply.

The sun is streaming through the windows onto the bed and by the look of it, it seems to be early morning.

Jo pushes the blanket aside, reaching for the clothes.

She briefly touches her lips, remembering how amazing it felt to be that close to Shea once again. Jo has never felt anything as perfect as last night, and the best part was how right it felt to have Shea safely held within her arms. Jo made a promise to Shea last night, one she intends to keep. The captain is hers now. But her words weren't wrong. Shea is a wanted criminal.

But maybe that could change?

A silk purple scarf on the large standing mirror catches Jo's eye, and just like before she takes it and uses it as a belt to tie off her pants. The gray blouse she's wearing makes her eyes sparkle. She looks around for a ribbon to tie up her hair but comes up empty, and her hair consequently falls loosely around her shoulders; it looks almost silver from all the sun. Before heading up to the quarterdeck, she stops by her own cabin and grabs her normal boots. As she shrugs on the last shoe, she briefly considers taking her blade she stole from the armory and threading it through the scarf next to her hip but ultimately decides to leave it. A quick stop at the kitchen and she notices that there are men still loitering around the galley, so she figures they haven't arrived in Lycos just yet. She grabs a small piece of bread from Strom and heads up top.

Aster is the first to see her as he's swinging from the foremast tying some new ropes under Tero's watchful supervision.

He waves down, calling her name, and she giggles at him, waving back. She doesn't see Shea on the quarterdeck, so she makes her way to the afterdeck staircase and to no surprise finds her at the map table with Mister James and Caen.

"Good morning," Jo says, announcing her presence.

Caen and James mutter a good morning, their eyes never leaving the map.

But Shea looks up.

At first she has a blank expression on her face that makes Jo's stomach clench in knots, but then a soft smile spreads across her delicate features and Jo breathes a sigh of relief.

"Good morning," Shea returns with a wink.

"Hi, James!" Aster's shout startles them all, and they each look up to see Aster on the foremast waving at the helmsman.

Caen laughs deeply and Shea chuckles, patting the embarrassed young man on the back as he turns bright red but waves back at the cabin boy.

Aster stumbles slightly, not paying attention to what he's doing and they can all hear Tero screaming at him to watch it.

James's face turns stark white and he mutters for permission to go check on everything below.

Shea smirks and sends him on his way.

He doesn't need much encouragement and takes off running toward the foremast; and Jo has to hold on to the railing from laughing as she sees poor Mister James start climbing up the rope ladder to save Aster from hurting himself.

Jo takes a breath to calm herself and then turns back to Shea at the navigation table.

Caen is now at the helm taking over for James.

"How close are we to Lycos?" Jo asks, looking down at the map.

"Close, an hour more and we should be arriving at port. James will be taking us straight in. We've lowered our colors, but there's not much we can do about the sails," Shea explains.

"We'll just have to hope the dock master is feeling extremely charitable today," Caen continues. "After all, last I heard our ransom has tripled. Again."

His voice is weary.

"Aye, it's risky at best," Shea states.

"I still don't understand why we don't dock near the cliffs and meet V there. We could make our way over land," Caen explains, though he seems to be repeating an old argument as Shea is already shaking her head in disagreement.

"We don't have that kind of time, and Soren has alerted us that he arrived in Arethusa yesterday thanks to Caeruleus."

At the sound of his name, Caeruleus purrs from above, swooping down on the wind over the deck and landing on the table. Jo tries not to show her unease with the Lionbird.

From her previous encounters with him, he doesn't seem to like her. Shea pets the top of his head and he meows sweetly, but when his eyes land on Jo, he hisses, flicking his tail in her direction.

Jo's eyes narrow; it's ridiculous to be this annoyed with a

bird, but she steps away anyway, leaning with her back against the rail.

Shea's eyebrows rise at the interaction, but she ignores it in favor of continuing her argument with Caen.

"The coronation is in two days. We have just today to convince Ceto to help us and tomorrow to ride to Arethusa. We have to arrive at the coronation ball tomorrow night and warn Mariner."

"Fine, but I still feel that we're risking the ship by docking in Acheron," Caen growls.

They're alerted to James's returning presence as he takes the stairs two at a time. When he reaches the top, he discreetly bends at the waist to catch his breath and then walks the rest of the way to the helm, taking the wheel from Caen, who storms off down the stairs.

He stops at the top briefly to voice one more remark, "But you're the captain. Captain."

He continues down the stairs, barking orders at various members of the deck crew.

Shea grimaces and runs a hand over her face. She shoos Caeruleus away, who takes off after Caen, landing on his shoulder.

Jo honestly wonders how the mangy blue nightmare knows exactly what Shea wants, as if they're mentally connected. Jo pauses. Considering how much she knows about magic now, for all she does know, they could be.

"You look tense," Jo comments, dismissing her thoughts.

Shea looks up, glaring. "Why thank you, my dear, you flatter me so."

"I'm sorry," Jo chuckles. "I meant what's wrong?"

"I wonder? Maybe it's because I'm sailing my ship and crew into the lion's den for a reason I can't really seem to explain."

Jo nods; she walked into that one.

"Did I mention how much I appreciate it?"

Shea laughs and crosses the afterdeck to stand next to Jo at the rail.

She smirks. "Aye, you might've said something along those lines."

Her eyes flick to Jo's lips; it's slow enough for Jo to catch her and it makes the princess smirk.

"I'm going to protect you, you know," Jo tells her.

"That's supposed to be my line," Shea teases, but there's unease in her eyes.

"You may know how to navigate the sea, Captain, but inside the throne rooms, that's my arena. I was born into it, I'm not going to let her take you," Jo states, her eyes boring into Shea's.

She takes Shea's hand in hers and squeezes.

"You might not have a choice"—the captain pauses—"Ceto and I, there's a lot of bad blood there."

"I know."

"Do you? Jo, I need you to understand. I have serious crimes against the empire; I might not make it off the port alive. If that happens, I won't be able to help you anymore, and the crew will leave you. Caen has smoothed the waters with the *Duchess* for now. Most of them are willing to help, some even like you and hope that for putting the queen of Arethusa back on the throne there will be some great reward—"

"I can do that—"

"But that's not enough. A small group at best and if this goes south? If I die? Caen will have to side with them. You'll be alone. I worry for Aster, but he's part of the crew, Caen can protect him. But you? I can't promise your safety."

It's a lot of information to absorb, but Shea's last comment catches Jo off guard.

"Which is why I've sent word to a friend of mine."

"Who?" Jo demands.

"It's just in case. She'll help you start a new life."

"No."

"Jo."

"No, Shea, regardless of what happens, I'm going back. I have to save Arethusa even if I have to do it alone. But nothing is going to happen. We're going to be okay."

"Gods you're so stubborn," Shea notes, rolling her eyes.

"I'm not the only one," Jo teases and pulls Shea into her side.

Shea struggles slightly, not appreciating the public display, and just about growls when Jo lands a big kiss right on the side of Shea's forehead.

There's a chuckle from behind them as they pull apart. James is laughing, and Jo can't help but laugh along with him as Shea turns around with a sharp glare.

"You want me to call Aster up here?" Shea asks him, her eyebrow arching.

James turns a nice shade of pink and quickly shakes his head.

Jo grins and whispers into Shea's ear to distract her from torturing poor Mister James.

"You look nice today by the way."

Shea raises an eyebrow in her direction now, looking down at her own brown peasant top and dark pants tucked into her leather boots. Her curly red hair is braided, falling low down her back. She's wearing her purple captain's coat and her feathered hat. If Jo didn't find her so damn adorable, she'd almost be intimidating.

Shea snorts in disbelief and gestures for Jo to get ready. "We'll be there soon, best to grab that dagger you nicked from the armory. Tell Aster to find you a weapons belt."

"I didn't steal it from the armory," Jo objects once again.

"That's funny because I don't remember a sword being an accessory to that dress I picked you up in."

Jo scoffs and takes off down the stairs.

"You guys are so mushy," James complains from the helm.

"One more word, James, and you'll be doing Aster's job for the next week. I'll even make you switch rooms and I might just make you share with him."

Jo giggles at James's stuttering, a sense of pride swelling in her chest at how powerful her girlfriend is.

"Land ho!"

Someone yells from the crow's nest, and Jo looks out ahead

where the peaks of Lycos can be easily seen. Everything is going to be fine, but Jo figures it might not be a bad idea to grab that sword from her quarters.

A SHEEP IN LION'S CLOTHING

Shea

THE WIND PICKS UP THE KNOTS, and the peaks are no longer vague shapes in the distance. In fact, they're so close, Shea can almost see the famous obsidian towers of Lycos.

The crew prepares to dock.

Shea alerts Caen that he'll be coming with them to the palace and then has the unfortunate pleasure of alerting Aster that he won't be.

"I need you to stay here," Shea commands for the third time.

"This is so not fair! I should be going with you. You could get hurt, or something could happen, I need to be there!"

"No," Shea orders, grabbing Aster's arm and marching him farther down the hall to his quarters.

"You are going to stay in your room until Mister Tero comes to get you, and when he does, you are to do what he says when he says, got it?"

"No," Aster repeats, "I'm going with you. I can't lose you!"

"And I can't lose you!" Shea bellows, shocking Aster into silence.

Shea's body deflates a bit and she pulls Aster against her,

hugging him. He returns the hug tightly.

"I need you to be safe. I won't be at my best if you're in there, and if something happens, I have to be at my best today." Shea pulls back, her palms cupping his face.

"Understand?"

Aster is reluctant but eventually he folds, nodding his head. They walk hand in hand to Shea's quarters until they're standing on either side of the doorway.

"I'm coming back for you, kid, I promise."

Aster is looking down at the ground and Shea knows he's doing his best not to cry.

"Be careful," he offers.

Shea nods, closing the door with Aster inside. And before he can change his mind, she takes out the master key and locks the door. The knob rattles slightly and then she hears Aster yelling.

He hits the door a couple of times, and she walks away with her head held high, knowing her "child" is at least safe.

Once she's back on deck, the men gather around her.

"You all know why we're here, even if some of you don't understand." She glances at Caen, who doesn't meet her eyes. "This day could end many ways, and I just want to say that it has been a privilege to sail with you all. It has been an honor as one of the crew and as your captain. I hope that today the gods stand with us in our favor. But if they don't and I am not permitted to return to this fine lady, I hope you all sail on strong. This is a fine ship, and a better crew."

Shea draws her sword and points the tip in the air. The men draw their swords as well, but instead of repeating her last sentiment, Mister Tero steps forward with a hand over his heart.

Jo watches uneasily.

Caen shifts in his stance.

"To the captain, ma'am," Mister Tero declares with a smile.

"To the captain," every crew member shouts.

They all cheer and Shea smiles; she wonders and hopes that

from somewhere Paetre can see how strong and magnificent his ship has become.

"Right then, prepare to dock," Shea orders. "To your stations!"

James yells from the helm.

The crew sheathes their swords and takes off in all their directions.

Shea readies herself, making sure she has enough coins for the bribes. Jo stands close to the gunwale, looking out at the port as the capital city of Lycos overtakes their view.

Fine vessels and ships scatter across the vast port of Acheron. Buildings of black marble and obsidian glitter in the sunlight. There's black sand on the shore and on the ocean bed that darkens the waves, casting a menacing shadow around the coast. The grand palace of Acheron envelops the center of the city; onyx bricks gleam in the sun, casting dancing shapes on the glittering darkness. There's a general gloom over the area. Even the sun casts gray light on Lycos. Shea can see the slave market from the quarterdeck. The market takes up most of the port as slaves stand on the giant auction platforms and kneel at tent-covered booths.

They continue the never-ending auctions through day and night, rain or shine. The port market is booming with ruffians, pirates, and people of distinguished fame. Women in giant gowns and strange clothing walk along the water's edge, slaves following behind with umbrellas.

"It's so...harsh," Jo mumbles, looking over the city as a whole.

She sees no hamlets or smaller homes shrunken beneath the looming black marble towers. Though there are obviously beggars and child thieves running amok through the market streets.

"Welcome to Acheron, the city of pain," Shea mutters, gritting her teeth.

No alarms have gone off yet.

Shea keeps her eyes on the wooden walkways, waiting for

guards to swarm, but there's nothing.

They pull into port easily, as they've done many times before. The crew extends the gangplank, and Caen goes down first to pay the dock master. Jo surprisingly decides to accompany him. Shea visits Tero before heading down after them.

She hands him the key to her quarters. "You let him out only when it's safe, and if the guards begin to board, you grab James and you smuggle the two of them out. Hide them the best you can and then give them this." She hands Tero a pouch of coin. "James is smart enough to find passage, but you tell Aster to wear his hair down no matter what. He can't let his ears show, not here."

"It'll be fine, Shea."

"Promise me."

"I promise, Captain," Tero states, taking the coin purse gently, along with the key.

Shea shakes his hand, but he pulls her in for a hug.

"Come back, kid," Tero utters before letting her go.

Finally she makes her way toward the gangplank and down onto the port walkways.

Caen paid the man, and the port master is already gone by the time Shea arrives. She's also just in time to hear the end of Jo and Caen's argument.

"I'm not going to let anything happen to her."

"You can't promise me that, princess. This place is out for Shea's blood. You don't understand the risk."

"My people are worth it."

"Exactly, they're worth more than her life to you!"

"That's not what I meant—"

Shea makes a point of pretending not to have heard them. She purposely steps on a loose board and the creak luckily catches their attention. They're both silent by the time she reaches them.

"Where to?" Jo asks, clearing her throat.

"We have to make it to the western entrance of the palace. I figure if we stick close to the Seams we won't have any trouble almost being spotted."

"The Seams?" Jo inquires.

"The underground of Lycos," Caen discloses.

He pushes past Jo until he's at the front of their little group and starts weaving through the crowd. Once they're off the wooden port walkways and onto the cobblestone, Shea takes in how little the place has changed since the last time she was in Lycos. The market vendors are still covered in scraps of material, it's loud and rough, like the black volcanic sand lining the seashore. Shea subconsciously reaches out her hand and takes Jo's, making sure she stays close and out of danger. As they start to make their way toward the alleyway leading to the Seam, royal guards flood out onto the market street.

Men, as only men can join the palace guard in Lycos, come out of the woodwork. Exiting from buildings and alleys. Their deep purple chainmail and dark red uniforms look warm in the heavy heat. Their dual-ended spears point at the trio as they make their way around, encircling the three of them with nowhere left to go.

Shea pulls her sword as Caen wields his hammer, but they both can tell it's too late. From the back of the ambush, a soldier makes his way through the crowd, his helmet obscuring his face. Finally he parts his way through the sea of Lycons.

"Drop your weapons," he orders, and Shea doesn't want to do it.

But she takes one look at Jo, who's trying to act tough, holding her sword at half-mast, and sighs. Shea drops her gold sword to the ground and it clatters on the cobblestone.

Jo looks over, puzzled, but does the same, letting her sword fall to the ground. Shea brings her hands up in a surrendering gesture.

Caen glares at her angrily. "What the Underdeep are you doing?" he seethes.

"Drop your weapon, Caen, we won't make it out," Shea whispers and gestures with her eyes toward Jo.

Caen growls. He grumbles but ultimately throws his hammer to the ground.

Five guards swarm in, two grabbing Shea and two grabbing Caen, while one grabs Jo. Three from the side pick up their weapons.

"Oi, careful with the hands, darling," Shea jokes bravely, and the head guard who gave the orders chuckles darkly.

"Captain Shea, I'd worry less about their hands and more about your head."

"Come up with that one all on your own? Have to say that's probably why it needs a bit of work."

The leader storms toward her, looking down on Shea with disgust, and that's when she sees it. She recognizes the pig nose and the brown-muck eyes. She lunges at him, almost clipping him in the chin, but the two guards rein her back.

"Marlo, you disgusting pig!"

Caen's head snaps to the side, recognizing the name, and he is successful in throwing off his two men, but four more tackle him to the ground before he can get any farther.

"Guess the cat's out of the bag." Marlo smirks, taking off his helmet.

"You know this guy?" Jo discerns.

"Yeah, he was our way into the palace," Shea spits.

"You sold us out," Caen roars, his breath heavy as he struggles from underneath the four soldiers pinning him to the ground.

"Let's just say the price for your head has increased enormously since we last talked; even you couldn't outbid Ceto. You made her angry, Shea."

"And how angry would she be to know how many times you —"

Marlo backhands Shea with his gauntlet, bringing her down to one knee.

Jo shrieks in dismay, struggling against the guard's hold.

Caen stops struggling and allows the guards to bring him up to his knees. His fighting will only make things worse, but his features darken to the point of murder. Shea sucks in a breath, adjusting her jaw; Marlo isn't finished though.

He grabs her by one of her ears and Shea bites back a yelp as he brings her back onto her feet.

"You'll do best to stay quiet, elf, or I'll alert Ceto to the slave who would have smuggled you into the palace," Marlo threatens.

"He's your agent," Shea snarls.

"He's a creature just like you. And you're both on the losing side of life. It's just the facts."

Marlo laughs in her face.

Shea wants to rip his cheek out with her teeth, but she won't give him the satisfaction of growling like an animal.

"Cuff 'em," Marlo orders.

The guards at her sides cuff her hands to her feet using black chains, and then for an added effect they use a steel gag, the kind that covers the lower part of the face just under her nose to keep her quiet—a common item that slave owners in the empire use on their property.

They place manacles on Caen's and Jo's wrists, but they don't get the same full-bondage treatment.

"Let go of me! You have no right," Jo snaps. "I demand to see Empress Ceto."

"Don't worry, girl, we're taking you to her right now. Let's go."

The guards begin the march. They push Caen and Jo ahead of Shea.

Marlo sticks to the main road, so he can get his time in the sun. Guards flank either side of the three of them while pig face leads the battalion from the front, showing the prisoners off in the streets and straight through the inner city of nobles.

Courtiers and merchants of wealth jeer and point from their compartments in the obsidian towers. The farther into the city they get, the more elaborate the architecture becomes. Spirals of gold connect in a terrace over the streets, covered in magnificent violet roses. The road itself is lined in a deep blue material, as if they're walking on one large pillow.

It's a dark paradise and it feels like the most dangerous place a person can be.

Finally the gates of the Acheron Palace appear up ahead, covered in fire and greased with scents of rose oil and incense. The gate burns around the entire palace, and at a heat that would incinerate anyone who tries to squeeze through the bars. Which is why getting inside requires an inside man.

But if the hood was actually telling the truth at any point, there might be another way in—and perhaps another way out. The gates are pulled apart with heat resistant steel chains collected from mines on the outskirts of Oceanus.

The small free country had once been a part of Lycos. The duke who ruled the once imperial province wanted freedom for his people against the tyrannous empire. He rose up against the emperor of the time through the help of an unexpected ally, the elves. It's the only battle in Nereidan history where elves united with humans to conquer a mutual enemy. Using Taurus magic, they created an unreachable mountain pass filled with dangerous charms and human traps on the border between Lycos and Oceanus, a natural gate to ward off the empire. Lycos has been trying to take back the free state ever since, and that was a hundred years ago.

After a few moments, they're granted entrance to the palace, the undead beating heart of Lycos. Shea has no choice but to keep moving at a slow place. Her hands and feet are bound; she doesn't even have her voice to fake bravado. It doesn't look good, but she keeps her focus on conserving her strength and looking for a way out.

Jo keeps turning back to get her attention but Shea keeps her head down, looking at the path ahead. She can't get distracted now.

They walk up the onyx steps to the giant black doors, the entrance to the center of the empire. The doors open before them and it takes Shea's eyes a moment to adjust because the inside looks pitch-black. But the more her eyes adjust the more objects inside come into focus, and she realizes that the light inside the palace is green. Torches of viridescent fire light the halls. The chandeliers above are also lit with a mysterious green fire. The windows of the palace are a dark crystal, and the green light seems to bounce off the chambers, creating a haunting glow.

The floor is covered in a purple silk. Shea rolls her eyes at how completely menacing the place is.

Farther in, the windows are replaced with open-air arches that look out over the city. Gray light streams in, mixing with the iridescent glow.

"Why is the fire green?" Jo whispers as she looks around. Even though Shea can't voice it, her mind supplies the answer: elves. Enslaved elves roam the halls casting charms and enchantments under the watchful eyes of the guards.

Shea shudders as she sees one elf in particular with a collar wrapped around her neck. The tips of her ears have been severed. Cropped, as the nobles call it. They consider it high fashion, a clean look for their animals.

Another set of doors are up ahead, these made of jade and reaching high toward the vaulted ceiling. It takes three guards to push the doors open. On the other side is the throne room. But instead of dark black and roaring green fire, there are bloodred silks and fabrics that wrap around the walls and floors, cushioning every surface.

In the center far back of the room is the throne, made entirely of gold, onyx, and rubies. A golden elephant lies around the menacing throne with spiked rubies protruding from the carved animal's tusks. The chair itself is made of onyx. Spikes of the black stone extend toward the ceiling at the top of the throne. Red cushions made of velvet line the seat and back.

Chandeliers of precious stones hang from above, but these roar with red fire. From the center of each magnificent chandelier, incense of sage and blossoms fill the room in a smoky haze. Men and women of varying ages sit along the side of the running carpet up to the throne on elaborate plush pillows.

As they step farther into the room, there's a distinct difference between the owners and the slaves. The nobles sit lavishly on the giant pillows, comfortable and clothed, in fine gowns of reds, greens, and deep purples, real gold thread embedded through every stitch. While the slaves, all elven, writhe beside them or at their feet in scanty, revealing sheer robes portraying scenes of erotic behavior.

Shea does her best to ignore the disgusting display as the guards propel them down the aisle. Marlo seizes Shea's chains and jerks her forward until she's in front of the throne.

Shea's eyes remain focused on the floor.

Sadistically, he uses the shaft of his spear to force her to her knees.

Caen is brought to her left and Jo to her right, but they're left standing.

Beads of sweat erupt on Shea's brow. She ignores the itching nerve, the desire to wipe it away, and instead straightens her back as much as she can. She refuses to show fear even in her vulnerable position.

And then, once she's gathered enough breath through her nose, she looks up at the cruel figure lounging in her throne.

THE UNDERWORLD'S EMPRESS

Shea

EMPRESS CETO'S CARAMEL EYES meet Shea's viridian green. Her cheshire grin reminds Shea of a cat that has finally caught the flighty bird that used to tease the feline in the window.

She's spared no expense to intimidate; her obsidian hair is pulled back and braided around her head before falling in ringlets down her back. The crown upon her head is made of jagged black diamond and rough rubies that look as if a mere touch would slice anyone's palm open.

Ceto leans forward under the red light casting a warm glow to her brown skin, and the gold tendrils painted up and down her bare arms look less delicate and more like war paint.

The elaborate maroon dress sticks to her frame as if it had been painted on, the deep satin resting against the curves of her figure provocatively.

An elven male with bright auburn hair and light skin hovers at her side, kissing the length of her neck, but she keeps her eyes on Shea.

It doesn't escape the captain's notice that the slave looks like a male version of herself.

Shea rebelliously casts her eyes to the ground and grits her teeth at Ceto's satisfactory laugh, filling the room with the rich sound.

The liner around Ceto's eyes makes them darker, almost ghoul black. Shea can feel the bitch's gaze raking over her body and she can't help it as her eyes flicker up to Ceto with a challenging glare.

"Well done, Captain Marlo. I highly doubted you could do it, but you've proven your worth." Her voice is a chilling contrast to her looks.

While she may appear young, her voice is rich like old honey and Shea notices Jo's eyes widen in surprise.

Caen is staring at Ceto warily.

He's subtly examining the room, looking for all the possible exits and outcomes. But there's only one exit that they all know of and they'll only get to leave through it with Ceto's permission.

"Your Majesty, it is urgent that I—" Jo speaks quickly without permission, but chokes off when the guard holding her punches her in the stomach.

Jo gasps for air, falling.

Shea lunges, without thought of the consequences, trying to catch Jo.

But Marlo jerks her back by her hair, effectively stopping her. He backhands Shea again for her movement and she hits the ground, groaning.

Jo's eyes connect with Shea's and they share a moment on the floor, reaching out with their minds to comfort one another.

Marlo grabs Shea by the ear and pulls her back up. She yelps this time out of surprise but luckily the gag muffles it.

He keeps his hand in her hair, holding her still in front of Ceto, who absorbs the commotion with a smile.

"Boys, please, there's no need to be so rough with our guest," Ceto playfully scolds. "It's best to wait until spoken to, dear, manners and all."

This time Jo remains silent, but her scowl speaks volumes as she steadily raises herself back to a standing position.

Shea rolls her eyes at the small feminine giggle that pops out of the imperial monster.

"Marlo," Ceto acknowledges and his head snaps toward her.

He bows awkwardly with Shea's hair in his grasp.

"Yes, my Empress?"

"I think it's safe to say you've earned the title you seek. Lord Marlo has a nice ring to it. Don't you think?"

"Yes, Your Worship," Marlo gushes.

"Very well, we'll see it done. Lyle?"

Ceto gestures to the elf kissing her neck, and he swiftly gets off the arm of the throne and stands at attention, waiting for her command.

"Very good, darling," Ceto praises, as if Lyle is a prized dog.

It makes Shea's blood boil.

"Will you show Lord Marlo where he needs to go?"

Lyle nods and bows.

He smiles at Marlo and points to a door off the side of the throne room and begins to walk there.

Marlo looks questioningly at Ceto and once she nods in approval, his hand briefly squeezes Shea's hair tightly, pulling at the roots before letting go to walk after Lyle.

"Oh, Marlo," Ceto whistles, and he stops in place, frozen like prey before a predator, "remove the gag before you leave. My dear pirate and I have a few things to discuss."

Marlo coughs. "Of course, ma'am."

He hurries back to Shea and unclasps the binding. It falls away from her face easily.

"You can go," Ceto allows.

Marlo makes a quick escape to the other side of the door before he's asked to do anything else.

Shea wriggles her jaw with a click after having it clamped shut for so long.

Ceto stands gracefully. Her movements are calculated as she descends from her throne to where Shea is kneeling on the silk ground.

Every step matches the beat of Shea's heart like a fearful march, counting the beats toward Shea's demise.

Finally the empress stands before the redhead, the maroon train of her dress falling far behind her. Ceto reaches out her hand, purposefully slow, and her long black fingernails catch the underside of Shea's chin, bringing her head up so their eyes meet.

"I've waited a long time for this," Ceto murmurs.

"Now that you mention it, you have aged quite a bit."

Ceto laughs but it's hollow. The slap isn't unexpected, and Ceto's nails cut Shea's cheek in the process.

The black-haired empress grips Shea's chin forcefully and the elf is pulled upward until she's on her feet. Ceto stands about a foot and a half taller than Shea, but she doesn't let it intimidate her; she stares down the monstrous cow even from her chained position.

"I will teach you to respect your betters."

"Is that before or after you kill me," Shea growls.

"Oh, my dear, death would be too good for you. There are worse things in life."

"You may be right. But as long as I'm alive, I will never stop fighting against you."

"Promise?" Ceto grins with what looks like a mouth full of razors but Shea doesn't stand down.

"Caen, you look as brooding as ever," Ceto comments, but her eyes never break from Shea's gaze.

"Your wretchedness, eaten any babies lately?" Caen sneers, taking a step toward the empress.

Spears block his path immediately but he shows no remorse.

"Charming as ever, as well," she drawls before finally turning on Jo.

Ceto's eyebrows furrow slightly. She saunters toward the princess, inspecting her like she's a rare antiquity.

"I know you," she tells Joana.

"Crown Princess Joana, the future queen of Arethusa," Jo replies stiffly.

"Arethusa? Oh, Queen Doris was an admirable ruler. I liked your grandmother very much."

"Thank you," Joana responds, her expression guarded.

"You look like your mother, Queen Triteia, though. I suppose you can't have everything." Ceto chuckles and Jo's expression sours. "Aren't you supposed to be dead?"

"At the moment? Yes."

"Well you look nice. For a corpse."

"I was kidnapped," Jo explains, ignoring Ceto's taunt, "and held in Shea's custody at the behest of a faction within my own court."

"So why did you come here?" Ceto questions, but she looks to Shea.

She wanders back to stand in front of the captain. "She outbid your original hire?"

"I'm just helping a friend out," Shea surmises, keeping her face neutral.

"Is that what you told her?" Ceto cackles. "Oh, Shea, you don't have any friends. You don't even have a generous bone in your body. You should learn quickly, princess, pirates are only out for themselves."

"I'll keep that in mind, but for now I need her," Jo replies, wrenching her arm out of her guard's grasp.

It catches the Lycon soldier off guard and he quickly reaches for her, but Ceto waves him off.

He lets Joana go reluctantly.

"I apologize, but where Shea's going, she won't be any help to anyone," Ceto says, clasping her hands in front of her in a mock apologetic gesture.

"I can't let you take her. As one ruler to another, help me take back my queendom. I know that you and Shea share history, but I'm asking that you allow me to take her under my sanctuary. I need her support," Jo states, coming closer to stand next to Shea until their shoulders touch. "Arethusa needs your help. Ally with me. Help me take back my throne, and on my honor, I will do whatever I can to pay off any debt Shea has procured."

Ceto stands speechless for a silent moment. Then, her features dissolve into a large grin; a loud laugh full of mirth explodes from her lips, and she cackles all the way back to her seat on the throne.

"What a touching speech. I'm moved really. I would be happy to negotiate allying with you to take back your queendom, though the price will be steep. But Shea is nonnegotiable. A few weeks back she crossed the line of no return. I cannot release her."

Ceto acknowledges the look of confusion on Jo's face at her comment and explains further, but this time she speaks to Shea.

"I see crown jewels weren't enough for you, you had to go and steal the crown princess of the neighboring queendom."

Shea smiles, raising her shoulders to express ignorance. "What can I say, I like pretty things. Your pearl caught a nice price on the market."

Jo's eyes widen in realization. "You stole the Pearl of Lycos?"

Her eyes narrow at Shea. She supposes that would have been a good piece of information to let her in on.

"Guilty," Shea retorts.

Jo reaches her hand up to her forehead, holding it in exasperation.

"The court appreciates your admission," Ceto snarls.

A loud yowl fills the room, though it's slightly muffled, catching Shea and Jo off guard, but Ceto continues speaking as if it never happened.

"I apologize, princess, but as far as the captain is concerned, she has condemned her fate."

"It's okay," Shea whispers to Jo.

"No, it's not," Jo growls back.

"Perhaps, if we were to give the pearl back to you, could we talk about Shea's release then?"

All heads in the room swivel to Caen, who has been standing quietly listening to the entire ruckus. A soft smile lays upon his face as he awaits Ceto's response to his query.

"Possibly, but as your captain spoke, it's already been sold —"

"What if I could give you the buyer?" Caen responds.

"Caen? What are you doing?" Shea demands.

A loud creak fills the throne room as the giant jade doors are pushed open by the guards on the other side.

Another loud trill echoes through the throne room, this time clear, and Shea feels her entire body freeze over.

Standing in the doorway is a tall elven woman she's never seen before wearing a black satin dress with long sleeves and a silver choker with multiple layers around her neck. Her hair is pulled up in a high braid that falls over the front of her left shoulder, proudly displaying her pointed ears with the tips capped in silver. The woman is beautiful, but what really chills Shea to the bone is the blonde standing beside her with ghostly purple eyes and an oh-so-familiar smile.

Caeruleus sits on V's shoulder as V follows the mysterious elven woman farther into the throne room.

"More guests! How charming. Countess, what an honor it is," Ceto drawls, waving her hand for the guards to shut the door behind the two women.

Caen steps forward while Shea is jerked back to stand at the side.

She watches Caen greet V and the countess that Ceto mentioned.

"Empress," the countess bows.

She then turns to Jo and curtsies deeply, extending her palm.

Jo places her hand in the elf's, cautiously, but is relieved when the countess only kisses the back of her hand.

"I was not expecting you today," Ceto reiterates, casting a curious glance to Caen.

"I'm here on behalf of an old friend, Mistress Venus of Arethusa," the countess explains, turning back to Ceto.

"Your Majesty," V murmurs.

Ceto acknowledges her with an appreciative look.

"I'm afraid I'm a little busy to discuss business today, Thetis."

"Countess Thetis and Venus are here to bargain," Caen clarifies, "for Shea's life."

"In what way?" Shea growls, taking a step forward only to be jerked back by the guard again.

She glares at Caen, hoping he'll turn to explain to her, but instead he continues to ignore her.

"Not possible," Ceto chuckles darkly. "I would not give up this opportunity even for—"

"Even for the prized Pearl of Lycos?" Venus concludes, producing the pearl itself from her cloak.

Ceto stands abruptly in shock. She descends the stairs with haste and snatches the pearl from Venus's hand.

"How did you—"

"A lucky break. I serve many in my establishment, and the captain on her last visit was careless. I assumed I might fetch a better price in Arethusa until a friend"—Venus looks toward Caen, who nods—"asked for my help. So I came to Thetis, so that I might barter with you."

"The pearl for Shea's life," Caen demands. "We leave and we promise to never enter nor interfere with Lycon business again."

"You can't just decide this for me," Shea snarls as she struggles against her captors, but she's knocked on the back of the head by one of the guards. She falls to the ground with a grunt, holding her skull in pain.

"It's an interesting offer, but what proof do you have you would be true to your words?"

"Because if she tries to return, I will hand her over to you myself," Caen states.

Shea hears the words.

He speaks clearly and yet Shea can't quite process them. She's still clutching her head. Jo is at her side, her hand on her back rubbing circles, but the betrayal makes Shea numb to Jo's touch.

"A delectable offer. You must give me the night to think it over."

Caen agrees, but they both know she's not asking for permission.

"Wonderful, well then, I think that leaves only one order of business and I'd prefer to do that alone."

She snaps her fingers on her left hand and the soldiers stand at attention. "Guards, escort Shea and her companions to a room within my quarters. Princess Joana will be given her own room after our little chat, and then, Thetis, if you'd like to join us, we'll all have dinner together. Now, won't that be nice?"

Shea looks up from where she is kneeling on the ground. She growls, "No, I won't leave Jo with you."

"I'm afraid you don't really have a choice. I'd be on my best behavior, darling. Your future is still in my hands. Lyle?"

BETRAYAL IS BEST SERVED

Shea

LYLE APPEARS AT THE DOOR where he led Marlo out. He gestures for the guards to follow him with the prisoners, leaving Jo behind with Ceto.

Shea shuffles out into the hall, followed by Caen and Venus with Caeruleus, who is kneading into her flesh happily on her shoulders.

Thetis elects to stay behind, taking a seat on one of the pillow chairs near the throne.

Shea chances a look back over her shoulder, but the princess waves her on.

They step through the door, and the red disappears, replaced by the black obsidian blocks and the haunting green fire lighting their way once again.

Shea is kept to the front of the line near Lyle, while V and Caen stay right behind her with two guards behind them.

The walls tighten the deeper they go into the castle, and it's as if the hall is beginning to close in around them, like a serpent constricting its prey.

But the hall opens up into their destination, an elaborate compartment. The first room is surprisingly warm and inviting, with colorful oranges and yellows filling the décor. Large chairs and pillows have been placed around for company to sit.

Murals of their patron goddess Scylla are displayed in a sympathetic story over the smooth onyx walls.

An open grand arch to the side of the sitting room leads to a private dining area. The dining set inside is long, made of gray stone, and a multitude of chairs with high backs and purple cushions surround the entire table. Crystal goblets and silver plates lie waiting for their next opportunity to be used.

As they shuffle farther in, they notice quite a few doors toward the back of the apartment stretching along a hallway lit by green fire, but it doesn't seem as sickly as the palace halls. This green reminds Shea of the deep color of trees or wet grass after a storm.

The guards separate.

One takes Caen to his room with V following behind.

The other two guards follow Lyle to take Shea to hers. They shove her through the entryway to her new quarters while Lyle explains that the entire compartment is available to her. This is a quarter of Ceto's main wing. Guards are posted at every exit; any sign of resistance or escape will be met with a termination of agreement.

Shea nods her understanding, and both soldiers remove her arm and foot restraints. There's a moment where everyone freezes, waiting for the pirate to attack but Shea just continues to stand there looking down at her hands, rubbing her wrists.

"Very good," Lyle tells her with a release of his held breath. "Dinner will be in the compartment. Once the empress is finished with Her Highness, we will begin preparation. You should expect to eat in a couple of hours. Maids will be in to dress you after Princess Joana arrives."

Lyle motions for the guards to follow him out, leaving the chamber entirely to Shea.

Curiously she follows them to the open door and watches

as all of the guards and Lyle leave the compartment. She's sure if she looks there will be soldiers stationed outside the main doors. Shea may no longer be bound, but she's still trapped. She looks down to the other end of the hall and finds Caen standing in his doorway to his own chambers staring fixedly at her.

His expression is filled with pain and guilt. Good, it should be, Shea thinks.

He takes a step toward her, but she holds up her hand; he can save his excuses. She steps from her doorway and into the compartment without a word. Caen doesn't attempt to follow her.

Making her way to the dining room, she inspects the fine dishes and chalices placed elegantly on the table.

"He did it to save you," V tells her, announcing her presence as she strolls into the room with her hands on her hips.

"It doesn't matter," Shea seethes. "I would rather have died. Or suffered Ceto's fate than let her get back that damn pearl."

Shea keeps her attention on the crystal goblets. She refuses to even look at the brothel owner.

"What good would that have done? The pearl is a symbol, taking it does no damage to the slave trade or her wealth. He did it to protect you, it's not fair to guilt him for saving your life."

"I didn't ask him to!" Shea snarls, glaring up at her.

Her temper flares wildly and she can't hold back her grief at failing Paetre.

"You're right. The pearl is a symbol and that's what makes it so bloody important. It is a sign of the empire's success, all of its triumph, its legacy. And Paetre and I took that away from her. News of the pearl being taken spreads cracks in her immortal image across Lycos. It shows she isn't invincible. For the pearl, for Paetre's legacy, my life would have been worth all it wrought."

"So she gets the pearl back, it doesn't prove that she's not vulnerable. You standing against her is what shows the slavers that Ceto's time is coming to an end. You show Nereid every day that Ceto isn't untouchable! From the first moment you defied her, you've created cracks in the Lycon armor! With you gone, there isn't anyone strong enough to bring her to her knees," V reasons.

She steps closer and grasps one of Shea's hands.

Shea glares at V and scoffs. "So? That's part of the deal, right? Even if I live through this, I can never enter Lycos again. I can never interfere again. I chose to lay down my weapon and surrender because at least I had taken something that would make my sacrifice worth it. I made her furious, and therefore, she would always remember that no matter how hard she tries to destroy me, I still did what everyone said was impossible. In that way, I won."

"Damn it, Shea, I don't understand how you can be so oblivious! There are people who care about you, people who don't wish to see you dead or, worse, pawned off as a pleasure slave to some sadistic noble that Ceto sees fit. Don't you care about what Caen thinks? What I think?" V growls.

Shea pulls her hand out of V's grasp and walks to the other side of the table. She reaches out, picking up one of the black diamond chalices, ignoring the mistress's tirade.

"Don't you care what Jo thinks?" V murmurs.

Shea nearly drops the chalice, the question catching her off guard.

"It's not about us," Shea mutters. She puts the goblet down and leans on the table with both hands, looking across the surface until their eyes meet. "And this isn't about me. This was Paetre's legacy, and I failed him the moment you gave Ceto that pearl back."

"He asked you to get out," V states.

Shea groans because of course she'd bring this up.

"That's what you told me after he died. He wanted you out. To live while you still had life left. You can do that now. You can go to Orena, start up a fencing business for gods' sake, or you could even start an entirely new life," V insinuates, crossing around the table.

She pushes her way close into Shea's space until they're standing mere inches apart. "A noble one. With Jo."

Shea doesn't step away. "This is my life. I can't give up knowing that people like me are being carved and sold for the amusement of humans like Ceto. I found my purpose, what right do any of you have to ask me to give it up?"

They lapse into silence.

V isn't really sure how to continue and Shea feels unwilling to.

"I'm sorry," V offers.

Shea shoots her a half smile. "I suppose fate will decide," she says, and then pauses.

Her brows furrow and she has to ask, "The meeting point?"

V nods.

"The map to the vault? Did he ever show at the neutral meeting ground?"

V snorts and shakes her head. "No. I waited two days before getting out of dodge with the pearl. If he had it, we'll never know."

Shea curses, all of it had been for nothing. So many lives ruined since the start of this job and the reward isn't even real.

"She's beautiful," V says, breaking Shea out of her wallowing. "Even more so than I remember."

It's a moment before Shea realizes who V is talking about and when she does her ears tinge pink.

"She's a princess."

"So? I'm a goddess. Your taste certainly hasn't changed."

Shea laughs, rolling her eyes. "Right."

V chuckles and they both turn their backs and lean shoulder to shoulder against the table.

"How'd you know anyway?" Shea asks.

"You kidding me? Caen can't rant enough about her. He's probably the biggest gossip I know."

Shea grins.

The laughter fades.

"You like her?"

Shea nods. "Yeah. I really do."

"I told you." V looks away, and Shea takes her hand.

"Told me what?"

"That the Fates would take you from me."

Shea opens her mouth to respond, but V interrupts her. "It's okay. I can see that you're happy. You're one of my favorite mortals, Shea. Don't you ever forget that."

Shea's eyebrow rises, but she smiles at the unusual comment.

Then V leans in. Her lips softly touch Shea's in a somber kiss. It's bittersweet, and it's the perfect goodbye to everything they've been through together. They break the kiss and V looks as if she's about to say something when her eyes widen at something behind Shea.

Shea turns to see Jo standing still, watching the two of them with a blank expression.

"Jo," Shea breathes, smiling. "How'd it go?"

"Fine. I'll tell you about it later. I'm going to get ready for dinner," Jo answers briskly and simply walks away to her room.

Shea is slightly put off by Jo's dismissal, but she decides to chalk it up to stress. Jo says they'll talk about it later and they will.

"Are you sticking around?" Shea inquires, but she really already knows the answer.

"I think I've done enough damage. But hey"—V catches her attention, placing her hand on Shea's cheek—"think about what I said. He doesn't deserve your anger."

Shea doesn't respond but she does pull V in for a tight hug. She walks her the rest of the way to the entrance of the compartment, careful to stay behind the doors. Watching Venus leave is like watching the end of a chapter closing in a book about her life. Shea waves goodbye, and though it feels so completely final, a small part of her whispers that she'll see her again.

(NEVER BE) ENOUGH

Joana

JO TRIES TO SUBDUE the overwhelming panic once the door Shea left through closes behind her captain. She keeps her head high, and when she turns back to look at Ceto, she finds the empress looming over her.

It's to incite shock and so Jo does her best to ignore the instinct to take a step back.

Ceto smirks in approval, and instead she takes the step back. She gestures for Jo to join her on the seat next to the throne, which Jo only now notices. It's an elaborate wooden chair with intricate carvings in the seat's back. Jo sits carefully and sees Thetis, the elven countess who came in with the blonde woman, Venus, lounging on the pillow seat closest to the throne.

"So, it must be an interesting tale on how you tamed the feral duchess of the sea. Shea seems quite under your thrall." Ceto giggles as if they're discussing a schoolgirl's crush.

Jo forces herself not to clench her hands into fists.

"I'm not here to talk about Shea. I'm here to discuss your aid in taking back my queendom."

"Spoilsport," Ceto whines. "Very well. I'd be more than happy to help you with your current situation, but I'm afraid the decision falls upon my court, you see?"

"So you can't help me?"

"Not just your mother's pretty face, good," Ceto coos.

Jo grips the arms of the chair, finding it harder to hide her displeasure on her face.

"So why am I still here then?"

Jo stands to leave, but Ceto slams her fist down on her throne, making everyone in the room freeze. She watches as the courtiers on their silk pillows stop their debauchery and drinking, all of them except for Thetis, who accepts a glass of wine off a gold tray from a serving girl.

"Sit down. We are not done with our discussion, princess," Ceto orders calmly with a terrifying grin stretched across her features.

Jo thinks about resisting but instead sits as instructed.

"Now the court would not be happy if I didn't consider them in the decision. But I offer a solution. You are aware of the rebel situation I have in the northwest? A group of freefolk men and women calling themselves the nation of Oceanus." Ceto explains the free state with a look of disgust, as if this rebellion hasn't been going on for over a hundred years.

"The country of Oceanus is an independent state free from Lycos," Jo corrects. A snort issues from in front of her, and she notices Thetis laughing into her wine.

"Their situation is not authorized by the empire," Ceto snaps, "and thus they are traitors to the crown. So I propose a trade."

Jo has an idea of where this is going, and she doesn't hold her breath when her thoughts come to fruition.

"You help me take back a piece of my empire, and I'll help you take back your queendom. I know you have trade negotiations helping Oceanus stay in power and have been supplying them with border barriers and weapons in exchange for their fishing cove export. All I ask is that you help me get a small army in and let me take back what's mine. As soon as you're back in power, of course."

"They're free people, Empress Ceto," Jo refuses. "They

fought for their independence and they won fairly. I cannot take their land in exchange for mine. It wouldn't be right."

Applause fills the throne room and Ceto and Jo both look to see Thetis giving the princess a resounding ovation.

What surprises Jo even more is the fact that Ceto says nothing. She merely glares at the elf as if Thetis is immune to Ceto's power.

"Then I'm afraid I can't help you," the empress states, "neighbor or not."

Empress Ceto rises, descending the steps from the throne. She walks past Thetis, shooting daggers at the elven countess, but continues on.

"Wait!" Jo shouts, standing.

Ceto stops but doesn't face her.

"Wait," Jo repeats.

"Yes?" Ceto drawls, turning very slowly toward the blonde.

"Perhaps..."

"Yes...?"

"We can discuss this more over dinner?"

Ceto grins widely and claps her hands in excitement. "Oh splendid, darling, I knew we could come to an arrangement. I look forward to discussing our alliance. There should be a dress laid out for you in your chambers, I'm sure you're tired of your rags."

"Thank you, Your Majesty," Jo mutters with a shallow bow.

Ceto nods, acknowledging her lackluster gratitude, and this time continues the rest of her way out the jade doors.

Once Jo is behind locked doors, Ceto summons one of her guards closer to her.

"Send a message via magic mirror. I want to know who's leading the Arethusian coup"—Ceto shoots a glance back at the jade doors—"and who has the better offer to best serve our empire."

The guard nods, and Ceto resumes her stroll down the hall.

AN AFFAIR TO REMEMBER

Joana

THE SOLDIERS WHO STAYED behind come closer to escort Jo to the apartment, but the countess, who is still lounging on the large pillow near the throne, orders them not to move just yet.

"You lasted longer than I thought you would," Thetis teases.

She doesn't try to stand and Jo steps closer to the countess, looking down at her.

"You're a countess?" Jo questions.

She looks the elven woman over with a bit of disbelief.

"Of Lycos," Thetis confirms. "You can spare me the shock. I'm just as conniving and backstabbing as anyone here. And that's all you need to succeed in the empire."

"That's comforting," Jo sighs.

"It should be. So you're doing all of this for red?"

Jo raises her brow, confused.

Thetis rolls her eyes. "The pirate we all came here to save. Well, you did. I came here to pay a debt."

"To Venus?"

"No, to the dark, handsome bald man in a vest," Thetis snarks. "Yes, of course Venus. Or did you miss our little entrance?"

Jo snorts and steps back, annoyed. There's no need to stand here and be insulted. Jo starts to walk toward the side exit, but she's stopped again, this time by a standing Thetis, who swiftly grabs her arm none too gently.

"You don't want to make demon bargains with Ceto."

"I don't really have a choice," Jo barks, wrenching her arm out of Thetis's grasp.

"What are you really doing here?" Jo continues.

"Well, to make a long story short. I'm doing what Captain Lara is trying to do. Just empire style. I'm trying to end the slave trade."

Jo doesn't believe her.

Thetis frowns, noting the disbelief on Jo's face, so she explains, "I was kicked out of Erebos, the capital city of the elves, for my taste in magic. I've worked my way into this court through sweat, blood, and sex. Arethusa needs you. Your father isn't as strong as you think," Thetis mutters but forces her hand onto Jo's mouth to stop her from objecting.

"Don't argue, just listen. If you help Ceto destroy Oceanus, you destroy a large haven for outcast elves—"

Jo rips Thetis's hand off her mouth. "I don't want to—"

"Then don't!"

"How else will I take back my throne?"

"With me," Thetis tells her. "I can help you take back Arethusa. I won't say how, but if you decide that becoming a queen instead of a pawn under Ceto is more important, then you can find me at my tower at the center of the Seams."

Thetis reaches past Jo, handing the two remaining soldiers a slip of paper that Jo realizes is money. They both take it easily, never casting Jo a glance. Thetis turns away, heading toward the same jade doors that Ceto left through, when Jo calls after her.

"What about Shea?"

"What about her?" Thetis laughs.

"If I turn away from Ceto, could you help me keep her safe?"

Thetis is quiet. Her expression is thoughtful, and when she finally speaks, it's stilted, as if she is choosing her words carefully. "The thing about elves. There's a reason we live in the woods. We don't do well in cages. No matter how pretty the bars may be. But yes. I could keep her safe for you."

Jo hears what Thetis is saying. But the last sentence takes a thousand weights off her shoulders. She smiles widely and tries not to laugh when Thetis bows dramatically before exiting the throne room. As tempting an offer as it is, how can Jo know whether Thetis is telling the truth? She said it herself. She's conniving, cunning, and has backstabbed whomever she needed to make her way to the top.

Jo supposes it comes down to the lesser of two evils, and she already knows what that is. She gestures for the guards to lead her on to the compartment. It's not long before they navigate through the winding corridor and end up in an apartment of what Jo is sure are a part of Ceto's chambers.

Jo mumbles a thank you to both men and steps into the sitting room, absently noting the directions to her bedchamber from one of the soldiers.

The compartment entrance shuts behind her. She takes a couple steps inside, and when she looks up, she sees Venus kissing Shea by the dining table.

The kiss appears to be short and chaste, but Jo's heart shudders in her chest. Her stomach flips and she fears she'll throw up right there and then. Jo's Shea, and the blonde bitch, Venus, break apart. Venus spots her immediately. The other blonde notifies Shea to Jo's presence, and the elf turns toward her smiling in what looks like pleasant surprise. The pirate doesn't even respond like she's done anything wrong.

Jo can feel her blood boiling in her veins. She wants to take off one of her boots and launch it at Shea's head, but instead she stays poised and calm. She answers the captain's question the best she can about what happened with Ceto.

Jo explains she'll talk to her later and escapes from the room quickly. Once she passes through the arch leading to the hall of doors, she slips behind the wall, spying on the two women. She listens to the rest of their conversation and watches Venus leave.

Jo tries to excuse the kiss as nothing more than a goodbye, but it only resolves her feelings. She doesn't want her pirate kissing anyone else. She doesn't want anyone taking Shea away from her. She departs as quietly as she can, slipping into her room to change for dinner.

THE LAST SUPPER

Shea

THEY REEMERGE FROM THEIR ROOMS in formal clothing a couple hours later. Jo could hear shouting from the room to her left as she was getting ready. She could just barely pick out Shea's voice before the elf quieted down, and with reluctance, Jo went back to getting dressed.

Two elven slaves arrived to help the princess get ready, and before Shea, she might not have thought much about them. But now it's almost painful as she silently allows them to dress her. She can't help but admire the dress Ceto picked for her. The pale blue looks almost white in the right candlelight. The only thing she doesn't like about the dress is the fact that it's an unusual two-piece.

She wraps her arms across her stomach, feeling exposed. The top bodice stops right under her rib cage, the fabric covered in soft tulle that accentuates her breasts. The sleeves cap her shoulders and white roses made of silk follow the neckline. The bottom of the dress rests comfortably on her hips and flows all the way to the ground in a small train. The way it shimmers reminds Jo of scales, making her feel like a mermaid.

Which then also makes her wonder: Are mermaids real? And if so, has Shea ever seen one?

The attendants do her hair, braiding it into a bun just above her nape, and then place a tiara of white roses on her head. They add some glitter to her cheeks, and she feels like her old self again. She looks in the mirror and she likes what she sees.

When she steps out of her room, she looks to her right and sees Caen emerge from his room in fine brown robes, the same color as rusty clay cliffs. Gold patterns are etched along the pant legs and down the front of the shirt. It looks comfortable yet extravagant.

Jo can tell he's uncomfortable though, as he keeps tripping in his formal shoes while trying to close the door behind him. She offers him a tentative wave when he sees her, and the tension seems to roll off his shoulders. He steps toward her with a determined expression. She braces herself for an expected yelling match, but instead he offers his arm with a gentle smile and gives her a nodding bow. She takes the peace offering and returns the smile. They have an understanding.

They're just about to go out to the sitting room to wait when the door to their left opens to the sound of cursing. A redheaded ball of fury is pushed out of the chamber. She stumbles, trying to catch her balance on her heeled shoes. As much as Jo feels angry about the kiss she walked in on, she can't help but notice how beautiful Shea is.

She's leaning against the wall, taking deep breaths as if trying to will herself to stand. Green eyes shine through her furious features, red curls framing her face. The half-up braid takes none of the volume away from the full body of Shea's curly hair, and Jo feels her breath catch as she notices the small tiara that's been placed on the captain's head. It's built in the same fashion as the consort's crown of Arethusa. Carved ivory impersonating white coral leading into two sapphires representing Poseidon and Amphitrite. Silver waves connect the ivory together and hold the sapphires in place. It's so well done that it makes Jo wonder if this is the real tiara that's supposed to be in the royal vault of Arethusa and Ceto has somehow stolen it.

She unconsciously curls her nails into Caen's arm and he grunts in pain. The sound snaps Jo out of her thoughts and she apologizes. She knows what Ceto's doing, and she doesn't appreciate the manipulation. But the surprise makeover doesn't end there as Jo takes in the dress they've forced Shea into.

The purple is the same shade as the Lycon flag. It's sheer and hugs the curves of Shea's figure in a tailored A-line. There's a purple silk slip underneath the sparkling see-through material, but it doesn't do much for Shea's modesty. Jo gulps as the dress causes a warm feeling to pool in the pit of her stomach. But that warmth quickly drains away when Shea finally straightens. She pulls her shoulders back and stands tall, turning to face Jo and Caen head-on. Caen drops Jo's arm in shock. Jo feels her entire body go rigid.

Shea doesn't really look at either one of them but at the wall behind their heads, as if unable to meet their eyes.

The dress is cut low and it displays the brand that Ceto carved into Shea's chest years ago. That warm feeling is now replaced by nausea as Jo takes in the silver choker, a collar, wrapped around the elf's neck. The message isn't subtle. All those slaves they'd seen earlier in the throne room flash before Jo's vision, and she remembers they all were wearing leather collars around their necks. Hanging from the silver choker is the cruelest piece of it all, the Pearl of Lycos. As if the brand isn't enough, Ceto makes her final point. Shea belongs to Lycos.

Jo takes a hesitant step closer to her. She reaches her fingers out, grasping the pearl lightly, and Shea doesn't even flinch. Jo can feel Caen step up behind her. Now they know what the earlier screaming had been about.

"I'll kill her," Jo snarls.

She wants to rip this thing off Shea's neck. The tiara is a mockery, another point made by Ceto, and Jo hates the possessive thrill she gets from seeing Shea wear it.

"Not if I do first," Shea growls, looking up into Jo's eyes.

They burn like the green fire in the palace, but beneath it all there's a dull edge to them, riddled with defeat. Jo can't help but feel she had a hand in putting it there.

"If she thinks I'll have anything to do with her, she's mistaken. I won't see you treated this way," Jo seethes.

She drops her hand from the pearl, turning on her heel to find Ceto, but Shea stops her by her arm with an empty smile.

"We all have our parts to play tonight, princess. Even you. We need her help," Shea reminds her.

Jo wants to object and tell her about Thetis, but Shea speaks again.

"I'm fine. My pride's a little wounded, but we can do this. Besides, I like the tiara." Shea winks. "The ladies said it was Arethusian."

Jo looks up at the ceiling, taking a deep breath, trying to cool her emotions. Shea's comment on the tiara makes her chuckle softly.

"It is," Jo confirms, pushing a curl back from Shea's face. "The consort to the queen traditionally wears a tiara or crown like that."

"Fitting then, don't you think," Shea teases.

A sense of calm washes over Jo and she admires how Shea pushes forward. If Shea won't let this ensemble affect her, then Jo will keep her head up as well.

Caen has been watching their exchange silently, and he smiles, pulling them into a bear hug. Once he releases them, Shea offers Jo her arm, which she takes with a grin. She leads her into the sitting room with Caen following behind.

Ceto is sitting in a large chair with a high back, emulating a throne—it must have been put there while they were all getting ready. Lyle is here as well and he instructs them to bow before the empress. As they bow, Jo catches sight of Thetis lounging on the couch.

Ceto is also in new apparel. She's wearing a large headpiece that looks like the sun is sitting upon her crown, with spikes spiraling off the design. Her dress is bright yellow, and the way it moves on Ceto's body, it's as if gold had been melted onto her skin and cast into a dress. It looks obscenely heavy.

Thetis, however, is in a more reserved evening gown. Her hair falls loosely down her back, and her dress is a soft gray that reminds Jo of the dress Shea wore on their date on Orena. Instead of shoes and heels like the rest of them, Thetis's feet are bare except for some kind of jewelry that crawls from her toes up her legs like jeweled vines.

"You all look splendid," Ceto remarks, leering at Shea. "I know how much you admire the pearl, my dear. So I thought I might lend it to you for the evening."

"Well it does look much better on me, that's for sure," Shea rebuffs.

Thetis chuckles at the comment and laughs harder when Ceto shoots her a glare.

"Oh, lighten up, Ceto, the girl's got spirit. I can see why you want her. Personally, I think she'd do much better under my wings," Thetis teases.

She moves her legs off the couch and offers the new party a seat. Caen takes the offer and Shea goes to sit next to Caen, but Lyle steps in front of her. He points to a large pillow next to Ceto's throne at the empress's side.

Shea tries to move around him but the guards along the walls take a step in, so Shea relents with a sharp breath, not wanting to cause any trouble. She reluctantly takes her seat at Ceto's side.

Jo wants to scream, but she bites her lip and sits gracefully in a chair opposite the couch.

"You're too easy on your property, Thetis, this one would need a firm touch." Ceto grins, acknowledging the bid for Shea's life.

Jo wants to wipe that smug look off Ceto's face.

"Of course the disfigurement of her shoulder will lessen the price." Ceto frowns. "Unfortunately I let my temper get the best of me. Though, I believe you were a part of the law that passed outlawing the branding of our slaves. Isn't that right, Countess?"

Thetis takes a goblet off the tray that Lyle is serving around the group. She takes a sip before answering more calmly than Jo would have. "It damages the merchandise, C, it's bad for business."

And Caen can't take it anymore. The room erupts into a debate about the humanity of branding slaves, but Jo doesn't participate.

Instead she watches Thetis, who casually puts her opinion in, taking regular sips from her glass. By the middle of the conversation Thetis has almost convinced everyone in the room of her stance on abolishing branding without sounding like a free elf supporter.

Jo glances toward Shea, who is staring at Thetis with an arched brow. She must feel Jo's gaze because she turns, catching the princess's eye, and shoots her a weary smile that Jo returns.

But watching Thetis makes Jo wonder if a life of nobility could be possible for Shea. Thetis is fighting from the shadows, but still fighting nevertheless.

Jo smirks into her own goblet, and scoffs. Shea could never be this subtle.

"Enough politics for the evening," Ceto groans.

She reaches down and grabs Shea's arm, standing from her chair. She pulls Shea up with her, catching the captain off guard as she struggles to get her feet under her in those ridiculous heels.

Ceto releases her once they're both standing, and Shea rights herself quickly, not wanting to add to the humiliation by falling over. Everyone waits for Ceto's next move; the empress claps her hands together and grins.

"So? Who's hungry?"

SAY SOMETHING

Shea

IT CAN'T GET ANY WORSE. Shea doesn't think she can handle it if it does.

If Ceto isn't terrible enough, the humiliating collar and traitorous Lycon countess only makes matters worse. Those high-rise windows are suddenly looking pretty enticing. She tries to resist sending daggers at the countess, as Jo ogles Thetis like someone who is siren-spelled.

It leaves a heavy feeling in the pit of her stomach.

The collar feels warm around her neck. There's panic in the back of her head telling her it's too tight, but she keeps her hands in her lap and ignores the urge to reach up and adjust the damn thing. It's not worth the attention it would cause.

After Ceto's dramatic announcement, dinner is finally served. Shea is placed on the empress's left-hand side with Thetis across from her and Caen to Shea's left, leaving Jo on the other side next to the countess. So Jo gets to sit right next to the new, hot, and free elf. Fantastic.

At the very least, the conversation has moved on from Shea's auction and brand.

It's bad enough being forced into this dress and made to wear a collar like some pleasure elf. Though so far, with how this whole evening is turning out, she wonders whether she should slip one of the dinner knives into her dress. Just in case Caen and Jo are killed and Shea needs to slit her wrists sometime into the night to escape Ceto's insane plans.

The empress begins to discuss the invasion with Jo somewhere between the soup and salad. Shea tries to listen, but she finds her attention waning. The conversation dissolves into the background.

She pushes her fork around her food, trying not to squish the tiny octopus still moving on her plate. So this is what royal cuisine looks like. Shea would take Strom's meals any day.

"Hey," Caen whispers, catching her attention.

His voice is quiet next to her and none of the others look up from their conversation across the table.

"Hey," Shea replies.

She wonders if she can sneak this poor octopus off her plate without anyone noticing.

"I'm sorry I didn't tell you," he says.

Shea shrugs and then looks over at him, careful not to bring attention to themselves. "I understand why you didn't."

He tries to explain anyway. "I knew that if we came empty-handed she'd have you gone faster than I could think of a plan out of the castle."

"I get it," Shea reassures him. "I mean, I didn't at the time, but I get it. It makes sense and you gave us time, which is what we needed."

"We're going to get out of here," Caen promises.

Shea tries to smile.

"Maybe, but if I don't, it's okay. We had a good run, you and I."

"We did but we've still got a lot more to do."

Caen's hand finds hers under the table, and she squeezes it before focusing back in on the conversation in front of them.

"I'll need at least thirty to forty men to make sure I make it into the castle. I don't know who's still loyal, so I'll need the extra manpower to hold them off while I confront the council," Jo explains.

Thetis nods.

"That sounds about right," she agrees.

Jo shoots the elf a big grin, which hits Shea right in the chest.

"It'd be possible to spare that many," Ceto begins but stops when a messenger comes through from the sitting room into the dining area.

He bows before handing Ceto a letter.

Ceto opens it, not bothering to hide it, and reads the contents silently in front of them. It takes her a few moments.

"Yes indeed," Ceto mutters.

She hands the letter back to the messenger, who takes it away and leaves.

Shea notices Thetis and Lyle making eye contact but chooses to ignore it, as it seems everyone is doing in this place. She even thinks she remembers one of the ladies' maids who dressed her talking about Lyle.

"It seems we won't be making an agreement after all," Ceto states and snaps her fingers.

The guards step off the walls and close around the dining table, keeping them all seated.

Shea tenses, as does Caen, while Thetis and Jo look around warily.

"I don't understand," Jo says, curling her hand around the fork on the table. Clever girl, Shea notes.

"It seems I've been given a better offer by the resistance in Arethusa."

"You know who it is," Shea growls, leaning toward Ceto, but a guard thrusts a spear in between them and places a rough hand on her shoulder to keep her still.

"Yes, I do. And I'm sorry, Joana, but it seems that they're quite insistent on you not returning. They've offered to pay handsomely for your death."

"You backstabbing bitch," Jo yells, slamming her fists on the table.

"Oh, darling, no, our empress is only doing what's best for

us," Thetis tells her sweetly.

Thetis calls Lyle over, who has the wine jug, and lifts Ceto and her glass up for him to pour.

"Thetis is right, it wouldn't be fair to my country if I didn't consider our options." Ceto nods in approval, taking the glass from Thetis. She takes a deep sip.

"Arethusa will never agree to help take back Oceanus for Lycos," Jo declares, to which Ceto laughs in her annoying, childish giggle.

"Yes they will, because they won't have you. I'll tell you this, my dear, you would be a much more challenging opponent, but I think I'll stick with this new ruler." Ceto laughs, but it sounds off as she slurs the last word of her statement.

Jo and Shea catch each other's eye as the princess notices it too.

"Your Majesty, are you okay?" Thetis asks.

"Why wouldn't I...be?" Ceto responds, but her speech sounds slow.

"I don't think she's feeling so good," Shea remarks, wrapping her hand tightly around the dining knife.

"Something's off...guards..." Ceto tries to call, but her body collapses forward and her head lands heavily in her dressed salad.

The guards tense around them. Shea grabs the knife, turning to stab the guard that has his hand on her, but the guard next to him runs him through instead. In fact, it happens around the room with various guards killing the others without so much as a word. The room remains silent as no one is really sure what to do.

"Right in her salad!" Thetis is laughing at Ceto, bent over in her seat chuckling hard, and Shea notices Lyle is smiling as well.

"Hang on, what in Hades just happened?" Shea questions.

"We're breaking you out," Thetis singsongs.

She snaps her fingers, and the guards get to work checking the halls and removing Ceto from the table to one of the rooms.

"Okay but why?" Caen responds, not sure whether to move from his seat.

"Because we have a deal," Jo states, standing along with Thetis and shaking her hand.

Jo comes around the table to Shea. She gives her a hug and Shea returns it the best she can, still utterly confused, dropping the butter knife back onto the table.

"You need to get going, ma'am, the sedative will only last for so long and we need to have everything stationed for when she returns so she doesn't suspect you," Lyle informs her.

The remaining guards signal an okay, and one comes over with a large cloak that he hands to Shea.

"No," Shea objects, refusing the cloak, "we're not going anywhere with you until someone tells me what the bloody Underdeep is going on."

"She's rather thick, dear," Thetis drawls to Jo, who glares at the countess. "Look I'm the same as you. I want to help Joana get back on the throne. I just happen to achieve what we want through politics instead of thug work."

Shea can feel her temper flaring, but she tries to keep it at bay for Jo's sake.

"So what? You thought you'd sedate the empress and get away with it?"

"It wouldn't be the first time." Thetis winks.

"And the reason we don't kill her now?" Caen asks.

"There are worse evils in Lycos than that bitch," Thetis utters, glaring at the brute.

"Look, Shea, she's a little unorthodox," Jo says, sticking up for Thetis, "but I trust what she has to say. She can help."

Shea looks at Jo, really looks, and try as she might, she can't seem to refuse that beautiful face.

"And who will she be suspecting instead? The one who drugged her, I mean?" Shea asks, taking the cloak hesitantly with Jo still partially in her arms.

"I believe your friend Marlo volunteered to take the fall."

Thetis laughs.

Caen smiles wickedly in approval, pushing back from the table. "That's good enough for me."

He goes and grabs all their clothes from the three back bed-chambers.

"My lady, we're clear to go," the guard alerts, and Thetis hums in acknowledgment.

"We best get going then."

"Wait." Jo stops, her hands reaching up to Shea's neck to take off the collar. "We're not going anywhere with that still attached."

"Oh no," Shea remarks, covering the pearl with her hand and stepping away, "I'm not losing this thing a second time. Regardless of what it's attached to." Shea chuckles, letting Jo know she's okay.

Jo raises her eyebrow but shrugs and relents, letting Shea keep the pearl.

Caen gets to the door first, following one of the guards out of the compartment.

Thetis follows behind flanked by two soldiers at her sides and Lyle directly behind her.

Shea slides the cloak over her shoulders and lifts the hood to cover her face. She holds out her hand to Jo, who hesitates but takes it anyway. The final guard holds up the rear. It's slow going, but Lyle directs them quickly through the halls; they stop periodically to let loyal guards pass. Shea's step stutters when they see a group of slaves up ahead, worried they'll sound an alarm. But as soon as the slaves see Thetis, they simply bow and let them pass. They're going deeper and deeper into the castle and Shea shoots Jo a worried glance.

"We're only going farther in, how are we going to get out?"

"Patience, my dear," Thetis responds, overhearing Shea's remark.

Finally they make their way down and through what Shea begins to realize is the slave quarters. Thin blankets are scattered along the stone and there's no furniture to be seen. It doesn't take long for her to understand that the blankets are beds. Some are cushioned with straw underneath.

They're treated like animals. Dogs locked in the basement of an extravagant empire. The farther they go, the more slaves they pass, ages ranging from children to elders, some even on their deathbeds. All of the children smile and whisper, running up to chatter at Thetis and Lyle about something or another.

Shea can overhear their words and the language shocks her. They're speaking elvish. She can only pick out a few words, but the language washes over her and suddenly the collar around her neck feels much tighter.

"She's like their fairy godmother," Jo whispers, and Shea nods in reluctant agreement.

Even the adults bow as Thetis walks past; the two guards at her side take off at a small signal from her, and Shea notices bags hanging on their backs.

The soldiers take out bread and other nourishment, handing the supplies to the adults to pass out. One of the guards even hands a small boy a doll.

"We're here," Lyle announces.

The slave quarters are the dungeon, Shea realizes, when she sees the inner river that runs through the palace at the other end of the castle. The smell of rotting wood and the sea fills her nostrils. Shea can't help but breathe it in, relieved. A couple elven men stand close to the river where two wooden boats float on the surface.

"There's no way to pass the gate," Thetis explains, turning to the trio, "so you have to go under. The underground moat from the castle goes through the old evacuation canals and leads into the Seams. It's funny what something forgotten can do."

As much as Shea hates to admit it, she's starting to like this woman. They're loaded onto the boat, Caen, and three of the guards in the first and then the other guard, Thetis, Jo, and Shea in the second. Lyle stands on the stone bank alone with two slaves waiting at the turn wheel to open the gate leading to the canal.

"You're not coming?" Shea asks, but she can already see it on his face.

He smiles at her and pulls his shirt down, revealing his left peck. It's covered with the same brand carved into Shea's chest, but she notices his was done through burning, not with a knife.

"My place is here."

"Thank you," Shea tells him, and he gives her a small bow before gesturing for the two elven men to raise the gate.

The gate rises slowly, and the guards in the first boat and the guard and Shea in the second boat pick up the oars and start to paddle through. The gate shuts behind them, and a sense of relief runs through Shea as she realizes that her life could have ended a very different way today. They paddle on through the caverns. The darkness growing as they float away from the light of the slave quarters. Thetis and Caen light the two candles attached to the bows of the boats so they can see where they're going.

The rocklike cavern is filled with old rooms and irons off on the stone banks surrounding the river. Shea can tell that this once used to be a part of the palace. A giant staircase of stone leading to what's now the ceiling is off to the side and skeletons scatter the edges on platforms of stone. As they get closer to the mouth of the cavern, rapids lay in the way between them and their exit. They navigate through as best they can, water extinguishing the lights on both boats until they're left in total darkness. Jo goes to relight the candle, but Thetis stops her.

"We're almost there."

They float in uncomfortable silence, and then Shea sees the opening. Gates block the exit, surrounded by locked chains, but they continue heading straight for it. The first boat smacks into the gate and the guard quickly gets to work undoing the chains until he calls for Caen to help him push it open.

The gate opens with a screech but no one comes running. It's dark outside, and they slip through quietly, the guard stopping their boat so that he can close up the gate.

Shea recognizes where they are as they row down the canal. They're in the Seam. Small shelters of wood planks lean against stone houses that line the edge of the canal. Animals roam over narrow walkways and what look like makeshift bridges across the river. It's quiet, but Shea can feel dozens of eyes watching, waiting for something they can steal or kill, anything that they can trade for money or food.

They keep paddling down the river until they come to the heart of the Seam. A black tower, nowhere near the size of the palace but certainly large, lies in the center.

Soldiers guard the perimeter and the gate is covered in white roses much like the flowers Jo is wearing tonight on her dress. Shea decides to ignore that little detail and instead focuses on trying to get out of the small boat without falling into the canal from the stupid heels.

As soon as she's on what looks to be black granite, she kicks off the obnoxious heels and stomps barefoot over to Caen. She grabs both of her black boots out of his arms, throws them on the ground and slides her feet in, reveling at the comfort.

She can hear Jo laughing at her from behind, but she doesn't pay her any mind. The white rose gates open and Thetis walks through, escorted by one of her guards; the rest disperse toward the perimeter.

Caen shakes his head at Shea's display but gestures for her to go ahead.

Jo follows next to Caen.

The entry hall is magnificent. Black columns of marble extend around a circular entrance with grand steps leading up into a foyer. The ground is pearlescent and the room itself is white, which creates quite an offset from the rest of Lycos. A woman in a nice dress appears, running down the grand staircase, her hair pulled up so her elven ears are easily identified. She lands in front of Thetis and gives the countess a quick bow before ascertaining whom her guests might be.

Shea watches warily as other elven workers on an elevated level look down over the railing, staring at them. After a hurried conversation, the older woman takes off back up the stairs and Thetis turns to the trio with a delicate grin.

"My housemaid is setting up rooms for the night for all of you to sleep, and then tomorrow we'll get you set up with a carriage to take you to Arethusa."

"I thought you didn't believe in the slave trade," Shea comments gruffly, eyeing the servants who all quickly step away from the railing when Thetis looks up.

"None of these people are forced to be here and all of them are paid. For many, leaving Lycos isn't an option. As I said, you'll find choices in Lycos tend to be between rocks and hard places. I just so happen to be one of the rocks that offer protection, you never know when you might need that," Thetis responds.

Her eyes flash at Shea coldly as if she resents Shea's accusation, but Shea holds her ground.

"She didn't mean anything by it," Jo interjects, looking worriedly between the two.

Shea glares at Jo's insinuation but keeps silent.

"I'm sure." Thetis nods. "Now while Azula readies the bedchambers, why don't we retire to my drawing room. There are some things that need to be discussed."

Without another word she turns away, and Jo follows without question. Caen looks to Shea for approval, and she waves him on. As much as Shea might not like her, Thetis is still her rescuer, and the least Shea can do is act grateful.

Up the stairs, the foyer is no less grand than the entrance. The light is warm and, unlike the green fire in the palace, a normal orange. The farther into the tower they get, the more the interior begins to change. Walls of dark green cover the tower and rugs that look and almost feel like soft grass line the floors. Exotic plants that Shea hasn't seen in years line the walls in various places. There are paintings of the gods in between arched windows and Shea stops right outside the drawing room, the last door down this hall, as she spots a painted history of the elves. The painting depicts Erebos in its prime with elven priests teaching magic to the children. She looks to the next picture, farther away from the door, and begins to turn in a circle—all of the images are of elven lore. At the end of the hall, she notices one picture in particular hanging alone on a large wall.

It draws her closer and she knows what it is without having to look at the plaque underneath. The blue vines weaving around the dark circle of black are as haunting as they are inviting. The priests and priestesses are standing around the black entrance to the Underdeep, the realm of the sea gods.

"Did you ever see it before you were taken?"

Shea jumps, not expecting to see Thetis standing so close; she looks back but everyone else is inside the drawing room.

"Don't worry, I have a fire roaring and tea being served. We won't be bothered out here."

Thetis steps forward and places her hand on the painting, brushing it with a soft sigh.

"No," Shea answers the question from before, "I was too young to be claimed, and I don't remember other claimings. I've never had the courage to really go back."

"Even if you did, you're an outsider now. They'd never show it to you. I was once a priestess though; in my teens, I washed the vines and brought tribute. I prayed every morning to the gods."

"What was it like? Growing up there," Shea can't stop herself from asking.

"Strict. But wonderful," Thetis murmurs. "We are an old race, we were here long before they"—Thetis gestures vaguely back toward the room—"and if we're not entirely killed off like game for sport, we may be here long after. We are the gods' people, their first."

"Which is why we were given magic, I know the story. My foster mother told it to me when I was small," Shea interrupts, remembering the hour-long lessons that Dari would make her sit through, practicing herbal and plant magic, but it was never Shea's specialty.

"Though we are discouraged from using it to its fullest potential," Thetis mutters, casting her eyes down. Shea shoots her a questioning look, but she doesn't have to voice her query, as Thetis continues.

"I was banished from Erebos for the practice of Underdeep magic; did your foster mother teach you about that?"

Shea can remember the tales. The claiming happens when elves present with magic. They are forced to go into the Underdeep, the realm of the sea gods. Their own elven people send down children who will become priests and priestesses to the gods of old. They're then claimed by their patron and sent back. Some elves never come back the same; at least from the tales Dari would tell. While in the Underdeep, elves would see dark magic or accidentally stumble upon spells too powerful for the mortal world and were cast out for trying to wield the forbidden enchantments. The Elder Council hoped that by severing the condemned elf's connection to Erebos and the Underdeep portal, it would weaken their magic, but that was not always the case.

"I was claimed by Triton, the son of Queen Mother Amphitrite and All Father Poseidon. It was a huge honor to my family," Thetis tells her, recalling the events from long ago.

"What was it like?"

"What?"

"In the Underdeep?" Shea asks, staring into the black paint on the canvas; the deeper she looks the more she feels like she can see eyes staring back.

"Dark, suffocating at first, and a cold that seeps deep into your bones. But then you see it and it's like nothing I can describe. It's magic, Shea, and it's very real."

Shivers crawl down Shea's spine and she wraps her arms around herself, staring at the painting.

"When you're claimed by Triton"—Thetis's voice breaks

slightly, but she seems to catch herself and continues—"you have to claim your conch shell. You learn to manipulate water through sound. But in order to get your shell, you have to travel to the white cliffs of Achelous, the crying god cliffs."

"Sirens," Shea whispers.

"Yes." Thetis laughs in approval but the sound is chilling. "They're children of Triton. You have to convince one to give you a shell without it killing you. I met one, but I made a mistake. Instead of her killing me, however, she saw something in me," Thetis says with irony, as if that last statement is an inside joke. "She taught me how to access my own magic. And once I learned how to manipulate water through the shell, I learned to manipulate people."

"The council found out, I assume."

"Yes. I grew greedy with the siren power, and so I was banished. I found myself in Lycos and was taken into Ceto's court once they knew of my abilities. I committed many crimes against my people. Our people."

Shea doesn't bother to correct her, too enraptured in the story. But... "Why tell me all this?"

"Something's coming, Shea. And I feel like you're to be a part of it. As is Joana. There's power in you, but you shield yourself from your roots. Someone is calling to you, and you've used their magic while neglecting their claim."

"I don't understand."

"We are the gods' people, we serve them. Triton put me back on my path by giving me a great blessing," Thetis tells her.

They stand close, face-to-face. "I see how you look at her. Jo," Thetis clarifies. "I have no need or want to come between you two if you have fears. I gave my oath as a priestess and regardless of what I want, I belong to Triton."

It takes Shea a moment to process this information. What Thetis is saying is big, bigger than her, and there's just something about it that Shea's gut tells her she needs to believe.

"Thank you," Shea finally says.

Thetis nods, smiling warmly and more genuinely than Shea has seen of her so far. The smile fades though, and that plastic one Shea finds familiar once again resides on the countess's face.

"You need to face what's inside of you, Shea. Because you're more than protection spells and illusions."

"How did you—"

But Thetis walks away toward the drawing room. Shea stays behind to give herself a moment to compose herself. She takes a deep breath, glancing back at the Underdeep painting, and then heads to the door. When she steps inside, her nose is filled with a sweet scent of flowers and fresh air. There's a waterfall on the far wall, and Caen and Jo are sitting together by the fireplace with mugs in their hands, speaking with Thetis, who is sitting in one of the armchairs across from them.

But what surprises her even more is the person sitting on the ground in front of the fire.

"Aster?"

"Shea!" Aster yells, standing quickly.

He runs over to give her a huge hug. She stands in shock, blinking over his shoulder at Jo, who's laughing, and then pulls him away to look at him.

"How did you get here? Are you alright? Where's James?"

"Calm down, mother hen, he's fine," Caen chuckles, taking a sip of his tea.

Shea scowls at him.

"I'm fine, James is fine," Aster explains. "Thetis brought me."

"Tero was supposed to keep you two safe. I locked you in the room." Shea glares, placing her hands on her hips.

"Well. Um, I may have blasted your door...using some old blasting powder I had under my bed. But don't worry, I told Tero and James that I'd put the door back on and clean the scorch marks when I got back. James decided to stay behind to take care of Tero and the ship, what with you and Caen gone."

"Your Mister Tero practically begged me to take him off his hands, and junior here wouldn't take no for an answer—something he must get from his mother," Thetis huffs, rolling her eyes in exaggeration.

"Captain," Aster corrects at the same time Shea growls, "Do I look old enough to be his mother?"

The rest of the party in the room doesn't answer, but Shea can't help but pull Aster in for another hug.

A blur catches Shea's attention as the housemaid from before comes running into the room. She whispers something into Thetis's ear. Then the maid runs right back out as if she's scared to be alone with anyone she doesn't know.

"Ceto is awake and furious. Her guards are combing the palace as we speak, as well as sending reinforcements to the docks."

"Then we need to leave," Shea states, pulling away from Aster but keeping her arm over his shoulders.

Aster slips his arm around her waist.

She continues, "Our ship is not safe, nor our crew."

Caen agrees, standing, but Aster cuts him off, looking up at Shea. "Actually. The ship isn't there anymore."

"What?" Jo exclaims.

"They left?" Caen worriedly asks, but Aster shakes his head.

"No! Countess Thetis managed to get a message to us. James got us out of the dock and now they're heading to Oceanus to wait for us at the major port."

"How did you—" Shea asks once again.

Thetis smirks. "I have my ways."

"So they're safe?" Jo reiterates.

"For now," Thetis answers.

"Good," Caen interjects, setting his mug down on the coffee table in front of him. "We'll start fresh tomorrow and head up to Oceanus. We can sneak up there and hopefully get the Underdeep out of here."

Shea breaks away from Aster, stepping toward Caen and Jo.

"Actually I was thinking we send the crew a message via Caeruleus."

There's a meow from up above and at this point Shea really

isn't surprised.

Caeruleus swoops down from wherever he's been hiding and lands on one of the large branches of the tree next to the waterfall. Shea hurries over to him, scratching his head and laughing as he purrs and tries to paw at the pearl resting on her neck.

"Caeruleus. Have them meet us in Arethusa. It'll be faster to ride straight there than make a stop in Oceanus," Shea orders the Lionbird, and he looks about to take off when Caen whistles.

Caeruleus stops and Shea turns to her old friend.

"I'm sorry what?" Caen growls, standing with his hands on his hips.

"What?" Shea responds.

"You want to continue on to Arethusa? Are you out of your mind?"

"We have to get Jo back to the queendom before the coronation."

"It's over. We have no manpower, no way into the castle, it's time to pack up and go home," Caen states, his voice rising as he steps around the couch.

He storms over and stops once he's looming over Shea, his lip curled back and his eyebrows furrowed.

"There have been setbacks, yes, but we've all agreed that getting Jo back on the throne is best for everyone," Shea argues defensively, crossing her arms over her chest.

Jo stays silent but does stand, watching from the couch.

"We don't mettle in land folk affairs. That's the rule, the one rule that every pirate with salt understands. Paetre understood it, so why the bloody Underdeep don't you?"

"I'll remind you," Shea orders, her voice deadly calm, "Paetre is dead and I am captain."

"No. This whole trip your mind has been clouded. You're right, you're not Paetre, but you're certainly not yourself. This whole time you've been thinking with your pants rather than your mind."

"Caen, that's enough," Jo objects.

"You stay out of this," Caen snaps. "This all started with you."

"You will not speak to her that way," Shea's voice booms, her hand going to her waist to grasp at her sword subconsciously until she realizes that it's not there.

Caen watches the movement.

He stares at Shea, offended.

"We promised to help Jo get back on the throne," Shea repeats.

"No, we promised to get her back home. Thetis has said she'll give her a carriage and even some men. That's enough, we've done our part."

"I'm sorry, but I don't see it that way!"

Aster takes a step back, not sure what to do. Thetis gestures for him to come stand next to her and he does, waiting anxiously for the conclusion of this argument.

"You'd risk your crew for her?" Caen shouts.

Shea gets right up in his face and bellows back. "Yes! Don't you get it? I'd give anything for her!"

There's silence after that. Their faces are inches apart, both breathing heavily.

"Then you don't deserve to be the captain of the *Veiled Duchess*," Caen states.

It's like a shock through her system. Shea's face crumples and her eyes narrow. "What?"

"You put the crew first. You protect our own."

Caen steps back away from her. His arms cross in finality, as if commanding Shea to change her mind.

"Caen. Please," Jo's voice shakes, and she steps closer to the two of them. "Think about what you're saying. If this is about money, I'll pay the men—" Jo tries, but he cuts her off.

"No, this is about the code. You need to choose, Shea."

Shea feels like the world is spinning. Jo erupts and starts screaming at Caen, who ignores her. Aster joins in pleading with Caen to stop this madness. He questions whether Caen has the power to remove Shea as captain. But he does, he has that right as quartermaster. Shea feels like she's floating and she knows she doesn't have long to answer. She looks past it all. Thetis is in the corner—smiling, of all things. Shea watches her features and it's like the world slows down around them.

Thetis's lips part: "Choose."

The whisper somehow carries all the way across the room to Shea and it makes her heart stop beating. And so she chooses.

"I choose her."

"What?" Jo breathes; her hair has fallen in loose tendrils around her face from all of her screaming.

They're all sweating. Aster is breathing like it's hard to do so, and Caen simply repeats Jo's question.

"What?"

"I resign," Shea tells him, clearing her throat, and then she continues louder, "as captain of the *Veiled Duchess*. I hereby relinquish control of the vessel and place Caen as captain."

"Captain," Aster whimpers, collapsing on the ground, his head in between his knees.

Jo pushes past Caen, who looks completely confused. She grabs Shea by the shoulders. "There's another way. Okay? I'll go. With Thetis's men, maybe I can win."

"I'm not letting you go alone," Shea tells her with a sad smile. "I can't. So I resign. As per pirate code, my resignation is left up to the new captain to do with me as he sees fit," Shea finishes.

She steps around Jo, who now also looks to be in shock, and opens her arms, exposing her chest.

"What do you say, Captain?" Shea spits out the title, looking Caen dead in the eye with no small amount of remorse. "You going to take my life?"

"No," Jo yells, stepping in front of Shea, between her and Caen.

"Just try it," Jo snarls.

"I wouldn't," Caen croaks and then clears his throat, shaking himself out of his daze. "I leave your life to you."

Shea nods and her body goes limp. She feels like a puppet whose strings are about to break at any minute and then she'll fall. The housemaid comes scampering in again, running up to Thetis; she whispers once more and then runs back out again.

"The bedchambers are ready; perhaps we should all retire for the evening and pick this up again tomorrow."

"I think it's best if I leave tonight," Caen replies, turning his back on Shea. "I thank you for everything you've done," he tells Thetis, "but if I might trouble you for a horse to make my way to Oceanus?"

Thetis nods. She picks a bell up off the table near the armchair. She rings it and the poor skittish maid steps back into the room, looking down at the ground.

"Azula, show Mister Caen to the stables. Miss Nessa will be able to take it from there. She'll get you set up with a horse and some provisions."

Caen thanks her once more and begins to walk toward Azula before he stops and glances back. He looks like he's about to say something to Shea but instead speaks to Aster, "Come on, son, time to go."

Aster shakes his head, keeping his head in his lap.

"Aster, I order you to get up. You get moving."

Aster looks up with tears in his vision and stands, wiping the water out of his eyes. But instead of following orders, he takes a stiff stance.

"No, sir. I resign as well."

"Aster, go," Shea orders.

"It's you and me, you said. At the beginning when you found me. Well, it's you and me now. I'm not going."

Caen sighs and takes a step toward him, but Aster takes a step back.

"You know what," Caen mutters, "fine. Shea?"

"I've got him," Shea responds, not looking at Caen.

Caen sighs again, turning to leave once more when Shea stops him.

"Caen."

Caen turns so quickly that she thinks he might have whiplash. There's a look of hope in his eyes and she steps toward him. She reaches up to her neck, immediately going to the choker. At first she can't find the cinch and fears that the choker is complete metal all the way around, but after pulling hard enough, the cinch gives and choker comes off.

Caen stares at the pearl now in her hand, and she holds it out, offering it to him.

"Take it. It belongs to the crew."

Caen hesitates but takes it and shoves it in his pocket. He leaves. The door shuts behind him and he doesn't come back through.

Fifteen years of hearing him fuss over her well-being, of this and that, and Shea just about collapses on the floor.

Jo yelps as she sees her go down and kneels beside her.

"Why did you do this?" Jo whispers.

"Because that's what you do. For the people you love."

Tears flood Jo's eyes and Aster walks over, kneeling on the ground too. They all embrace each other, and they stay together until someone behind them clears their throat.

"That's all very well, but I'm exhausted, so if you wouldn't mind taking this to your chambers," Thetis drawls with a smirk.

Jo and Aster laugh while the tips of Shea's ears turn red.

STAY WITH ME

Shea

ZULA RETURNS FROM ESCORTING CAEN, and Thetis instructs her to lead them to their rooms.

Jo thanks Thetis and apprises her of their plans to leave about daybreak as the journey is far. Even leaving that soon, they still won't arrive until evening. Thetis approves Jo's requests of course. She lets her know that a carriage will be prepared for them. Thetis even enlists Caeruleus to take a letter to the allies in Arethusa, for them to get ready to stop the coronation. Azula finally shows them to their chambers, but they only find two doors.

"I'm sorry but I think there's been a mistake, there's three of us," Shea softly explains, trying not to scare the flighty elf off.

"No mistake," Azula mutters with her eyes watching the floor. "Countess said that the boy was to have one room and that you and the princess would share a room."

Oh she did, did she?

Shea looks up at the ceiling in exasperation and Azula takes her chance, bowing before scurrying away.

"I can sleep in Aster's room if you like," Shea starts, but Jo waves her off.

"Aster, have a good night, we'll fetch you in the morning to leave."

Aster salutes Jo with a grin and rushes inside his room before Shea can shuffle in behind him. Shea stares at his closed door slightly dumbfounded.

"Shall we?" Jo inquires; she opens the door to their chamber and walks into the room.

Shea is tempted to go find Thetis and demand another room but instead she takes a deep breath and enters, almost laughing at the sight.

White petals have been placed all over the floor and on top of the giant bed. Sheer fabric hangs off the walls mystically and the eggshell blue reminds Shea of the water closest to the shore of Orena, bright and clear. Candles are lit at varying points around the chamber, casting delicate shadows around the room. There's even a bath off to the right.

Shea notices that her old clothes and bandages, along with a nightgown, have been placed on a vanity together. As have new day and nightclothes for Jo. The blonde points toward the bath, asking to go first to change, and Shea lets her. The door closes behind her, and Shea gets to work changing in the bedroom. She first takes off the ridiculous dress and it falls to the floor without a sound.

Next she goes for her hair, pulling out all the pins and what feels like needles and shakes her curls out until the wild mane falls loose down past her shoulders. She's still wearing the consort tiara, but she decides to leave it. She wants to wear it for a little while longer.

Underneath her work clothes she pulls out the simple white nightgown made of thin cotton. She pauses, considering her bandages, but discards them near her peasant blouse, slipping the sleeping gown overhead with nothing underneath. She takes a quick glance at the bath door before admiring the tiara in the mirror on the vanity.

As she smooths out her gown, she hears the door open to the bath. She hurriedly takes off the tiara and places it under her clothes before Jo can see. She looks up toward the bath and finds the princess in a similar slip, but this one is light pink, making her skin look a little flush. Her blond hair is also loose and the light blond seems to have become even lighter over their adventure at sea and on land.

"Hey," Jo murmurs, stepping back into the room.

Shea takes a step forward and Jo closes the distance until they're standing right in front of each other.

"Hey," Shea whispers back with a crooked smile.

"You okay?" Jo asks, but Shea knows it's just a formality; Jo knows how she truly feels. Shea answers anyway.

"I don't know. I've only ever had the ship. I don't know what's next."

"You've got me," Jo laughs awkwardly, and Shea smiles even more.

"Yeah. Yeah I do."

Jo steps closer until they're inches apart. The candlelight flickers through the room, and their shadows dance along the light blue walls.

"I saw you," Jo takes a breath, "with Venus."

"Yeah," Shea acknowledges, she remembers.

"The kiss?" Jo asks.

The realization occurs to Shea and she finally understands Jo's weird mood.

"It was a goodbye," Shea tells her honestly, hoping she understands, "nothing more."

"Okay." Jo looks away after that, but Shea can still tell there is something wrong.

"You don't believe me?"

"I do, I just, I thought I was going to lose you," Jo confesses.

Shea places a hand on the side of her face as a couple tears fall.

"I'm here," Shea whispers, soothing her.

"I thought Ceto was going to take you—and everything she did, I just wanted to kill her."

"I'm not worth that," Shea chuckles.

"Yes! You are," Jo exclaims, putting her hands on Shea's hips and pulling her close. "You're not the only one who has someone they love."

Jo leans forward, hesitating for just a moment, but when she looks into Shea's bright green eyes, Jo smiles and presses her lips against Shea's in the softest, lightest of touches.

The kiss is sweet and chaste, much like V's, but then again not at all.

V's was a goodbye, but this—this feels like a hello to the start of something new. Jo pulls back. Shea lets her hand drop from Jo's face to her shoulder.

"I want to make love to you," Jo tells her.

Shea doesn't really understand the statement at first. But then it sinks in and she has to step out of Jo's hold. This isn't a brothel. It isn't some one-night stand that Shea can leave on the shore tomorrow. This is bigger than all that, and once it happens, she can't leave. Whatever happens, Shea must face the consequences, and suddenly after all she's faced, she finally feels scared.

"Will you let me?" Jo asks.

Those sparkling blue eyes tear into her in earnest, and Shea huffs because there's that starlight shining through once again. She takes an unsteady breath, closing her eyes; the better question is, is she ready? Shea wants to laugh at herself, throw her head back and let out a good hearty chuckle. She's had sex before, many times, with many different people, male and female. So why is this any different?

Maybe because she's never loved anyone before, says a little voice in the back of her head.

It makes Shea open her eyes. Jo is staring at her now with a little worry, fear of rejection, and she wants to cry—all of her experience and an emotion turns her into a virgin. A virgin of love, how pathetic, but it still begs the question: Is she ready?

"Yes," Shea answers.

Jo's smile is so bright that it nearly knocks the redhead off her feet. The princess steps forward, closing the gap Shea created, and begins to undo the string at the top of her own nightgown. Jo leans in, kissing her deeply as her hands deftly work at the strings. Shea reaches up to do her own, but Jo stops her.

"Wait," she says and finally unfastens her gown.

Shea watches as Jo pushes her slip off her shoulders and lets it fall to the floor in a pile around her feet. Shea takes a breath. Jo is beautiful. Her breasts are smaller than hers, but it matches the blonde's body perfectly. The white unmarred skin is as smooth as churned milk, and Shea thinks she can see a little definition in the princess's stomach. She's so tall and lithe that it suddenly makes Shea very self-conscious of the scars marring her own body.

Shea subconsciously reaches up to cover her brand with her hand, but Jo catches it instead, taking it to her lips and kissing it with such affection. Shea's eyes catch on Jo's hair below, noting the white curls. And right on the side of her hip, Shea notes a small imperfection, a beauty mark that only adds to the beauty of Jo's body. Jo slowly reaches for the fastening on Shea's dress.

She freezes, her hands almost catching Jo's wrist to stop her, but she stops herself instead. Shea lets her hands fall to her sides. She can't help clenching her hands into fists before she forces her body to relax. Her strings seem to unfasten faster than Jo's, and Jo gives her a look as if asking if she can push the fabric past Shea's shoulders.

She nods and the fabric slips to the ground in a rustle, making the only noise in the room besides their joined breathing. They're naked before each other, and Shea feels her body trembling. She wants to put her hands over herself to hide the scars and keep them hidden from Jo's perfection, but Jo doesn't let her. The princess lets her fingertips skim along the jagged white scars scattered all over the pirate's body.

Jo kneels down in front of her, examining the bite mark scar on Shea's leg from a wolf attack in Knowman's Canyon. Shea looks away, embarrassed, and nearly squeaks, biting her lip to suppress the sound when Jo presses her lips against the scar.

Next Jo trails past Shea's vibrant red bush and up to her hip where a long, jagged scar rests from a Lycon man who'd tried to run Shea through. She kisses the scar there, too, and the next on her abdomen from a rigging accident, all the way up in between her breasts, until Jo's standing once more staring at the brand carved right over Shea's heart.

"You don't need to," Shea mutters, her ears red.

Jo doesn't reply; she simply leans in and presses a deep kiss to the brand as if her kiss could burn itself over the carving and replace it there, forever. Shea moans in pleasure and gasps as Jo's hands rise up and grip Shea's breasts, kneading and squeezing them in pleasure. Her head moves in between Shea's breasts, sucking a mark over the redhead's sternum as her hands continue to massage the two tan mounds. Shea's breath hitches as Jo's thumb rubs over her perked nipple.

She watches Shea's reaction with hooded eyes, smiling, and lets go of Shea's breasts. She steps closer to the elf, wrapping her hands familiarly at the back of the captain's thighs.

Shea's eyes widen, and at the slight pressure, she jumps up and wraps her legs around Jo's waist and her arms around her neck. There's a moment of silence where Jo is holding Shea without too much effort and Shea is hoisted on Jo's hips— their eyes meet and everything else falls away.

Shea's head falls forward until their foreheads are touching and they breathe together in perfect unity. Then they're moving. Jo walks Shea backward until finally they lean downward, and her back softly hits the large bed. Jo quickly climbs on top of her and it feels like the night in Shea's cabin where they kissed languidly until they passed out in each other's arms.

But it's so much more intimate than that. Shea almost feels vulnerable as Jo pulls back, looking over the elf's body with lust to the point where Shea closes her eyes, trying to push away just how overwhelming this moment feels. Shea gasps as a sharp pain sparks her nipple and her eyes fly open to see Jo's fingers pinching the sensitive skin.

"Look at me," Jo commands.

Shea wants to close her eyes again, but the hand on her nipple tweaks it again, drawing another gasp.

"Look at me," Jo repeats. Shea looks at her, her vibrant green eyes meeting the cold starfire blue, and Jo tells her unflinchingly, "You're beautiful."

Shea's eyes prickle, and she can't understand what's happening when it hits her—she's about to cry in the middle of sex. This can't be happening.

But this isn't just sex, this is something more and it's scaring Shea down to her bones. Jo leans over her and presses a deep kiss to her flushed lips. The warmth through the touch spreads deep into her body, setting her skin ablaze. Every touch of Jo's wandering hands across her flesh raises bumps along her skin. From Shea's lips, Jo moves her mouth to her neck, nibbling her ear in between her teeth and then down toward her collarbone, worrying the skin there, just to the point of pain but only for what feels like a second. Shea knows she'll have marks in the morning.

From her neck, Jo's head continues to travel down, as do her hands, pushing Shea's legs apart until her hips rest between them. Jo's hands return to Shea's chest, gripping her right while her mouth closes in on Shea's left nipple, and Shea feels her wicked tongue flick the shivering flesh with delicious suction.

Shea can't figure out where to put her hands and so she clenches them into the top blanket of the bed, holding on or else she fears she might float away. There's this whining noise that fills the room and Shea distantly wonders where it's coming from until Jo's teeth rake across her nipple and Shea realizes it's coming from her. Another moan escapes her lips as Jo drags her tongue across Shea's chest, circling around the redhead's right nipple before latching onto that one as well.

Finally Shea's sword hand leaps off the bed and into Jo's hair pressing her breast deeper into that divine mouth, and a low moan escapes Jo as Shea's hand tightly tangles into the princess's hair. Jo relinquishes the nipple with a teasing bite that draws a needy whine from Shea's mouth.

A tear escapes Shea's eyes and Jo looks up and reaches, wiping it away while planting a sweet kiss onto Shea's lips. But then she's back to trailing farther down Shea's body, peppering her abdomen with light kisses all the way down past her bush until she arrives at Shea's glistening sex. Shea lays her head to the side, looking through her eyelashes down at Jo, who is staring at Shea's womanhood like it's something to be revered.

Jo shoots Shea a confident smirk that makes Shea blush before she places a hand on both of Shea's thighs. Jo blows a soft breath over Shea's quivering center, admiring its beauty and the way Shea's tan skin shakes under her touch. Slowly Jo leans in and Shea watches, entranced, waiting for the moment when Jo's tongue touches her most intimate part. Even knowing it's going to happen doesn't prepare her for the wave of pleasure that comes over her as Jo's mouth kisses her sex. Shea tangles her hands back into the covers, holding on to them as Jo's tongue runs along her skin.

"Jo," Shea moans. "Gods."

Jo giggles slightly at Shea's last sentiment and the sound sends a vibration straight to Shea's aching nub. Shea's hands snap from the sheets to Jo's hair, tangling into the soft blond, pulling her closer to Shea's dripping heat. Shea tries to spread her legs more, feeling the stretch in the hollow of her hips. The suction is mind-blowing and the drag of Jo's teeth on her clit has Shea arching her back into Jo's mouth. Sweat is beading at the sides of Shea's forehead as suddenly she feels something enter her.

A small insistent pressure dips inside and Shea recognizes it as a finger, Jo's finger. Jo focuses on Shea's nub, sucking and worrying it gently between her teeth as she pushes her middle finger inside slowly. Jo begins to pull back until just the tip is inside and then she pushes her finger back in, fucking Shea at an agonizingly slow pace. Shea whimpers, her hands tightening in Jo's hair. Jo hisses at the stress against her scalp.

Jo picks up the pace, sliding her finger back and forth, grazing the top of Shea's walls until finally Shea's arching her back wildly. Jo smiles against Shea's essence, kissing it sloppily as she aims for the right spot, causing Shea to moan loudly again.

"Fuck, Jo," Shea cries, pressing herself back onto Jo's hand as Jo adds another finger to Shea's opening. Jo keeps fucking her harder until her hand is smacking against Shea's outer lips. She's quaking under Jo's touch. Jo crawls back up the captain's body continuing to finger her faster.

As Jo reaches Shea's mouth, she adds a third finger, kissing Shea like she wants to swallow her whole, and Shea kisses back for all she's worth. Her body snaps and it's like a flood breaks through a dam she never knew she had locked inside her. It roars into her blood and her body hums as Jo keeps kissing her through her orgasm.

Black spots threaten to overtake her vision as she feels herself desperately seeking oxygen. Finally Jo breaks the kiss and Shea gasps for air like a dying woman as she crashes down from her climax. Her body feels drained, but Shea manages to help Jo as she grabs Shea around her middle and flips them until she's straddling Jo at her waist. Shea continues to breathe heavily, Jo doing the same and she leans down lazily kissing Jo with a smile. Jo pulls on her hips manipulating Shea's body until she's only straddling one thigh. Her own thigh is in between Jo's legs and Jo slowly begins to rock against her, grinding against Shea's leg.

The angle is slightly off, but Shea pushes Jo's legs farther apart and widens her straddle as well. Then she leans forward, holding her weight on her left arm and begins to grind lightly. It feels good and Shea rocks her hips, rubbing her thigh a little harder against Jo's sex, making her moan in pleasure. Shea's still slick from her orgasm and it makes Jo's thigh wet and comfortable. Jo pulls Shea's head down and kisses her hard on the mouth, keeping their grinding rhythm going. Shea wonder's if Jo needs more stimulation, so while she's kissing Jo, she snakes one hand down, intending to reciprocate the fingering. But the moment Jo feels her finger edge down around her folds, she pulls back, breaking the kiss, and reaches for Shea's hand, bringing it back up to her breast.

Shea looks at her, confused, but Jo doesn't look distraught; she simply smiles and shrugs, "I was never one for penetration."

Shea nods in acknowledgment, filing that information away for later, and leans back down to kiss the princess. The elf's movements become more erratic as her womanhood is still sensitive from her first orgasm and she can feel another building. She huffs a chuckle into Jo's mouth as they're still making out through the grind and she can hear Jo's breathing becoming staggered as well. They break apart and Shea enjoys the ride, their hips rocking together in perfect synchronization.

Shea catches Jo's eyes wandering down toward her sex, and she's not sure what she's going to do until the princess's right hand moves from Shea's hip to instead rub the redhead's clit. Shea's throws her head back in extreme pleasure as she feels Jo massaging her nub in constant circles. The pressure is murder, and the pace makes Shea want to scream. Sweat is leaking down Shea's brow and Jo's skin glistens in the dying candlelight.

"Tell me you're mine," Jo demands, and it makes Shea's eyes snap open to Jo's.

She feels delirious, like she's been drugged the same way Ceto was, completely strung out with mindless pleasure.

"What?" Shea murmurs, not quite coherent, rotating her hips against Jo's thigh.

"Tell me you're mine," Jo repeats, putting more pressure on Shea's clit, rubbing it harder.

Shea moans in agony. "I'm—I'm yours."

Jo keeps at it though, and Shea can feel that same pressure building inside like before.

"You belong to me. You always will," Jo moans, losing herself to the possessive ecstasy overwhelming her.

"I'm yours," Shea repeats, "I'm yours."

"You're mine."

Jo's nail scrapes against Shea's clit and Shea screams,

orgasming again. Jo bites down on her lip and her sex spasms against Shea's thigh. Both backs arch and there's a moment where it feels like they'll never come down from the roaring in their ears. Finally, Shea collapses on top of Jo. Both of them breathing hard, their chests rising and falling together. It feels like hours pass before Shea can finally find the strength to fall over onto her side next to her princess, who actually tries to keep Shea on top of her.

Jo maneuvers Shea until she's half lying on top of Jo, her head resting on her chest. She kisses Shea's forehead softly, smelling her hair. Their hands tangle together.

It's a few moments after when Jo asks, "Did you mean it?"

It's hard for Shea to even think, she's so tired. "Mean what?"

"Are you mine?"

Shea freezes because she wonders if she did mean it. Did she say it because she wanted to make Jo happy, or was she simply thrown into the moment and babbling whatever sounded right? And if she did mean it? Then what? What's going to happen next for her without *The Duchess*? Things have certainly changed from before.

"It's okay if you didn't…"

Jo trails off, pressing another kiss to Shea's forehead and pulling her closer. With more effort than Shea cares to admit, she turns her head to look up into Jo's eyes, and for the first time since this whole affair started, the blonde is the one who looks vulnerable. She looks almost nervous. And it makes Shea smile.

"I meant it," Shea answers.

The smile that Jo gives her is bright and it makes Shea laugh. She has to look away, giving their connected hands a light squeeze. Shea can still feel the grin on Jo's face against her head as she begins to close her eyes sleepily, and she wonders if it's possible to stay like this forever.

THE POINT OF
NO RETURN

Shea

SHEA WAKES TO A DARK ROOM. The candles must have died sometime in the night. She's lying naked on her stomach, her hair falling over her face. She presses her hands out to feel for Jo but instead finds empty space. There's the sudden urge to panic, but she suppresses the sensation and instead sits up in bed, flipping her hair out of her face.

Images of the night skim across her mind as she rubs the sleep from her eyes. She bites her lip, trying to stave off the huge grin that threatens to overcome her features, but it doesn't help as it spreads across her face anyway.

She gets up, walking carelessly toward the heavily draped window, and pulls the material aside to catch the first light starting to edge over the city. Light streams through the room and she heads to the vanity where her clothes are still hanging over the chair. She picks up the bandage, taking a breath before holding her arms up to begin binding her breasts. A quick knock erupts from the door.

Before she can answer, it pushes open and a head pops around the corner.

Aster is looking back behind him talking to someone, completely oblivious to Shea's naked form, before finally turning to speak to Shea.

"Captain, the carriage is ready. Theti—"

Aster does a double take. His eyes widen as he takes in Shea's appearance and freezes.

Shea smirks, dropping her arms while she waits for the boy to continue. He turns a bright shade of red before smacking his hand over his eyes like they've been burned out of their sockets.

"Oh my god! Why are you naked?" Aster screeches.

Shea laughs. "Serves you right for barging in. You were saying?"

Aster lets out a choked noise. "It's fine, I'll tell you when you're done."

He hurries to step out, but Shea calls for him to stop. "Nope, it's okay, I'm just binding my chest. Go ahead."

"But, Captain—"

"Aster," Shea scolds and he lets out a groan, keeping his hand over his eyes.

"Thetis told me to wake you and tell you that the carriage is ready. The blinds are down and there will be border patrol, but she swears they won't bother the carriage marked under her sigil."

"Good," Shea remarks, finishing the bandaging and going for the pants next. "Who will be driving?"

"I will," Aster responds, peeking through his fingers and letting out a sigh of relief when he notices Shea's mostly clothed in pants and bandages.

"The foreman is letting me borrow one of his uniforms."

"Good, and Jo?" Shea asks, slipping on her blouse.

She tucks it into the pants and then goes for the belt. It's heavy as she tries to pick it up with one hand, but when she looks down to assess the problem, she sees her old blade made of pure gold is attached by the hilt.

Aster must notice her relief at the sight of the blade and tells her, "Caen got his hammer too before he left."

Shea looks up at that and she can tell her boy regrets saying his name.

"And Jo?" Shea repeats, ignoring the awkward tension.

"She's good, dressed and waiting for us downstairs. We can take off as soon as you're ready; we should be in Arethusa in approximately twelve hours at a steady pace."

"And if we hurry?"

"Ten."

Shea nods, clicking the belt into place.

"I'll meet you at the carriage."

Aster gives her a teasing salute and takes off, not bothering to close the door. Shea shakes her head after him. She takes a quick look in the mirror, evaluating her state of dress. She plays with a red strand.

She really should put her hair up, but a memory of the night before replays in her mind of Jo twirling the curling red tendrils, and she decides to leave it down. Shea shivers remembering the ghost of a kiss gracing her lips before heading out the chamber door. She realizes she's not exactly sure where the carriage is and runs into a maid who directs her to the kitchens.

In the early morning light there's something peaceful about the tower; it doesn't feel as dark and ominous. Shea once again examines the vast amount of elven tapestries scattered along the walls, images and symbols that Shea doesn't even completely recognize.

Finally she arrives at the kitchens, where she finds Thetis and Jo talking over cups of tea. Shea feels slightly uneasy and wonders whether she should interrupt when Jo looks up and sees her. The worry fades away as she meets the blonde's eyes, which light up like blasting powder when the princess finds her.

Jo excuses herself from her seat next to Thetis and walks straight for the ex-captain. The redhead watches her warily, not sure what to do, so she continues to stand awkwardly in the entrance to the kitchens.

Jo stops in front of her before grabbing Shea's hand and bringing it up to her lips, placing a delicate kiss on the back.

"Good morning, my lady," Jo murmurs.

Shea opens her mouth to respond but then closes it as she's suddenly being led through the kitchens and sat in the seat where Jo was before.

Shea's eyes meet Thetis's, where she's sitting across from her sipping her tea and smirking at the other elf like she knows something Shea doesn't.

The kitchens are huge. Machines designed to cook at large capacities are in every corner. On stone walls, hanging herbs and meats are either drying or setting. All of the servants are elven women. Some old and young but all of them laughing and working together as they prepare the day's meals.

Jo laughs when she notices Shea's awestruck expression at the harmony before commenting, "Isn't it wonderful? Thetis and I were just talking about how this is her favorite spot in the house. It feels happy here."

They're right, it does, and Shea finds herself cursing once again at how much she admires the countess.

"So how'd you sleep?" Thetis asks as she hands Shea a cup of tea.

"Very well, thank you," Shea returns, glaring.

She assumes this is the countess gloating.

"The rooms were lovely," Jo adds.

"Well hopefully when you're back on the throne you both might visit again sometime."

"I don't think I'll be coming back to Lycos for a long time," Shea mutters, blowing on her tea.

"Yes, I suppose not," Thetis chuckles.

Aster strolls in through the door, dressed in Lycon coachman attire, and everything sets in with what they are about to do. There's no going back.

"Ready?" Jo says.

Shea searches Jo's features and then nods. "Yeah. Ready."

"Ready!" Aster exclaims, straightening his costume.

"I've alerted my contacts in Arethusa," Thetis informs them. "They know you're coming. They'll be able to get you to your father's quarters. I'm sorry I can't do more."

"Wait, you're not giving us any guards?" Shea snaps, raising a brow.

"Unfortunately with the increased border patrol, it would look too suspicious," Jo explains.

"But don't fret, darling, I've sent another letter for further aid with your blue catbird, you might have some backup yet."

Shea guesses that's the best they can hope for. She recounts the odds: an twelve-hour journey to the Arethusian capital, no aid except for help getting into the castle itself, and just the three of them—one ex-captain, a teenager, and one crown princess whose fighting experience consists of light self-defense—facing a mysterious violent uprising all alone.

Right, should be fine.

"We best get under way then." Shea claps, standing from her seat.

She reaches her hand out and Jo takes it with a smile.

"Alright." Thetis grins. "Nessa?"

A small woman comes around the counter with a large basket. She hands it off to Shea, who takes it gracefully before turning to Thetis. "What's this?"

"Provisions for your journey," Thetis elaborates. "Some loaves of bread, cheese, small meats, and fruit."

She sighs; this woman really has thought of everything.

"Thank you, my lady," Shea murmurs before she does something she never thought she'd do genuinely for anyone—she bows to Thetis.

When she stands, she can feel Jo's proud gaze on her, and Thetis looks surprised. The countess quickly regains her facade and nods appreciatively, giving Shea a genuine smile back. Aster scrambles forward, bowing to Thetis just like his ex-captain, and Thetis chuckles, ruffling his hair. Jo curtsies and the dark-haired woman curtsies back to her.

Finally the countess leads the trio out the side door of the kitchen and down a few steps into the stable. A large carriage waits, attached to two beautiful black horses. They're massive in size and Shea wonders if they're magical in nature. She walks toward the door to the carriage with the basket, but Aster stops her.

"I got it!"

He opens the carriage door and undoes the steps so that Jo and Shea can climb inside. She holds out her hand to Jo, who takes it with an easy smile.

"Your Highness," Thetis calls out from the stone steps by the kitchen side door. Jo looks back.

"Good luck."

The princess nods once more, and it's only then that Shea notices how her hair is half pulled up, the bottom falling loose down her back. She's wearing a powder-blue peasant dress with drawstrings at the top and white material peeking out of the sleeves. The shoes are brown, flat and simple, and there's a small pink flower adorning the back of her hair, and in this moment, Shea can't remember her ever looking so beautiful. The pirate memorizes every detail, as Jo looks the part of a strong monarch on her way to take back her queendom.

The redhead gets in after placing the basket of food on the seat across from them. Aster folds the stairs away, and Shea shuts the door on the outside world. The inside of the carriage is light yellow with frills of silk and ribbons. The windows are heavily framed with curtains, but right above the seat in front of them is a small rectangular window that looks out from the driver's feet. No one can see in unless they're looking for it, but Shea can see out and it settles her anxiety of being closed in. Aster climbs on and settles into his seat; all Shea can think is thank gods she taught him how to drive a couple summers ago.

He knocks on the roof of the carriage that he's ready, and Shea looks to Jo, who gives the signal to go ahead. She knocks back, and with a jerk, they're on the road. The carriage is tense on the way to the border, both women too uneasy to speak. A same worry lies in the back of both their minds that there's some magical way Ceto will find them and she'll come to take Shea away. Jo keeps Shea's hand in hers and occasionally squeezes lightly. They sit quietly in each other's presence, Jo's head falling onto Shea's shoulder. It feels like hours before they hit the patrol, but the moment finally arrives.

"Halt!"

Two patrolling guards step up to the carriage, while the rest deal with other travelers coming in and out of Lycos. Aster hands them the paperwork that Thetis must have given him and the guards look it over with feigned interest.

"We're going to need to speak with your mistress," the lead guard orders, handing the paperwork back to Aster, who takes it gingerly.

Shea moves forward off the seat and Jo scrambles to pull her back, but she waves her off, bringing a finger to her lips in a quieting gesture. Shea peers out the secret window, watching the exchange while Aster scrambles for a response.

"I'm sorry, gentlemen, but the mistress has requested she not be disturbed."

"Look, elfling, the orders are passed down from the empress herself. The countess has to verify her leaving."

"Guys, come on, please don't make me," Aster begs, and Shea doesn't have to guess that it's genuine.

As a pirate, it's a great skill to be an excellent liar. Aster has asked her on more than one occasion about how she became so good at bluffing, and for a while she played it off until she realized if he ever found himself in a situation he couldn't see a way out of, the best thing he could do is lie. So she told him. The best lies are told with a bit of the truth. Find anything truthful in the lie he needs to tell, remember an old feeling he had or a moment where he felt what he's saying, and use it. Shea sends a silent prayer up to Poseidon, hoping that Aster heeded that lesson.

"Why? She beat you for it?" the guard asks, laughing. Shea's hand grips the hilt of her sword tightly.

"Worse, don't you guys know the sigil? This is Countess Thetis. She has magic," Aster whispers like he's letting them in on a secret.

The lead guard looks at him with extreme doubt, but the other's face lights up with acknowledgment.

"Kinsey, that's the elven countess, the one with the voice," the second guard hisses, taking a step back from the carriage.

"Please, guys, I'll do anything, just don't make me disturb her; she'd hang me portside by my ears and I'd tie off the rope all with her say so. She'd probably string us all up."

Shea has to cover her mouth not to laugh, she'd threatened Aster with that very sentiment when he refused to clean his room—clothes and books were spilling out into her own quarters with how much crap he had on the floor. He hadn't known Shea very long and she remembers he got to work quickly after that.

"Alright, shut up. Let me think," the lead guard grumbles. He looks Aster up and down, and his gaze shoots to the carriage before he finally throws his hands in the air.

"Alright, kid, move along. But don't you be telling anybody or I'll have your ears for the market."

"Yes, sir!"

Aster whips the horses, making them move along, and Shea slumps back against her seat. Jo, having been watching Shea's reactions, looks at her quizzically, raising a questioning thumbs- up. Shea chuckles and raises two thumbs-up back.

"We're through?" Jo whispers.

"We're through," Shea responds and they laugh together.

"Good job, Aster," Shea whispers through the window, and he stomps his foot lightly three times to let her know he heard her.

OUR ROOTS
ARE DEEP

Shea

WHILE THE MINUTES GETTING to the border passed slowly, the hours to Arethusa fly by. They stop for food about halfway along the Trident's Fork Road that runs up and down Nereid, but so far there are no guards, Arethusian or Lycon, nor bandits that bother them.

It's like the sigil on the carriage carries more protection than merely just inside Lycos. Night begins to fall and they all feel as if they're chasing the light fading before the horizon.

When they're back in the carriage, Shea instructs Jo to get some rest. They'll want to be awake when they get there. And they didn't exactly get much sleep the previous night.

"What about you?" Jo asks as she takes a fur blanket from under the seat and wraps it around herself, leaning her head against the carriage side.

Shea kisses her lips softly. "I'll be fine. I'm going to keep Aster company for a while. Get some rest."

Jo nods and lets her eyes close while Shea goes to the door. The carriage is already moving, but she's had enough practice holding on to moving carriages. She hops out the door, hanging on to the side by the metal railing on the roof. She shuts the door behind her before she begins working her way around to the front.

It's all green land this far inland, and the trees curving over the road obstruct the light even more, causing spots of shadow to dance between the trees. The jungle atmosphere of Lycos morphs slowly into the great plains of Arethusa. Finally she makes it to Aster's side. He hasn't even noticed her yet, so she decides to tell him gently.

"Hey," Shea murmurs and Aster looks to his side, jumping when he sees her, only jerking the reins slightly.

So much for softly, Shea shakes her head.

"Triton, you scared the crap out of me. Get up here." Aster scoots over and Shea pulls herself up easily onto the driver's seat.

Shea holds her hands out for the reins once seated properly, and Aster gives them to her gladly, taking a moment to stretch.

"You doing alright?"

"Just like watch duty," Aster remarks with a smile.

They sit in comfortable silence looking out at the way the grass almost turns purple in the orange light of the sunset.

"Do you think you made the right choice?"

Aster turns to look at Shea with furrowed brows. "What do you mean?"

Shea shoots him a pained smile and then turns her eyes back on the road. "Coming with me, with us, instead of with Caen."

"Of course."

"I don't know, kid. I can't offer you the same protection out here as I could as the captain of the *Duchess*."

"Is that why you think I came with you?"

Shea shrugs. "Maybe. You know I can still remember the day I picked you up?"

Shea tells him before Aster can say anything.

"You were so young, and I thought if one good thing could come out of this trade, it'd be setting you free."

"I remember," Aster mutters, his eyes looking off the side of the carriage.

"And then, when he sent you to my chambers? I knew I couldn't let him live. Caen nearly killed me…"

Shea trails off, her hands tightening on the reins.

"I can't believe you're fourteen." Shea laughs, and she can see him smile out of the corner of her eye.

"You were incredible," Aster tells her. "I'd never seen an elf so powerful."

"Well, now you've met Thetis."

"No, you're way better than her," Aster exclaims matter-of-factly.

A small swell of pride enters Shea's chest and she revels in the comment.

"Cap?"

"Hmm?"

"I didn't take your offer to be cabin boy because it meant protection."

"No?"

"To me that's not all you were offering."

"I don't—"

"Family." Aster laughs and Shea looks at him with a raised brow.

"You gave me a family. And while I love Caen, and James"—Aster blushes at the older boy's name—"and even Mister Tero…Shea," Aster continues, making her look at him, "you're the closest thing I've ever had to a mom—"

"I'm not a mom—"

"And a sister," Aster finishes, placing his hand on her shoulder, and Shea stops her argument and lets the claim be. She lets the words sink in before she replies.

"I don't want to see you get hurt," she comments.

"I don't want to see you hurt either. I figure we all have a better shot if I tag along anyway," Aster bluffs, puffing his chest out.

Shea ruffles his hair affectionately. "Leave it be, woman," he gripes.

Aster continues "fixing his hair," but the whole conversation—Shea can't decide if it's made her feel better or worse.

"Why don't you head below?"

Aster starts to object, but Shea quiets him, "Come on, you know I can operate with little to no sleep just fine. Besides, I'm too restless to close my eyes. No sense in both of us up here, get some rest. If you truly are ready to storm the castle, you're going to need it."

Aster decides not to argue and instead makes his way down the side of the carriage. Shea listens for the door opening and closing before knocking on the roof. Two knocks sound right back and Shea lets herself relax.

From the looks of the area, they're about two hours off, and from the invitation Thetis received, they should arrive an hour before the coronation ball, a party the night before the coronation ceremony, begins—plenty of time to get in, find Jo's father, and stop the rebellion. Shea yells for the horses to speed up and the carriage jolts slightly as the horses begin to move faster. The sun sets beyond the trees, and Shea silently thanks Aster that he had the idea to light the lanterns early. About an hour later, light shines between Shea's feet, alerting her that Aster and Jo are awake. They're close to the city, so close in fact that as Shea breaks through the tree line and into the glades she can see the castle walls.

Arethusa's large castle sits at the top of a cliffside on the far end from the docks, which lie to its left. The walls are massive, made of white stone spanning from the dock to around the castle. The only way around the walls are the cliffs or to sail into port with papers; otherwise you have to go through the mainland gate into Thalassa by carriage or horse.

Shea pulls off to the side of the road. She places the reins onto the hook by the seat and jumps off, knocking on the door. Aster swings the door open, and he looks over to see the castle.

"Time to switch," Shea says.

Aster nods and jumps up into the driver's seat. Jo pokes her head out the door, and before Shea can stop her, she's out of the carriage and looking at her beautiful city.

"Thalassa," Jo whispers before letting out a huge holler. "We made it! Gods she's as beautiful as I remember." Jo laughs, placing a hand over her mouth, her eyes tearing up.

Shea watches, not making a sound.

"I never thought I'd see the white wall again."

Shea smiles and walks toward her, stopping next to her.

"We can do this."

"Thank you." Jo smiles.

"We need to go though; it's still another hour to the palace, and we want to make it before the coronation ball."

Shea pulls on Jo's arm to get her back into the carriage. Jo hesitates but then climbs back into the coach. They start moving again and this time they get ready. Jo grabs one of the cloaks she found under the seat and begins tying it off at her neck. She hands one to Shea too, who does the same. Shea inspects her sword, making sure it's battle ready.

"This is it," she tells her.

There's a knock from above and they stop breathing. Shea looks out the small hidden window—they're already at the gate. The guard halts them, but as soon as Aster hands them the identification papers with an invite, they're ushered through.

"Jo," Aster mutters.

Jo moves forward, kneeling on the seat under the window next to Shea.

"Yes?"

"Which road do I take up to the servants' quarters?"

"You're going to go up to the castle, but instead of following the other guests, follow the delivery road; we're going to have to ditch the carriage and make the rest of the way on foot. The coach will be too noticeable."

"Right, you got that, Aster?"

"Loud and clear."

The coach makes a sharp left and soon Shea can see the

other carriages with family sigils following a long line up to the palace.

"Now we wait," Jo states.

But it's not as long as they hope. The line moves quickly, running up the winding roads to the palace. Shea instantly recognizes the courtyard up ahead, but instead of veering toward the marble steps, their coach turns down a small dirt road off to the right. It's not cobbled but instead full of gravel that makes the wheels of the carriage bump along the way, but finally Aster pulls off the road into some bushes. Aster jumps out and opens the door.

"We're here." Jo nods and gets out first with Shea following close behind.

Around the corner are many peasant wagons with food and other various products being carried by servants through the entrance to the kitchens. Shea recognizes the entrance and realizes this is the way they snuck Jo out the first time. Fate has led her right back to where it all began.

Thetis's voice flashes through her head, and Shea wonders what fate has in store for her after all. She pushes her cloak higher, covering her face the best she can.

"Okay, you guys wait here. Thetis gave me the name and description of who we need. I'll be right back," Aster explains and takes off, leaving them behind.

Men and women in all kinds of working uniforms are walking through the entrance, so Aster blends right in.

"I'm nervous," Jo mumbles.

She's clenching her hands together, fidgeting slightly. Shea turns to Jo, placing her hands on her shoulders. "There's going to be two hard parts, okay?"

Jo nods hesitantly.

"Okay, one is getting into the castle. Once we're in, we're in. We just have to keep our heads down."

"And what's two?"

"Getting to your father without being seen."

"I don't understand why we don't just walk in the front

door," Jo reiterates her sentiments from earlier in the carriage.

"Because we don't know who's working for who. A guard or a lord or a lady could offer to escort us somewhere and it could be to the gallows instead of your dad. We have to make it in quietly."

As much as it pains her, Jo agrees with the plan once more—she knows Shea is right.

"Hey."

Jo and Shea jump. Shea's hand goes for her sword until they see Aster with an older elven woman trailing behind. She's in nice attire, like she's one of the intended for the ball.

"Aster," Shea hisses, "I thought you were getting a servant?"

"Lady-in-waiting," the woman clarifies before Aster can respond.

"Lady Catherine sends her best," she continues.

Jo gasps and steps forward. "Lady Catherine of Arethusa?"

"She is still loyal to the crown, Your Highness. She was happy to receive Thetis's message of your survival."

The lady-in-waiting curtsies.

Shea waves her hand for the woman to stand.

"Look, that's great and all, but how are you going to get us into the castle?"

"Don't worry, I have a plan, follow me and keep your hoods up. Lad, if you'll escort me?"

Aster quickly offers up his arm and the lady takes it. She walks away without another word, gesturing for Jo and Shea to follow. Shea stares a moment, hesitant, but she starts right on their heels until Jo pulls her back.

"No," Jo whispers, "wait. Follow my lead."

Jo counts subtly under her breath; Shea can just barely hear her. Then they're off, following behind the lady-in-waiting and Aster at a distance of about three feet. Shea rubs her hands at her side. Her skin is prickling with nerves, as if she's never done this before. But this is different, there's no backup. No one's coming. There's a guard at the entrance to the servants' quarters and he stops them as expected.

"Ma'am, the entrance to the ball is in the front," the guard lectures, speaking to the newcomer of their party.

"Yes, sir, thank you. I am Lady Catherine's matron lady-in-waiting; unfortunately, our junior maidens were separated due to a carriage mishap. As you can see, they are not dressed for the ball." The matron gestures back to Shea and Jo, who subtly hold the front of their cloaks closed so he can just barely see their clothes while obscuring Shea's sword.

"I see." The guard nods.

"Lady Catherine wishes for them to go to their chambers so that she may have her ladies with her to enter the ball; it's only proper."

"I should really clear this with my captain—"

"Of course, sir, and you must understand that I'll need your name when Lady Catherine asks about her party," the matron smiles sweetly.

The guard shifts uncomfortably, and Shea has to hand it to the stuffy courtier—it makes her think of Thetis.

These politics really can get you in anywhere.

"No need for trouble. Give her ladyship my regards."

"I will, sir, thank you."

They walk past the guard slowly, careful not to make a mistake, staying in position. Shea tries to match Jo's steps as carefully as possible until finally they make it into the kitchen. Once past the kitchen and into the hall, the matron pulls all three of them around a corner.

"Alright, you're safe for now. My lady?"

"Yes," Jo whispers.

"Can you make it to your father's quarters from here?"

Jo looks down the hall, back and forth, and nods. "Yes, thank you. I know where I'm at."

"I'm sorry we can't do more."

"You've done plenty," Jo soothes.

"We'll take it from here." Shea clears her throat, and she extends her hand out to shake the matron's, who takes it graciously.

"We're rooting for you, Your Highness," the matron tells Jo.

The older woman curtsies deeply once more before looking around the corner and taking off down the hall.

"Are we sure we know where we're going?" Aster clarifies, peering about nervously.

"Yes. Whenever I wanted to see my father, I used to sneak through the servant passages to enter his chambers, trust me. I can get us there from here."

Shea draws her sword, and for the first time she notices Aster has a dagger concealed in the back of his pants; he draws it carefully and she gives him a look.

"I know how to use it," Aster grumbles.

Shea rolls her eyes. "I'm sure. Jo?"

The princess looks over to Shea.

"Lead the way."

They take off down the hall. Two close calls almost stop them in their tracks as they hastily make their way up the many stairs to the west wing tower. So many thoughts are running through Shea's head, and she tries not to think about how nervous she actually is to meet Jo's father. Now is not the time, Shea chuckles to herself.

They keep climbing the steps, and Shea's actually almost out of breath, wondering how any of these royals can be so pudgy with how many stairs it takes just to get to their rooms. Then Shea remembers that these are the servant halls. For all she knows, the prince could be carried up any of the royal stairs. She decides not to mention that theory to Jo.

Finally at the top of the steps, a single plain wooden door rests before them. It feels almost anticlimactic, but Shea decides she'll take easy over anything else. Jo goes to grab the knob, but Shea stops her.

"Jo."

Jo turns and looks at her. Shea sheathes her sword and with confidence walks straight up to her, grabbing her face in her palms, and she pulls her down for a heated kiss. She hears Aster gag behind her, and she reaches out to push his face backward.

It lasts a moment, one perfect quiet moment. Then they carefully break the kiss, and Jo smiles.

"Thank you," Jo whispers.

"Whatever happens? I love you," Shea tells her.

Jo's eyes widen and she scans Shea's face, looking for any trace of doubt, but there isn't any.

"It's okay," Shea says.

She doesn't expect an answer.

"Let's go."

Jo kisses Shea once more before turning to the door. Shea unsheathes her sword again and holds it at half-mast; Aster does the same with his dagger.

The door clicks open with a soft sound, but the creaking is like nails raking against wood. Jo walks in with the two pirates close behind. Inside the chamber, red fabric hangs down the wall; quilts and banners with family sigils decorate the cherry wood panels. A large wooden desk stands off to the side, scattered with maps and papers. Shea realizes they're in a study. Farther into the chambers are two double doors that Shea assumes lead to the master bedchambers. Jo leads the group, peeking first through the crack in the double doors into the bedroom; she must like what she sees because she begins opening them.

Shea stays vigilant, taking up position at the back of the group and watching the door they came through to make sure no one surprises them. After a moment, Shea turns her eyes forward to take in the large bedroom. A huge four-poster bed stands against the back wood-paneled wall. There's a tall wardrobe off to the left side of the bed and a floor-length mirror next to it.

A gentleman with silver-blonde hair and a short beard is examining his reflection in the looking glass as he fastens a pin to his sash that partially covers the traditional navy Arethusian suit, dark blue pants with black dress boots and a white high-collared, long-sleeve button-up with a long coattail navy jacket on top. He's wearing a more masculine version of the crown Ceto had made Shea wear, coral, black pearl, and deep blue sapphires connected around his head in a thin silver band. Shea glances back through the double doors once more and sees a family portrait tapestry off to the side, hidden in the corner.

"Dad?" Jo croaks, and Shea's head snaps forward.

The man freezes, looking up in the mirror as he catches sight of the three of them. He looks a lot like Jo, but what catches Shea off guard are his eyes, the same cold blue starfire as Jo's.

"Joana?"

He turns, staring at her, and she walks toward him until they're almost touching.

"Is that really you?" he gasps.

He holds out his palm, touching her cheek, and she nearly melts into it. Shea lowers her sword but she doesn't sheathe it. Aster follows suit.

"Yes. I'm home." Jo grins.

"They said you were dead. That—that pirate," Prince Mariner stops and looks up, his eyes hardening as they land on Shea.

"You," he spits.

He steps past Jo, storming toward Shea, who stands tall. No matter how much she might want him to like her, she won't let him intimidate her.

Jo grabs his arm, holding him back.

"No, Dad, it's okay! She saved me."

"She stole you!"

"Yes. But she's made up for that. Captain Shea helped me uncover a plot to overthrow me," Jo elaborates.

Prince Mariner turns on his daughter curiously. "A plot?"

"Yes! Shea was paid to kidnap me by someone within our own court. A navy ship was sent after us to make sure I was dead and that Shea died as well. We managed to overwhelm them, and the lieutenant confirmed the story."

"We believe the orders came from a Lord Tyber," Shea

finally speaks. She ignores the glare she gets from Mariner. "He wants to overthrow the matriarchy and put you in charge."

"Lord Tyber? He's here at the ball tonight. I should send for him; we should get to the bottom of this."

"You can't," Shea orders, stepping forward with Aster close behind.

"And why not?" Mariner snarls.

"Because Lord Tyber was able to send an entire navy ship without your knowledge after your daughter. Who knows how far his influence spreads."

"My men follow my orders."

"Dad, you should listen to her," Jo objects.

"Do you trust me?" Mariner asks his daughter.

"That has nothing to do with—"

"Silence, pirate. Joana, do you trust me?"

"Of course, Father," Jo replies, taking his hand in hers.

"Then trust me when I say my men are loyal. I'll call them up here and we can figure out how to catch Tyber. Now, do we have an accord, Captain?"

The sentence brings silence and Shea stumbles back as a memory resurfaces. One from the night she was hired to kidnap Jo.

"Okay, let's do this," Jo agrees, but Shea is lost in thought, those words swirling through her mind.

Mariner walks toward the wall, reaching out to ring the guard bell, when it hits Shea right in the gut. No lord, no matter how powerful, could send out an entire fleet without the reigning power signing off. Especially when the reigning power is already a leading member of the military.

Do we have an accord, Captain?

"No," Shea barks. "Stop!"

But it's too late. The moment Mariner rings the bell, there's barely a second before a flood of Arethusian guards come running into the chambers.

Shea reaches out, grasping for Jo, but Mariner pulls her away, grabbing her roughly by the arm.

"You son of a bitch!" Shea snarls as the guards circle around the four of them.

Aster turns so he and Shea are back-to-back, their weapons pointed out at the guards who all have swords of their own.

"Drop them," Mariner says, his voice a deadly calm.

"Dad, stop! They won't hurt anyone."

"Jo, listen to me," Shea says. She looks up at the ceiling, wondering how the gods can be so cruel.

She takes a shaky breath and says, "It's your dad."

The room's silent and Jo shakes her head. She looks up at Mariner, who's smiling at her with a smug expression. "No. No, it's Lord Tyber. No, no, it—" Jo stutters, shaking her head. "It can't be."

"Sorry to disappoint," Mariner sighs dramatically. "But Lord Tyber? Really? The man is a complete idiot."

Shea takes a step forward angrily, but the guards press their swords farther in, causing her to stop in her tracks.

Aster closes the distance, keeping their bodies close.

"You'd murder your own daughter for the crown?"

"I murdered my own wife and mother," Mariner admits. "I tried to kill Joana in her crib, but unfortunately my mother became a little more creative in keeping us apart."

Jo's complexion is ashen.

Mariner drags Jo closer to him and takes a dagger from one of the nearby guards. He holds the blade against Jo's throat.

"Drop your weapons," Mariner repeats.

Aster drops his dagger upon seeing Jo's position, but Shea tries to hold her ground.

"I said. Drop. Your. Weapons," Mariner shouts, nicking Jo's neck.

Jo gasps and it's enough to show Shea he's serious. She drops her blade, but no one rushes at them just yet.

"Captain," Mariner chuckles familiarly, like they're old pals, "I gave you a job to do. Yet here she is. I paid you."

"Actually you were supposed to pay V. But seeing as we never saw a lick of that money, consider this our return policy," Shea hisses, her nails digging into her palms to keep her from doing something stupid.

"Cute. But you see, when I tell people to do something, they do it. Do you want to know why?"

"I don't really care." Shea shrugs.

"Because I teach them why I don't ask twice."

Mariner snaps his fingers, and two guards come from behind, dragging Aster out of the circle.

Shea yells, reaching for Aster's hand, which they clasp together. Jo screams, struggling to get out of her father's hold, but he keeps her steady. A guard grabs Shea by the hair, forcing her to let go of Aster.

"No! No, it was me," Shea screams, turning to Mariner. "Take me!"

"Don't fret. You should be thanking me, Captain. I'm teaching you a lesson, as well as your boy here. I'm sure he has a bright future in piracy."

Two guards hold Aster down. He's struggling as hard as he can, but they're both so much bigger than he is. Shea screams. She goes to pick up her sword and slaughter all the guards in the room, but as she lunges for her blade, the guard's grip tightens in her hair, keeping her down, his blade going to her neck.

Mariner even presses his dagger closer to Jo's throat as a warning. Shea's helpless. More helpless than when she was at the mercy of Ceto, collared and paraded around like property.

"Stop it, just stop. Dad, we can end this now," Jo pleads, but her begging falls on indifferent ears.

She tapers off, tears falling silently.

"Now," Mariner taunts, ignoring his daughter's words, "the price of treason is usually death, which we'll get to, Captain. But I think the boy is no more than an accomplice, so we'll let him off with a warning he'll remember."

One guardsman folds Aster over his knee. He holds Aster's body still as another man pushes Aster's head back and holds it to one side. A guardswoman with a ragged-edged knife strides toward them. The position they've placed Aster in unsettles the pit of Shea's stomach. The guard holding Aster's head drags his hair back, exposing his right ear.

Shea gasps, "Aster."

She head-butts the guard holding her hair and tries to rush past the surrounding guards, but she's forced back with the swing of a sword. A soldier rakes his blade across her right upper arm, slicing deep. Shea grunts and grips her bicep as blood seeps through her shirt. She yanks the cloak off, tied uselessly around her neck, letting it fall to the ground.

Aster is still struggling feebly. His body is barely moving as the guard with the serrated knife stops in front of him.

"Aster," Shea calls again. He looks up at her with his big round eyes, tears brimming to the surface. Shea breathes past the instinct to cry.

"Look at me."

"Cap'n," Aster sobs.

Shea gulps. "Son, look at me."

The endearment slips out before she can stop herself.

"I'm here," she croaks.

And the guardswoman is on him. She holds the tip of his ear, and Aster starts struggling harder.

"No," he screams. There's movement from behind Shea, but she doesn't bother to look.

"Dad, enough," Jo chokes.

"Aster," Shea mutters, "keep your eyes on me."

And he does.

Aster keeps looking at Shea as the guard carves the top of Aster's ear off. Slicing the point clean. He screams, and it brings Shea to her knees.

His eyes clenched tight in agony. Shea keeps her eyes on his. She doesn't look when the guard throws the tip of his ear at her feet. She doesn't look. She keeps her eyes on Aster, who's sobbing in pain.

Humans will never understand the sensitive points at the tip of elven ears. It's like they've just cut off his arm. The trauma is roaring through him and all Shea can do is kneel there and not cry. Because she doesn't get to cry after what she's done.

"You bastard!" Jo screams, and she starts struggling in her father's arms. But the reveal has left her weak, and Mariner easily holds on to her.

"Very good," Mariner praises Aster like he's some kind of dog.

But that's how royalty sees them, as nothing more than bad dogs. Shea can barely move. The world is moving so slowly around her that it's as if she's merely a ghost in the chambers.

"Now the other," Mariner orders.

The guards holding Aster readjust. Shea's head snaps back to Mariner and he stares her down. Bile rises at the back of her throat, and she suppresses the panic boiling in her gut. Aster is thrashing harder than before. Feral noises escape his small shaking frame like a tortured animal being burned in a cage.

"Please," Shea pleads.

Mariner grins.

He walks forward, bringing Jo with him to the edge of the circle.

"Beg."

Shea purses her lips; everything in her is telling her to spit in his face, but Aster's sobs hold her back.

"Beg," Mariner repeats, powerful and clear.

"Please. Please don't do this," Shea mutters, the volume of her voice gradually rising, "I swear. I'll do anything, please."

There's a moment of silence. Shea can't even look at Jo, though the princess is trying to catch her eyes. The guards are still moving and Mariner is staring Shea down until she finally drops her gaze in submission.

"Wait," Mariner says.

Everyone stills. Aster's sobs quiet to hiccups and Shea breathes in a ragged breath of relief.

"Make sure she watches," Mariner commands.

Shea's head snaps up. "No!"

The guard who was holding her hair a moment ago is joined

by another; they swarm in and hold her steady. They grab her arms, yanking them behind her back, and drag her to the other side of the circle to face Aster.

The one from before forces her head up to look at him as her boy is turned over onto his left side. The tip of his right ear is still on the floor in front of her. She wants to look away, but they're holding her tight. She could close her eyes, but she forces herself to watch as the guardswoman who cut Aster the first time brings the knife back down, severing his remaining tip.

Aster's body jackknifes. Instead of releasing a scream, his body simply goes limp in the arms of the guardsman holding him over his knee. His left tip is tossed to floor next to the other one. Shea stares down at both points numbly.

The guardsman brings Aster forward and dumps him on the ground in front of her. The boy's curled in a ball, holding what's left of his mutilated ears. Shea struggles against the two holding her back and she breathes a sigh of relief that he's passed out from the pain.

"I think we understand each other better now," Mariner speaks.

A chill runs down Shea's spine.

"Guards, escort the captain and her boy down to the dungeon. To await Shea's execution."

Her captors lift her off the floor and begin dragging her toward the front chamber door. Another simply picks Aster up and throws him over his shoulder.

"Actually…"

The guards pause at Mariner's thought. The prince drops Jo, and she falls like a doll, likely still in shock. Mariner stalks toward Shea. He grasps her chin sharply in his hand and forces her to look him in the eyes.

"I know an empress who would pay handsomely for you." Shea weakly tries to shake Mariner off, but his grip tightens; she winces in pain.

"Take them below and notify Ceto that we have a little present. She can take her. As an agreement of our alliance." The guards nod, bowing before him.

"No, Dad," Jo mutters, pushing herself weakly off the floor. "Wait."

"As for you, my dear," Mariner gloats, clutching a blond handful of his daughter's hair, "there's a cushy prison cell with your name on it for the rest of your life."

He throws Jo forward to one of the guards, but they don't catch her and she falls again to the ground. Shea's body jerks, but she resists the urge to go to her, not wanting to make this situation any worse.

She doesn't struggle as a guard places manacles around her wrists. The guardsman grabs her by her wounded bicep, and she hisses in pain as she's pushed toward the threshold.

"They'll never accept you," Jo grunts into the floor, not bothering to try and get up again.

"Jo," Shea warns.

Mariner struts toward his daughter, pulling her up with a firm grip on her arm.

"What was that?" Mariner asks sweetly.

"You will never truly be king. As soon as a new woman of noble connection is old enough, they'll replace you," Jo whispers, her voice a hoarse scratch. "Or they'll want you married."

"I will never be dethroned," Mariner snarls.

"You will," Jo laughs. "But if you spare Shea's and Aster's lives, I will give you the throne, and I will help you keep it. I will support the patriarchy."

"Jo, stop," Shea demands.

Shea is trying to catch Jo's eye, but the guards shove her through the doorway before she can. She digs her heels into the stone, anything to hear the last of the conversation. There's silence. Mariner huffs and Shea can hear him pacing back and forth.

"Talk," Mariner hisses.

"What about Ceto," Jo inquires.

"I will decide after I hear what you have to say."

WATER IS THICKER
THAN OUR BLOOD

Joana

"**Y**OU ABDICATE COMPLETE claim to the throne, you publicly support male rulers, you will marry a male ruler of my choice at my time of dying to reproduce male heirs. And you make the council see things my way," Mariner muses, pacing back and forth in front of the four-poster bed where Jo is chained to the bedpost.

"In return, you spare Shea's and Aster's lives," Jo reminds him. "You will not hurt either of them anymore."

"There's no way I can let them go, they'd only retaliate."

"Then," Jo stutters, thinking quickly, "you place them in a comfortable home within the queendom, I mean *kingdom*, in protective custody. You give them some semblance of a life."

Shea would be screaming her head off right about now, Jo thinks, closing her eyes. She knows Shea would rather die than have her freedom taken away, but Jo can't bear to let them die. She was wrong about everything—she'd led Shea into a trap, and she'd maimed Aster for the rest of his life. The nausea from the mutilation still sits in her chest. And all the while she did nothing.

All that training, all that strength Shea supposedly saw in her, and she couldn't even rise up to stop them.

"Yes." Mariner shrugs. "That can be arranged. But they'll only stay that way while you follow every order to the letter."

"Yes, sir," Jo responds.

Mariner laughs out loud; he claps his hands together before adjusting his sash.

"You killed Mom?"

The question is soft and innocent.

Mariner groans and looks at her like she's a child asking why he'd taken away her favorite toy.

"Yes, I did."

"Why?"

Mariner walks toward her and kneels so they're just about at eye level.

"Because she took my birthright from me."

"I don't understand. She was Grandmother's daughter; it was her birthright to rule."

"I really don't feel like having to pull out the family history books, I've got a ball to attend."

"You hurt the people I care about tonight, you owe me this decency. You hurt me. Why?"

Mariner snarls, "Because I am the rightful heir to the Arethusian throne. Queen Doris is my mother."

"What? That doesn't make any sense."

"Your mother wasn't my sister, if that's what you're thinking. My mother couldn't believe her luck; she chose to bear a child with my father because he came from a long line of sisters, powerful women. She couldn't even look at me the day I was born," Mariner sneers.

"Triteia was born a day after I was. They hadn't announced my sex to the court yet and so your grandmother had a brilliant notion. Your maternal grandmother was one of Doris's maids so she ordered her to switch children. I would still be raised at the palace, but officially Triteia would be Doris's heir."

Jo sits stunned in silence. She'd always known her grandmother could be cruel, but switching your child because of a preferred sex was unthinkable.

"My father couldn't handle the lie, and so he was exiled for treason. He tried to speak out against her. Fool. Doris even sent your maternal grandmother away because she was no longer permitted to be around Triteia. They looked too much alike, you see. She died of grief, or so I was told. Even I had no idea of my true patronage."

"Then how?"

"My father, he found me years ago at a small port in Oceanus. The freefolk were in the beginning stages of independence and my dear fiancée sent me as diplomat."

"And he told you?"

"Everything! Who I really was and that it was my birthright to rule Arethusa. Just because I was born the wrong sex meant that I was forbidden from the crown? No. I decided that I would rule," Mariner snaps. "This is my land! My kingdom. So I went back, and I married your mother."

"Did she know who she was?"

Mariner clears his throat and actually looks ashamed. He shakes his head. "No. I later learned she knew nothing...But—but she was still partisan to the crime!"

"So you murdered her because she was a girl and your mother was a conniving witch?" Jo screams, lunging at Mariner, but the chains stop her.

Her hands are wrenched behind her back, pulling at the bedpost where she's tied. She stands tall, finding some of her courage.

"No," Mariner replies like he's speaking to a half-wit. "First I murdered our surrogate carrying our first child. I couldn't risk a daughter being born. I had been kind at first, only making the surrogate miscarry. But she got pregnant again, you see, so I had to take more drastic measures."

Jo wants to cover her ears. Every word is like poison. She can't even recognize him; now all she sees is a pathetic excuse of a man grasping for power like a spoiled child.

"Of course after that, your mother started to suspect something. She grew distant toward me, cold. Then she decided to risk childbirth and have you. She went away during it all. So there was nothing I could do, but as luck would have it, her body just wasn't meant to withstand pregnancy. She became ill after you were born and was weak for many years after, until finally a little slip of poison put her out of her misery."

Furious tears start to brew at the corners of Jo's eyes. In that moment she wishes she could be incapable of crying. Her tears feel like molten coals slipping down her face.

"And Doris?"

"Heart attack, officially."

"Unofficially?"

"I slid my knife into that woman's chest as she looked into my eyes and begged me for forgiveness." Mariner laughs, grabbing Jo's face brutally, forcing her to look at him.

"And it all could have been avoided if she'd just given me my birthright."

"She didn't give you away because you were a boy, Father," Jo tells him, her voice monotone. "She gave you away because when she looked into your eyes she knew she'd birthed a monster."

Mariner backhands Jo with enough force that she falls back and her head hits the post that she's chained to.

"Perhaps," he chuckles, flexing the hand he slapped her with. "But my blood runs within your veins, my dear; who knows, you might have as much monster within you as I do."

Jo's ears are ringing and her hand instinctively flies to her head but the chains restrict the movement. There isn't any blood trickling down her neck but it'll bruise.

"So it's settled. Your life for that of your pirate. I have to ask though. Why save her? What is she worth to you?"

"It's not something you're capable of understanding," Jo hisses, attempting to stand once more.

Mariner's brow furrows and then his eyes light up with

understanding. He lets out a hearty laugh.

"Well, it seems the tale of the captain's charms are not exaggerated. You gave it up to an elf? No more than an animal? I take it back, my dear, you're nothing like me. You are so much less."

"She is more brave, more powerful than you could ever be! And she loves me as much as I love her. And that's something you will never have."

"No," Mariner answers. "But I'll have the crown. Guards!"

Two guards hurry in. They walk straight for Jo.

"Take the princess to her quarters; get her cleaned up and ready for tomorrow. She doesn't leave her chambers."

"You'll release Shea and Aster," Jo demands.

"After the coronation tomorrow, yes, but not before."

They unlock the chains from the post and grab her by both arms.

"Now how about a proper goodbye for your future king?"

Mariner holds out his right hand with two sapphire rings adorning it. Jo does her best and with movement so slow it's almost torturous she curtsies low, taking her father's hand and kissing his ring.

"Did you ever love me?" Jo asks, though she already knows the answer.

"If things had been different," Mariner answers, "maybe I could have."

The guards lift Jo to a standing position so that she's forced to look up at her father.

"Long live the king," Mariner says with a cheshire grin.

"Long live the king," Jo repeats plainly.

Then she's taken away, out the main double doors and toward what she used to consider her bedroom—but would now, forevermore, be her cell.

BOUND APOLOGY

Shea

THE DUNGEON IS COOL AND DAMP. Shea's breath is labored as she takes in deep gulps. The air feels thick, as if she's breathing in the ocean, drowning, and it burns against her lungs.

The guard holding Aster takes him down to the far cell and dumps him inside on the stone floor. He groans and Shea hopes he's not waking up just yet. The two guards holding her usher her toward the cell opposite his. She begins to struggle.

"Please," Shea yells, holding her arms out against the bars. The guardswoman to her left squeezes the cut on her bicep and Shea grits her teeth against the pain.

"Please, let me be with him, you don't understand the pain he'll be in," Shea begs. "Please."

The guardswoman looks to the guardsman on Shea's right, and he shrugs. Seeming to come to some sort of agreement, they turn her around and throw her into the same cell as Aster. They don't bother removing Shea's manacles, but she doesn't care.

She gathers Aster up in her arms, looking at his maimed ears. It's a clean cut, which she thanks the gods for. It'll heal well, if she can get it cleaned soon, with minimal scarring. If anything, it will look fairly normal to humans, but the elves will know, and it will be seen as shame. She wants to scream; she wants to run her sword through Mariner and watch as the life bleeds from his eyes. She wants to murder both guards that held Aster down. Then she'll hang the one who cut him from the bow of her ship.

Until she remembers she doesn't have a ship. Or a crew or even her sword, as the guards took that as well. She's alone in a cell waiting to find out if she's going to die in a couple hours while the boy she holds dear as family, as her child, bleeds in her lap. She shuffles back, with him in her arms, so she can lean against the wet wall. She rips her blouse, on the side of her sliced upper arm and gathers the material so she can staunch the bleeding on both of Aster's ears. She doesn't bother with the cut on her arm.

Instead she leans her head back and curls Aster close to her chest so he can rest. Hours pass, and Aster still hasn't woken up. She's tied the tattered pieces of her sleeve around his head and so that it covers both ears, but not his eyes. Shea's been holding him continuously, looking for any sign of movement, but she doubts she'll see any. She occasionally places a hand above his mouth and nose, and when she feels the shallow breath her heart keeps beating.

Cutting, there's an actual word for this, it's a punishment saved for only the deepest offenders against the elven city of Erebos. To have the tips cut meant you were no longer elven. Now it's a common practice in the slave trade known as cropping, not just because it's high fashion but because if the enslaved elves are no longer recognized by their own kind, then they have nowhere to escape back to.

Shea bangs her head back against the wall; it hurts but not as much as the pain in her chest. She wishes she could take back everything. She sends a silent prayer up to whatever deity might be listening, but if she was them? She wouldn't listen either.

Shea leans her head back gently this time and just stares up at the prison ceiling. A guard comes by another couple hours later to alert them that Shea's execution won't be happening just yet. When Shea asks why her life is being spared, she simply gets, "The princess made a better offer."

The guardswoman doesn't say more and leaves, ignoring Shea's request for fresh water and bandages. It's some time after the soldier leaves, Shea's starting to go crazy from all the silence, then Aster whimpers in pain. Shea looks down, holding him closer. He's shaking from the stress. She rubs his arms, trying to keep him warm.

Finally his beautiful light green eyes open. He's pale. His bottom lip is trembling.

"Shea," he croaks. Shea shushes him, kissing his forehead.

"It's okay, I'm here."

"I'm sorry. I should have done more, and I should have stopped them. They—"

He shuts his eyes and a single tear falls down his cheek.

"No. Hey," Shea growls, tilting his head up to make him look at her. "You did everything right."

"I let him take Jo."

"No, you didn't. There was nothing anybody could have done," she tells him. She leans her head back against the wall, forcing the tears to stay at bay.

"I should have saved her," Aster moans.

"No. It wasn't your job. I should have been ready. You both were mine, but you—you are my child."

Aster gazes up at Shea, his eyes watering at her admission.

"And I failed you," her voice cracks, "and Jo."

"No," Aster argues.

"Yes I did. I promised I would protect you both, but I—I promised you first. This is all my fault."

And she can't hold it back anymore. She begins to cry.

"I'm so sorry. I should have never gotten involved with all this. I should never have kidnapped Jo. I endangered our crew and ship. I hurt you. Gods, Aster, I hurt you. I'm so sorry."

Aster pulls Shea in and they sit there hugging each other, Shea crying softly.

"I should have listened to Caen. And to Jo. I messed every-thing up," Shea murmurs. Her arms and legs feel like pins and needles.

"No," Aster tells her.

He pulls back to look her in the eyes. "We did what was right. We're pirates and we fought for justice. I don't know any other pirate powerful enough to do that."

"Crazy ones?" Shea chuckles.

Aster gives her a pained smile.

"I'm proud to call you my captain. I'm proud," Aster enunci-ates this to make sure Shea is paying attention, "to call you my mom."

Shea doesn't know whether to cry or smile so she settles for both.

"My sacrifice was mine to give," Aster continues.

Shea shakes her head sadly. "I broke our laws, I interfered with the land folk, and my crew got hurt."

"I thought what makes us pirates is that there are no rules. How I see it, you did what you thought was best for us. I think if Caen was here, as stubborn as he is, he'd agree with me. You're a great captain because you're a great leader. And leaders make mistakes. But the best ones learn from them."

"Gods, kid." Shea tearfully smiles. "When'd you get so smart?"

"I got it from my mom." Aster winks.

Shea laughs, pulling him back into a hug. There's a knock on the bars and Shea glares up, holding Aster close, ready for anything.

"That was beautiful," Caen states, leaning against the prison bars, spinning a ring of keys in his hands.

He's dressed as an Arethusian guardsman.

"Caen?" Shea chokes.

"Surprise," Caen tells her, unlocking the cell door.

Aster rolls off her, not quite ready to stand and Shea pushes herself up using the wall so she can look down the hall. She spots James and a couple other crew members also dressed as guardsmen.

"What in Hades are you doing here?" Shea hisses as Caen gets to work unlocking her manacles.

They come off easy and Shea rubs her wrists before bending down to pick up Aster.

"Rescuing your stubborn ass," Caen replies.

She attempts to lift Aster up, but a sharp pain shoots down her wounded arm and she almost drops him. Luckily Caen is there for the save. He grabs Aster and picks him up, damsel style.

"He okay?" Caen raises a questioning brow, noting the bandage wrapped around Aster's head.

"He's hurt," Shea explains, straightening up. "Why did you come back?"

Caen pulls out a letter with a seal on the front and Shea recognizes the sigil.

"Thetis sent you?"

"She's pretty convincing when she wants to be. Besides, after Aster's speech, I only made it to the ship before I was telling the crew we had to go after you."

"But the crew?"

"Took a vote; they want you, Captain. We're pirates. A strong leader is hard to come by."

"Rule breaker," Aster teases.

Caen smiles down at him.

"How ya feeling, kid?"

"Better now that you finally came to your senses."

"We need to get him out of here, think about our next move," Caen says.

He walks out into the hall with Aster, and Shea's right behind him. She grabs him by the arm and turns him gently so she doesn't jostle Aster.

"Caen, I'm not going anywhere. I still have to save Jo, and Arethusa," Shea states, though she could live without the latter.

Caen rolls his eyes. "I know, kid. We've already had this

fight. That's why I brought two teams. Group one will stay with you and me in the palace; no way we're getting back inside these walls if we leave. The rest will take Aster back to the ship?"

The plan ends in a question. Then Shea realizes he's waiting for her approval; the small consideration makes her smile and she voices her agreement. They meet James and the others at the entrance to the dungeon.

"You alright, Cap?" James inquires, gesturing to her arm, but really he's already scanning Aster and checking his wounds.

She claps a hand over the wound, wincing.

"You're hurt?" Caen demands, handing Aster over to one of the crew. He takes a closer look at Shea's arm.

"I'm fine. A quick bandage and I'm ready. You guys need to get moving. James, you got a way out?"

"Met up with the lovely Lady Catherine's matron, apparently elves really like to stick together." James glares at Aster, who sheepishly smiles.

"Yeah," Shea sighs.

She listens to the rest of the plan and then orders them to move. Aster tries to argue, but a stern look from everyone silences him. James grabs his hand, briefly giving it a squeeze, which makes Aster blush in embarrassment. Then he nods to the crewman holding Aster and gestures for him to take off with three of the other men. Which leaves, including Caen and James, ten behind.

"What time is it?" Shea questions.

"Early morning about, I'd say around four, ma'am," a crewman answers.

"Which means we've got about five hours until the coronation," Shea concludes. "Any suggestions?"

The man on lookout whistles. "We got incoming soon, so we best figure it out quick."

"We've got a room. But we're going to need to move fast. That arm going to be a liability?" Caen asks.

He rips a piece of his shirt off for Shea just as she had done for

Aster and ties it off quickly.

"I got my wits. Let's go."

"Two men are going to have to stay behind to keep the pretenses up here, so no one wanders in," one man says; he looks to his friend, who smiles. "We'll stay behind, pretend to be guarding the cell."

"Thank you," Shea says, it's a huge gamble but she's not leaving any men behind today.

Caen nods and whistles for the lookout to start heading down the hall. James steps through the entryway, looking to his right to make sure there aren't any guards passing by. He ushers the other men forward, and Shea does her best to keep up with Caen. She looks back at her two crewmen and gives them a small salute. They do the same and then stand at attention inside the dungeon.

They creep down the halls at a quick pace. Shea realizes they're going in the opposite direction from Prince Mariner's quarters and instead are heading farther into the castle, to the east wing. Just as they're coming up on what Shea assumes is the guest quarters, they round the hall and James runs straight into another man.

All of them freeze, a couple of the pirates drawing their swords, but as Shea sees the face of the man they've just run into, her eyebrows rise.

"Soren?"

The lieutenant from the Arethusian navy ship who aided them is sitting on the ground rubbing his forehead.

"Good, you got her. Lady Catherine was sending me down to see what was taking so long."

"Easy, navy." Caen smirks, putting his sword away. "We don't fail when we're sent to do something."

Soren glares up at Caen but takes the offered hand from James. "Very funny. Let's go before someone sees."

Soren leads them down the guest quarters hall, and Shea can't help but admire the billowing light blue curtains, which look just like sails, connected to the white marble arch windows lining the walls. Toward the end of the hall, before it leads to more steps and more rooms, Soren stops and knocks rhythmically on a grand white door.

It opens to a woman dressed in a long white nightgown wrapped in a shawl.

"Soren?"

"We got her, let us in."

The woman hurries aside, and the crew usher Shea to the front. They push her into the room with Caen and Soren at her back. The room is dazzling. Crystal chandeliers, a long wooden dining table with a small drawing room, and three bedrooms can be seen at the back.

Sitting at one of the dining chairs is an old woman in blue lace wearing an intricate lace headdress covering her silver hair. The woman who opened the door goes to stand behind her with another young woman; she guesses they are her maidens. But sitting in the chairs on either side of the older woman Shea recognizes none other than the crones who raised Jo, Rhea and Gaea.

"Hello." Shea smiles with an awkward wave.

"This is the girl our surrogate daughter fell in love with?" Rhea gripes as the last of the men trickle through, and the door shuts and locks behind them.

"I remember her being much prettier at the ball," Gaea observes, sneering at the captain.

Shea bites her tongue. She supposes she's looked better. Her high-waisted black pants are stained with dirt from the dungeon, her black boots are scuffed as well, and she's missing the right sleeve of her royal-blue peasant blouse with gold leaves sown into the unlaced collar. Even her hair falls in frazzled ringlets loosely down her back. And she can't forget the bloodied fabric tied around her bleeding bicep. She grits her teeth and chuckles in acknowledgment.

"Yes. It's good to see you both as well." But the woman in the center is looking at her with a pleased smile.

"Are you Lady Catherine?"

The woman's smile widens and she gestures for Shea to come sit down. Shea sits across from all three of them and hisses when her arm bumps against the chair.

"I'm going to fix that up," Caen tells her and then orders the men, "Go relax, we're not going anywhere yet."

He kneels down next to Shea's right arm, giving her bicep a more thorough examination.

"Caen, it's fine," Shea mutters, trying to stop his fussing, but she's utterly distracted.

She can't take her eyes of the elderly woman across from her; there's something about her that Shea recognizes. And the older woman seems to notice Shea's intrigue as she just keeps grinning, turning her head slightly as if showing off her features.

"You remind me of someone," Shea states.

"Do I?" the woman replies airily.

"So you are Lady Catherine," Shea tries to clarify but is cut off by one of the old hags.

"Well of course she is! Who else did you think was helping you," Rhea snaps, and Shea glowers back at her.

"I am Lady Catherine," Catherine confirms, her voice soft and familiar.

"Why are you helping us?"

"Thetis is an old friend of mine; she wrote to alert me of the coup and let me know that Joana was alive. Best letter I ever received," Catherine laughs.

And right in that moment, Shea sees it.

"You remind me of Jo."

"Well thank you, dear. I'll take that as a compliment considering how beautiful my granddaughter is."

"Granddaughter?"

"Yes."

"You're Mariner's mother?"

"No. I was Queen Triteia's real mother."

Shea's head spins at the implication. Politics aside, and Shea's hatred for royalty once again reinforced, Shea finds herself missing one fact.

"What you're suggesting...I doubt the reigning party would have wanted you around. I'm sorry, but how are you alive?" Shea inquires, thinking of the awful stories she'd always heard from Paetre about Queen Doris. Doris had been his Ceto.

Gaea snorts, causing everyone to look at her, her dark face almost completely shadowed by the candlelight.

"What a rude thing to ask. I see Joana has a lot of work to do if you're to become Arethusa's queen consort."

Shea's eyes widen, but she instead decides to ignore that comment. She'd rather not think about the possibility of a title right now.

Catherine laughs at Gaea's remark.

"It's a fair question, Gaea. I was a lady-in-waiting to Queen Doris, pregnant at the same time she was. If news had gotten out about Mariner's true parentage, well needless to say, the country wasn't in a stable place back then. She wasn't the only one who approved of the idea to switch our children."

Catherine looks away from Shea's gaze, her features lost in thought.

"She was a hard woman, Doris. But she loved her country, and though most would say otherwise, she loved her son. She didn't really want to give him up, but she had to. So she faked my death and displaced me so that my daughter could eventually know me and Mariner would have a reason as to why he was living at the palace."

Shea sits back in her seat, ignoring Caen's protest—Soren found needle and thread and Caen had just started stitching her up.

Shea looks at him, confused at how he's taking all of this so easily. He shrugs and grabs her arm once more.

"Royals," Caen mutters.

Shea relents and allows him to stitch her up. But this new information has her thoughts reeling.

"Wait. Joana said she knew you—"

Shea starts, but Catherine shakes her head.

"Not as a grandmother. Merely an old courtier."

"Not that old," Rhea snaps, primping her hair.

Shea's eyes narrow on the two rude crones.

"Did you know?" Shea questions.

Rhea laughs and Gaea rolls her eyes. "Of course we bloody knew," Gaea snorts.

"We were Doris's other two lady's maids, you dolt."

Shea takes a breath, counting to ten, honestly thanking Poseidon Jo didn't pick up either of her guardians' dispositions.

"This is a lot. One of my men though, they made it sound like you were an elf?"

Catherine gestures vaguely to one of her maids, who goes to her side and carefully unlaces the ribbon at the side of headdress. Shea nearly falls over in her seat, getting another curse from Caen, as she sees two points sticking out from beneath Lady Catherine's long silver-white hair.

"You're an elf!"

"She's really not that bright," Rhea sighs.

She ignores the hag and the needle weaving through her skin, though it bloody hurts. She winces but keeps her attention on Catherine.

"But Jo doesn't have points. I would know; in fact, I've checked."

"Jo's grandfather was human, which made Triteia half. A fact Doris hid easily as her points weren't well-defined. Not to mention elven slavery hadn't been abolished yet and it couldn't be well-known that Doris had an elf in her court. And then Mariner of course is also human; Jo doesn't have enough elven blood left in her to be elven, but I love her anyway." Catherine smiles and it makes Shea grin in return.

She has one of those smiles, Shea decides, like Jo. It's impossible not to smile back when they smile so beautifully at you. Catherine leaves the headdress off and finally Shea asks about the other surprise visitor in the room.

"So how do you know Soren?"

"Thetis relayed the information about the navy men who

came back from the attack. I figured you would need all the help you could get if you're going to take down my son-in-law."

"And you're both fine betraying your possible king?" Shea asks, elevating one brow at the light and dark hags.

"We serve the queens of Arethusa, not some wannabe penis that's gotten too big for his britches," Gaea snipes, and Rhea leans across the table, giving her wife a high five.

Everyone stares at them with wide eyes, and even Caen has to stop his stitching.

He chuckles and shakes his head in amusement.

"Alright." Shea grins.

Caen grumbles for her to cut the thread and she leans down and bites it clean so he can tie off the stich. She stands and gestures for the men to gather around the table. Caen and Soren stand at either side, and all the women on the other side, including the young lady's maids, lean in.

"So how do we stop this coronation?"

FIT FOR A QUEEN

SERVANTS BUSTLE AROUND JOANA'S chambers while she stands on a wooden platform in front of the floor-length mirror letting them finish dressing her. She stayed up the rest of the night after everything happened; she couldn't find the will to sleep knowing Shea and Aster were locked away somewhere in pain.

Pain that she'd caused.

All in one morning she was expected to support her father, who she now knows murdered her mother, grandmother, and unborn older sibling. Rise from the dead to give her blessing and help her monstrous father become king.

Obviously the occasion called for a new dress at Mariner's request, which is exactly what has the maids panicking as they scramble to finish her white abdication gown, with blue wisteria blossoms, most likely purposeful on Mariner's part. Her late mother's favorite flowers trail down the bodice in decorative designs, flowing into a small train behind her. Her hair is pulled up into a tight bun with a braid along the side, and a simple silver band wraps over her forehead. She looks like she would've on her own coronation day, and she doesn't fail to notice the mockery.

But she keeps her head high and her face plain and lets the

maids fuss about her appearance. The door opens without a knock and Mariner steps inside.

"You look lovely. Absolutely regal."

"Thank you, Father," Jo replies.

Mariner shakes his head with a grin.

"Your Majesty," he corrects.

"Your Majesty," Jo reiterates and returns her gaze to the mirror.

"Do you know what you're going to say?" Mariner asks with a lilt to his voice.

"Yes."

"Why don't you share it with me."

It's not a request, so Jo begins her speech of how traumatized she was by the whole kidnapping. How she dreamed of getting home but realized she couldn't go through with becoming queen. That she believes in her heart that her father should become the first king of Arethusa. That it is Amphitrite's wish and her will should be honored. Therefore, Joana of Arethusa abdicates the throne and crowns Mariner as king.

Mariner claps.

"Splendid, my dear, and good touch about Amphitrite, couldn't have written it better myself."

"How's Shea, and Aster? Are they alright?"

"The guards say they're well, and they'll continue to be as long as you do as you're told," Mariner threatens with a sharp smile.

"Now, say thank you for the dress."

"Thank you," Jo murmurs.

Mariner gestures for her to continue.

"Your Majesty."

"You're welcome. I'll see you at the doors to the throne room in an hour and not a moment later. It's time to take my rightful place on the throne."

Mariner exits the room, and it's not until a maid screeches at her side that she realizes she'd taken a pin from the dress and stabbed it into her palm. She stares at the blood and wonders what horrors might be hiding inside.

Could her child hold the same evil that her father does?

It's in that moment that she makes a decision—if she can help it, she will never produce children. The pin is disposed of and the bleeding stops quickly. The dress is complete, not a moment too soon, as the guards arrive to take her to her final destination.

BEST LAID PLANS

"**Y**OU'RE INSANE," GAEA REMARKS, examining the plan etched out on the table.

"I agree," Soren comments, rubbing his hand down his face.

"I think it'll work." Shea grins.

"Not to mention it'll be fun," Catherine laughs. "Those uptights won't know what hit them."

"Question?"

Shea looks up and sees James raising his hand.

"Yes?"

"Do we get to keep any of the jewelry we steal?"

"Absolutely not!" Rhea screeches, glaring at the young man.

"I would." Catherine winks.

Now if this is how Jo is going to be in her later years, Shea could get used to it.

"Okay, so the plan is to commit a fake robbery of the court and expose Mariner for the treasonous murderer he is?" Caen clarifies.

"Pretty much."

"Well I like it, and I'm definitely keeping whatever I find," Caen responds, crossing his arms.

There's a rhythmic knock at the door, and Catherine's matron who had helped Shea, Jo, and Aster get into the castle walks in dressed in a fine gown and veil. She pushes the veil back.

"My lady. The coronation is in an hour; we need to get you dressed," she says, and shoos the young maidens to the back chambers, who honestly had been no help at all, simply flirting with the crewmen. The matron walks over to Catherine and helps her up from her chair.

"Well, I guess we'll see you in there." Catherine smiles and starts heading toward her bedroom.

"We best be going as well," Rhea grunts, getting up as quickly as she can manage, and Gaea starts moving as well but wobbles, and cracks can be heard from their stretching bodies.

Soren reaches out to help her, but she smacks him instead.

"Watch it, boy, or I'll hit you where the sun don't shine."

The two old crones take each other's hands and move to the door before stopping. They both turn back to look at Shea.

"You best not lose, elfling," Gaea growls.

"Or die," Rhea mutters. "We don't need some dick running the show. You've seen Lycos."

"Lycos is run by a woman. Empress Ceto," James tells them, confused.

"So? She's got more balls than any man on the continent," Gaea snaps.

"And look how well that's turned out."

And with that, the crones slam the door on their way out. James hurries and locks it behind them to prevent them from coming back.

"I like them," Caen announces with a smirk.

"Of course you do," Shea mumbles, rolling her eyes.

"You're going to need a weapon," Soren tells her and, to her disappointment, hands her a sturdy iron blade that is definitely not her gold one.

"Sorry," Soren tells her when he notices her expression, "apparently Mariner is using your sword as the coronation blade. A trophy of sorts."

"I'm gonna kill him," Shea mutters, inspecting the blade. It'll do.

"Soren, you'll seal off the exits with your men?"

Soren nods. "They know the princess is alive, they're ready to fight for their queendom. The guards might be tough, but they're not soldiers. We are."

Shea holds out her hand with a grin and Soren takes her forearm with a strong grip. They nod in alliance.

"Go, we'll be close behind," Shea orders.

Soren leaves with a bow and heads out the door to ready the navy men.

Now she has to ready her own men; she turns to the eight souls looking at her and hopes she won't let them down.

"This could go south," Shea speaks to her small crew. "You sure you wanna do this?"

Caen steps closer to her and then turns so he's at her side. He's with her. The other men glance among themselves and then James steps forward with a grin.

"We're with you, Captain. Till the end."

"Alright then." Shea smiles. "Weapons?"

Caen removes his hammer from his back and takes a swing, careful not to knock over anything important. The rest have swords.

Shea nods approvingly. Time to go. The men draw their weapons. She takes another look at the map and commits the hallways to memory.

"Remember we're going to try to keep casualties to a minimum with the guard. Aim to hurt, not to kill," Shea reminds them, leading the party toward the door.

"And Mariner?" Lady Catherine asks, exiting her bedroom dressed.

"He's mine," Shea orders.

Lady Catherine sighs. For a moment, Shea thinks Catherine doesn't approve.

"Knock him dead," she finally answers, "for my daughter."

Shea curtsies with as much effort and precision as she can.

She wants to give Catherine her respects. Then Shea throws open the door.

"Let's go."

RISE OF THE PATRIARCHY

Joana

THE GRAND DOORS TO THE throne room stand between Jo and the rest of the court. She stares absently at the white marble entry and knows once she steps through them, Arethusa will change forever. She is about to condemn her people, the very people she has put before everything, to live under Mariner's absolute rule, and all she can think about is how much she wishes that Shea were here, standing beside her.

She wishes she could hold her captain one last time. She wishes she could tell Aster how sorry she is. She stands there waiting, wondering if the woman she loves is thinking about her or even still loves her at all. She feels selfish, like the airheaded royal Shea made her out to be in the beginning, and for the first time she almost believes it too.

Mariner saunters in from the left hall, dressed in a white suit. His dress shoes are the color of ivory and at the hem of his slacks miniature conch shells are embroidered in silk thread all the way around. His jacket flows to the ground in a train and his dress shirt is embroidered over the pocket, as is the tradition.

But instead of the usual Arethusian symbol of their goddess Amphitrite's face and a dolphin creating a half circle behind her head, there is a red trident embroidered in her place.

"What do you think of the new coronation robes?"

"You look wonderful, Your Majesty," Jo answers, keeping her voice neutral.

"Out with the old goddess and in with the king, wouldn't you agree?"

He's baiting her. It's utter blasphemy and Jo can't bring herself to say anything, so instead she nods, hoping that will suffice.

"Shall we?" Mariner asks, holding out his arm as if he were a gentleman, and Jo reluctantly takes it.

Mariner nods to the two guards—no, navy men, Jo realizes, slightly confused at their presence as she takes in their uniforms. They open the doors. The music begins and the court turns to see Mariner walking down the aisle to the throne. Mariner steps forward, Jo at his side, and they enter together.

The hall erupts in whispers and gasps as Mariner leads Jo to the front of the ballroom. The Arethusian priestess, in charge of leading the coronation, calls for the music to stop. But Mariner simply smiles and waves to the audience; he continues to drag Jo up to the front as if strolling to invisible music. The room is in evident shock as courtiers stand around dumbly staring at their supposedly dead princess.

Once at the thrones, Mariner bows to the crowd and gestures for Jo to do the same, and she does. The crowd bows back out of habit, and Jo can see the members of the council coming to the forefront. She even sees Lord Tyber, who apparently does support her father. He looks around nervously at the other members of the Council of Nobles, tugging at his collar.

"I have wonderful news, everyone," Mariner shouts gleefully. "Due to an undercover mission, my daughter was rescued from where she was being held captive. Apparently the dread and now dead pirate, Captain Shea of the *Veiled Duchess*, marooned her on an island to the south of Lycos. Empress Ceto has sent her back to me on good faith and as a show of a strong future alliance," Mariner continues.

He's grandstanding, but even he can see he's quickly becoming old news. The long-lost princess has returned, which means there's no need for him; unfortunately, he's more powerful than they realize.

"Now my daughter wishes to speak," Mariner starts, clapping drowning out any comments to be made by the now forefront council.

The other courtiers follow suit, awkwardly trying in vain to understand exactly what's happening. Jo spots a few familiar faces in the crowd, Rhea and Gaea, and she even sees Lady Catherine, who helped get Shea, Aster, and her into the castle.

"It's so very good to see all of your faces again," Jo murmurs before she starts her long monologue of how her trials have made her unfit to rule and how she knows it's time to make a change and crown the first king. When she's done, the former whispering has turned into loud cries, and Jo wants to come clean. She wants to expose Mariner for the murderer he is and destroy him. But she can't lose another person at his treacherous hands, so she smiles. She smiles so the whole world can't see she's splintering to the core.

"I trust the princess, we should honor her wishes and crown Mariner," Lord Tyber shouts, and a faction of his party applauds and cheers. The rest of the room looks around warily, and as her gaze lands on the other members of the council, she realizes they're not buying it.

"It is the princess's prerogative to choose her successor," a councilwoman commands, a woman who has served on the council since the reign of Jo's grandmother Doris, and the rest follow suit, nodding in agreement. She can see the old woman imploring her to speak up.

"Well then?" Mariner asks, turning to Jo, and his glare is firm; one wrong move and her friends are dead.

"We came here to crown Prince Mariner," Jo answers, and the priestess steps forward with the royal crown. "Let's make him king."

Half the room erupts in applause. The old councilwoman shakes her head in disappointment, but her own faction stays silent next to Tyber's elated one. Mariner surprises Jo slightly, taking her firmly but gently by the arm and leading her back to the thrones. He guides her, instead of to her normal seat in the ruler's chair, to the smaller consort seat next to it. And doesn't that burn just a little?

"Prince Mariner," the priestess's voice echoes through the ballroom, "step forward…"

Mariner winks down at Jo in her small, mocking throne and turns on her, walking back toward the court. He stands tall in front of their subjects, listening to the priestess begin the coronation rites.

Jo can't watch; instead she looks over at the massive fountain off to the side, of a proud Queen Amphitrite standing in a blast of marble water on a silver chariot with two mighty dolphins leading her, a smaller trident than that of Poseidon's in her grasp.

She studies Amphitrite's beautiful but powerful face, and as Jo stares, she can't help but think Amphitrite's marble features look very disappointed.

FARTHER TO FALL

Shea

THERE'S NO MORE HIDING. Captain Shea and her men storm the halls of the castle toward the ballroom. Back to where it all began.

They take down three guards easily on the way. The first rushes at her with a cry, and she sidesteps as he lunges his sword for her chest. He stumbles forward at the momentum and she grasps the back of his coat, nearly pulling him off his feet. She wraps her arm around his neck, his back bending as she chokes him to the point of passing out. He hits the ground with a thud. The other two guards stand frozen on the spot and Shea snaps her fingers. Caen and James step forward, grinning.

Caen swings his hammer, bashing his guy right into the wall. He crumples in a heap, groaning; he won't be getting up and he won't be following them either.

James jumps, tackling the left guard using his body to swing him around and to the ground. He lands with the man's head between his thighs. He's careful not to snap his neck, but it takes a moment for James to incapacitate him.

"James, no killing," Shea warns.

"I'm not," James groans, squeezing harder, "he's just taking some effort to subdue."

The guard's head falls to the side, unconscious. Shea gestures for whomever to check their pulses before the pirates move on.

Finally they arrive at the marble doors. The sun is shining through the water, streaming over the windows, and Shea reluctantly admits she likes the palace in the morning.

Two armed navy men stand at attention watching the nine of them warily. Shea's hand goes to the hilt of the iron blade she's been forced to work with, but Soren comes jogging from the left corridor.

"Wait, they're my men. It's okay."

"The perimeter?"

"It's sealed," Soren answers her. "No one is getting in or out. Mariner's treason ends today."

"By Poseidon I hope so," she mutters a prayer.

Shea unsheathes the sword, letting it rest on her shoulder.

"How many guards are inside? No way the inner ballroom is left unattended?" Caen questions as he cracks his neck in preparation.

"I've got the three on the inside who will take care of the back guard as soon as these doors open," Soren explains. "There are six up front. Three on either side of the thrones."

"Nothing we can't handle," a crewman from behind grunts, and the rest murmur their agreement.

A female voice carries through the small cracks in the monstrous marble door, and it's time. The coronation is under way.

"Good luck." Soren grins.

"You too," Shea shoots back.

She waits until he's taken off for the other entrance into the ball before nodding to the navy men at the door. "Open it."

They salute her with respect, and it gives her all the more confidence as they clasp the large handles and pull the doors open. The ballroom is just like Shea remembers. The water falling over the open arched windows, the blue and white banners stitched across the vault ceiling, and the Amphitrite fountain standing proud. There are just as many people too, and all heads turn to the back, wondering who's coming through the doors. Shea vaguely hears grunts to both sides as she steps in and realizes it's the inner guards being taken down.

Time to begin the theatrics. Shea clears her throat and offers her audience a big smile.

"Good morning, ladies and gentlemen. I hope you've been enjoying the coronation. I'm Captain Shea Lara"—Shea bows, exaggerating the movement with an eccentric grin—"and this is a robbery."

She points ahead to where Mariner is kneeling before a priestess with a crown in her hands.

"Nobody move," Shea shouts, and there are screams and whispers from the courtiers as four men fan out into the crowd, taking down anyone who might think themselves a hero. Whispers break out among the people, and Shea swears she hears someone whisper she's supposed to be dead.

Shea whistles, alerting Caen, James, and the other men, gesturing to the six guards coming their way. Caen laughs heartily and charges forward, slamming his hammer into the first. He hits the second over the head, and as soon as he goes down, Caen walks over him, squishing his feet into the man's back.

Shea holds back, letting them do the work and pretending to be bored while leaning on her iron sword and checking her nails. Playing the part of the evil pirate perfectly.

Caen easily takes on the third guard. Shea mockingly rolls her eyes, scanning the audience, and needless to say, they're buying it. She watches while James and the others dispatch the remaining three.

One particularly skilled fighter is their first casualty of the morning, as he almost kills one of the crewmen, leaving James with no other choice but to run him through. The guard goes limp and the crewman who was being pummeled underneath him pushes himself out from under the deadweight.

Shea keeps her expression blank, moving up the aisle. Inwardly she wishes there had been another way; she didn't want any more casualties for Jo.

Shea saunters toward the priestess and Mariner, who hasn't moved from his kneeling position, probably still in shock.

Shea uses the subpar sword like a walking stick, as a noble would, and the taunt seems to jolt Mariner enough to stand. Shea's eyes shoot past him toward Jo, who she finds sitting in one of the thrones behind him. Jo rises at the sight of Shea, not bothering to hide that gorgeous luminescent smile on her face.

"Hello, Mariner," Shea drawls. "Miss me?"

At the sight of her boasting smile, Mariner's hand goes for her real sword, her beautifully crafted pure gold one on his waist.

She scolds him.

"No, hands off," she orders, extending the pitiful iron blade toward his chest.

He relinquishes his hold on her gold one.

"That is a beautiful crown," Shea remarks to the priestess, neither sword nor eyes wavering from Mariner. She can see the priestess shaking in her periphery, and the pirate grins. "I'd like to wear it."

The priestess hastily moves forward, and Shea has to wonder: Does no one in this country have a backbone? The lady places the crown delicately on the captain's head and with her free hand adjusts it nicely.

Shea sighs. "Thanks. Now while I have you all here..." She laughs, waiting as her men gather the guards up to keep watch on them all together.

Caen stalks closer to the front, leaving the other men to guard the captives. He keeps his eyes on Mariner as Shea turns her back to him to face the crowd, all the while keeping her sword pointed at the prince's chest.

"I'm going to tell you how this court got my attention," Shea begins.

"We care not for your lies," a man yells near the front,

dressed in fine robes. He seems to be standing with a group of people dressed similarly in the national colors. Shea uses what intellect she has to assume they must be the council. Which makes loudmouth over there Lord Tyber.

"Lord Tyber is it?" Shea hums questioningly.

He nods warily.

"Ah yes, I'll get to you soon for damaging my ship," Shea growls, and he shrinks in on himself nervously.

Mariner attempts to slowly retreat a step while Shea's back is turned, and Caen whistles. Shea doesn't turn. She instead yells back to her princess, "Jo, darling, would you be a dear and restrain your father?"

Mariner snorts. "What's she going to—"

He's cut off with a grunt. No one even hears her move as Jo roundhouse kicks her father forward at the back of his head. He lands on his hands and knees, just barely catching himself.

Jo goes to his throat and holds him steady in a chokehold. Shea glances back to see her position and make sure she's alright. She smiles—looks like those lessons Shea gave her paid off.

"Got him," Jo grunts.

The crowd is silent; no one is really sure what to do. Not even the guards, who have awoken from the attack. They're now just staring at their former crowned princess in dismay.

Shea turns her attention back to the courtiers, and she has to swallow down a bit of laughter as she sees her four men she'd sent into the crowd actually stopping and collecting jewelry. Shea nods to the display between Mariner, who is struggling lightly, and Jo holding him back.

"Yeah! I'm in league with the princess, shocking, I know. See, I was contracted to maroon her on an island at the edge of the world. By one of you." Shea gestures with both arms out to the crowd.

"Preposterous," Lord Tyber shouts.

The rest of the council steps away from Tyber, watching him with great concern.

"Not entirely," Shea responds. "I am guilty of kidnapping the princess, but really, you all made it too easy. Of course we had help from a much higher power than I expected. I was taking her to Tenaro where I had been instructed to maroon her, when I got to know her," Shea starts, bringing down the theatrics.

She begins speaking to the people of Arethusa plainly.

"Your princess is stronger than you ever could have hoped for." Shea is watching the reactions of the council, and while most of them still look stern, she can tell she has their attention.

"My ship was attacked by your navy. Who told me I had murdered the woman still in my custody, and that they had been given orders to sail out to Orena days before the kidnapping to wait for my ship. They were given orders to stop a murderer, before the murder had even happened, and with no evidence to even suspect me. We quickly found out the orders came from a Lord Tyber and that instead of investigating the ship, it was to be blown to Hades. Fortunately, we took down your navy, and when they found the princess alive, they were more than a little confused."

Shouts erupt from the crowd and Shea can see Lieutenant Soren and three navy men close in from behind, pushing their way through to the aisle and continuing toward the pirates.

"I can attest to the story," Soren shouts, coming up to stand beside Shea.

"And who are you?" a lady courtier questions.

"I am the lieutenant who was charged with blowing up the princess under Tyber's orders."

"You tried to murder the princess," another councilwoman shouts, pointing at Tyber.

"I was only following orders," Tyber snaps back.

Mariner groans at the man's idiocy.

"Whose orders?" an old councilwoman interrogates.

"Prince Mariner's," Shea answers.

Every head swivels back to the front of the ballroom.

"We arrived at the castle late last night hoping to seek aid from Joana's father," Shea continues her story.

"This is ridiculous," Mariner claims with a strained smile.

Shea opens her mouth to counter him, but Jo bellows instead, "No. I'm sorry that I lied to you all this morning, but I was coerced by threat to say what I did. Last night my father in his chambers confessed to the murder of my mother, Queen Triteia."

The room erupts into chaos; men and women alike begin shouting their outrage and disbelief.

"And my grandmother Queen Doris," Jo continues, "and the unborn first child of my father and mother, as well as the surrogate who carried the baby." Jo seethes, the barely controlled rage dripping from her voice.

A choked noise escapes from Mariner, and Shea realizes Jo's grip has tightened.

"Murderer!" Someone shouts from the audience and more voices join in.

"Bastard!"

"You have no right to rule!"

"I—" Mariner chokes out, trying to speak, his hands starting to claw at Jo's tight grip.

"Jo," Shea calls softly.

Jo's eyes snap to Shea and there's a flicker of something that makes Shea believe she's not going to stop, before Jo finally loosens her hold so Mariner can answer.

Mariner coughs thickly, growling, "I have every right."

He seethes.

"I am the true son of Queen Doris!"

It happens before Shea can even realize what he's done. Mariner's elbow flies back and hits Jo square in the stomach. It's fast and hard, and Jo folds over, releasing him, trying to catch her breath. Then he's up, drawing his sword. He reaches for Jo, forcing her to stand, as he places the blade at her throat just like last night.

"It's over, Mariner," Shea states, her sword tense and at the ready.

She throws the crown off her head to the ground.

"No! It's my right! My birthright!"

"No," Lady Catherine speaks from the crowd, and the people part like the tide pulling back from the shore. "The people of Arethusa will never recognize you as king."

Everyone cheers in agreement, but Shea steps forward nervously as she watches Mariner quickly losing control.

Jo is gagging, still trying to catch her breath from the blow to her gut.

"Don't make this worse," Shea tells him, and she sees it in his eyes: How can this get worse?

He ventures farther back onto the throne platform until his body is pressed against the wood paneling behind the thrones.

"You vile little elfling, I should have killed you when I had the chance," he spits. "Let your whore sit on the throne for now"—he shakes Jo forcefully—"I will return and claim what is rightfully mine."

One of his hands snakes behind him to the wall panel as Caen shouts, "You've nowhere else to go."

Shea hears the click of gears turning before it touches human ears. There is a way out. Shea sheathes the iron sword and her right foot hits the ground at a run as she storms toward them. The panel Mariner is pressed up against slides open and he doesn't hesitate as he pushes Jo at Shea to block her path.

The door is already closing and Mariner is through. Jo hurtles toward Shea, and Shea uses as much momentum as she can. She can hear footsteps behind her, but they're too far back to make it through before the door shuts. Shea grasps Jo. She spins them around, memorizing each feature of Jo's beautiful face, the movement feels so slow. Shea throws Jo toward the steps in front of the thrones and jumps through the secret passage.

She slides past the closing panel just as it shuts behind her.

Shea gathers her breath, and she can hear Caen's exasperated shout from the other side, "Did anyone know that was there?"

Jo's breathless voice carries through the wood as Shea pushes herself off the floor.

The banging from fists echoes throughout the secret passage, and Shea gets a mere moment to look around the room before pain shoots up her injured arm, Caen's stitches having broken open. It's a dome, the ceiling low with candles lit all the way around, and there's a dark arched exit on the other side; the ground is like sand or dirt. It's an arena. On her feet, she groans. Blood is seeping through her ripped shirt.

She's barely looked up from her wounded arm when a huge fist fills her vision. The punch almost knocks her off the ground. Shea lands half kneeling, with one hand on her knee and the other holding herself up. When she tries to push herself up to stand, she makes the mistake of looking around to find Mariner, and he lands another solid punch to her face, this time sending her sprawling to the floor.

Shea gasps, spits, and licks her bottom lip, tasting blood. Out of the corner of her eye, she sees the iron blade that has slipped out of her too big holster off to the side. She scrambles, grabbing it, and manages to turn onto her back and block the blow as Mariner brings down her golden blade.

She catches it with the iron one.

Shea kicks out her legs and he's close enough that it causes Mariner to stumble back. It gives Shea enough time to find her feet and a defensive position.

"All my plans...What does it matter to you? You have no allegiance!"

"You're wrong. I have two, one to my crew. And one to your daughter," Shea growls.

The pounding on the secret door becomes more insistent. Mariner and Shea circle each other, their shadows flickering on the walls from the candlelight.

"She's just another slut in your lineup," Mariner spits.

"You really don't know your daughter."

Shea makes the first move. She catches him off guard,

but the gold sword roughly connects, blocking her blow. He winces at the awkward angle, but he parries the next hit, blocking each offensive strike. They break, eyeing each other uneasily.

"I'm not some royal who was taught to fight in the courtyard." Mariner laughs. "I was a soldier."

"I'm sure you were a great show pony," Shea mocks.

Mariner shouts in anguish, attacking with more vigor than Shea expects. She blocks the blows easily, matching his footing expertly, but he's right. He's not bad at all. She spins, narrowly missing a lunge, but dances out of reach just in time.

"How do you think this is going to end?"

"With your head on a pike," Shea snaps.

"No, not us." Mariner grins. "You and her."

Shea dances out of his grasp once again, sliding under his legs before slashing him across the back. Mariner cries out, reaching vainly for his back in blinding pain. Shea quickly falls back into a defensive position. Mariner growls when his hand comes back with blood. He looks over to Shea with a harsh expression before chuckling. It catches Shea off guard as she tries to keep her focus.

"She'll marry, you know," he continues his blathering. "Someone of good standing because you're no one. You have no value to give her or her people."

Shea blindly makes the next move. She lunges, but it's off-kilter and Mariner dodges easily out of the way. She tries to shake off his words, both mentally and physically, knowing instinctively what they are—a distraction. She's used similar tactics.

"You think she can just ignore your crimes? What happens if she can't pardon you, when you cross the line one too many times? You're a pirate after all." Mariner parries Shea's every blow.

And his strikes come back with more strength, landing harder and harder every time. Shea doesn't anticipate his next move, and she gasps when she feels his foot go behind her ankle, swiping her feet off the ground. Shea lands on her back. Her breath leaves her body for a quick moment. Her vision blurs, and when it comes back to her, her eyes widen and she rolls to the side as Mariner's sword plummets into the ground where her head used to be.

She leans back into the floor, using her arms and legs to jump up to a standing position. She grasps her sword before he can take it.

"She'll have no choice," Mariner says, swinging his sword in a taunting circle, "but to sentence you. Do you think she'll watch? As you're led to the block? As the executioner severs your head from your body? Do you think she'll cry?"

Shea bellows, storming into an offensive position, slicing and slashing the weak iron blade, desperately trying to catch him off guard. She continues to push his voice hopelessly out of her head as he blocks every laughable blow.

"Either way," he breathes, "you can't stay. Oh you'll promise her, but you'll leave. It's not in you to be kept. She'll be heart-broken."

Shea shakes her head, blocking a particularly hard thrust.

"Because everyone leaves her. You'll be the final blow. You'll break her."

Shea lets out a guttural scream, bringing the sword down one last time. But the strength of the gold outweighs the iron and the sword is flung from her fingertips. He swings the sword and slices behind her kneecap. Shea falls to her healthy knee with a pained shout. She looks up in defiance. He doesn't hesitate as he slashes the blade down across her left eye. Shea screeches in agony, falling helplessly to the ground. Her hand goes to her wounded eye, covering it as hot blood runs down her cheek. Mariner kicks her in the stomach, flipping her hard onto her back, so that she can look up at him with her remaining good eye.

There's a loud boom and Shea sucks in a sob as she tries to glance back at the paneled door. Dazed from the trauma, she thinks she can see splinters of wood as someone pounds their way in. Her right eye flutters back in time to see Mariner lunging his sword down at her heart.

Her reflexes shoot up and she catches the gold blade between her palms. Shea groans as the sharp edges cut into her hands, and she uses all of her strength to stop the blade from coming down even farther. Mariner kneels, pressing the sword down until he is sitting on her waist so she can't move. He admires what used to be her left eye, sneering, his fingertips brushing her left upper cheek, both sides swelling from the first two punches. The gold blade moves slowly between her palms, as the blood partially slicks the way and he presses his weight onto the hilt causing it to press closer to her chest. Shea grunts at the force.

"She'll forget you, when you leave," he says, and Shea fears she's going to pass out from the pain. "She'll move on. You'll be a distant fling she once had in her youth. She won't even remember your name. Just the elf she fucked a couple of times." Mariner laughs.

Shea whimpers, the blade's edges slicing the inside of her palms.

"You'll die alone, maybe drunk like I found you. A scarred, one-eyed old maid all used up."

She manages to maneuver the sword a little farther up until it's hovering over her left shoulder instead of her heart. The sweat and blood on her palms is enough for the blade to slip through. Her hands falter, and she cries out as the sword plunges into her shoulder. She manages to get a grip on the blade once again before it can go all the way through.

"You might as well let go," Mariner drawls. "Your kind is going extinct anyway. Wouldn't you like to be with your people?"

He snarls and pushes the blade down as hard as he can. There's no sound as the blade runs straight through. Shea gasps, her back arching and her mouth open in a guttural cry. Both of them are so engrossed in each other they don't hear the panel slam open. Her senses overtake her as Mariner twists the blade just above her chest, damaging the muscle and nerves to the point it feels as if the blade were dipped in fire.

"Well you're not drunk or old, but looks like you get to die alone anyway," Mariner hisses.

Her vision blurs, but a wet squelching sound fills her ears. She opens her right eye and tries to focus on Mariner. There's something that wasn't there before. The iron blade that was ripped from her hands appears—run straight through Mariner's chest.

He chokes, gurgling in his throat, releasing the hilt of the gold sword embedded in Shea's shoulder. His hands touch the end of iron sword protruding through his chest. Jo's furious face appears at his side.

"She is not alone. And the only one dying today," Jo says, taking the blade out and stabbing him straight through once again, "is you."

Blood spills past his lips, and he opens his mouth, either gasping for air or trying to speak, but neither happens. Instead he falls sideways off of Shea, and Shea's head follows his slumped-over body. His dead pale blue eyes stare unseeing straight into Shea's dying green one.

"Shea," Jo gasps, rushing forward.

She tries to gather Shea up in her arms, but Shea shouts when the sword embedded in her shoulder tugs, pinning her to the ground. Instead of moving Shea, Jo pushes her dead father away until she can sit by and hold Shea's head in between her palms. Black spots are filling what's left of Shea's vision.

"What has he done to you?" Jo whispers.

Shea can just barely feel Jo's fingertips brush against her damaged eye.

"I didn't need it anyway," Shea chuckles, her breath rasping.

"No," Jo tells her, wanting to pull Shea's upper body onto her lap, "stay with me. You have to stay with me."

"You were amazing," Shea grunts; her shoulder is a ball of pain, but Jo's here, and Shea feels so tired.

"So were you. I'm here, love. I've got you."

"We got him," Shea mutters.

Jo smiles and kisses the top of Shea's forehead, tears streaming down the princess's face.

"Yes, we did."

"It hurts," Shea tells Jo, and a single tear falls from her right eye.

"I know, love, we're going to get you fixed up."

"Shea!" Caen roars, rushing to her side. He moves Jo out of the way, and Jo comes to Shea's other side.

"Son of a bitch," Caen growls, taking in the damage. "We need to get her moved if we've got any chance."

Caen shouts to the crewmen filing through the secret door to find a board of wood to carry Shea on. He quickly stands to help them move faster. Shea's fading attention falls back to Jo.

"I wish we had more time," Shea says, her remaining vision slipping.

"We have all the time in the world because you're not dying. Because I love you and I'm going to marry you, Shea, and we are going to be a family, you, Aster, and me, Hades even kids of our own. I promise you the world, Shea Lara, if you just hold on. Hold on for me," Jo commands.

She wipes her nose with her hand and then glares at the sword still embedded in Shea's chest. "This stupid thing."

Jo grabs the handle, and Shea pushes herself to speak, to say something, "Jo...no."

But Jo takes the sword out. It's like a rush of relief, and she can feel her life force pouring from the wound.

"Joana, no!" Caen snarls. "She'll bleed out!"

Shea's lips twitch into a harsh semblance of a smile because of course the princess would be the death of her after all. Her eye closes, and Shea swears she can hear the sound of the ocean as she falls deeper into darkness.

THE ACCORD

Shea

PAIN. INHUMAN, TORTUROUS PAIN. Agony, red and then black. But out of the black, colors of blue and teal spin threads, threads that make up a giant quilt like the seabed covering Shea's vision. Gold flashes throughout the material, and when she reaches out to touch, it's wet and thick like tree sap.

Daughter, something whispers from the blue. It chills Shea down to the core of whatever she is now. A ghost?

He's coming…

She tries to shout back: Who? Who's coming?

The storm is coming…

A sensation of cold. Energy flows through her body, and as she looks out into the aether, she can just discern the outline of a massive city with black pearl gates before the water crashes over it. It suffocates her and pulls her back to an unknown surface. Shea gasps for breath, her eyes snapping open, though something soft is covering the left one.

Bright light tortures her vision in her right eye as it slowly recedes into shapes and normal color. Material of light blue and gold cover the top of what she realizes is a bed. It doesn't take long for the pain in her shoulder to overload her senses, and she gasps, going to grab it with her other hand, but she is stopped by something cold and strong.

Shea looks to see a manacle wrapped around her right wrist.

"What the—"

Her vision slowly adjusts, and as the last of the black spots recede, she can finally see the room around her. A white marble fireplace is straight ahead of the bed, and off to the side is a door. There's a long, low dresser in the corner with bowls, instruments, and bandages scattered across it and a tree next to it.

Someone moans off to Shea's side.

She turns over and sees Jo sitting at her bedside, her head lying on the bed, and her arms used as a pillow. Her hair is pulled up into a loose bun with pins stuck throughout with pearls at the end and she's wearing a pink dress that looks made for royalty. Shea watches her silently, not wanting to wake her; instead she attempts to figure out how much rotation she's got in her injured shoulder and finds she has surprisingly good motion for an injury this extreme; she must have been out a long time.

"You're awake."

She jumps and finds Jo looking at her, her head in her palm, propped up by her elbow.

"No thanks to you if I remember," Shea teases.

And she realizes she hasn't lost her touch for awkward comments, as Jo pulls back, horrified. "I am so sorry. I didn't think and I knew better. I just couldn't bear seeing you that way and I wasn't thinking."

"Hey," she soothes, reaching out the best she can with her injured left arm and pushing a couple white-blond strands of hair off her face. "I'm here, okay. I'm okay."

"Nol stitched you up. He said the first twenty-four hours were crucial, but when he checked your bandages around the seventh hour, he said your improvement was something he'd never seen before," Jo tells her, and there's wonder in her eyes that Shea wishes would go away.

"Can't get rid of me that easily." She winks, burying the

voice she'd heard in her sleep. She'll think about that later.

"Wait," Shea jolts, realizing what Jo just said. "Twenty-four hours? How long have I been asleep?"

"About two days," Jo answers, then chuckles. "Longest two days of my life."

Shea doesn't answer. Instead she has to lie back. She schools her features. With a wound like this and the blows she took to her head, she should have been out a lot longer, weeks in fact, but she doesn't tell Jo that.

"Well, I'm awake."

"Yes, you are." Jo smiles.

"Now what's with the cuffs?" Shea asks, raising a brow and wriggling the manacles.

"Ah, well the council took some time coming to terms with your help. They're a little untrustworthy at the moment," Jo says, and Shea can't help but snort in amusement.

"So? Am I speaking to the future queen of Arethusa?" she questions.

"They're crowning me tonight," Jo responds, pushing a strand of hair behind her ear.

Shea watches the movement and remembers Lady Catherine.

"Jo, Lady Catherine—"

"Is my grandmother? I know. She came to me after it all happened and told me her side of things while Nol had you in surgery. Caen was pacing the halls like crazy and he was mad at me for pulling the sword out of your chest and nearly killing you, so…Catherine kept me company."

Shea laughs. Good, she's happy they managed to connect.

"Looks like you've got some real family after all," Shea teases, and Jo rolls her eyes.

"So where is the great ball of worry?"

"Caen? Outside, he hasn't left the door, keeping it guarded."

"Aster?"

The thought hits her like a wave, and suddenly she's pushing herself to sit up in bed.

"Hey, whoa," Jo commands, helping Shea lean up against the headboard when she sees her wince. "He's okay. He's even been by, but James escorted him back to the ship. He's still got some healing to do, mostly mental, but for now he's okay."

Shea sighs in relief.

"Everyone's okay?"

"It's hard to believe, isn't it?" Jo chuckles and Shea agrees.

"So I guess the last thing to do is for me to head out of here."

"Maybe," Jo answers, lightly rubbing her forehead. "Or you could stay?"

"Am I not free to go?" Shea inquires, and Jo shakes her head.

"No, of course. I have a pardon with your name on it already drawn up once I become queen. It exonerates you to present date though, so whatever you do after this…"

"I'll be a Grace," Shea grins.

"I don't know how much you remember before you passed out, but you could stay. And…marry me."

"What?"

"Well, as queen, I need a consort. And I want that to be you."

"Jo," Shea starts, searching for the right words, "I love you, but as crazy as your dad was, he had a point. I don't think I'm built for this life."

"You once asked me to give up everything for you," Jo begins.

"Yeah, and you said no," Shea reminds her with a raised right brow.

"You're right," Jo acknowledges. "I wasn't strong enough. So let me ask you what you once asked me. Do you think I'm worth it?"

"That's not fair," Shea grumbles.

"Our love never will be," Jo laughs.

"It's always going to be one or the other isn't it?"

"After tonight, there's only one way."

Shea nods.

"Look, I promised you the world, Shea Lara, and I will do anything to make sure I can keep that promise."

They lapse into silence, and Shea thinks about how she's just gotten her ship back. But she also thinks about how much she loves Jo. And then, a light flickers on.

"Okay," Shea tells her.

"Okay?" Jo repeats.

"Yes, but first, I have a stipulation for you."

"Stipulation?"

"Call it a condition about our engagement."

"Proceed," Jo teases.

"I will marry you, but…"

"What?"

"You have to catch me first."

"Shea," Jo boasts, "I've already caught you."

Shea doesn't respond, instead she merely catches Jo's face in her injured arm's palm and brings her forward.

"Kiss on it?"

Jo smiles and leans forward, kissing Shea deeply. Shea wraps her arm lightly around Jo's neck, pulling her close, and subtly grabs one of the pins out of her hair. She keeps the kiss going as she pushes the pin into her manacled hand and begins working on the lock. Just as she thinks she has it, she moans loudly to cover up the click.

As fast as she can, Shea pulls the manacle to Jo's wrist as Jo places her palm on the side of Shea's face. And as they break apart, Shea clasps the manacle around Jo's forearm, locking it in place.

"What—" Jo's forehead wrinkles in confusion as she looks down at her now manacled arm.

Shea rolls out of bed as softly as she can in the opposite direction, away from Jo, while the queen-to-be stares after her, stunned.

"How did you—"

Jo looks down, tugging on the manacle, but it's locked in place. Shea grins and pushes herself off the bed, nearly tumbling onto the floor.

"Walking…Right, I know how to do that," Shea mutters.

"Oh, you've got to be kidding me," Jo growls, pulling on the chain.

"Now remember you kissed on it; I'll marry you when you catch me, and I'll try not to make it too long of an engagement." Shea grins.

She goes for her clothes at the end of the bed as she realizes she's only in her bandages and undergarments. Shea is almost finished dressing when she has to grab the bed frame to steady herself—a wave of dizziness distracts her.

She grasps her head lightly, feeling the bandage over her left eye, and glances to the mirror over the dresser.

"You shouldn't be up like this," Jo yells. "You need to sit down."

Shea waves her off. "I'm perfectly capable."

She stumbles to the dresser, looking into the mirror hanging on the wall. She examines her clothes, her brown pants and teal peasant blouse obviously new as the lack of tears and blood is evident. Her gaze travels up to her long, curly red hair that springs wildly in all directions, tamed only by the bandage wrapped around her head and left eye. Shea reaches up to pull it off.

"Shea, you shouldn't do that," Jo warns, obviously struggling with saying something.

Shea unwraps the bandage, closing her right eye. And once it's completely off, Shea looks.

"Caen," Jo shouts.

"Tattletale," Shea whispers, but her one good eye is glued to the impossible vision in front of her. Though she was expecting a black hole where her left eye used to be, she sees it still intact. Her eyelid is there as well, as if magic had stitched it back together, but there's a long gash that stops right above her brow and below her upper cheekbone. What shocks her, though, is the color—her normal vibrant green has completely bled away, and in its place is pure white.

No pupil, just white.

It's slightly unnerving, and yet Shea is mesmerized by the

fact that in forty-eight hours after an impossible injury, her body has healed itself to extraordinary lengths.

"Caen!" Jo shouts again.

The door to the bedchamber flings open and in storms Caen with Nol directly behind him.

"What's wrong?"

Jo points to Shea, who has since broken her transfixion on her new appearance and is back to struggling to get her boots on.

"Oh, she's just mad that I promised to marry her but not until she catches me first. So, we need to go if I'm going to get anything done in between the time before she does," Shea explains, wriggling her right foot until it pops into the boot.

"How are you—" Nol starts, but Caen cuts him off.

"So the first thing you do after being pardoned is chain the future queen of Arethusa to the bed?"

"When you put it like that, it makes it sound dirty." Shea winks, smirking over at Jo, who rolls her eyes in exasperation.

"Caen, she shouldn't be up," Jo demands.

But Caen's already helping.

"You need me to carry you?" Caen asks.

"Possibly, but I'm going to try walking first."

"Don't worry, Your Majesty, I'll make sure she gets plenty of rest," Nol tells Jo, bowing while also staring at Shea curiously.

Shea slips on her other boot and Caen reaches out his hand to help her when she sees her gold sword at his waist.

"My sword," Shea coos, "you really do always come back to me."

Shea caresses it slightly.

"Don't do that when it's attached to me," Caen exclaims.

"Sorry," Shea mutters and clears her throat.

She's about to limp out of the room when Jo calls after her. "Shea!"

Shea turns back to her with a smirk. "Yes, my love?"

"You really want to do this?"

"I really do."

Jo looks up at the ceiling of the bedchamber as if weighing her options, and then she stares Shea down from under her eyelashes while she asks with a sweet smile, "One last kiss for the road, darling?"

"Oh, I don't think so; it'll give you something to look forward to." Shea curtsies the best she can and Jo laughs in frustration.

They're down the hall as quick as they can be as Jo's last scream echoes after them.

"Shea!"

Halfway to the horses Caen has to carry her, but Shea doesn't fuss—she was stabbed after all. It's a short ride to the docks, and once there, Shea requests to be let down.

Nol runs ahead to alert the crew they're shipping out of here fast. Caen helps her hobble to the ship.

"Gods, you're trouble. How are you awake?" Caen groans as he helps her to the beginning of the onboarding plank.

"I don't know. But we'll figure it out later; besides, you wouldn't want it any other way," Shea jokes, and she accepts the kiss Caen places on the top of her head.

Once on deck, the crew stops everything they're doing, staring at the woman they call captain. They all place their hands over their hearts and salute. Shea stands tall and proud, grinning widely before she's nearly brought to the ground by a short ball of energy.

"You're alive!"

Aster shouts, hugging Shea tightly. Shea groans loudly and Caen separates the two of them, grabbing Aster by the arm. The crew laughs. Shea cracks a smile once she's recovered enough.

"I appreciate the love, guys," Shea shouts, and they all mock and jeer. "But you see I've made a bet with the queen. It's time to run, boys. So, James?"

James leans over the rail of the afterdeck. "Aye, Captain?"

"Take us out!"

"Aye, Captain!"

"Mister Tero!"

"Aye, Captain! Let's get those sails up, lads, bring the plank up, come on, you mangy deck rags," Tero shouts.

"Aster, you fit enough to help Mister Tero?"

"Yes, Cap." Aster salutes and runs off after the old bos'n.

"Aster," Shea calls after him.

"Yeah, Cap," Aster shouts back.

"We made it." She smiles. And he smiles widely back before he's scampering up the rope ladders to the second post of the foremast.

"Captain." Caen offers his arm, and she takes it graciously, heading up the stairs to the afterdeck.

"Captain." James nods, stepping away from the helm. "Would you like to do the honor?"

Shea pauses but then continues to the helm, taking the steering wheel.

"Weigh anchor," Tero screams.

"Weigh anchor!" Aster repeats.

"The ship is ready, ma'am," Caen tells her.

"Let's take her out," Shea orders.

The ship creaks as the wind catches the sails and starts moving the *Veiled Duchess* out of the harbor.

Aster shouts from the mast and Shea grins as the sea breeze hits her face. The horizon stands before her and the sun gleams over the waves as the *Duchess* departs from Arethusa.

"Where to, Captain?" Caen asks, pulling out the maps on the compass table.

"Somewhere we've never been before. Set a course north, let's see where the wind takes us. Expect the royal Arethusian navy on our tail."

"Yes, ma'am." James nods, though he looks to Caen, confused.

"Didn't we just help them?" he asks.

Caen huffs, looking back at Shea and shaking his head. "I'll tell you later."

The crew is bustling down below, and as the wind blows, hitting the mast, Shea keeps her eyes on the horizon.

Caeruleus yowls from above, flying over the ship—he's returned home.

Alone in her thoughts as she guides her ship, she thinks about the voice she'd heard in her dying dreams.

He's coming.

The storm's coming.

Thetis's voice filters through her mind as well, *Something's coming, and I feel like you're a part of it.* Shea knows they're right. She can feel it in her bones. And now with this miraculous healing, she has more questions than ever. And she knows whatever it is, it's coming soon.

And unknowingly, it's coming for her.

EPILOGUE: PART ONE

THE OLD BELLS ARE RINGING. Bells they never thought would ring again. The great council of elves in Erebos chant, trying to protect their people in the great temple of Poseidon.

He's coming.

He rose from the depths, and now, he's coming.

"Ami!"

One of the older priests calls to their leader, her bright fiery red hair glaring in the torchlight as she focuses her power on keeping the darkness on the other side.

"He's going to come through," another high priestess shouts.

Ami can feel the sweat falling down her mortal brow. She's too old and his power is too strong—she can feel the dark energy bang against the boundary once more. The high priestess looks back at her elven people, shaking and cowering. This was all they could save safely inside the temple and away from him. Most of the claimed children are out there, taken as his militia rose from the Underdeep portal. No doubt he'll use them for their gifts.

"Erebos has fallen," Ami whispers.

One by one her fellow council members fall from exhaustion. She can feel the boundary getting weaker and weaker.

He'll break through at any minute. The temple is at the center of Erebos, not far from the Underdeep portal; if she can just get to the roots, she can use the magic there to resurrect the border. He'll be locked out.

For now.

But it'll leave Nereid completely defenseless and at his

whim. The temple shakes, and old stone falls from the ceiling. She feels the last of her fellow council members fall. It's only her against him. She glances back to the statue of Poseidon, standing tall with his net and trident.

"Forgive me, my love," she whispers.

She drops to the floor at the release of power. And the boundary falls. The pounding stops, and one of Ami's fledgling priestesses flees to her side, checking to see if she's alright. There's silence outside the temple and they wait. The door blasts open; the remaining elves cover themselves, protecting their bodies from the blast.

He walks in.

He's tall, his hair a dark auburn and his eyes a vibrant, pale green. His skin is so light he looks almost translucent, covered in his black priest robes, the symbol of Aquarius scrawled across his chest.

Ami looks around; it seems that most of her people remain uninjured, but what pulls the breath from her body is what the dark elf carries.

Triton's conch shell.

Ami's heart squeezes in her chest and she prays to Poseidon to hear her. The council members all begin to stand, and Ami goes to do the same, but she sees her old friend Merric, another priest on the council, shake his head. He knows she's the only one who's strong enough to push him and his Underdeep militia out of Erebos.

"You will all kneel. I am the one true king of Nereid. Together, we will take back our world from the humans."

"This is not who we are. We're guardians, not warriors," Merric shouts, standing his ground against the dark elf. The dark elven priest steps forward, his militia of followers rushing past him, creatures that were once elves now twisted and contorted with bodies made of the sea and flesh.

They take the other elves into custody, but Ami projects enough magic that they move right past her and her fledgling priestess, just enough that he won't notice. Ami sees her opening. She nudges her fledgling, who looks up and sees the crack in the wall made by the blast. It's enough for Ami to slip through. If she can make it to the Underdeep, she can take them out of Erebos. She just has to get past the boy.

No, the man—the man they all helped create.

"No," the elf chuckles, glaring Merric down, but Merric keeps his ground. "You're not warriors. That's the problem though." He advances on the Elder Council. "You've let the lesser beings take and enslave us. You've exiled your own. You are as much to blame for our extinction as the gods who abandoned us and fled their halls."

"There's not enough of us to win," another council member speaks. "What you're talking about is impossible."

"We are the children of gods, the legacies of power," the man preaches, and Ami has had enough of false prophets for now.

She holds her fledgling's hand and rises, inching them toward the crack. But as she's just about there, her magic falters, and one of the militia creatures snarl. The dark elf turns, seeing both of them, but it's too late. Ami has slipped out through the crack into the city. She turns to grab her fledgling, but the girl is pulled back in by the creatures.

She doesn't have time to waste. She takes off running through the ruined city. Uncontrolled magic flutters against every part of her skin, and she looks back in time to see the roof of Poseidon's temple blown off. Pieces of rubble hit the ground around her, and the city's square is filled with screams and cries. She passes the Atlantis fountain, and it's not far now. There's so many screams echoing through her head and around her, she wishes she could tune them out.

And there it is. A black hole in the ground of Erebos with teal-blue and black vines encircling the circumference and white veins curling up them, pulsing. It's a long drop, which she knows well; she just has to reach out and touch it. But a voice stops her at the circle's edge.

"Hello, Ami."

Ami stops, her chest huffing; she keeps her hand outstretched, just about touching the portal, but turns back to face him.

"Hello, Perses." Perses is standing there, and she can almost the see the face of the boy, the teen they threw to the depths of the Underdeep, never to be seen again. What fools they were.

He has Merric in his grasp, her old friend. Perses's hand is wrapped around his throat with incredible strength, the shell in his other palm.

"You look just as you did." Perses smiles, and Ami knows that smile. She used to love it on a much kinder face.

"I can't say the same about you."

Perses chuckles and releases Merric. He drops to the floor, and she pleads silently for him to stay still, not to move and anger the beast. But he gets up and starts running away, and she has to close her eyes as a trident made of black water appears in Perses's hand. He turns sharply on his foot with great power and precision, and throws the trident beautifully. It flies through the air, and Ami drops to her knees so she's now touching the vines as Merric drops to the floor, dead. His power has grown, that he can now produce water from the air, she notes. As she touches the vines, raw energy fills her core and her eyes glow a pale white.

"Today," Perses exclaims, "we declare war on the human race."

The dark priest turns back to her. He doesn't quiver in fear and he knows that there's no stopping her, but he doesn't look angry. He's deadly calm and it scares Ami even more.

"The weak will be ripped out, and the gods' people will remain." He nods to Ami like he's giving her permission. "I have work to do."

Ami starts chanting. The clouds rumble above and a loud crack erupts as a streak of lightning strikes the ground between them. Perses is no longer standing in front of the leader of Erebos; instead he's at the border of the Eastlands with his creature militia behind him. He reaches out and finds an invisible, impenetrable border keeping him out. Well, impenetrable for now.

Perses looks up at the storming skies and smiles as a drop of rain falls on his face. He knows he's watching him even now.

He turns and bellows to his militia, "A storm is coming!" They screech and cheer as Perses smiles wickedly to no one in particular. "And they won't know what hit them."

EPILOGUE: PART TWO

"I don't know."

"No," the lavender-eyed blonde growls.

"I underestimated him," the man continues, gazing into the pansy shell connected to a leather cord around his neck.

A scene plays out on the ancient sea urchin skeleton: a man with red hair being banished from the elven city of Erebos by another redheaded elf.

"Clearly," the woman snaps, scanning the man and taking in his appearance.

He's aged since she last saw him; his hair is no longer auburn but a shoulder-length gray. He's still as handsome though; any mortal would fall blindly for a chance to be with him. His facial hair, normally a long beard, has been trimmed short, and it brings back a seaside summer from long ago entailing stolen kisses and meaningless whispers. He's just as broad and muscular, and she finds the smell of fish and bait less endearing than it once was.

They're standing in her tavern staring each other down. How has it come to this? She wonders. This mortal life she's built for herself is finally coming to an end.

The lady of the Slippery Serpent walks to a short table by the fireplace, pouring herself a drink. Her hands shake as visions dance through her mind of consequences they've brought upon themselves.

"Aphrodi—" A glare cuts the older man off and he begins again with her preferred name. "Venus. We have to stop him."

V chuckles, taking a heavy sip of rum. "We don't have the

same power anymore. Amphitrite is gone. Triton is missing. The others, well, the gods split up a long time ago. Even your own kingdom has closed its gates. But," V mutters, her eyes closing, contemplating, "but there is someone in Nereid. Someone who might be able to stop him."

"Who? You've just said it yourself. He's more powerful than us now."

The old goddess suddenly looks her age, and this time when her eyes open, they're a stunning green.

"Who better to go up against Perses than his own sister."

The old man scoffs, strolling over to where V stands and pours himself a drink.

"She has barely scratched the surface of her potential. He trained with his brother, a god; she wouldn't stand a chance."

"You don't know her," V snaps. "You asked me to watch over her, to get to know her. Well, I know her. And I'm telling you, if anyone can stop him? She can. She just—she'll need our help, your help. She needs her father."

"I'm not what I once was," he barks, collapsing in the giant armchair, his troubled features looking just as his daughter's did when she sat there weeks ago in this very room. It makes V smile.

She kneels down in front of him and their eyes meet. "Poseidon. None of us are as we once were. Nereid is going to fall if we do nothing. Our world needs us and we need her."

Poseidon's head dips, eyes closing, and his eyebrows wrinkle.

"What if she fails? I don't know..." He sighs at the emotion welling in his chest. "I don't know if I could take the loss."

"We'll make sure she doesn't."

The pansy shell around his neck suddenly glows a bright blue. He opens his eyes, looking down at the image displayed on the shell.

"She's beautiful," Poseidon murmurs.

V laughs. Oh yes, she is. It's quiet then. The air in the room —V can still feel it. The vibration of ancient magic makes the very hair on her arms stand straight. She can almost taste the power filling the bedchamber. She takes a deep breath, pulling it in, and then stops when she notices Poseidon smirking at her. She straightens, smoothing out her dress.

"How much time do we have?" V questions.

"A year, maybe less," the old sea god guesses. "He'll need time to prepare, regroup now that he's been banished from the Underdeep and Erebos."

"We should find her now then," V states, moving to step away from him, but Poseidon grabs her hand, stopping her. He looks up in to her eyes and says, "No."

"No? Why not?"

"She needs time to heal."

He releases her hand, but she doesn't move. His own palms reach for the pansy shell, and he closes his eyes, letting his dying power flow into the shell and through the aether toward his unconscious daughter. Sending her the warning she truly needs for the times coming. He releases the shell with a harsh breath once it's done.

"I've just sent her a message. Now she knows something's on the horizon. When he makes his move, we'll make ours. But for now, we need to find my son, Triton, if we'll have any chance of getting through the magic shield surrounding Erebos."

V reluctantly agrees. "A year then?"

"A year."

"Then we better make the most of it."

Suddenly a thought crosses V's mind after all this and it makes her chuckle.

"What?" Poseidon inquires.

"I never thought I'd tell her. Who I really am. How the Underdeep did we get here?"

"I'm starting to believe that's what happens. When mortals and gods come together. Nightmares, angry children, and the world as we all know it begins to end once again."

"Not all bad comes from our unions with mortals; there's

beauty, love." V laughs, though it's empty, and when their eyes meet her eyes are glossy. "Very good things."

"Maybe," Poseidon acknowledges.

He breaks her gaze and focuses his attention on the image in the pansy shell of his daughter, now awake.

"Let's hope Shea will be the ultimate good."

To be continued in book two of the Veiled Duchess series, *The Veiled Descendants*.

Coming next summer.

GLOSSARY

Acheron Capital city of Lycos, translates in elvish to the City of Pain.

Aphrodite Greek goddess associated with love, beauty, pleasure, passion, and procreation.

Amphitrite Greek goddess of the sea, wife of the god Poseidon, and one of the fifty (or one hundred) daughters (the Nereids) of Nereus and Doris (the daughter of Oceanus). Poseidon chose Amphitrite from among her sisters as the Nereids performed a dance on the isle of Naxos.

amidship The middle of the ship.

Arethusa Northern queendom on Nereid ruled by a matriarchal line.

Atlantis Kingdom of Poseidon and the sea gods.

bos'n A warrant officer or petty officer in charge of a ship's rigging, anchors, cables, and deck crew.

bow Front of a ship.

bowsprit The slanted spar at a ship's prow jutting out in front of the ship. It is usually used as a lead connection for a small navigational sail.

broadside A general term for the vantage on another ship of absolute perpendicular to the direction it is going. To get along broadside a ship was to take it at a very vulnerable angle.

cabin boy/girl   A child employed to wait on a ship's captain or passengers.

captain   Captains were selected because they were respected, not because they were feared. When electing a captain, the crew looked for someone who was capable of commanding and navigating a ship. Also, it was crucial that captain had courage and skill in sword fighting and leadership.

claiming   When elves are claimed by the old gods and trained in their specialty of magic, they are claimed priests and priestesses. Some elves come into their magic without being claimed due to many elven children being born outside of Erebos in slavery.

crow's nest   A small platform, sometimes enclosed, near the top of a mast, where a lookout could have a better view when watching for sails or for land.

Eastlands   Elven country on the east coast of Nereid, home to the last of the free elves and guarded entrance to the Underdeep.

Erebos   Capital city of the Eastlands where elven clans gather for the Elder Council meetings, claimings, and other events.

first mate   First mate had rank just below the captain. He would take control of the ship if the captain could not perform his duties any longer. However, pirate ships usually did not have first mates; quartermasters performed their duties.

forecastle   The section of the upper deck of a ship located at the bow forward of the foremast.

galleon   A large three-masted sailing ship with a square rig and usually two or more decks.

gangplank　A board or ramp used as a removable footway between a ship and a pier.

Grace　A Charis or Grace is one of three or more minor goddesses of charm, beauty, nature, human creativity, and fertility, together known as the Charites or Graces.

gunner　Gunners were leaders of small groups who operated on the artillery. They watched for the safety of their men and usually aimed the cannons themselves.

gunwale　The elevated side edges of a boat, which strengthen its structure and act as a railing around the gun deck. In warships the gunwale has openings where heavy arms or guns are positioned.

helm　The steering wheel of a ship, which controls the rudder.

hold　A large area for storing cargo in the lower part of a ship.

hull　The body of a ship.

longboat　The largest boat carried by a ship, which is used to move large loads such as anchors, chains, or ropes. Pirates use the boats to transport the bulk of heavier treasures.

Lycos　Southern empire on Nereid ruled by emperors or empresses who come into power either by force or birth. Capital of the elven slave trade.

mainmast　The longest mast located in the middle of a ship.

Metis　Capital city of Oceanus.

Nereid　Island continent home to four countries: Arethusa, Oceanus, Lycos, and the Eastlands.

Oceanus   Free state, which won its independence from Lycos over a hundred years ago. Ruled by a lineal position called the governor and a senate.

pinnace   A light boat propelled by sails or oars, used as a tender for merchant and war vessels; a boat for communication between ship and shore.

poop deck   The highest deck at the stern of a large ship, usually above the captain's quarters.

port   The left side of the ship when you are facing toward her prow (opposite of starboard).

Poseidon   God of the sea, earthquakes, storms, horses, and ruler of the Underdeep, the underwater realm of the sea gods.

quarterdeck   The afterpart of the upper deck of a ship.

quartermaster   After captain, the quartermaster has most authority on a pirate ship. As a captain's right hand, he was in charge when the captain was not around. He had the authority, and he could punish men for not obeying commands. Quartermaster was also in charge of food and water supplies.

queendom   A queendom is when all power is concentrated in a central female figure. A matriarchal monarchy ruled by a strong queen.

rigging   The system of ropes, chains, and tackle used to support and control the masts, sails, and yards of a sailing vessel.

scuttle   A small opening or hatch with a movable lid in the deck or hull of a ship.

Scylla   A legendary monster that lived on one side of a narrow channel of water, opposite her counterpart Charybdis.

spyglass   A telescope.

starboard   The right side of the ship when you are facing toward her prow (opposite of port).

Thalassa   Capital city of Arethusa.

Triton   A Greek god, the messenger of the sea. He is the son of Poseidon and Amphitrite, god and goddess of the sea respectively, and is herald for his father. He is usually represented as a merman, which has the upper body of a human and the tail and fins of a fish.

Underdeep   The underwater realm of the gods.

ABOUT THE AUTHOR

Sophia Menesini lives in Martinez, CA, with her husband and their two small Chihuahuas, Ziggy and Zeppelin. *The Veiled Threat* is her first novel. Sophia is an avid tea connoisseur and lover of Scotland with an unconventional memory for obscure Disney and Broadway song lyrics.

CPSIA information can be obtained
at www.ICGtesting.com
Printed in the USA
LVHW091429020320
648710LV00001B/68